C000174023

The One I Want

New York Times Bestselling Author

S.L. SCOTT

Published in the United States of America
ISBN: 978-1-7371472-0-6

Cover Photographer: Kyla Jeanette Photography

Cover Models: Karlie Place & Colin Ringas

Cover Designer: RBA Designs

Editing:

Marion Archer, Making Manuscripts

Jenny Sims, Editing4Indies

Rebecca Barney, BBarney Books

Proofreading: Kristen Johnson

Beta Reading: Andrea Johnston

ALSO BY S.L. SCOTT

To keep up to date with her writing and more, visit her website:
www.slscottauthor.com

To receive the Scott Scoop about all of her publishing adventures,
free books, giveaways, steals and more:

CLICK HERE

Join S.L.'s Facebook group here: S.L. Scott Books

Read the Bestselling Book that's been called **"The Most Romantic
Book Ever"** by readers and have them raving. We Were Once is
now available and FREE in Kindle Unlimited.

We Were Once

Audiobooks on Audible - CLICK HERE

Complementary to The One I Want

Never Got Over You

We Were Once

Everest

Missing Grace

Finding Solace

Until I Met You

The Everest Brothers (Stand-Alones)

Everest - Ethan Everest

Bad Reputation - Hutton Everest

Force of Nature - Bennett Everest

The Everest Brothers Box Set

The Crow Brothers (Stand-Alones)

Spark

Tulsa

Rivers

Ridge

The Crow Brothers Box Set

Hard to Resist Series (Stand-Alones)

The Resistance

The Reckoning

The Redemption

The Revolution

The Rebellion

DARE - A Rock Star Hero (Stand-Alone)

The Kingwood Series

SAVAGE

SAVIOR

SACRED

FINDING SOLACE - Stand-Alone

The Kingwood Series Box Set

Playboy in Paradise Series

Falling for the Playboy

Redeeming the Playboy

Loving the Playboy

Playboy in Paradise Box Set

Talk to Me Duet (Stand-Alones)

Sweet Talk

Dirty Talk

Stand-Alone Books

We Were Once

Missing Grace

Until I Met You

Drunk on Love

Naturally, Charlie

A Prior Engagement

Lost in Translation

Sleeping with Mr. Sexy

Morning Glory

From the Inside Out

THE ONE I WANT

S.L. SCOTT

PROLOGUE

Andrew Christiansen

IT'S A LIST.

As if I have nothing better to do with my time, I now have five more things to check off a list. There's no getting out of it because my mom made me, *a grown man*, pinky swear before I left California, and I always keep my word, or in this case, my pinky swears. So here I am with ridiculous to-dos as if I didn't already have enough on my plate.

1. Lie in the grass in the nearest park at 9:17 AM on a sunny weekday.
2. Eradicate negative vibes from the apartment on the sixth Thursday after arrival.
3. Perform in front of an audience. *(Work doesn't count, Andrew)*
4. Read Shakespeare on the steps of the New York Public Library just after midnight.

Number five . . .

"What is my mom thinking?" I can't even bring myself to read number five without scoffing. It's like she doesn't know me at all. If she did, she'd realize *that's* the last thing on my mind.

I review it once more before tucking the list under a magnet on the side of the fridge. I've gone over this list more times than I can count. Would she know if I didn't follow through? I ask myself that question every time I read it.

This week is not the time to drop this guilt trip on me. I can't believe I'm even considering it. I can't. "Sorry, Mom."

Maybe next week.

Or not.

1

Andrew Christiansen

Two weeks and a few days later . . .

WHAT AM I DOING?

Why am I ruining a perfectly good shirt with grass stains and the scent of the outdoors?

How did I get talked into this?

Cookie Christiansen. My mom has me acting like a fool in the middle of Manhattan. I'm the CEO of a billion-dollar company, dammit. Why do I even entertain her New Age nonsense?

Guilt made me do it. That and not wanting to disappoint her.

I lie in the grass, staring up at the blue sky. The occasional cloud floats by, but it's a beautiful spring day. Sure, it's not LA, but if I close my eyes and let the sun warm me, I'm almost tricked into believing I'm back home again. Maybe that was my mom's plan.

When I open my eyes, I check the time. 9:14 on a sunny Monday. I have three minutes to go. This may be utterly ridiculous, but the longer I lie here, the easier it is to forget that I'm supposed to be at work right now. Probably in a meeting, but I push those thoughts aside and inhale deeply, making the most of it.

Closing my eyes again, I release a breath as visions of sitting on the shores of the Pacific Ocean back home, long drives in the convertible I had to leave behind, and game days with friends on Sunday afternoons return.

Stress from work rarely allows me time to enjoy the present. After officially launching our Seattle office two months ago, I shifted my full attention as CEO—pro tempore—to expanding Christiansen Wealth Management beyond the three offices. Although headquartered in Los Angeles, the New York market has the greatest growth potential. Once this office is bringing in the numbers we're used to seeing in LA and then grows beyond that, I can expand into a southern city like Dallas or Austin.

This world is full of wealth. It's my job to find these whales and bring them onboard. My father's eyes are on me, and Corbin Christiansen never accepts less than excellence. That's what I intend to give him. Sometimes, I feel the weight of his legacy—a vision implemented with enormous success—is on my shoulders. Sometimes—no . . . always— all eyes are on me, not only to make this company bigger but better than my father did.

My younger brother, Nick, chose a path that led to his professional and personal happiness. I've not been given the same luxury as I continue to sacrifice my personal life for this company. For my family.

So, this distraction by my mom does nothing to help me

reach my goals. Giving her crazy ideas five minutes of my valuable time is already giving her notions more credit than I should.

Ridiculous.

Ocean.

Convertible.

Friends.

I get my thoughts back on track, releasing the tension and closing my eyes again. Reaching out, it almost feels possible to touch the water again, surf at sunrise, or even sit in solitude after a long day.

Agh!

My stomach tenses as my eyes fly open. Reflexively, my head digs deeper into the grass as I'm met with two dark, round eyes surrounded by a lot of hair and a yap. "Um, what are you doing, dog?"

Perfectly content to stand on top of me, he pants and then sits, comfortable in his lack of training. Not sure if he'll bite me, I look to the side. Is anyone looking for this dog? It barks again, not scaring anyone, least of all, me.

"What? What do you want?" I look around, wondering where his owner is. "Where'd you come from?" I ask him, narrowing my eyes as I continue lying on the ground like an idiot. There's no way one of these prissy dogs would survive on the streets. Its white, brown, and black coat is too clean to make me think this dog is anything less than pampered on the daily.

Since it's staring at me like I have a pocket full of treats, I hold my hands up. "I have nothing for you. Now scram."

"Hey!"

I turn and see a woman in a baggy sweater flapping against her sides and a skirt pressed to her shapely legs as the excessive fabric flows behind her. Arms covered in the chunky knit material flail in the air, and I may be wrong, but it appears she's holding a leash in her hand. "Hey! Grab the dog. Please—"

Her words are swept away with the wind, causing me to miss the last part. The dog woofs again, though, and I put two and two together, swiftly taking hold of him. His tail wags, and then he leans in to lick my face. His breath stinks.

Another good washing is in order to rid the smell of saliva from my face. Great, another delay in my day.

Since the dog seems to consider us friends now, I sit up and then stand, tucking the dog under my arm.

The woman slows her pace as she approaches. She may be out of breath, but relief brings a smile to her face. Dipping forward, she squeezes her side and then holds up a finger. "I need a sec."

Despite the body she's trying to hide under those baggy clothes and her white Converse, I think it's safe to assume she's not a runner. I point at the dog. "Is this your dog?"

"Yes," she says through huffing breaths. Finally standing upright, she smiles at the dog. "Oh my God, you saved me." She tickles the dog's little head and goes nose to nose with him to whisper, "Who's a little rascal? You are."

She's quite stunning. Her green eyes with a hint of brown are bright with happiness (so what if it's because of the dog. I'm not threatened by the fuzzball). Her dark blond hair is twisted on top of her head with wild strands loosened from the run, and her lips have a gentle covering of pink that matches her heated cheeks.

She reaches for the dog, but I should really ask a few questions and keep him firmly anchored to my side. "Hi," I start, wiggling my nose in hopes of evading the stench of the animal. At this rate, I'll be taking another shower when I get home.

"Hi." She grins and then wraps her hands around the fuzzball's body, but when I don't release it, she asks, "Are you going to give the dog back?"

"How do I know it's your dog?"

Her eyebrows practically hit her hairline before her eyes narrow, and her gaze slices through the air between us. Holding up the red leash and collar, she says, "Obviously, it's my dog."

"What's its name?"

"Are you really doing this?"

"If it were your dog, wouldn't you want me to ask a few questions before handing it over to any crazy person who tried to steal it?"

Her head tilts, annoyance pursing her lips to the side. "It is my dog. And his name is Rascal."

Looking down at the dog, I grin. The name is fitting, for sure. "Hi, Rascal."

Little dog slobber coats my chin, so I angle him away from me. His back paws scratch against my side, giving him leverage to lunge forward. The woman adds, "See? Now may I have the dog?"

"I'm not sure that's proof it's your dog since he seems to like me just as much. I don't want to give Rascal to any old person."

"Old?" *Of course, that's all she got from it.*

With a chuckle, I hand her the dog. "I think that's my cue to exit." I rub the top of the little fuzzball's head. He's kind of cute, I guess. "See ya, Rascal."

As soon as I move my hand, she slides the collar over his head and then kisses his nose. With a know-it-all grin on

her face, she turns back to me. "Thanks." Her eyes go wide.
"Oh shit."

"What?"

She holds the dog away from her body and then sets
him down quickly. Standing back up, she says, "I'm so sorry.
I can pay for the dry cleaning."

"Why?" I ask dumbly but then catch on quickly. Looking
down, I see the smear across my shirt. "Shit. Guess it's me
who stinks." Grabbing a clean spot, I pull the shirt away
from my body. "I was heading to the office."

Reaching forward, she ghosts her hand in front of me as
if that will help. "I'm so sorry."

Annoyed, I look between her and the dog, both wearing
similar worried expressions. Exhaling heavily, I then say, "I
need to go."

"I really am sorry. It's such a nice white shirt. Hopefully,
it will come out. I'm sure it will. I have a great dry cleaner if
you need one. *What am I talking about?* We're in Manhattan.
Everyone in Manhattan has a great dry cleaner. It's basically
a requirement, like having a favorite coffee shop, deli, and
takeout place."

Her rambling about all the things I have back in LA is a bad
reminder of what I'm missing here. A dry cleaner is just another
thing I need to figure out and, by looking at the stain, quickly.

Her unease has me feeling the same, so I turn to leave.
Caressing my arm, she says, "Wait. Let me pay for the
cleaning."

My gaze meets hers again, where she keeps every
emotion in the forefront. I don't need her sympathy, though.
Standing here awkwardly, Rascal staring at me from beside
her feet, I add, "I got it."

"I feel terrible, though." She steps closer again. "I have a trick for getting ryegrass and fescue out. It might work for the poop."

"What's fescue?"

"Technically, it's turf type tall fescue and perennial ryegrass." My staring at her doesn't deter her from continuing. "The grass. You have stains. Make a paste with a few drops of hydrogen peroxide and baking soda. Let it sit for at least thirty minutes. Rinse in cool water, and then wash with your normal detergent. That works for me when I get plant stains."

Disbelief has me wondering if I should run or take notes. "Does that happen often?"

"Not anymore." She sighs in defeat. "Anyway, it's a lot of work. A good dry cleaner will make it look brand new."

There is no way I'm getting this shirt dry-cleaned. It's going right down the garbage shoot. "Don't worry about it." My tone is harsher than I intend, and just to prove I'm in a complete asshole mood, I shoot Rascal a glare. The small dog causes me to grin, lessening my bad mood. It's really hard to be mad around him, even if he did just cost me a few hundred bucks. "What kind of dog is that?"

"He's a papillon. Sweet as can be and usually really clean." Looking around, she says, "People are supposed to pick up their dog's poop. It's frustrating when they don't." It's not until that moment that I realize she's still touching my arm. When I glance at her fingers, she's quick to pull them back.

As if the smell is getting to her, she wiggles her nose in disgust and takes a few steps back. "I didn't bring enough money to cover the cost, but I can send—"

"It's okay. I can cover the cleaning. As for the smell, I don't think I'm so lucky."

"Sorry about that." The apology drapes her expression, pulling it down.

Well, shit. "Look, don't worry about it. I'm glad you got your dog back."

"Yeah, me too," she replies, shyness creeping in, deepening the pink on her cheeks. Looking down, she smiles at the dog, who seems content to sit by her side all day long if asked.

I should leave because I'm already late for work, and "my mom made me go to the park at 9:17" isn't a valid excuse —*Wait, what time is it?* I check my watch, but when my eyes deceive me, I ask, "Do you have the time?"

Her gaze shifts to my wrist before she pulls her phone from a little satchel she has tucked under the bulky sweater. "Nine twenty-three."

"What? That makes no sense." I tap the glass face of the watch and then toggle the bezel. When the hands don't move, I twist the crown. A twelve-thousand-dollar watch, and it's stopped? That's about right for how my day's going.

The blonde *(so what if I noticed how much her hair varies in the sunshine)* angles her neck. "Your watch stopped. That's a bummer." When her eyes return to mine, she adds, "Nine seventeen."

"What?"

She touches the face of my Rolex and then the heat of her fingertips graze over my skin. "It stopped a few minutes ago on nine seventeen."

"Yeah, but you said nine seventeen."

"Yes."

"How long have we been standing here?"

"Not more than ten minutes."

My heart kicks in my chest. "I mean exactly. How much time has passed?"

Looking at me like I'm a weirdo, she laughs humorlessly. "Um, six or seven minutes tops."

Fuck. "I should go." Before I let myself believe my mom has had a hand in this twist I didn't see coming, I turn and walk away. When I reach the path, I glance back. How can I not?

Who is she?

Have I been set up?

Scanning the area, I half-expect my mom to jump from the bushes and tell me I told you so. Fortunately, that doesn't happen.

But the woman is still standing there, watching me as if we're friends and she knows I'll return. Rascal tugs on his leash, trying to run toward me. He yaps twice. As much as I can't help but think he's talking to me, I turn back around and exit the park. Blending into the crowd on the sidewalk, my mind files through everything from the list pinned to my fridge to the fact that my hard-earned watch is somehow a part of this witchcraft.

Giving my watch another once-over, I twist the crown for the hell of it. I stop and blink once in disbelief because the hands are now rotating as if nothing happened. *What the hell?*

I start walking again and pull my phone from my pocket to check the time because I legit think I'm going insane. Tapping the screen, it reads 9:24. Until now, I've never had issues with my watch. I need to send it to get fixed and forget about this nonsense.

I may be rushing, but since when is that a crime? I slow, wondering why I'm getting dirty looks. "What?" I ask, throwing my arms out and staring down a man who raises his nose in disgust.

An older woman behind me pinches her nose. "You smell like shit, young fellow."

Oh shit. I look down, remembering the dog doo smeared across my nice white shirt. I shake my head. It's gross, but the world will survive, although I'm thinking my shirt won't.

I'm already making quite the impression in my first few weeks in the city. I could be mad, but I'm not that bothered by people avoiding my personal space, to be honest. Straightening my shoulders, I walk like I don't give a shit *or have it on me.*

But then I hear a familiar bark and turn back. The woman from the park rushes toward the nearest shop as if I didn't just bust her for following me. "What are you doing?" I ask. "Are you stalking me?" I might be jumping ahead of myself, but better to settle it now. A lot of weird stuff was happening at the park. Is she to blame?

Despite Rascal's joy to see me, obstinance stiffens her shoulders, and she scoffs. "You wish." Her hand flies out. "It just so happens that I'm walking in the same direction. So what?"

"Defensive," I reply, analyzing her body language. Crossed arms. Straight line across her lips. Half-mast eyelids as she glares at me.

"I'm not defensive. I'm offended. You just called me a stalker."

"My bad."

"You're bad, all right." She angles her chin up, and adds, "You can go about your day now."

I'm tempted to chuckle, but I'm thinking it's wise to restrain myself. "I will. Good day."

"Good day, sir," she says to my back as I walk away.

I stop again, but this time, I don't look back. Forcing myself to walk forward, I continue through the upscale neighborhood to the next block. I busy my attention on the architecture until I hear Rascal bark again.

I knew I shouldn't have talked to a stranger. She may be hot, but she could also be deranged, using her dog as a ploy to trick her next victim to her lair. What am I even talking about?

When I turn back this time, she sidles quickly up to a coffee shop window, pretending to know the people sitting on the other side.

By how they turn their backs to her, they don't reciprocate. "Nice try," I tease.

Glancing at me, she huffs. "I'm walking in the same direction. It's no big deal, for God's sake." She punctuates the words with an epic eye roll as if I'm putting her out. Huffing, she grabs Rascal, clutching him to her side.

"His feet have—"

"Shit."

"Exactly."

Anger fills her chest, and she shakes her head, exhaling it loudly with a foot stomp. "Ugh! I'll go this way."

As. If. I'm the nuisance.

Me?

Why am I even sticking around to have this conversation? Why am I bothering? Going in different directions— that's us. She crosses the street, and I turn the corner, both of us heading back to our own lives and hopefully never seeing each other again.

I continue toward the building up ahead alone. *I'm good. I'm fine.* Alone is how I thrive. I'll be here a year or two. That's nothing. I have plenty of work to keep me busy.

Work.

I'm here for work. That's it. I have a plan in place, and

nothing and no one will keep me from achieving my goals. I'll go in, change my shirt, and get to the office.

The doorman opens the door for me and nods. "Welcome home, Mr. Christiansen."

"Thanks, Gil." When he coughs, turning his head away from me, I ask, "Is it worth noting I've had a shitty morning?"

"It was noted the moment right before you arrived."

Funny guy.

2

Juniper "Juni" Jacobs

IT's NOT THE FIRST TIME I'VE BEEN CALLED A STALKER . . .

New York has changed. Apparently, I can't walk in the same direction as somebody else without people assuming I'm following them home. Despite how sullen the guy at the park was, I'm not letting his mood taint mine.

As I look out the window, the Manhattan streets are busy below, but the sun is shining above. It's a beautiful spring day, and I need to make the most of it.

After giving Rascal a bath, I blow-dried his hair before returning him to his owner, Mr. Clark. I turn up the music and finish getting ready, feeling good after my shower and hoping I've successfully gotten rid of the smell.

Walking around the apartment, I gather my stuff.

A book to pass the time if I have to wait.

Stationery and pen to take notes.

Snack. I scribble an S on the end. A single snack would be a flat-out lie.

Wallet.

Charger.

Phone.

Mints.

I'm traveling light, except for the nonfiction book I'm bringing with me. Sometimes, these meetings take ten minutes, and sometimes, I'm left waiting for two hours. I feel better prepared. I swing the straps of my bag over my shoulder and grab my bottle of water on the way out the door.

Sixteen flights down, I enter the lobby and am greeted with a warm grin. "Good afternoon, kiddo."

"Hi, Gil. How are you today?"

Standing, he comes around from his desk to get the door. He once told me I'd put him out of business if I kept beating him to it. I glance at the camera hanging in the top left corner that's filming our every move and slow my pace to let Gil catch up. He's not as fast as he used to be. He replies, "It's a beautiful day, and the Yankees are up."

"What inning?"

"Fifth."

Just outside the building, I slide my sunglasses over my eyes while still under the protection of the awning. "We'll take it."

"Darn right, we will. Where're you off to?"

Turning, I walk backward a few steps. "I have a meeting with the agency."

"Good luck, Juni."

"Thanks." Turning back, I wave over my head. "Have a great day!"

"You too."

Down one block, I push into the coffee shop and stand in line. My morning should have been more easygoing, but I've lost some steam after that encounter in the park.

Chasing a dog who loves to escape more than Houdini was the workout I didn't see coming.

Looking at the daily specials, I decide I'm not in the mood for anything but my usual, finding comfort in the familiar. It's not a phrase I live by, but I remember hearing my grandmother telling me that, her voice a faint memory these days. The tears had stung as they rolled over my skin, but the warmth of my mom's favorite sweater and the comfort of my grandmother's hug made it better. *At least that night.*

When it's my turn, I step up to the counter to place my order. "Good morning, Barry."

"Good to see you today," he replies. I doubt this college kid has hair on his chest, but he's managed to develop an ego to rival most men I've met in this city. I guess being cute is a curse he's learned to abuse. "Your usual?"

"Yes. Thank you." He's normally flirty, but I'll take the reprieve.

Moving off to the side, I mentally tick through my week's to-dos. For a woman with few commitments, I have a mountain of things to tackle. Nana always warned me about burning the candle at both ends. *I miss her.*

I reach into my bag for my phone to schedule in some fun when I hear, "Got the time?"

The deep voice is familiar. He's standing in a suit tailored to his fit build, the medium gray fabric set nicely against a crisp white shirt and black tie. I give a half-smile, unsure if I'm under friendly fire or the warm smile is real, considering how things ended earlier. "Depends on who's asking."

"Good point." Chuckling, he seems less . . . angry than he was when he called me a stalker. He's also drop-dead gorgeous. Everything about him is put together, even his hair, which tempts me to run my fingers through it just to muss it up like it was this morning. *What am I thinking?*

Crossing my arms over my chest, I raise an eyebrow at him. "Is this a coincidence, or are you stalking me?"

I don't get the laugh I was going for. Instead, his smile disappears, and shame stiffens his shoulders. "About that. I owe you an apology. I don't know why I said that. I've watched too many movies, or maybe it was that weird look in your eyes."

Reaching up, I touch the corner of one eye. "What weird look?"

"That one that silently accused me of stalking you."

I give him a full grin as amusement works its way through me. "Serves you right." He laughs. There's a formality to it, but it feels natural for Mr. Uptight. "You may have thought I was nuts, but I wasn't the one lying in the park for no reason."

Waffling his head, he says, "There was a reason."

I'd been trying to keep my eyes off him, not to seem like the stalker he called me, but this brings me back to him. "Which was?"

"It was nine seventeen."

"I suppose that makes sense . . . *to a crazy person*."

He finally releases the tension that fills his shoulders along with a chuckle. "Touché."

Barry, the barista, leans over the counter and shouts, "Andrew?"

Tall, dark, and too handsome for his own good standing next to me steps up to the counter, thanks Barry, and then turns back to me. I see the debate in his eyes when he glances toward the door. Does he need a reason to leave, or is he looking for a quick escape? I can't worry about what comes next because I'm stuck on his name. "Andrew?"

"Yes?" Then it dawns on him, awareness awakening his expression. "Guess we haven't gotten that far."

"No, we haven't." I stare at him, still intrigued by the secrets he appears to hold in his dark brown eyes while trying to imagine him living life as an Andrew. "I wouldn't have guessed Andrew."

"Oh, really? What do I look like to you?"

"Mocha latte!" Barry calls out as if someone just offended him. My guess is the guy to my right based on how Barry's glaring at him. I also note an impatient tap of the fingers before I glance back at Andrew. "That's me."

When I step up to the counter, Barry whispers, "I added a bonus half-shot of espresso and just a hint of peppermint syrup. Just how you like it when you have a rough day."

"Thank you. You're the best."

His voice is still low, only for my ears when he asks, "You coming around tomorrow?" I swear he glares at Andrew.

"Depends on a job I might have."

As if I just made his day, he replies, "I hope I see you tomorrow, June."

Does that mean he's rooting against me getting the placement? Sure sounded that way. Andrew is now the one staring at me when I walk away from the counter. "June?" he asks with the slightest tilt of his head.

"No. That's not what I like to be called. He got it wrong the first time, and I felt bad correcting him." I take a sip of coffee.

"Why would you feel bad?"

Shrugging, I say, "Because then he'll feel bad every time he sees me. June is no big deal."

"But that's not your name. What is your—?"

"Aren't you late for work?" I look at him, remembering

he was in such a hurry this morning. "Or wherever you're going?"

"Figured it didn't matter now, and I need a hit of caffeine."

The midmorning rush for caffeine crowds the coffee shop, and I'm bumped from the side. "I'm going to get out of the way." It's not exactly an invitation, but I can't help but think I wouldn't mind him leaving with me. I start for the exit.

Andrew is swift enough to reach the door and open it. "After you."

"Thanks." On the sidewalk, I'm not sure what to do. Do I keep walking, never to look back, or do I stop and chitchat with Andrew? *Andrew* . . . I can see it fitting now that we're back in the sunshine—the suit, the chivalry, the comfort he exudes in his own body. I decide to take a chance and toss an opener into the mix. "Well . . ."

"Yeah." He glances around, making it really hard to read him, though I don't think I was doing a stellar job of that previously anyway. When his eyes settle back on mine, he adds, "I'm sorry for accusing you of stalking. I don't know why I said that."

I don't know why I like how he runs his hand over his hair, dipping his chin down and peeking at me, but I do. "Maybe you find women a foot shorter and a lot smaller than you intimidating, or maybe Rascal made you nervous. He can get pretty vicious if you try to take his food away."

"Why would anyone take his food away?"

I laugh lightly, but he doesn't. *This guy is so serious. Intense.* "Don't worry. No one's taking his food from him." This time, I look around before catching him check his watch. "We don't have to stand here awkwardly if you have someplace to be."

"I do, but it's not so awkward standing here with you."
He tucks his hand in his pocket and jiggles what sounds like
keys.

The silver metal of his watch catches the light just
above the gray fabric, and I say, "I see your watch works
again."

"It does." Pulling his arm up in front of him, he studies
it. "I'm not sure what caused it to stop. The—"

"Universe?"

His smile reminds me of how he looked this morning
before he got grumpy. "I was going to say that."

"Jinx, you owe me a coffee."

His smile wiggles wider. "I think we're both supposed to
say it for it to count as a jinx."

"Work with me here." He's very nice looking, smiling
and all. Fine, he's hot when he's uptight as well, so I seize
the moment. "How about tomorrow? You heard Barry. He'll
have my order ready to go."

His eyebrows knit together, but then they recover. "Are
you asking me out?"

"No. I'm collecting a debt." I twist my lips to the side,
tightening the reins on my grin.

Andrew doesn't bother with the same restraint. A smug
smirk practically consumes his stupidly handsome face. "I
never leave debts unpaid. Should I prepay Barry now, or do
you like to collect your debts in person?"

"Always in person. Don't want to be stiffed."

"It's not so bad being stiff."

If I had pearls to clutch, I'd do it just for effect. "Oh my,
Andrew. Did you just insert a sexual joke into our innocent
conversation?"

"Were we not flirting?"

"I have a feeling you never misread a situation."

He shrugs. The lax gesture doesn't suit him as well as that designer one does. "I should probably get going."

"You're always going."

"Yeah, duty calls. I should have been there hours ago."

"What kept you?" Shaking my head, I look down briefly. "Sorry. I tend to ask too many questions."

"That's okay. I have one for you. What time do you want your coffee?"

He might be flirting with me this time, but I'm not going to embarrass him by calling him out. "I'm fairly open. What works best for you?"

"Seven thirty. Is that too early?"

"It's not." I start to walk away. "See you tomorrow, Andrew."

He stands still, looking smug as ever, but then his lips part, and he reaches out. "Hey, I didn't get your name. I want the one you like to be called."

My cheeks heat. Twice in one day. It's been a long time since I've felt this giddy. It's been longer—*going on two years next month*—since I've even dated. "Juni. I like to be called Juni."

"See you tomorrow, Juni."

3

Andrew

Knock. Knock.

I drag my tired eyes from the monitor, my gaze traveling across the large office when my door opens without permission. "I don't want to be disturbed."

"You never do," Nick replies, my brother's tone light. He's been like this since he got married two years ago—smiling all the time, whistling for no reason, no tension found in his body. Basically, he's not like he used to be at all and definitely no longer like me. "Why are you here so late?"

"Because Mom sent me on a mission, and I foolishly played along."

He chuckles and sits across the desk from me. He's wise enough not to kick his feet up on my desk. "Oh, yeah? What's she up to?"

I could cite the three reports I still need to go through tonight, but what's a few minutes with my brother? I push the keyboard away and lean back in the cushy chair. "That remains to be seen. Right now, she claims it's having me settle into a new city, but I have a feeling there's more to it. She didn't give me a crazy list of things to do in Seattle."

"Wonder why the sudden focus on your life in New York?"

"I have a hunch—"

"You don't work off hunches."

"Typically, but that's all I have to go off of this time. Ever since you found your one and only, her focus has shifted to me."

Chuckling, he sits forward. "I'll be honest, I thought her New Age beliefs were nonsense, that she was traveling down a dead-end street when it came to me. Now I'm a believer."

"What changed your mind?"

He raises his left hand, and the light from my desk lamp gleams off the metal wrapped around his finger. "I met Natalie."

"I thought you met her on a drunken weekend in Catalina?"

"That too."

"I don't understand."

He snaps his fingers. "Keep up, brother. She's not helping you settle into life on the East Coast."

Rubbing my right temple, I scowl, regretting that I allowed him to come in. "Now I'm completely lost."

"For the smartest guy I know, you sure are dense some-times." He stands and rests his hands on my desk. "I'll let you in on a little secret," he says conspiratorially. "Mom's matchmaking."

"No . . ." I tick through the list again—park, perform, Shakespeare, exorcism, and the one that shall not be vocal-ized or even given a second thought. Arguably, all of them have nothing to do with anyone else other than the fifth and final. "She's being subtle if that's her motive." *And how on earth can she do that from California?*

"Only time will tell. In the meantime, the last thing I want to do is make her feel like a failure."

"I know there was no big production in you and Dalen calling things off—"

"Can we not do this?"

He studies me. "You weren't in love with Dalen."

"No, but she's a good friend."

"Hence, my point. The spark wasn't there. As Natalie would say, she wasn't your person. So, if Mom's really trying to fix the unfixable, let her. Maybe you'll both come out winners."

Bored by my love life being the topic of conversation, I return my attention to the doc displayed on my monitor. "I need to get back to work."

"Look, I get it, Andrew. You put your life on hold for years, worked your ass off, and have been rewarded. You're married to your job. But one day, you're going to wake up and wonder if an actual life was worth the sacrifice."

"Until regret sets in, I have three reports to finish before morning, and you have a wife waiting for you to return home to, so if you'll excuse me . . ." I don't need to look up to know he's staring at me, most likely disappointed. I can feel it. But the silence stings, so I give in, not something I often do. "What?"

What I expected isn't written in his expression. Though I don't understand the sympathy I do find. He finally says, "Natalie is waiting on me. We have reservations at eight thirty at this great restaurant in Tribeca. It's been there forever, long past being trendy. If you ever need a place to take a date, Asado is the place. Try the empanadas."

My stomach growls, reminding me that I forgot to eat

lunch. Mostly because I was distracted by Juni and those hazel eyes of hers, the delicate curve of her neck where it meets her shoulders, and those lips—bare and licked with care as we stood on the sidewalk.

What the hell am I thinking?

She was a hurdle in my day, at best. At worst, I was shit on. So yeah, the fond thoughts of the two encounters twist into annoyances. *A debt . . . I scoff.*

A loud clap snaps my mind into the present, and Nick asks, "You want to share whatever's on your mind because I have a feeling it's not the accounts you're working on?"

"No."

"Figured, but since you didn't hear me the first time, I thought I'd repeat myself. Natalie and I are hosting a dinner party on the twenty-fourth. I'm giving you three weeks' notice, so save the date. You're not getting out of it. No working that Saturday night or saying you're too tired. I'm RSVP'ing for you now."

He heads for the door. After he opens it, he looks back. "Let us know if you're bringing a plus-one."

"I don't know anyone in this city who could be a plus-one, so you're stuck with me coming alone."

"Natalie can set you up on a date if you'd like. She has plenty of single friends looking for love in all the wrong places."

"Wrong is right, so I'll pass."

"The offer still stands. Anytime you're ready, just let us know."

"I think Mom's rubbing off on you."

He chuckles. "Have a good night, man, and don't work so hard."

The door closes before I can think of a comeback, and silence invades the space like he was never here. Enough light still claims it's still day when I look out the windows, but night's coming in quick. I won't make it home before nightfall at this rate, so I bury my head in work and get these reports done.

I look up, my body stiff from sitting too long. Stretching my neck to the side, I realize darkness has only taken over outside. It's past ten. *Again.* Work has stolen another night out from under me.

But as I pack up, Nick's words return. *"One day, you're going to wake up and wonder if an actual life was worth the sacrifice."*

Scrubbing over my face, I attempt to fight the tiredness that's overcome me, but I'm done for the night. I'll blame the start of my day since that threw everything else off.

The monitor goes dark as I grab my jacket and slip it on. When I open the door, most of the lights are turned off, and the vacuum roars somewhere down the other corridor. No other employees should be here, but I do a quick walk around just to make sure. Working late is practically in the CEO's job description, but for others, I'm hoping they find the balance that eludes me.

I nod to the cleaning crew on my way out. I know I'm not the only one working in this thirty-five-floor building, but it sure feels like it as I ride down in an empty elevator. This may be a first for the bustling building.

The lobby lights are dimmed, and the security guard is caught up in a cop drama on his covertly hidden phone from the sounds of it. I say, "Good night."

"Good night," he replies, glancing up as I pass.

The car is at the curb waiting, the door open when I approach. "Good evening." I slip into the back with a quick nod of my head.

"Good evening, Mr. Christiansen."

When the door closes, the weight of the day drains from my body. I never needed someone to drive me around in LA, but I appreciate the luxury here in Manhattan. Usually I bide my time, checking emails, text messages, and listening to voicemails. Tonight, I take a deep breath and just relax.

At my apartment building, Gil opens the door for me. "Seems we're working the same schedule today, Mr. Christiansen."

"Seems that way. Good day?"

"Great." His answer makes me realize it's been a while since I've felt the same. He asks, "You?"

"Not too bad," I reply, trying to keep my mood from souring as I head upstairs.

My state-of-the-art apartment has a programmed ambience set to begin prior to me walking in the door—soft music not overpowering the view—to welcome me home.

Home.

I don't let that sink in. It's a rung on the ladder, two years at worst, sooner if I have my way.

A quick push of a button on my phone has the bathroom filled with steam by the time my suit hits the bed, and everything else lays at the foot of it. The heat envelops me, and when the hot water hits my shoulders, my tension begins to melt away.

Closing my eyes, I step under the spray. Usually, I'd recount my day, but tonight, Juni outweighs that habit. I have time for this . . . *or her.*

Not sure why I'm trying to convince myself. Nick is right. I'm married to my job, and I don't see a change in that commitment anytime soon. So why get involved with someone in New York when I plan to move back to LA?

Nick is a prime example. He came here for work and stayed when he met someone. That's not my plan. I'm not even open to it. Though I imagine my mom would have a field day if she knew my focus even slipped for a minute.

The bottom line is I'm not interested in strings or complications. I'm not sure if that's what Juni is, but by how our lives have already tangled together, there's a strong possibility.

I take several deep breaths to calm my mind, letting it fog over like the glass of the shower, my muscles easing under the pounding of hot water. Resting a hand on the marble wall, I lower my head and close my eyes. I can't stop my stomach from growling, reminding me that a small bag of Fritos and an apple at four won't tide me over for long.

After pulling on a pair of sweatpants, I try to figure out something quick to make for dinner. Loud music begins as soon as I set the mustard on the counter.

Surely, playing music that loud is against the rules, especially after eleven. This wouldn't fly in the building where I lived in LA. It was filled with lawyers, doctors, agents, and even a few celebrities, looking for peace from the outside world, not to have it shattered. That's why I lived there. If I wanted to party, I would have lived on Sunset or in The Hills.

I finish making my sandwich and eat while I move from vent to vent, listening with the rapt attention I usually reserve for my work. I'm quick to narrow it down to three vents in the living room as I eat. Tomorrow, I intend to find out who's at the other end. *I don't need another stress. Not. Here.*

The kitchen only takes a minute to clean, and then I make my way to the bedroom. In the bathroom, I stare into the mirror, not recognizing myself as easily these days. I've aged beyond my years, the stress of building a family empire wearing into my skin. I run my hands over my jaw, feeling how the long hours add to the growth. I didn't shave every day in California because I didn't have to. But from what I've seen of this city, even from my brother, the professional community takes a more formal approach.

I pull out my razor blade and set up for the morning. Organizing things now feeds my need to control things. I brush my teeth, floss, and then climb into bed. After a day of being surrounded by TV screens blaring while watching the stock market, this is much-needed peace.

I'm not that lucky, though.

The upbeat melody from the offending neighboring apartment sneaks in. I bury my head under a pillow. *Shit.* Seems to be a running theme today.

4

Juni

WHAT IF I GET THERE EARLY? DO I STAY AND WAIT TO ORDER? Or do I order and then take the coffee, telling Barry the bill will be paid as soon as a certain man who lost a jinx shows up with the money?

Oh wait, they won't even make the coffee until it's paid for. *Hrm* . . . I could arrive fashionably late, but that would be rude. I have no idea what to do. It's been a long time since I met someone of the opposite persuasion for coffee. This flirting-dating business has me feeling woefully unprepared for this meetup. And with someone I find extremely hot, in spite of his ever-changing moods.

I'm making a mountain out of a molehill. It's coffee. *Nothing more.*

Anyway, a molehill is all it can be since I have a job today. I grab my bag and hurry downstairs.

Pete is helping Mrs. Smith to the curb. The door closes behind them as I cross the lobby, determined to ignore the wilting row of variegated snake plants against the far wall. I lose. Again.

Pushing the door open, I hear Pete say, "Sorry about that, Juni. I didn't see you coming."

I never mind opening the door for myself. It always makes me feel too pampered when I leave it to the door-men, but they don't appreciate me stealing their job.

"No worries, Pete. I can handle the door."

He tips his head. "We're always looking for help if you want to cover a shift or two."

"I appreciate the offer," I reply. "I'll keep that in mind." As he helps Mrs. Smith into a taxi, I stroll the block, admiring the trees blooming in their large planters and the birds flying with a blue sky as the backdrop.

When I turn the corner, I spy Andrew pacing the side-walk with a phone to his ear. The tips of my fingers run the length of the smile he brings to my face before I bite my lower lip. I shouldn't fixate on such shallow things like his looks or the way his suit hangs on his body just as nice as yesterday's did. And my tummy definitely shouldn't tighten when I eye that cliff dive of a jaw on full display. But I'm pretty sure I'm not alone, nor the first one to admire this man for his physical attributes.

Men like him get plenty of attention. The last thing he needs is mine.

But that smirky grin he's wearing when he sees me also doesn't help settle the butterflies flapping around my stomach.

Keep your eyes on the prize, Jacobs. *Coffee, that's it.* Nothing more. The last thing I need in my life is some guy who has me imagining growing a garden, barbecuing on the weekends, strolling through Central Park, or dining out.

Nope. I don't need any of that . . . *that* . . . fantasy stuff in my life.

I'm not interested in changing. Cut bait and get out is working just fine.

"Hello, Juni," he says, a grin so devilish that my knees weaken, causing me to stumble over my own feet in my stride.

My arms fly into the air as a high-pitched squeal escapes my throat. "Oh my God!" I exclaim, catching myself. Technically, my face stopped the momentum against his chest, but we don't need to get caught up in the minutia of the details.

Fortunately, he's quick with his hands and also stopped me from plowing into him . . . well, any more than I did already. Pushing off him, I try to catch my breath, which was also lost in the fall. I straighten my skirt before brushing my hair back from my face and failing to keep the embarrassment from heating my face.

A small section of hair falls from his prior-to-seeing-me perfectly coiffed hair, and he asks, "Are you okay?"

"I'm okay." *And utterly mortified.* But I swallow down that admission.

His kind smile quirks up on one side. "If it makes a difference, you saved it at the end."

"As did your chest. *Oh no!*" I reach for his shirt but stop shy of rubbing the fabric that's now covered in makeup that conveniently matches my face. Covering my mouth in horror, I say, "I'm so sorry." His expression hardens as he stares at his shirt, but he doesn't say anything.

As for me, I think all of Manhattan can hear me swallow. I add, "I'm sorry. I can't fix it, but I can have it cleaned. Again, you probably have your own dry cleaner, but you can send me the bill. Or I can just buy you a new shirt. That won't help you right now, but—"

"It's okay." Nothing about his tone has me believing it's actually okay, but he's kind enough to pretend. "Two out of three leaves me one ahead."

"Yeah, I'm thinking I'm bad luck for you."

His eyes are more golden when he looks in my direction as the sun awakens the avenue. The hard lines of his forehead finally soften, and he says, "I don't believe in bad luck. Things happen for a reason."

"So I was meant to ruin two of your shirts in two days?" I laugh. It's light but releases some of the guilt. Only some of it. "Look, I feel awful. How can I make it up to you?"

"No need." He checks his watch and then glances over my shoulder. "I hate to cut this short, but I need to get to the office. Can I buy you that coffee?"

I'm quick to the door and open it. "I should be buying you a coffee."

Andrew's hand covers mine, and I find my breath escaping me. His body is close, all six-two, maybe six-three of him, shadows mine. "After you. I insist." His voice is low, as if a secret was shared, and those butterflies are awakened.

I slip my hand out from under his, careful to only steal a glance at him. "Thank you," I whisper before entering the coffee shop. When I look forward, Barry's eyes are on me, and a smile on his face, but they're quick to dart behind me to Andrew. His smile disappears. If there was a way to steam milk with fury, he's mastered it.

As Andrew and I wait in line for our turn to order, I ask, "Are you sure you have time for this? I don't want to keep you. It was only a playful joke anyway. My feelings won't be hurt if you need to leave."

"Are you trying to get rid of me?"

"No," I reply with a light laugh. "Like I said, I just feel bad. First the shirt and now I'm keeping you."

"The line is moving fairly quick. I should be fine." We both move forward, and as I study the pastry counter, silently debating between the chocolate croissant and the banana muffin, he says, "You look very nice."

Instead of looking up at him, I look down at my clothes. It's not a shining star of an outfit or anything, but I guess it's flattering. Over my shoulder, I say, "That's very kind of you to say." Keeping my voice down, I say, "Thank you."

"You're welcome." Confidence is built into every syllable this man speaks. And although I'm fairly certain he's hard to catch off guard, I'm thinking I'm doing a fine job of it.

Turning all the way around, I take him in from feet to neck and then spend a little time on his face. "You look very nice too, Andrew."

He chuckles, and says, "Thank you, Juni. Speaking of, that's a very interesting name."

"Thanks. My mom loved it." Sure, he did the polite lead-in comment like so many do, but I don't feel like delving into my past right now. My name is too tightly woven into that topic. So I leave it be and find relief that we're called to the counter.

I expected Barry to greet me, but I get the new barista—Jen. Barry doesn't even make eye contact with me, much less with Andrew. Apparently, I've gone and destroyed his dreams of us being together. I can only hope the poor kid will go on to find his soul mate in another customer.

I order, and then say, "I'm buying."

"No, she's not." He leans in, and the magic of his smile makes Jen blush. "You see, Jen, Juni here won a jinx yesterday, and I owe her a coffee. So this is on me, okay?"

Jen gives him a wink. "I've got your back."

"I knew you would," he adds. "Also, make that two muffins, and I'll have a regular coffee."

"Your name?"

"Andrew."

He pays, and she slips his credit card back to him like she's slipping her digits across that counter. "Thank you, Andrew."

I move along. When he joins me near the pickup counter, I say, "Don't let me keep you."

His chuckle is loud, completely not appropriate for a coffee shop or anywhere inside at this hour. By the evil glares we receive, I think he's woken the dead, or maybe their caffeine finally kicked in. From where he stands beside me, his elbow fans out to tap mine. "You're not jealous, are you, Juni?"

"I barely know you." I kind of hate that he might be right. Yet here I am, completely lost as to why I even care.

By the lines beginning to leave their marks on the outside of his eyes, he scowls more than he should. Or maybe it's from smiling so much, but I doubt it. Each smile of his seems to be hard-earned. He's just so confusing. One minute, we're flirting, and the next, we're going back to our own lives like complete strangers.

Wait, we are complete strangers.

I think the most I've gotten from him is his first name, that he seems to be obsessed with crisp, white shirts— expensive, I might add—and he drinks his coffee black. *No surprise there.*

Leaning over, he whispers, "This is true, but maybe—"

"Andrew?" Jen is holding his coffee and the bag of muffins in the air for him.

I'm tempted to roll my eyes, but . . . *nah*, I roll them. I take my coffee from a pouting Barry, who tries to ignore me, and then I maneuver around Andrew to leave. He's picking up his order when he says, "Thanks, Jen."

I don't stick around to hear their cute little banter. *It's fine.* It doesn't bother me at all, but I don't need to be subjected to it either. Feeling snarky, I mutter to myself, "Here's your coffee, Andrew, all perfect and hot like you. Oh, and you're a stud muffin like this banana nut." *What am I doing?* I'm losing my mind, that's what. Outside, I take a deep breath, exhale, and then pluck the top off my coffee to sip.

The sidewalk is bustling with people trying to get to work. Leave it to Andrew to stand out like a superstar on a red carpet that's been rolled out just for him. He hands me the bag, and says, "I hate to run, but I have a conference call I can't be late for." Signaling to a car at the curb, he adds, "I can drop you somewhere if it's on the way."

"I'm sure it won't be. Anyway, I'm not in a hurry, so I think I'll walk."

"If you're sure." He leans on the top of the door, looking at me for what feels like an hour. It's mere seconds, but the lingering stare carries weight with it. "I—"

"It's okay, Andrew," I say, letting him off the hook. Raising the coffee cup, I suck in a breath. "Debt paid, and I scored a muffin."

"All right." He nods once, his gaze staying locked with mine. "Goodbye, Juni."

"See you around."

He dips inside the car and closes the door. I could stand around hoping for some big moment, a grand gesture, or a sign that we're meant to be friends, but that only happens in the movies. So, I click my heels together and head to my job. But hey, I got a free coffee and muffin out of this morning. *Slightly better than Jen, I suppose.*

5

Juni

THE ELEVATOR DOORS OPEN WIDE, REVEALING A DESK WITH gleaming brass letters hung above the receptionist's head. Although her eyes meet mine, a headset mic blocks most of her smile. "It's a great day to invest in your future with Christiansen Wealth Management. How may I help you?"

That's a mouthful. "I'm here to see—"

A finger cuts through the air, silencing me. She waves me forward and then holds that finger up again when I reach the front of the high counter. Her gaze dips down, and she punches buttons before releasing a hard breath. "Sorry about that. The calls are endless this time of day with clients freaking out about early market projections. I get it, but the New York Stock Exchange hasn't opened yet."

"I thought this was a financial advising company?"

"It is, but CWM bought Manhattan Financial to get a foothold in New York, which was a brokerage firm. They're headquartered out of Los Angeles." She quirks her mouth to the side and taps a pen against her cheek. "Though since

Mr. Christiansen, the eldest Christiansen son, moved to New York, I guess this is the headquarters. At least for now."

That's a lot of information in the span of two minutes. I like this fast talker. She stands and adds, "Now that you're all caught up on the company business, how can I help you?"

"I'm Juni Jacobs. I'm here for—"

"For *my* job. I'm Melissa." Smiling, she rubs her belly. "I'm off for maternity leave in a few days, so we need to get started right away. There's a lot to learn." She pulls a drawer open and points. "You can tuck your bag in here. It'll be safe. There are cameras everywhere."

I set my bag in the large drawer.

Wasting no time, she pushes the drawer closed with the tip of her block heel and then clips a box to her belt. "Follow me." As soon as we start walking, I see her press on the box, and then hear her say, "It's a great day to invest in your future with Christiansen Wealth Management. How may I help you?"

She looks back over her shoulder, holding her mic to cut off the sound, and quieter than a whisper, she mouths, "This is the atrium. Assistants, researchers, and data entry all sit here."

I nod just as she says to someone who's called, "I'll transfer you." Pointing to our right, she says in a normal volume of voice, "This is the conference area. Conference room one through five. They go from smallest to largest. One being the smallest. Employees have to book the rooms in the main operations dashboard for CWM. That way, there's never any confusion as to who has it when." She stops and turns to me. Grasping my arm, she sighs heavily. "It used to be my job. God, am I glad I don't have to mess with that anymore."

Her back is to me again, and not breaking stride, she

waves her finger in front of her, crossing out something I can't see. "The mailroom and brokerage division are housed one floor up. It's noisy and a different environment from down here. The stockbrokers watch the market like they're standing on the exchange floor. Technically, they should be, so yeah, it never made sense to me why they play the screens at such a high volume."

"Maybe for them, it's like staying in character. Method stockbroking."

"Ah. You mean because of all the yelling they usually do down at the stock exchange? They do like noise."

"Yes."

She ponders the thought, and then a smile slides into place. "Probably. Never thought of it that way. The cave is on the opposite side of the atrium." She starts whispering, "The accountants and HR are in this area on the left. They like quiet at all times. It's like a library over here. I've been shushed a time or two. And the financial advisors take up the offices on this side. The *window* offices."

Answering a call, she skips right over an office that appears to take up the space of two. The plaque reads CEO, but there's no name attached. There's also an open-door policy sign posted. "Last but not least, our legal department." Pulling me into the break room, she whispers, "Are you single?"

"I think that's against most company policies to ask."

"Oh, I know, but we're friends, right? My point is if you are single, there are so many hot guys. Some sexy married guys too, but that's against my personal policy." Rubbing her baby belly, she laughs. "Well, before and after I was married."

"It's a good policy to live by, no matter what your status is."

Opening the fridge, she pulls out a yogurt and points it at me. "I'd kill Kellan if he cheated on me." I'm thinking she veers easily from topic to topic. "As I was saying, if you're single, it's not against policy to date a coworker is all I'm saying, though they do frown upon it." After grabbing a spoon from the drawer, she hip-checks it closed. "Do you want a coffee or anything?"

"No, thank you. I finished one just before I arrived."

"I think that's it for the office layout. Each door is labeled, but if you do need help, you can ask almost anyone. Most people around here are nice. There are a few moody members of the CWM team, but we're careful not to talk about them." Cupping her hand to the side of her mouth, she rubs her belly again. "At least not until we get to happy hour. It's been a while since I've gone to The Watering Hole, though. Any questions so far?"

"About the office layout or happy hour?"

"Either." She laughs. "You're hilarious, Juni."

"Thanks." I give her a nod of appreciation, and then say, "I noticed there's no plant life."

She waves it off as if that's insignificant, as if breathing fresh oxygen isn't the basis of survival. "The last receptionist left a plant behind. I think it was a fern. Big leaves with a long vine."

"Sounds like a philodendron." When she doesn't blink, I wave my hand between us. "An ivy."

"Oh! Yeah, I don't know. It sat here on the counter until it died."

"Did you water it?"

Setting down the yogurt and spoon, she begins sorting through the papers left on a table. "Guess that mystery is now solved." With a burst of energy, she waggles her thumbs in the air. "Did you say you're all good with the office?"

"Yep. All good."

Marching past me with her snack in hand, she says, "All right then. Let's get back to the front desk and start on phone protocol. I have a baby shower to get to in the atrium before lunch. You think you'll be ready to cover the front?"

I have faith I can handle it. "I'll be ready, and you can enjoy the shower."

"That would be fantastic. We thought we'd have to move it to the reception area while I answered calls." And then she answers another call. "It's a great day to invest in your future with Christiansen Wealth Management. How may I help you?"

Although my temp career has had me working everywhere from offices to retail to once being hired for the Big Apple Circus for a week as a stand-in ballerina (all those dance lessons my grandmother insisted I take for poise paying off), I'm not sure what to make of this one.

I only took this job as a favor to the temp agency. They begged. Apparently, it was big money, and they wanted to land this account for future opportunities. They've had two others rotate through, but neither was a good fit. Now they're sending me, the best they have.

Agreeing to something steady for six to eight weeks will be a change in pace. I prefer variety to my days, and this job is feeling a lot like commitment. The last thing I want to dedicate my time to is something with the potential for permanency. That never works out well for this soul.

But I made the commitment, or had my arm twisted, I should say, so I'll follow through.

It's only six weeks, max eight, depending on when Melissa wants to return.

Weeks. *That's it.*

Not for a year or for life.

After completing Tuesday's task of organizing the supply room, we return to the front desk.

I'm told we restock the break room on Wednesdays.

We are supposed to verify conference room appointments and make sure they're ready to go next week.

And it sounds like I prepare to repeat the week's duty next week by ordering everything for delivery on Monday.

My ability to learn quickly growing up served me well on the junior circuit, my mind a sponge for information, my memory as sharp as a thumbtack. *At least back then.* It's not too shabby now, I must admit, but I'm not competing anymore.

The little reassurance doesn't do much for my stomach. I'm not sure what's making me a little queasy, but I swallow it down. As if that is an accomplishment in and of itself, I pride myself on being present in the moment and not letting fear take over. "I push this one and then transfer here, but add their employee number?"

"Exactly. The automation takes it from there."

Judging by how busy this position is, time is going to fly. She's already had me running the reception desk for two hours. She grabs her purse from the drawer and asks, "Are you ready?"

"Guess we're about to find out."

"You've got this, Juni. I'll be right inside if you need anything."

One hour on my own. Easy peasy. While I work, the entire office showers her with baby gifts. I can hear the laughter and her squeals of excitement all the way in reception. Barely able to hear my calls over Melissa's raving about Mr. Christiansen's gift, I get up to shut the door.

From my research, the directory lists two Christiansens, who I suspect are the owners, considering the company's name—*a lawyer and the CEO.* Apparently, one of them is winning the day with their gift.

Although I'm curious what it is, it's much quieter with the door closed.

Melissa practically floats through the door, leaving it wide open again. She taps the screen of her phone, bringing it to life, and then says, "It's lunchtime. This is how we shut everything down when we leave the desk for an hour or at the end of the day."

She goes through each step and then has me do it. When I get it right the first time, Melissa confides in me that she knew I'd catch on quickly the moment we met.

We ride down the elevator together. It's crowded, so we move to the back. She whispers, "The boss just gave me a silver baby's rattle from Tiffany and two extra paid weeks off. And here I thought he was the moodiest man I've ever met. Today he's my favorite." The herd exits the elevator, but I remain, my knuckles whitening around the railing.

Just outside the elevator, she turns back as if she just realized I'm not beside her. "Come on, Juni."

I move at the sound of my name but then stop in the lobby. "Does that mean you're taking eight or ten weeks for your leave?"

"Ten." She carries on as if she has no cares in the world. "My last day is Friday, and I cannot wait to work on my tan." She turns around again and waves me to her. "And nest, of course."

"Of course," I reply, going through the motions. Ten weeks is suddenly sounding like forever. Am I ready to take that on? Do I even want to? I need to call the agency again.

Outside the building, Melissa jets off to meet her

husband for lunch, and although she was kind enough to invite me, I decline. I brought my lunch from home, but more so, I need a minute or fifty-five to wrap my head around this change in plans.

No matter how much this city changes, some things always stay the same. If memory serves me correctly, there's a park two blocks up and one over.

Satisfaction sets in as soon as I see tall trees and soft grass covering the ground. I remember coming here with my grandmother when I was little since it was near the dance studio. I'd dance barefoot, and she'd clap as if I was the star of the ballet. I wasn't. I was quite terrible. I could blend in at the circus since the audience was watching the acrobats and the trapeze artists.

I find a spot under a tree and reach inside my satchel to dig out my lunch. My hand hits paper that crinkles under my touch, and I pull it out. I'd forgotten about the muffin because my morning has been so busy, but I'm pleasantly surprised to find the treat. Looking inside the bag, I find two. I'd forgotten he'd ordered one. Apparently, he forgot as well.

And now he's on my mind again. Too bad he's not here, or I'd share. Taking a big bite, too big to be proper, I attempt to chew.

"Juni?"

With him on my mind, my heart races, and for a brief second, I think it might be Andrew. It wouldn't be a total surprise since I feel like we're stalking each other at this point.

I am disappointed, though, when I discover it's not him. Unfortunately. If my mouth wasn't so full, I'd be able to say his name, but seeing a beautiful brunette on my ex's arm has me chewing a little slower. This muffin is a good excuse to hold my tongue.

Raising my hand, I mumble with a full mouth, "Hi."

When it comes to Karl, etiquette goes out the window.

I once trusted him. Of course, I did. He was the boy in the spotlight beside me, the one standing next to me on every stage as we presented our findings, the plant species we were studying, and whispering words of reassurance when my knees knocked from nerves. It didn't matter that he was also my biggest competitor.

I may not have set out to become a prodigy in the field, but it was in my blood to follow in my parents' footsteps. And from his own sheer determination, he was right there with me. We were young and talented in a field populated with botanists much older than we were. When no one else understood what we were going through, we relied on each other.

He's also one of the reasons I struggle to get too deeply involved—with work or in relationships. I'll never know if it was greed, ambition, or fame going to his head that made him do it, but I'll never forget what true betrayal feels like.

It's been eight years. I've read enough periodicals to know he succeeded and seen photos to recognize the changes I see in him now. I don't need to put on a show or pretend we're friends. We're not. I know that as much as he does. But I still have one lingering question for him. "Was stabbing me in the back worth it?"

When shame flashes through his eyes, he releases the woman's hand and shoves his in the front pockets of his jeans. For a moment, I almost expect him to say something kind. "Still bitter, Juni?"

I expected too much. "No," I answer honestly. "You did me a favor."

"How so?"

Tossing the rest of the muffin back in the bag, I push off

the ground and dust my backside. I pull the straps of the bag onto my shoulders and cross my arms over my chest. "If I'd won, I wouldn't be free."

It wasn't a great comeback or even the one that had played out in my head for the last eight years. There was never going to be a reward or revenge, but it felt good to finally get that off my chest.

I didn't live up to expectations, and even worse, I crashed and burned when it was my moment to shine. But as I walk across the grass with him standing there stunned, I don't have one regret leaving that life behind.

6

Andrew

"Commitment is the foundation of a business. Trust builds it." My father's voice fills the office.

"Did you start the jacuzzi, Corbin?" My mom's voice is heard in the background. "I brought the piña coladas."

Eyeing my brother sitting across from me, I rattle my head, needing that image out of it. Nick silently gags, so I finally say, "Sounds like you two have a busy night. We'll talk soon, Dad."

"Hello, Andrew," my mom sings in the background. "How are you, honey?"

"Good, Mom. Busy, but that's typical."

The sound of water splashing, and her giggles follow. "Hope not too busy. New York has so much to offer if you just give yourself some time to discover it."

"I know. I know," I say, sighing. "But it's a busy time of year, so—"

"So schmo, Andrew. Tell your brother to take you out.

He's lived there for years, he probably knows all the great places."

My eyes dart to Nick, who shakes his head, and then mouths, "Don't do it."

I hate sacrificing my brother, but I need the deterrent from my life. "Actually, Nick's right here." I shrug, inwardly chuckling.

She asks, "Nicholas?"

"Yeah, Mom?"

"How's Natalie?"

"Wow, that's how it is now? I give you the daughter you always wanted, and you give me the cold shoulder."

Both of my parents laugh. Water sloshes, and then my dad finally pipes back in, "It's not like that at all, son. Your mom talks about you all the time. When are you coming for a visit?"

"We're thinking next month."

My mom replies, "That works for us. The weather's been beautiful."

"It's California," Nick says, "the weather is always beautiful."

She says, "And your sarcasm is duly noted." Not letting anything bring down her mood, she splashes my dad from the sound of it.

Nick adds, "Sorry. You're right. The weather here has been a nice change from winter. I need to talk to my bosses about splitting my time between LA and New York for the seasons."

I say, "Your boss is right here."

"I'd love that," my mom replies. "I miss both of you so much. Nick, you should take your boss out for drinks. You know, schmooze him."

Listening to her plot with my brother is entertaining.

They go back and forth before he asks her, "What have you been up to?"

"I started doing sunrise yoga on Thursdays again." We nod as she continues, "Oh, and Andrew might be interested in this. Are you still there?"

"I'm here."

"I saw Megan and Dalen Dalery at The Polo Lounge last week. She just recovered from a brow lift and looked refreshed."

Nick's eyes dart to mine, and he asks, "Dalen had a brow lift?"

"No, her mother, Megan, silly. Dalen is much too young for that. Speaking of Dalen, she looked so pretty in a pink dress. Do you and Dalen still talk, Andrew?"

"Not much, but I get an occasional text here and there." It's strange how a sexual relationship can turn into a platonic friendship, but it did for us. After a few months, we realized the sex was great, but we didn't see a long-term relationship working out. The friendship was good, though. I think that's why it was easy for us to stay friends. I don't tell my mom that Dalen sends me texts with photos of her friends in hopes to set me up on a date. The last thing I want my mom to do is team up with my ex to play matchmaker for me.

Nick says, "Mom, Dad, we have another meeting to get to, so we'll call you soon. Okay?"

"Of course," my mom replies, "we have some relaxing to do. Your dad has taken to retirement like frosting to a cupcake." I feel like there's a lost opportunity by not using crumbs to a cookie, but she never mentions cookies. It must be the curse of being named after the sweet treat. "Take care of yourselves and have some fun. Love you."

"Love you," we both reply in unison.

I look at my brother. "You realize it's midday in California, right? Our parents are hot-tubbing it in the middle of a workday."

"I can only hope for such a glorious retirement."

He might have a point. "Coffee?"

"Definitely." He stands, ready to lead the way. "Break room or the coffee place downstairs?" Stopping just short of opening the door, he swears under his breath as he looks at his phone. "Shit. I can't go. Barbara just added a call onto my schedule."

"Who's Barbara?"

"My new assistant."

"What happened to Emily?"

He clicks his tongue. "She finally got the offer she was looking for." I have a feeling he's speaking in code, but it's not something I care to riddle through right now. He adds, "Just a heads-up. I'm trying to wrap up a contract before the weekend. I may message you to help on this call. You have time?"

"No, but I'll do it if it's important."

"It's important."

"Then just let me know."

"Thanks, Andrew."

He disappears, leaving the door to my office cracked open. I can't work with a lot of noise from the office. And although the Cave is usually the quiet side, something is stirring in the ranks. I get up but pause before I exit. I know the chatter will stop as soon as they see me. I won't eavesdrop, but sometimes, I'd like to be in on the goings-on around here.

Just as I step out, I overhear Justin from accounting ask Taylor, "Have you seen the new girl? She's pretty hot. I think

I'll go introduce myself and offer to show her around the office, like the supply closet."

Taylor asks, "I thought you had a girlfriend?"

"Always room for one on the side." Justin laughs. Taylor doesn't.

Neither do I. Making my presence known, I clear my throat.

Taylor ducks back into his cubicle, and Justin waves. Justin's the brownnoser in the office. An accountant who's gunning for my job. "Good afternoon, sir."

The corner of my eye ticks. I get that I'm the head of the company, but since I'm not quite thirty, being called sir still bugs me. Justin bugs me as well, but he's given me no cause to fire him yet, and he's good with numbers, so he remains. I'm hoping HR finally handles him. Naturally, none of them are around to hear him talk about this *special tour* he wants to give.

"Afternoon," I reply, now wondering who the new girl is. That's a line I won't cross, but he has my curiosity piqued.

My assistant, Mary, asks, "Can I do something for you?"

"No. I'm going to get a cup of coffee."

She's quick to rise. "I can get that for you."

"It's okay. I need the break."

"All right," she replies, sitting down again. She was hired right before I moved here. We're both still learning the ropes. She also does excellent work.

When I enter the break room, I exchange greetings with two of my top human resources employees. Guess this is where Laurie and Joseph hide. Probably to get away from Justin. I chuckle at my joke.

Laurie and Joseph have brought some of the top talent in the city to CWM over the past six months. I rely on them to add to the foundation we've laid and create a great work environment. Working with over a hundred unique person-alities is never easy, and they allow me to stay out of the fray. Most of the time. "Just overheard Justin being crass about one of his coworkers."

As they wait for the microwave to finish heating their food, Laurie asks, "What did he say?"

"He was talking about the new girl," I say as if I'm knowledgeable to who that is.

Joseph says, "I'll remind him of the company policy to show due respect to all employees."

"Thank you." I watch the coffee machine percolate but then turn to them as they whisper to each other. Trying for nonchalance, I ask, "Who's the new girl?"

Laurie replies, "We were just talking about her."

"I guess everyone is. Do I need to give you a warning?" I joke.

Laurie is closer to my mom's age, but she still blushes around me. This time her laughter precedes it. "That won't be necessary. It's the temp we hired to replace Melissa at reception while she's on maternity leave. Joseph and I were saying that we're hearing great things about her."

On cue, Joseph adds, "It's only been three days, but she's accomplished a week's worth of tasks and done them well."

"While juggling the phones, I might add," Laurie says. "She's very impressive."

"That's good to hear. Keep an eye on her. We're always looking for exceptional employees." *And maybe a new accountant down the track.*

Joseph pops the microwave door open to remove his dish. "Melissa has been an asset to the front, but she wants to move upstairs to the brokerage division." He turns to Laurie. "Maybe now is the time we consider it."

She says, "I agree. If things keep going the way they are

with Ms. Jacobs, we definitely need to consider it. Let's rede-fine the job description as well."

"I think Ms. Jacobs already has." They sound giddy. Laurie turns back to me and says, "Have a nice day, Andrew."

"You too."

I walk back to my office with coffee in hand, tempted to detour to reception to meet this stellar Ms. Jacobs. I'm not that foolish, though. I set the mug on my desk as I settle into the late afternoon.

As soon as my concentration returns, my phone screen lights up with a text from Nick. *Are you available?*

My brother may be a punk half the time, but in business, he's always shown me respect. *I'll be right there.*

A call that should have taken less than an hour kept us tied up for over two. When I returned to my office, I shuffled through a few emails and then got lost in the numbers on my screen. Mary checked in before leaving, but I lost track of time after that. I didn't even notice my office was dark until the door opens, allowing light to flood in. Nick asks, "Why are you sitting in the dark?" and then flips on the light.

Briefly blinded, I blink until my eyes adjust. "It wasn't dark when I sat down. What time is it?"

"Seven thirty."

"Phew. That's good. I can still get some stuff done." As he holds up the wall with his shoulder, I keep typing and ask, "Is there something I can help you with?"

"How are you, brother?"

My gaze shifts past the monitor. "It's been two hours since I saw you. You already miss me?"

Chuckling, he replies, "I miss partying with you when we had fewer cares. I miss hitting the waves at sunrise and then grabbing breakfast tacos from a food truck while trying to hustle to get to school on time." I sit back and listen because I miss those times too. "But I've been thinking about what Mom said earlier, about taking you out."

"You don't have to worry about me, little brother. I'm good . . . I'm fine."

"Yeah," he says with little faith in my words. "I can tell."

My brother is one of my best friends, always has my back, and can read me like a damn book. But the thing is, I *am* fine. I *am* good. The way he's staring at me like I grew a third eye in my forehead has me questioning my sanity, though. "What?"

"You're too uptight."

"I have good reason to be." I drag the keyboard closer and return to my work.

He makes himself at home on the other side of the desk, sitting there without a care in the whole fucking world. "You always have been, but if it's possible, you seem tenser than usual. What gives? Work? The move? Let's grab a drink and talk about it."

"Like you said, it's only seven thirty."

Nudging the desk with his knee, he says, "I didn't say only. Come on, Andrew. It's Friday night, and no one's left in the office but you."

"You're here."

"I'm here because I need to suck up to my boss."

"Ha!"

I'm given another shrug, and then he chuckles. "Only between these walls." He stands again, and as he walks to the door, he says, "Come on. I'm meeting Jackson, and I can introduce you to The Watering Hole."

"Natalie's brother, Jackson?"

"Jackson St. James, himself. Did you know he's brought

on four new clients this month, and not one of them is investing under a mil?"

I'm thinking he's not going to let me get out of this despite leaning back like I'm not budging from this chair. "I did know, but what about Natalie?"

"She has her own company."

"No." I toss a pen across the office at him. "I mean, she's not expecting you home?"

He flicks the light off again. "Why do you think I'm still here?"

I shake my head as the puzzle becomes clear. "Because besides Mom trying to marry me off, your wife is now sending you on the same mission? What is it with women not appreciating a single man? Maybe I'm fine being on my own. Not that anyone would know that since they don't ask."

"Actually, Natalie called it a sympathy offer since all you do is work. *Tomato.* Tomahto, though. *Am I right?* Wrap up, and I'll meet you at the elevators in five."

"What if I don't—"

The door closes before I have a chance to set a different proposal on the table—like me working another two or three hours and then going home. Ignoring him, I start analyzing the numbers on the screen again. I'm determined to figure out where the discrepancy is in this report.

But a beer, a bar, and blowing off steam do sound tempting. I won't give him the glory, but Nick's probably right. I *should* get out. I've been following the same routine since I arrived in this city.

Seattle kept me too busy to enjoy the fact that I was actually in Seattle. Am I going to repeat that mistake in New York? I might as well make the most of it since I won't be here forever.

Scanning the page on the screen, I realize there's

nothing I'm working on that can't be handled over the weekend. I always work then anyway. I close it down and grab my jacket.

Nick's waiting at the elevators when I arrive. I hadn't noticed earlier, but my brother's looking sharp. "Nice suit," I say.

"Back atcha."

I can admit the Christiansen brothers clean up well, but even messy, we can pull more than our fair share of attention. *Thanks for the good looks, Cookie and Corbin.*

He rests against the wall of the elevator as we ride down the twenty flights. I can feel the weight of his stare and turn back. "What is it?"

Grinning, he says, "I'm glad you decided to come."

"You didn't think I would?"

It's a subtle shake of his head, but I notice. "I wasn't sure."

Maybe I do owe him some credit. "Thanks for inviting me."

He reaches over and squeezes my shoulder. "Life's passing by."

Nothing more needs to be said. I know they want me to be happy.

Am I?

I'm not sure if I've felt that emotion in a while. I'll have to think about that.

We travel the rest of the way in silence. Outside, we catch the last of the remaining daylight before the skyscrapers engulf it. "I've been here, what? Three weeks and you haven't introduced me to your bar until now?"

"It wasn't for lack of trying." He pats me on the back. "It's around the corner."

It feels good to forget about work, to get out of the office, and not feel like I'm behind on a million things. I confess, "I miss the good ole days sometimes, too. What happened?"

"Life got in the way."

"Work piled up."

I was busy earning my MBA while working my way up the corporate ladder. There were rumors I got the job based on my last name, and I'm not stupid enough to think that didn't play a big part in it. But my dad had expectations of Nick and me. We exceeded them, and that's why we're here today. Not at the bar, but sitting atop a company that we've given our lives to.

One night hanging out with my brother feels like old times. My mood has improved, and I'm actually looking forward to it. He says, "Let's not let it get in the way again."

I shake his hand. "I'll hold you to that if you'll do the same for me."

"You're on." Holding the door open, he grins as if we're about to enter a secret world that only he knows about. "This is where tycoons to tellers, day traders to corner shop owners hang out. You never know if you're talking to a billionaire or someone just starting out in their career until you get into some drunken conversation with the stranger next to you. That's what makes it so great." He peers over the heads of the crowded bar and then adds, "Come on. You'll fit right in."

7

Andrew

MY WORRIES ABOUT WORK WERE FORGOTTEN THE MINUTE I walked into this place, my jacket discarded before the first game of darts, and my tie loosened after the second round of drinks.

The server tried to take up residence on my lap several times, pawing my arm and touching my hair. Margie's cute, and I'm not opposed to hooking up for the night, but I am opposed to expectations in the morning. She's already sticking to me like glue, which is not a good sign this early on. Add a jealous bartender scowling at me into the mix and I think I'll stay clear.

"Andrew?"

I look up to find the guys staring at me. "What?"

Nick asks, "What the fuck was that?"

"I don't know what you're talking—Oh." *Margie.* "She's not my type."

Jackson asks, "Hot, flirting, and wearing a shirt that reads 'ready when you are' isn't your type?"

Glancing a few tables over, she smiles at me just before my eyes go lower to the design across her chest. "I didn't notice."

"Wow," he says. "It was pretty damn obvious, but okay." Being Natalie's brother, Jackson is family, but he also works upstairs. It was his parents' brokerage firm that we bought. He's barely out of university, but he's been working his ass off to prove he deserves to be there.

"Don't worry about me. I'm good—"

"I know," Nick says. "*You're fine.* You always say that."

I level a glare at him. "I am, except I could use another whiskey."

As if her ears were burning, Margie's here and offering, "Another drink, handsome?"

Jackson wags his finger in the air. "Another round, Margie."

Still staring at me, she winks. "You got it."

Nick says, "She's definitely into you, man."

A guy leans back from the table beside us. "I'm not one to give unsolicited advice, but I know a thing or two about Margie. She wants three things from a man. By appearances alone, you have two out of three."

"What's that?" I ask.

Chuckling, he replies, "Looks and money."

After taking a sip of my drink, I say, "Trust me, my looks and bank account are the least interesting things about me." I'm confident I have more to offer than that.

Nick is laughing but manages to say, "We're going to have to trust you on that one, brother."

Jackson leans forward as if Margie will somehow hear us over the rowdy crowd, and asks the stranger, "What's the third?"

"A wedding ring."

I angle to get a good look at him by resting my elbow on the table. "She only dates married men?"

"No, she likes to break up couples."

He doesn't seem like a shit-stirrer, but I know nothing about him. "That's a damning accusation. How do you know?"

He shows his left hand where there's no ring to be found. "I once fell for her tricks."

"Luckily, I'm just here for the whiskey." I toast to that and then empty the glass.

"Wise choice," he says, setting the legs of his chair down again and rejoining his friends.

Jackson says, "I'm fairly certain it takes two to tango. He can't place all the blame on her."

I eye Margie across the bar as she rubs some other guy's arm, the bartender now glaring at that guy. I'm not upset one bit.

That doesn't change the fact that I'm reminded it's been too long since I was with a woman. Clearly, I'm not seeking a relationship, but companionship with some fun at the end of the night wouldn't be so bad. Turning back to my friends, I say, "I'm sure she'd appreciate the vote of confidence, though I'm not sure she needs it." Just as her laughter reaches my ears, I cut my fingers through the air in front of my throat. "I think I'm done for the night."

"Another round is on the way." Standing, Jackson moves around the table. "I'm gonna take a piss."

The bartender delivers our drinks and grunts when he sets mine down. Nothing else. Just a grunt.

Glancing between the glass and Nick, I ask, "Do you think it's safe to drink?"

"Since I'm the spare, I'll sacrifice myself to protect you, Sire."

We've had a long-running joke about me being the heir and him the spare. Nick and my mom never appreciated it, but I cracked my dad up a few times. Not that he liked me more, but he likes a good one-up, and that was mine. "You will?"

"No, I fucking won't. Drink it." He taps his glass against mine, and adds, "The guy's not going to kill his clientele."

That's true, so I drink. "Hey, I wasn't going to say anything, but since you know about the list, I might as well tell you that I already did number one."

"You gave in? What made you do that?" With a cocked brow, he sits back, crossing his arms over his chest.

"Figured it was the easiest, and that might satisfy her if she asks."

"Maybe. What'd you have to do?"

Sitting forward, I curl my shoulders. "Waste my fucking time, that's what. It was the reason I was late to work on Monday."

Chuckling, he shifts around in his seat and rests his arm on the back of the chair. "And look. You lived to tell the tale. Now what was number one?"

"I had to be lying in the grass at 9:17 AM on a sunny day. On a weekday, to be precise."

With his brow wrinkled, he looks as confused as I still am regarding this list. "Why?"

The liquor has loosened me up, so although I'm not usually the shrugging kind, I do it and then slump back down. "I don't know."

"What happened?"

"Was my life forever changed? *No.* Did I get dog shit on me? *Yes.* And then the dog's owner was stalking me." Rolling my neck to the side, I give it a good stretch. "We had it out on the sidewalk before I lost a jinx and ended up meeting her the next morning to buy her a coffee as payment."

"What the fuck are you talking about?"

"The debt for the jinx. It was actually quite funny because she—"

"Huh? It sounds a lot like you're talking about a woman you met while on one of Mom's missions."

"No, I'm not talking about the woman. She was cute but kind of weird. I was talking about 9:17 in the morning. It was just a coincidence we met at that time. Like I said—"

Jackson returns and drops into his seat. "What'd I miss?"

I say, "Nothing."

But my brother has to include the whole world in this embarrassing conversation. "Andrew met someone."

"How long was I gone? Five minutes?"

Nick laughs. "Not here. He met her the other day."

"Ah." Jackson discovers his fresh drink and holds it up. "Well, here's to meeting new people."

We tap our glasses together and drink, and then Nick says, "Speaking of meeting people. Some guys just walked in who I want you to meet."

And just like that, I'm reminded of why I'm in New York, of my goals, and try to forget about the distraction of the female persuasion.

I follow the direction of his gaze, and ask, "Oh yeah?"

"Big money, but they have shit portfolio managers. We could help them."

"First, we have to land their accounts."

He stands and dusts my shoulder. "We will. They're brothers like us. Work together. Play together. Make money together."

I look behind me. "Who are they?"

"The Everest brothers."

In my head, that statement should have had a bigger climactic build than it did. Everyone's heard of the Everest brothers. "Ethan Everest, the tech billionaire?"

"Tech. Shipping. Electric cars. You name it, he owns it, billionaire. That's the one. And his older brother, Hutton. Impressive portfolio. He holds interests in Europe and domestically. May not be a billionaire yet, but he's well on his way."

I take another long pull from the glass and then see them heading our way. "I love landing a whale. Two is even better."

"I believe the term is a pod." Nick and I look at Jackson. He clears his throat, and says, "Technically speaking, a pod is a group of whales."

A chuckle rumbles through my chest. "Let's land this pod then."

Nick stands and shakes hands with them. "Man, it's been too long," he says. "Where's Bennett?"

Ethan laughs. I recognize him from the tabloids to *Forbes*. He even landed on the cover of *Time* magazine twice for innovations. He replies, "We don't always travel in a group."

When I see Jackson open his mouth to correct him, I shake my head just enough for him to get the message. No one wants to be called a pod.

His brother adds, "It's hard to get all three of us in one place at the same time these days. I just got back from Brudenbourg, and Bennett took off to visit our property in Texas."

Nick stands to his full height, comfortable standing next to anyone, from a celebrity to a billionaire. "I forgot to mention to Andrew that you married royalty. It's an incredible story."

Hutton laughs. "Sure is."

With his glass in hand, Nick adds, "I want you to meet my brother. This is Andrew and my brother-in-law, Jackson St. James."

Ethan waves Margie over after introductions are done. No doubt she'll be all over him since he's easily recognizable. I didn't set out to be a bodyguard, but I guess I'll do what it takes to protect a friend or land an account.

For the past two hours, we've talked business over darts and gotten into the details of their life stories. "Fascinating stuff, man." Six drinks aren't going to kill me, but it's going to fuck up my morning. "We should get together and talk about your investment portfolios. I know you're working with Jenkins & Myers, but I'd like a meeting to show you how we're different and what we can do for you."

Ethan laughs. "I won't pretend to be offended that a casual chat turned to business because it usually does. Normally, I'd say no, but Nick's been a friend for a while, and I've done some research on CWM. What you've done with the company is impressive. I like the energy and new path you're paving in a stale industry. Have your lawyer call mine."

"Nick's my lawyer."

He chuckles again as we shake hands. "Even better."

I stand, knowing when to make an exit. After another round of handshakes, I leave the guys to drink another round. Since it's after hours and I didn't reserve my driver for the night, I hail a cab.

Unplanned drunken nights are fun, but it's been a while for me, and I'm feeling it. I have the cabbie drop me off two blocks from the building, hoping the cool night air and walk will help me sober up. The first one starts clearing the fuzz from my brain, and my vision sharpens.

But as soon as I reach the second block, I stop in the middle of the sidewalk because I must be hallucinating. "Juni?"

8

Andrew

RASCAL SEES ME FIRST.

And yaps, of course, causing Juni to look in my direction. Her hand plants on her hip, and a tilt of her head makes it hard to decipher if she's happy or mad that I'm here. I walk toward them, hoping it's the former for Juni. Rascal tugs on his leash, making me realize at least one of them is excited to see me.

I approach with caution since her expression is as unreadable as her body language, and ask, "A bit late for a dog walk, don't you think?"

"When you got to go, you gotta go."

"Truer words have never been spoken."

For some reason, that makes her smile. Her defenses lower along with her hand. "Have you been drinking, Andrew?"

I lick my lips, admiring her as she comes into view under the lights sneaking out through the windows from the lobby. "Why are you asking that?"

"The way you're walking, the slow drawl in your words," she says, ticking each one off the top of a different fingertip, "or maybe it's the first time I've seen you without a coat hanger holding up your shoulders."

"Very funny."

"I thought so."

"You think I can't have fun? I do all the time," I insist.

"One doth protest too much."

"Only stating facts, babe."

Babe?

"Babe?" she repeats as if she can read my mind.

Shaking my head, I mumble, "Yeah, I got nothing."

There's a melody to her laugh, a sweet song that sometimes slips out for others who are lucky enough to hear. I'm one of them.

I look her over again, realizing I kind of missed her. "It's been a few days since we ran into each other." Not a question. Just a comment.

"You mean literally, right?" Humor punctuates her words. "Hopefully, your shirt is safe tonight."

I chuckle. When the laughter dies down, I count the feet that divide us. Three. But I'm close enough for Rascal to jump up on my leg. He's a great distraction. Squatting down, I pet his head and scrub down his back. When I glance up at Juni, I ask, "What's with the name?"

"You don't think he looks like a Rascal?"

Chuckling, I stand back up. "Your name."

She smirks, and it's quite appealing on her. "You don't think I look like a Juni?"

Angling my head to the left, I twist my mouth to the side as if that will help me figure out the answer. "Oddly enough, you do look like a Juni. Both of you."

"You see two of me?" An alarm rings through her tone.

I burst out laughing again. "No. I'm just messing with you. As for the name, I've just never heard it before."

"Most people know it from *Spy Kids*. Juni Cortez." She moves closer to the building when a group of people walks by.

Spy Kids? That's a flashback. "I haven't seen that movie in ages. Decades, in fact. Juni was the brother, right?"

"Yes. He was sort of annoying."

I close some distance and rub my jaw. "I had the biggest crush on Carmen."

"She was awesome. The actress does Hallmark movies now."

"The Christmas ones?"

"They're not all Christmas," she says, shrugging, "but that channel, yes."

"I haven't seen any. My mom does, though."

"Right," she says between tight lips. "Your *mom.*"

"I didn't mean to insinuate—"

One of her hands comes up in front of her, and her expression softens again. "I know what you meant. It's okay."

Shit. I'm blowing this . . . whatever *this* is. "I like Juni on you much better."

Restoring the joy that fits her features so well, she looks down shyly. "Thank you, Andrew."

With my hands in my pockets, I rock back and then side-step but play it off like I intended to stumble to the right. *Distract.* "Did he do his business?"

With pinched brows, she jerks back. "Who?"

"Rascal. He's on concrete. Wouldn't he like grass better?"

She looks at him sitting contently by her side and then at me again. "Who wouldn't?" she says, thumbing over her shoulder. "That's why I took him to the park."

Looking past her, I don't see any grass. "Is that safe at night?"

"It has been so far, but I guess you never know." She lifts her wrist to show something dangling from it. "I also carry pepper spray."

The alcohol catches up with me, and I lean against one of the stone columns dividing the windows. "Smart." Looking down one side of the street and then the other, I ask, "What are you doing here?"

"You're nosy when you're drunk. You know that, Andrew?" Despite her words, she doesn't sound offended.

"Is that a compliment?"

I can admit that I earned that eye roll she gives me. "I'm trying to decide if it's good or bad to see you in this state."

"I'm better in California, if you know what I mean, but . . ." I raise my arms out. "I'm stuck here in New York for the next two years."

That gets her laughing. "I don't know what you mean, but I meant your condition." Her hand gestures down and then up again. "Your body's physical state, not the geographical location."

I narrow my eyes, but then I widen them again, preferring the view of all of her better. "Ah, so you *were* checking me out."

"Oh my God," she says, sighing, but I hear the lightness in her tone. "You're a handful—"

"More than, but it would be rude to brag."

"Too late." Coming closer, she lowers her voice. "I'm thinking I should take you home."

"Great minds think alike."

She doesn't even try to restrain her laughter. "Do you remember when you accused me of flirting with you?"

"I thought it was the other way around?" Gil sits behind the counter and occasionally looks in our direction.

"Oh right." She looks up at the stars, letting her gaze linger, and then to me again. "Anyway, your flirting doesn't bother me. I actually like it, but I'm wondering what's happening here."

When my gaze slides back to Juni, I can practically see the questions filling her eyes. Questions lead to commitments, and that's not something I can do. "I don't know what to say. I don't want to hurt your feelings."

A soft hum is exhaled as if I just fed her the best thing she's ever fucking tasted. I think . . . *Yeah*, I definitely need to readjust when she makes that sound twice.

Her reaction is unexpected and sexy as fuck. The tips of her fingers land on my stomach, and she drags them leisurely down two buttons as if we're old friends. I shift, trying not to be so obvious, because fuck, it's been a long time since I've slept with a woman. And she's hot and funny in a quirky way and standing right here looking at me like she feels the same about me. Not the funny part, but the hot part I mentioned.

"I'm so relieved to hear you say that, Andrew. I was thinking we could hang out more often—"

"Four times this week is fairly often."

"I was thinking we could hang out on purpose."

Running my hand through my hair, I say, "I'm open to the idea. Continue."

"Although the universe is doing a pretty darn good job, maybe we can make a plan."

"Plan a date?"

"No, more like going out together without it being a date. Go out as friends."

"Friends. Yes. I like this dating plan."

"It's not a dating plan. It's just friends going on a . . . ugh. I mean going out. Hanging out. Platonically. Now I'm getting confused. Platonically." She says that last word again, and then asks, "Is that even a word? Why does it sound strange and taste so weird? *Platonically*."

"Platonically. It sounds weird to my ears now too." When I yawn, and my eyes dip closed longer than is acceptable for standing on a street having a definition-defining conversation about a word, she tugs me by the sleeve of my jacket. "As fun as this is, as your friend, I think you should go home."

Tapping the tip of her cute nose, I admit, "I don't disagree."

"All right. Since you're drunk and wearing a Rolex and a designer suit on the street, Rascal and I will just make sure you get home safely."

"This is a first."

"Guess there's always room for another." Now that we're standing in the middle of the sidewalk again, she looks around. Unsettled, she asks, "Where do you live?"

My head bobs to the right. "Right here."

Her smile is honest and unassuming, unlike her eyes that seem to protect her secrets.

What am I doing? "I used to hold my liquor better." When she looks at the building, I study her profile, tracing the slightest of slopes down her nose to the peaks of the bow at the top of her lips. She really is quite attractive.

Puffing a breath, she sends strands of hair flying into the air in front of her, only for them to return and fall back in her face. Out of the corners of her eyes, she looks at me. "Let's get you home. It's past Rascal's bedtime, and I have a feeling it's past yours as well."

Before we reach the door, I stop her. My fingers slide up

the back of her arm while my gaze remains glued to her face —the sharp lines that lead from the apples of her cheeks to her cute little chin. "I think that's a good idea, but I also think I should make sure you get home safely."

"I'll be fine. Don't worry. I live really close, and I have Rascal to protect me."

Gil swings the door open, smiling as usual. "Good evening."

Just inside the door, she says, "Good evening." Turning back, I look at her, realizing she's not wearing any makeup. She's fresh-faced, and her hair is messy but beautiful as always. Words don't come easy as I take her in.

But with a clearing of Gil's throat, I step farther into the lobby as she stands just outside the door, an invisible barrier keeping us apart. Gil scratches his head as confusion rattles his expression. "Is everything all right?"

Juni scoops Rascal into her arms and then catches up to me. "Hey, I know you've been drinking, but I don't want you to forget about our plans."

I punch the button and then stop with my back to the elevator. "To hang out?"

Her smile is sunshine, though it's late at night. "Yes, to hang out. Drink lots of water, okay?"

"I will." Smiling, I say, "Thanks, friend."

"Wait." Grabbing her phone from her pocket, she asks, "What do you think about exchanging numbers? Then if we want to hang out or you need someone to protect you on your next drunken night out, you can text me."

I pull mine from my pocket and tell her my number. A text pops onto the screen, cementing the smile on my face. She releases a breath, and then says, "We'll talk soon."

"Yeah," I say, nodding as I back into the elevator. "Definitely. Good night, Juni."

"Good night, Andrew." The door closes, and I fall back on the wall, staring down at the screen. I decide to send her a text. *How do you feel about tomorrow?*

The door opens, and as I walk to my apartment, my phone buzzes in my hand. I stop to read her quick reply. *I love Saturdays.*

My fingers fly across the screen to respond: *Me too. I don't have plans. I was thinking if you don't have plans, maybe we could not have plans together.*

What is wrong with me? Why am I acting like a high school kid again? I really shouldn't feel this good, considering what I've drunk tonight, but there's just something about her I can't put my finger on. Another text comes in, making me grin like I'm guilty as sin.

I am. Thoughts fill my head, and I let my imagination run free with the images of how dirty Juni and I could be. The heat from when we touched still pulses through my veins. Instead of going to bed, I grab a bottle of water and then detour to the bathroom. I'm definitely going to need a cold shower.

With the water running, I slip my jacket off and toss it onto the bed. Leaning against the marble counter with a ridiculous smile on my face, I think about the last text she sent. *Sounds like a plan.*

9

Juni

NOW WE'RE FRIENDS?

Oh God.

Not that I'm opposed to having friends. Having them is great, but what happened? Why did I ask a drunk man if he wants to be my friend? So humiliating. *Why did I do that?*

Have I gone insane?

I sounded so desperate, yet I couldn't bring myself to stop. Once the words left my mouth, it was too late. I'm now two texts deep into making plans with him. Well, agreeing to not make plans but a plan to hang out sometime. *Oh God.*

When burying my face in a pillow doesn't ease the embarrassment flooding every fiber of my being, I consider other alternatives like moving to Alaska, or going on an extended trip to Texas, maybe joining the Navy, a stint on *Below Deck*, or even hiking the Pacific Crest Trail like Cheryl Strayed in the movie *Wild*.

Anything works that gets me far from being in the same building, in the same vicinity, or even the same state with him. I half giggle, unwittingly thinking about how he thought I meant the state of New York instead of his state of sobriety. He was drunk, all right.

As funny as that was, how am I going to face him when he's sober?

Oh, wait. I bolt upright. Maybe Andrew won't remember. I have a feeling he wasn't drunk enough to forget. One can only hope it's the opposite.

Flopping back down on the bed, I need to think clearly. I need to dissect the night through each minute, and then use my brain's muscle memory to trace and track.

It was a normal night, not meant to be more.

Mr. Clark called about Rascal needing to go out just before ten, so I grabbed my jacket since I had nothing better going on. It wasn't a big deal. I chose the grass pad down the street instead of hitting the rooftop patch. Sometimes it's not worth the fit Rascal throws when I'm trying to make him go on fake turf.

But unlike any other night, Andrew had shown up seemingly out of nowhere. Sure, I know he came from down the street, but with that tie loosened and the top button of his shirt popped open, I was taken by surprise.

The way his hair hung over his forehead as if he'd spent hours in bed instead of at a bar, or restaurant, or wherever he was that overserved him. The late-night scruff covering his jaw had me biting his lip—*my lip.* I meant I was biting *my* lip but wanted to bite . . . This might be a good time to drag the pillow over my head again.

At this rate of mortification, I'm never going to get any sleep. I roll to the side to check the time. 12:38.

Only two things will make me feel better. I'll start with food.

I drag the spices from the cabinet and the paneer cheese

from the fridge. I need comfort food tonight, and that means curry. It's New York, so I could order anything I want at this hour, but sometimes I just need to turn on some music to set the scene and do something to take my mind off things.

Even if just for a short time.

I turn up the music and start cooking. Moving around the kitchen, I dance in the fragrance of the spices. Since I'm using cheese as my protein, it doesn't take long to simmer everything together, but I go ahead and pour myself a small glass of wine. It may not take my mind off everything from earlier tonight, but for a brief time, it helps.

Twenty minutes to cook.

Ten minutes to devour.

I lose the motivation to clean the dishes afterward, but I'm never one to rush to clean up after a meal anyway. The process of cooking and eating should be enjoyed. Cleaning is such a chore. I fill the sink and leave them to soak until morning.

Turning off the music, I fall back on the couch, stuffed after eating my creation at the island. Like a bad date, the memories return for another round of torture. I wallow a while but then decide I have to resort to the only other option I have. *Gil.*

Pushing off the couch, I go to slip on my baby-blue, sheep-covered sleep pants and my fuzzy purple robe over my tank top. I tighten the belt and slip on a pair of flip-flops before heading down to the lobby.

The elevator doors open, and the newlyweds from the fifteenth floor—looking like they just walked off the runway —step back with mouths wide open. "Hi," I squeak out because sure, I needed to be embarrassed once more before bed.

Her flowing chestnut hair drapes over her shoulders as if

it considers it a privilege to be there. Her perfect red lips form a smile, but she can't hide the sympathy filling her eyes as if she knows I begged a drunk man to be my friend.

She's probably never had to beg for anything.

Cringing inside, I mutter, "We can't all be supermodels," with a roll of my eyes.

They let the girl having a mental meltdown have her moment by not saying anything, but don't think I don't notice the wide berth they travel when they pass to get on the elevator. If wearing pajamas in a high-rise lobby is considered an act of the insane, then call me cuckoo. I flip my hair and head toward the front desk.

Witnessing it all, Gil chuckles behind a fist. His laughter is contagious, and this time, I roll my eyes at myself and give in. "What? They acted like being dressed in your jammies is weird or something. They probably sleep in the nude, or worse, she wears those silky lingerie sets while walking around in those fluffy feather slippers with heels being glamorous for the entire city to see through their windows."

Trying to keep my imagination from running further than it has already, I plant my elbows on the top of the counter and rest my chin in my hands with a dramatic sigh.

Gil holds up a pink box of donuts. "Your favorite, strawberry frosted."

I take the pastry despite still being stuffed from the curry and rice. He may not have made them, but I feel the care in the sweet offering. "How do you always know exactly what I need?"

"I was here the first day you walked through that door as a precocious seven-year-old," he says, pointing at the front as I snack on the pastry. "My daughter used to babysit you, and my sweet wife, Nancy, baked your tenth birthday cake. I always grab an extra just in case you need a pick-me-up. Call me sentimental."

"Sentimental," I say, watching his smile grow wider. "But honestly, I hate you spending your hard-earned money on me. You don't have to." I bite off more than I can chew—in life and of the donut—but do it anyway.

"I don't mind, Juni." He kicks his feet up on the counter, and asks, "Now what can I do for you?"

There's always been a bond between us. He's been a voice of reason many times over the years, and despite me coming down here regularly dressed like a crazy person in the wee morning hours when I can't sleep, he never judges me for it. *It's called respect.*

"I feel stupid, and logically, I know I shouldn't, but I do."

"Does this have to do with what happened earlier tonight?" I nod and pop the last of the donut into my mouth. He says, "Listen, kiddo. I'm not sure what was going on, but you two were out on that sidewalk for a long time. By the time you made it inside, I was thoroughly confused. So, if you're seeking advice from me, I'm gonna need some details."

Fair enough. "Here's a little background to catch you up to speed. Rascal and I actually met him in the park last Monday. Don't tell Mr. Clark, but Rascal slipped right out of his collar. It's not the first time, and I've warned Mr. Clark about this happening before, but he insists Rascal is good when he walks him in the mornings." I lean down, and whisper, "I'm not trying to badmouth Rascal, but he's become a little terror lately."

I tap my chin, realizing things are much clearer in the lights of the bright lobby. If I think about it for more than a few seconds, the only connection I can make is Andrew. Meeting him is when Rascal's . . . let's just call them troubles began. And mine, if we're being honest. Obviously, Andrew is the problem, but I keep this revelation to myself.

"Anyway," I start again, "Rascal became a little escape artist and took off running faster than I could keep up. He ran straight to Andrew, who was lying in the grass at the park. I have no idea what he was doing, by the way. Enjoying the sunshine, maybe avoiding work, who knows?" I shrug.

"Okay, so . . .?"

"Right. So Rascal runs through poop that someone didn't pick up, which is really annoying. We share a jinx, and then I face-plant into his shirt. This all happened in one week." Gil's feet are back on the floor, and he's looking at me with confusion wrinkled into his remarkably smooth skin for a man of his age. When a polite pause allowing him to inject a question isn't taken advantage of, I continue because he is clearly keeping up. "So what I'm saying is—"

"Yes, what *are* you saying?"

"I'm saying that I didn't expect to beg the man to be my friend, but here we are. He's upstairs, living in the same building as me and probably sleeping soundly while I'm down here asking for advice."

His brows knit together. "What's the question?"

I sigh and begin pacing. I thought since he had a daughter, he'd understand the emotional turmoil of putting myself on the line for this stranger who took pity on me because I'm in need of a friend.

Clearly, I'm going to have to spell this out for him.

Stopping in front of his desk, I place both hands on the counter, and ask, "Do you see me hiking the Appalachian Trail or becoming a reality star?"

"Um, I don't really like either of those options."

"Because of Andrew, I obviously have to leave the

building for an extended period of time, basically until he moves on, so I need your help deciding where to go."

"What happens if you stay?"

I raise my arms wide before dropping them to my sides again. "There's a strong chance, and I say this from experience, that I'll run into him again. And then what? We actually become friends? Have you seen that man? He's gorgeous and has these flecks of gold in his brown eyes, like little buried treasures he's personally hidden for me to find. And I don't know why his grumpiness is so entertaining to me, but it inspires me to want to make him smile." Melting against the counter, I hold my arms wide and press my cheek against the cold marble. "What is wrong with me, Gil?"

There's silence. That's not unusual, but when it drags out, I tilt my head up, resting my chin on the hard surface instead. "What is it?" I ask.

As if two plus two finally equals four, he asks, "We're still talking about Mr. Christiansen, correct?"

My spine stiffens, and my arms fall to my sides. "Mr. Christiansen?" I ask slowly for the people in the back. That's me. I'm the people in the back. The image of brass letters rushes to the forefront of my mind as the words—It's a great day to invest in your future with Christiansen Wealth Management—tickles my tongue.

I suck in a harsh breath and then say, "I have to go." I'm already running for the elevator when I stop to add, "Thanks, and good night, Gil."

"Night, Juni."

Pressing the button, I then turn back again. "Don't tell anyone about this, okay?"

"You know I won't."

"Not even if he asks about me. Promise?"

He stands, joining me at the elevator. "Juni, you know I

can't lie. I'll do almost anything else, but my mom—*God rest her soul*—made me promise to always be honest."

I glance up to see what floor the elevator's on and then turn back to him. "You know I wouldn't normally ask this of you, but at least give me time and a little heads-up if he comes snooping around. Will you do that for me?" When he gets trapped in an internal debate, I add, "I know it's asking a lot of you, but please? No lying. Just a heads-up for me if he finds out?"

"I can do that," he replies without hesitation this time.

I wrap my arms around him. "Thank you, Gil. I appreciate it."

The elevator dings, and the door slides open. When I step in, I face him again. "I just need time to think."

"I understand."

I nod and give a brief wave before the door closes again. As soon as I land on my floor, I run into my apartment. Dropping the keys on the side table, I ignore the clang of metal when it hits a glass tchotchke. I don't pay any attention to the blinds still hanging wide open. Even the ticking of the grandfather clock in the back room doesn't bother me.

I'm on a mission, and nothing is going to sidetrack me.

Grabbing my laptop, I sit in the chair by the window and cross my legs. I settle the machine on my lap and log in. There's a slight shake to my hands as I type Andrew Christiansen into the search bar and press enter.

I quickly click images. I'm not here to learn about his past life. I just need to confirm he's not who I think he is. A CEO will have photos put out—professionally.

The average Andrew—and I say that acknowledging there's nothing average about this Andrew—won't have as many. Of course, social media plays a big part—*Uh!*

My hand covers my mouth as I take in the screen full of images.

Andrew surfing.

Andrew shaking hands with George Clooney.

I right-click save that one to analyze later.

Andrew in an LA movers-and-shakers, under-thirty magazine spread.

Andrew . . .

Andrew . . .

Andrew named chief executive officer of Christiansen Wealth Management.

I sink back and stare out the window.

Andrew isn't just a sexy new neighbor who I find mildly (*humor me here*) attractive and majorly frustrating to figure out. Andrew is Andrew Christiansen.

My new boss.

10

Juni

"I've been given no choice."

The door opens wider. "I didn't catch the ultimatum."

"Oh, there's no ultimatum. I'm just quitting my job before there is one."

"Are you not going to walk Rascal anymore?" Mr. Clark asks, scratching his head. Rascal whimpers at my feet. "Do you want me to pay you more money, Juni?" He ducks into his living room, leaving me standing in the doorway with the leash in hand. "I have a two-dollar bill around here somewhere."

"I didn't even know they made those anymore?"

He laughs to himself as he pulls the urn off his shelf. "I used to get them at the club." Looking back at me, I'm given a mischievous grin. He waggles his thick eyebrows, and then adds, "The ladies' club, if you know what I mean."

"Unfortunately, I do know what you mean." It's an image I'll spend the rest of the day trying to rid from my brain. I continue, "I don't need more money or any money for that matter. I walk Rascal for free, remember?" Rascal yaps. "I was talking about my day job. Also, put the urn back. You don't want to spill Mrs. Clark on the rug again."

He holds up a finger. "Right." Standing in front of the shelf, he kisses it, and says, "You always did like the sunshine, my darling," before placing it in a spot of sunlight. My heart melts as I hold my chest. Ninety-three years young and was lucky enough to be married to the love of his life for seventy of those.

When he comes back to the door, he asks, "How'd Rascal like his walk?"

I smile. His memory may be fading, but his heart is always in the right place. "I'm taking him now. We'll be back in a little while, Mr. Clark."

He's already lost interest and is settling into his recliner. "Thanks, Marion."

I never correct him when he calls me by my grandmother's name because for a moment, I can feel her with me again. She'd get a kick out of the sweet mistake. I shut the door and then kneel to have a chat with Rascal. "Upstairs today or to the park?" I release his leash, and he legs it for the elevators. "The park it is."

Gil will be gone, done with his shift for the weekend, but seeing Pete sitting behind the desk makes me wonder if I should run my idea by him.

"Hey, Juni, it's a beautiful Saturday."

"It sure is." I keep walking, thinking it's best if I don't put a damper on his day with my issues.

He pops out of his chair and opens the door wide for us. "Where are you and Rascal heading today?"

"I think a quick stroll around the park and maybe some ice cream from The Barkery down the street."

"I was just there on Thursday. Picked up some peanut

butter treats for Enzo. He devoured them. I bet Rascal would like the nutty nibbles."

Pete spoils his pit bull like a kid. It's really sweet. "We'll have to try them. Have a great day."

He's right. It's a beautiful day. The sun's shining, a blue sky is overhead, and flowers are blooming. Spring is just magical as the earth reawakens from the dormant winter.

Rascal tugs on his leash. He's only ten pounds, so I can handle him, but geez. "Slow your horses. Well, paws in your case. We're almost there."

Just as we enter the park, I freeze. Tensing my lips, I give Rascal my best evil eyes. "You little traitor. You tricked me."

I look down the path to where Andrew's stretching—sweaty hair with glistening skin and biceps he's been hiding under too many clothes since we met. "Oh my." I fan myself, and then ask Rascal, "How about Central Park today?"

He yaps his approval. It's so cute when he replies.

"Juni?"

Okay, maybe not so cute when he draws unwanted attention, though . . .

I head back down the path to the sidewalk, my pace rivaling Olympian speed walkers if speed walking is a thing in the Olympics. I'd probably win. I'd better. There's no point entering a competition to lose.

What am I talking about?

"Juni, wait up."

I turn back to see him actually jogging after me. *Shit.* I'm never going to outwalk his pace. Seeing the edge of the land-scaping, I'm left with no other choice. I duck behind the shrub and lower my head. It's not the most mature reaction to seeing someone you totally embarrassed yourself in front of the night before, but it's the only answer I have right now.

"What are you doing, Juni?"

I remain silent. Not because I don't think he can see me, but because I have nothing to say. And with the sun above, I don't want to be tempted by those warm brown eyes to say the wrong thing, like *I'm hiding from you.*

His feet come closer, and he squats down next to me. "What's going on?"

I've wanted to see these shrubs up close for a while now, so I don't regret the decision to duck inside. His white shirt clings to him, soaked through with sweat. The scent of a forest by the ocean fills the air between us, making me realize even his sweat smells good. His hair is free of gel and hanging down after a hard workout, causing the wet tips to stick to his forehead.

It's the tint of his cheeks that I find irresistible, the slightest red from his body's heat. He's incredibly good-looking and makes my mind go fuzzy. I rattle off the first thing that comes to mind. "Enjoying the weather?" I'm tempted to bury my head in the dirt to give him time to realize he would have been better off if he'd kept walking.

Rascal's not hearing of it and tugs me sideways. *Traitor.* Anything to get to Andrew.

Petting Rascal's head, he replies, "I am. I went for a run and was just cooling down when I saw you. Other than running away from me for some unknown reason, what are you doing in there?"

"Did you know," I say, taking a green leaf between my fingers, "that a large swath of the population confuses the doublefile viburnum for a small, non-concealing tree? It's actually a shrub and can spread easily if not managed. Not as bad as bamboo if we're looking for comparisons, which we're not." *Shut up, Juni.*

"That is interesting." For a second, I'm not sure if he's

being truthful, but the sincerity in his eyes relieves me and causes me to smile.

"I always thought so." But then I remember I do not want to have a conversation with this man, at least not right now, so I clap my hands together. "Well, this bush looks healthy."

He stands, but his eyes remain on me. "Are bushes and shrubs the same thing? I've always wondered that." He's cute when he wonders too.

"To a layperson, yes."

"What if you're not a layperson?"

Botany was never sexier than when Andrew is talking about plants. My heart patters against my rib cage, and I rest back on my hand. "No. One's denser than the other."

"A bush has denser branches. Is that right?"

"Yes," I reply, suddenly content spending all day hiding behind a shrub if I get to talk botany with him.

He takes a step back to give me space. Offering his hand, he asks, "Would you like help up?"

I'm already hating the distance, but I shake my head. "I don't feel comfortable accepting charity."

He scoops Rascal into his arms, making me jealous of the little guy, and then sits down where the sidewalk meets the dirt. "Then I guess I'll have to join you. That is, if you don't mind the company."

"I don't mind." And that's the truth.

As he scratches Rascal's back, Andrew says, "As a New Yorker, why do you know so much about plants?"

I laugh. "What does me being a New Yorker have to do with my knowledge about plants?"

When he shrugs and lets his shoulders drop, I notice how relaxed he is. No coat hanger posture in sight. "I figured most people live in apartments without gardens."

"Ah. Well, that is true, but once upon a time, I lived in the Berkshires."

"I've heard it's beautiful there."

I love that New Yorkers walking by see us in the bushes but don't say a thing. It's like we've seen it all. A woman sitting in a bush? *Okay.* Just another day in this vibrant city. "So beautiful. It's been years since I've been back."

"What's stopping you?"

I pluck a leaf from the plant and study the skeletal structure, running my finger along the spine and turning it over in my hand. "Myself." I glance up at him. There's a soulfulness that comes with this more laid-back side of him. I like it.

"I used to surf with my brother almost every morning before high school. We'd come rolling in just as the first bell would ring. Two kids from Beverly Hills—"

"You're from Beverly Hills?"

I bet not much embarrasses him, but for some reason, this does. Dipping his head down, he runs his fingers through his hair. It's dried messily, but not any less sexy. It might even be more so. God, I'm so shallow. And apparently sexually deprived.

He replies, "Yeah, don't hold it against me."

"Why would I do that? Is it an awful place to grow up? I thought it was always fancy when I saw it on TV."

Chuckling, he pulls a weed and then looks up at me again. "No. It's a fine place to grow up. I had a great childhood with few complaints."

"What few do you have? Maybe you should get them off your chest."

When he stands, I can tell the winds of his mood have shifted. "I think I'm good. You still want to stay down there?"

I hold my hand up. "I think I'm ready to stop hiding."

His laughter is heartier than usual. He takes my hand and helps me to my feet. "Do you want to talk about what you're hiding from, or should we keep things light?"

"Light. Definitely light." I tap the side of his leg as we start walking. "Nice shorts, by the way."

"Thanks." His laughter carries us the next block until we reach the corner.

I say, "I promised Rascal doggie-safe ice cream."

His arms cross over his chest as he looks at me. "Can't disappoint the little guy."

"No."

"Hey, Juni, before you go, I wanted to talk to you about last night."

Here it comes . . .

My face is already heating, just thinking about it.

I look down the street. I'm not sure what he's about to say, but it sounds serious from his tone. I mentally brace myself.

"I think," he starts, "I could use a friend. If the offer still stands."

"Really?"

"Yeah." He shifts to the side, looking down, and I recognize his awkwardness in the slight movements.

Forget the heat of my cheeks. It's my smile that I have to worry about. I think it's about to expand right off my face. "I'd like that."

"You would?" he asks, sounding hopeful.

"I definitely would."

Satisfaction fills his smile, and his eyes shine brighter. It might be the sun since he squints right after, but I'll take it because it's a good look on him. "Okay, we'll be friends then."

"Friends." I stick out my hand again, but this time when he grasps mine, we shake on it.

Our gazes linger as long as our hands stay connected, which is at least long enough for me to wonder if maybe there's something—*No.*

Friends.

That's all.

11

Juni

OFFICIALLY BEING FRIENDS WITH ANDREW DOESN'T SOLVE MY immediate issues. Mainly that I live in the same building, and he still doesn't know. *Oh, and he's my boss.*

During my first few days at work, we never ran into each other. I have no idea how luck was on my side, but it was a clean sweep for the week. So yeah, that we're working in the same office will come as a surprise to him as well.

This whole friends thing adds extra complications.

I do the only thing that's right. I march into work on Monday with a formal letter of resignation ready to send from my draft emails—one for the agency, who is really the only one I need to send it to, and one for Laurie, the head of HR at CWM. She's been so supportive that I feel I owe her the personal courtesy.

The problem is, I've enjoyed this job. Having a routine and accomplishing daily tasks has been fun, and exceeding their expectations is exhilarating. I may not be profession-ally trained for the job, but I think I've done well at picking up the skills required. Even with the position extending for ten weeks, I had just adjusted the dread of anticipation to return. Now I'm full of doubts again. Did I knowingly sabotage myself?

Does it matter anymore?

No. I need to walk away before I sabotage my new friendship. I email Laurie, set the calls to go to the answering service, and head to the Cave before the bossman shows up. It's a straight shot down the hall, but I look both ways just to make sure the coast is clear before I even step a foot through the main doors. I dash ahead but slow when I reach the other end of the walkway. I'm quick to study each plaque, finding Head of HR on the fourth door.

Knocking lightly, I wait to enter until I hear, "Come in."

I spin inside, my back pressing to the door, and a sense of relief washes through me.

Laurie asks, "Is everything all right?"

"Yes," I say, waving my hand like it's no big deal. I don't tell her I'm hiding from the CEO. That would just lead to questions for answers I don't have. "I'm fine." Approaching her desk, I continue, "I would like to speak with you about—"

"I just got your email." She angles her chair toward me and rests her arms on the desk in front of her. "I'm kind of surprised. This is a temporary job. You said you've enjoyed being here when I checked in with you last Friday. I felt like it was a good fit so far. Do you mind me asking why you decided to leave? You don't have to answer, of course, if you don't want to. I'm just curious if you can help me fill in the blanks."

I silently check off each point in my head.

1. The boss is sexy.

2. He'll think I'm stalking him. Again. He'll think I
   lied about knowing he works here.
3. I also, just by pure coincidence, live in the same
   building as him.
4. And finally, Andrew, aka Mr. CEO, and I are
   friends. I'm not positive, but I'm pretty sure he
   won't get a kick out of the previous three points.

None of the above appear to be viable avenues to travel down when explaining the situation, so I take a more obvious route. "I do enjoy the office and most everyone I've met . . ." I don't mention Justin or how he hangs around the front desk a little too long or makes me uncomfortable when he insists on showing me the new steno pads in the supply room. "I'm just not being challenged."

"I was afraid of that." If eyes could physically light up, hers do. "I'm also not upset to hear you say that. I know you're overqualified for the position, but you're very good at it."

"I appreciate that."

"Joseph and I were talking about offering you full-time employment, either up front or somewhere else in the office. We think you can find something challenging here at CWM that you'll enjoy." Leaning forward like an old friend, she says, "We want you to stay, Juni. You're efficient at multitasking and personable on the phone and to coworkers. Our office never looked better, and you put care into everything you do. You're special, and we would hate to lose you."

"Full-time employment?" That's not what I expected when I came here, and I'm not sure how it makes me feel.

"Yes. Is that something you're interested in doing?"

I thought I already knew the answer. That's why I sent the email. But now, hearing of the possibilities potentially changes things. My financial backing has allowed me to live life on my own terms and avoid getting involved in a job professionally. Dedicating my time and energy to professional pursuits did not turn out well once upon a time. When everyone counted on me most, I blew my chances at winning the grant my parents so desperately needed.

That money would have supported their team to continue their work after their death, and I failed.

Karl stepped up with my research in hand and won the judges over with my presentation. The worst part—*I let him*. I thought he was doing me a favor, helping me when I froze from the news I'd just been given. Instead, he shattered my heart more than it had already been broken.

Anger courses through me, and when I look down, I'm fisting my hands. Karl was right. I am bitter. To this day, his actions made me leave a part of my heart on that stage that I've never been able to recover. I lost my passion for botany because of him, and I haven't been the same since.

I can't fix the past, but with time and distance to the accident, I've learned nothing is worth sacrificing time with the ones you love—no job, no hobby, no passion. We get one chance at this life, and I want mine to matter.

Is a new opportunity in line with that thinking, or is it finally time to put my past to bed? "Can I think about it?"

"Yes, please do. And if you have questions, please ask. Joseph and I believe in you, Juni, and we think you'll go far with Christiansen Wealth Management."

"Thank you." I still haven't fixed the issues surrounding my relationship with Andrew, so why am I even considering this job? With my hand on the knob, I look back. "I haven't contacted the temp agency yet. I came to you first."

Laurie stands, pressing her fingertips to the glass-top desk. "I appreciate that."

"I'll wait to contact them until after I make my decision." She nods with a gentle smile. I walk out floating on cloud nine. My day has taken an unexpected turn for the better. Now it's up to me to decide which way I want to go.

Dark hair at two o'clock has me dropping to the floor. When I hear the voice— deep and sultry, commanding, and sexy—coming closer, I crawl into the nearest cubicle.

"What are you doing down there?" My stomach tightens. Justin's voice alone makes my skin crawl. And he adds, "Looking for a snack?"

"A snack is all you have to offer," I snap back.

I start to get up but halt on all fours when I hear Andrew's assistant ask, "What are you doing, Ms. Jacobs?"

I look over my shoulder, my eyes connecting with Mary first and then Andrew. "Juni?"

Trying to push up, I get caught and sent back to my knees because today, of all days, I had to wear a pencil skirt. I drop my head, humiliation flooding my face, and try again.

Laurie joins in the party. *Naturally.* "What's going on?"

Mary says, "Um . . . I think I hear my phone ringing." I hear the sound of her hightailing it out of here through her quick footsteps. I don't blame her. I wish I could do the same.

Andrew's anger consumes the air, and I finally say, "I'm stuck."

Justin stands, but Andrew demands, "Sit." As if he's a dog that's been punished, he scurries back to his chair.

A pair of black designer Oxfords, Italian by the looks of the leather and stitching, appears before me. I know they're Andrew's because there's nary a scuff in sight. He bends down. "Are you okay?"

I look up, my hair falling over my eyes. Through strands of hair, I see the anger I heard moments earlier now situated as ire in his eyes. He holds his hands out for me. When I slip my hands in his, an unfettered energy travels between us, a spark reaching his eyes.

He carefully helps me to my feet, where I brush the rest of my hair away from my face and straighten my clothes.

I dare to look into Andrew's eyes, already missing the little gold flecks that have been replaced with embers of fire. He says, "I'd like to see you in my office, Ms. *Jacobs*," and maneuvers around me.

He's quickly covering the distance to his office, but I say, "I should probably—"

"Now," he commands without breaking his pace.

I turn to see Laurie staring at me, a million questions surfacing in her expression. Shame fills me, and I start, "I can explain—"

"I think I should be present for this meeting." She returns to her office, and when she comes back out, she walks right past me with a pad and pen in hand.

Once more, I make sure my skirt is straight and in place before I start walking. I'm not sure if this is a walk of shame or I'm a dead man walking, but either way, the entire office is staring at me as I head to my own beheading. The door to the office I've been so good about avoiding is wide open.

I can't say I'm getting welcoming vibes from the inside when I approach, though. Taking a deep breath, I tug at the collar of my shirt and make sure the clasp of my necklace is at the back. I exhale and then walk in.

Andrew is staring at the TV on his wall like it's going to reveal the secret of life. It's not, just what the S & P 500 is at for the day. Laurie sits in a chair across the desk from him, leaving me to brave the fifteen feet by myself. I consider detouring to the couch because that looks like a better place to be fired. At least I'd be comfortable.

His eyes hit mine, freezing me to the spot. "I'd like to speak with Ms. Jacobs in private."

Laurie says, "I don't think that's a wise idea. Per company policy, a human resources representative—"

"I'm okay with it," I say. There's a tremble to my voice that I'm not used to anymore. I hate it. I also hate the fear this situation inspires inside me. Tamping it down, I add, "I'll be fine. I've done nothing wrong."

She looks back and forth between us and then sets her eyes on me again. "It's for your protection as well."

"I don't need protecting."

Andrew's eyes finally leave mine, and he says to Laurie, "If you must stay, I'll allow it."

"It's up to both of you."

"We're fine," we both say, the words rushing out at the same time.

Her gaze darts between us several times before she stands up and moves to the door. "Okay, then."

I'm still standing in the middle of the room like a damn lingerie model when the door clicks closed behind me. When I turn back to Andrew, he says, "I'm going to need you to explain."

"Can I sit down first?"

12

Andrew

THAT SKIRT.

Fuck. Doesn't matter how mad I am at her; I'm going to be dreaming of that fucking skirt all fucking night. I scrub my hands over my face a few times before looking back up to find her staring at me.

Wide-eyed innocence is written all over her face, despite that damn skirt that says she knew exactly what she was doing by wearing that today.

I angle my chair toward the couch because Juni, being herself, went for the unexpected option—the one not even offered. "Enlighten me as to what you're doing on the floor of my office in the middle of the day."

"Would you rather it had been at night?" She grins, but it drops again. "Is this a no-joke zone?"

"This is a no-joke zone." Resting my forearms on the desk, I have a thousand ideas running through my head, but not one of them makes sense. "I'm serious, Juni. Why were you on the floor in Justin's cubicle?"

A flicker of anger cruises through her pretty hazel eyes before she glances away. When she looks back at me, her composure has returned. "I wasn't purposely on Justin's floor. I've been avoiding him like I've been avoiding you."

"Why are you avoiding *me*?"

"Because you're the CEO."

I take a breath and sit back, wondering if we can actually get from here to there in the most direct fashion. "I don't understand, Juni. I need you to explain with more detail."

She sits forward, clasping her hands on top of her knees and studying her nails. When she looks up, she asks, "You want the truth?" with the confidence I'm more familiar with in her.

"I want the truth."

For a moment, I feel like she's going to tell me I can't handle it, quoting the old movie line. "I just resigned and was coming out of Laurie's office when I saw you and Mary about to come around the corner." *No teasing is heard.*

"What do you mean *resigned*? When did you start working here?"

"Last Tuesday. I was brought in to cover for Melissa while she's on maternity leave."

"The new girl . . ." I say to myself.

"Yes. I'm the new girl."

Speaking with such ease in this unofficial moniker they dubbed her, she doesn't even realize what Justin's been saying behind her back. "Last Tuesday, we met for coffee before work?"

She grins as if she's been waiting for me to piece this puzzle together. "I came here right after."

"This is getting close to the stalker issue again."

"I knew you'd go there. You always go straight for the heart."

"I think it's straight for the jugular."

"Oh, okay," she replies angrily, crossing her arms over her chest. "For the record, it may be jugular, but you accusing me of something I didn't do feels like a hit to the heart." She stands. "I didn't stalk you, Andrew. I didn't even know your last name until Friday night . . . or technically, Saturday morning. It's so hard to know what to call those wee hours in the middle of the night." She huffs. "Anyway, I didn't even know your name was Christiansen last week, or I would have told you I got a job here. Well, a temp if we're being accurate, but I quit, so it doesn't matter now."

I rummage through the rambling words to make some kind of sense of it. I'm not sure what to think, except that she looks ready to bolt. "Look, I don't know what's going on, or how I'm supposed to react. Should I be mad or freaked out that you're working in my office, and I didn't know?"

"What about happy?"

"Huh?"

She bends her ankle slightly to the side, drawing my attention to the black patent leather heels she's wearing. *Fuck. Focus, Christiansen.*

She says, "Try being happy that we've been given an opportunity. Like out of all the millions of people in New York City, divine intervention has played a part."

Normally, I'd tune out this spiritual stuff, but there's a part, *a tiny part of me*, that's wondering if she's right.

She adds, "The park. The coffee shop, and now right here in this office. What are the chances?"

"You forgot Friday night and how we ran into each other again outside my building."

"Right." She nods, pursing her lips to the side and looking away. "I almost forgot. Another act of the universe.

Or the temp agency, but really it's the universe that gave them the lead."

The temp agency? I'll ask Laurie about this next time we meet. As curious as I am today, I'm already late for my next meeting.

Motioning to the seat by my desk, I ask, "Will you sit and talk to me? I won't keep you much longer." I hate the taste of the words leaving my mouth. They're not only bitter, but also not sweet.

Eyeing me for a few seconds, she finally comes closer and sits down. I say, "Thank you."

"You're welcome."

"Listen," I say, lowering my voice. "I'm not sure if the universe is messing with us, but I won't be the one who drives you away. I've heard great things about the work you're doing here. HR even mentioned bringing you on full-time."

"They offered me a permanent position this morning."

"After just one week, you have my team begging you to stay. What will it take to make that happen?"

Her body appears lighter with a lift of her mouth's corners and a weight removed from her shoulders. "I was hired as a temp."

"Is that what you'd like to continue doing?"

"I'd be okay with that. I like it here."

I'm still confused, but I feel like we're miles closer to an answer. "Then why were you leaving?"

"Because we're friends," she answers instantly.

The answer takes me by surprise, and as I study her expression, I try to riddle through the intensity of her eyes. "Is that a personal rule you have in place for your professional endeavors?"

"No, I just thought you wouldn't like it."

My mouth falls open, not gaping but enough to exhale my shock. "Why would our friendship make you think I wouldn't want you working here?"

She pushes up and walks to the window. I know it's impossible to see the street from this floor, but when she presses her forehead to the glass, I know she's making the effort. Suddenly, she turns around, and says, "I don't want you to think I'm stalking you. I'm not."

"I don't think that," I confess with honesty. "I know we got off on the wrong foot when we met, but I shouldn't have said that to you. I didn't believe . . . *Well, not entirely.*"

I spy the crack of a smile forming on her lips. "An ex once called me a stalker, so I guess I'm a little sensitive to the term." Her tone is upbeat despite what she's sharing.

Not sure if I should go there, I ask myself, *what would Juni do?* She'd go there. "Were you stalking him?"

"I was absolutely stalking him." When she laughs, I join in because I shouldn't have doubted her for a minute. She sits back on the couch and crosses her ankles. My eyes trace the shape of her knees and down each curve of her legs, landing me on her shoes again. "In my defense, I was following him because I had found a note in his backpack. He told me to grab his graphing calculator from the front pocket. When I did, a note fell out. It was a time and a place. I showed up, he called me a stalker and psycho ex-girlfriend for everyone to hear, and then he walked off with the woman he married two years later."

"So he was cheating?"

"Yeah, but rumors spread faster than the truth. I might as well have been wearing a giant S across my chest and had crazy eyes for all anyone cared." Her gaze extends out the window as the memory appears to replay before her *not-crazy* eyes. "I didn't date much after that."

"Their loss."

The joy returns to her eyes when she looks at me, and she smiles. "I've decided I'd like to stay."

"I'm glad to hear that."

She slides forward on the leather. "Well, I should probably get back to the desk then." Raising her hands up, she adds, "I can rip the hem of this skirt trying to get up, or you can help me."

I stand and move around to the couch. "If you're asking me which I prefer, that might be different than what's appropriate for the office."

"Might?"

"Will be."

I offer her two hands palms up. When she slips her hands in mine, I caress the feel of them and help her to her feet. Standing toe-to-toe, she doesn't pull away as the heat builds between us. The tip of her tongue dips out to lick the center of her top lip, and I retreat, turning my back to her as I return to my desk.

She doesn't play fair for someone who's only supposed to be my friend. "Then I won't wear it to the office anymore."

"Let's not get carried away."

The blush I love colors her cheeks when she giggles—wait! Love? *What the fuck?* I turn to my monitor. "I, uh, yeah . . ." I run my hand through my hair, forgetting I had pomade in it.

"You? You need to get back to work?"

Refusing to make eye contact with her or that skirt or those sexy fucking shoes, I force my eyes to stay on the screen. Despite my eyeballs burning, I add, "Yes, I have a lot of work to do."

My willpower is shit, and as soon as her back is to me, I

do what I'd fire another employee for doing—I stare at her ass.

She looks back suddenly. I'm not sure that she actually busts me, but she smirks, which makes me think she did. I remind myself again that we're nothing more than friends, despite my pants currently being too tight for comfort. She says, "Have a good day, boss."

"Yeah, have a great fucking day," I mumble to myself.

"What was that?"

I look up again, this time with a smile on my face. "Have a great day."

"I plan to." The remark isn't snotty or sarcastic. It's as if once she sets her mind to it, nothing can stand in her way.

As soon as the door closes, a knock disturbs the peace of my office. Nick's waltzing in before I have time to rearrange my package. *Fuck.* "What?"

He pushes the door closed as he comes charging toward me. "You're bangin' the new girl?"

I jump and stalk to the door. "Keep your voice down, Nick." I double-check the door to make sure it's closed. It is, thank fuck.

When I turn back, he's leaning against the windowsill with his arms crossed and a smug smirk on his face. "I have to admit, big brother, I didn't think you had it in you for an ethics code violation." His arms go out. "But look at you being a rebel."

"No codes, ethics or otherwise, have been violated for your information." I roll my eyes and return to my desk, wondering if I'm going to get any work done at this rate. "And I'm not bangin' the new girl. This is how rumors get started." Shaking my hand at him, I add, "While we're on the topic, don't call her the new girl."

"She is the new girl. The next hire will be the new guy or

girl, and the cycle continues. Why are you so bothered by it?"

"Because she has a name. You should use it out of respect." I sit down in my chair and am about to reacquaint myself with how the market's doing this morning, but his silence demands attention. He's like the kid who you leave alone for too long—if you hear him playing, all is safe. It's when he's silent that trouble's brewing. "What?"

"You're very protective over someone you claim to barely know."

"Because I'm not fucking her doesn't mean I don't know her."

"How well?"

"Don't you have work to do, or do we need to find more for you?"

He glances at his watch before pushing off the glass and heading back to the door. "I have plenty, but I heard what happened. I wanted your take on it."

"And what is 'it' exactly?"

"Justin being called into HR." I don't know what that fucker did, but this is New York. I can easily find an equally, if not better qualified accountant in this city.

"I know nothing about that."

"Rumor has it he crossed a line with Juni," he says with emphasis on her name.

My hackles rise, but I try to remain calm. "Oh yeah? What'd you hear?"

Stopping before he opens the door, he says, "Don't worry about it. Joseph will handle Justin. Oh, and happy Monday."

"I'm noting sarcasm."

"Note it in my file, so it's official." He walks out laughing. For a lawyer, he sure laughs a lot. It's a nice change from when he used to mope around. I'm thinking it's not the work that makes him happy, but his wife.

I've never been in the market, but he makes it sound more appealing.

As I watch the TV, the numbers scroll by, but my mind is still elsewhere. Like inside Laurie's office. I wonder what was said or what he did this time.

I need to let HR do their job and not get involved. That asshole is just so fucking infuriating. My curiosity gets the better of me, and I stand. But then I sit. I should stay. They can handle it.

I practically have to sit on my hands. Leaning back in my chair, I decide to tuck them behind my head and stare at the couch where Juni sat.

My thoughts cross many lines with her.

Her legs.

Those lips.

The shoes.

Her hips.

Fuck me, I'm no better than Justin.

And knowing she's just across the office from me is distracting. Did I make a mistake by asking her to stay? I'm starting to think that seeing Juni every day will be a lot harder than I thought.

13

Andrew

I never know when I'm going to see Juni.

I just do.

She's suddenly there, behind a bush or on the office floor. I never know when I'm going to see her next.

Scanning the street when I arrive home, I expect to see her walking Rascal or coincidentally catching her as she crosses my path. Hell, skydiving onto the awning wouldn't surprise me at this point.

But even though I don't, her presence fills my air. My world is feeling much smaller these days. The part I don't understand is why I'm not bothered by it. For years, nothing sidetracked my goals, ensuring CWM thrives. It's been my only thought day and night. And now, it's as though my mission has shifted, and I'm stuck in the middle of a Tom Hanks movie.

Tut.

What am I thinking? We're not in a romance movie. This is real life.

Mine, to be specific.

But admitting that I wish I knew where she lived is the first step. If I did, I could be on the lookout or even parachute into her world for once. But I didn't even know her last name until this morning.

Jacobs.

Not what I would have imagined, but Juni Jacobs has some nice alliteration going on. Not that a form of figurative language is imperative when naming kids or couples, but there's a nice ring to it.

Shit.

Before I have a chance to justify my stance, I'm devil advocating against myself.

Corbin Christiansen.

Cookie Christiansen.

Dalen Dalery.

Ethan Everest.

Jackson St. James. That might be a stretch, but then the couples come into play. Cookie & Corbin. Nick & Natalie. Andrew & Juni . . .

Nope. Doesn't work. That's why being friends with each other does.

With my finger on the trigger, I hold the bottle of air freshener in the air, ready to press it. I had the displeasure of my neighbor cooking again, still completely disregarding how it affects others through what I can only figure is an outdated ventilation system.

Although there's no rhyme or reason that allows me to prepare for these international cooking fests, it occurs to me that this person follows some patterns.

They like cooking past what's considered dinnertime to the average American and always after ten PM. Sometimes as late as one in the morning—or early, depending on how you view such times of the day.

They like to set the scene with music to match the theme. I'm curious if they decorate as well.

Also, it's never something simple like a burger being cooked. There's an international flair to these meals. Mexican food last week. Indian over the weekend—in the middle of the night when I was trying to prevent a hangover from invading my head. And Italian tonight.

The scent of marinara wafted through the vents along with *La bohème* played at an offensive volume. Not a note was missed, not even in my apartment with those three closed vents. *Unfortunately.*

I went to bed early and in a sour mood.

The thing is, I'm not sure why. My grandparents used to drag us to the opera, so listening to it is not torture. I actually kind of enjoyed hearing it again since it's been so long. But my night was off, and I think I narrowed it down to something inside me.

I miss Juni.

Her pesky little tangents and the way she sees the world are totally different than I do. I've been a realist. Dreamers were younger siblings and people who weren't committed to a path before they knew how to walk.

There's a reason everyone calls me uptight, and it's not because of my own choosing. It's because I stepped up to the expectation plate and hit a homer for the home team—the Christiansens and our close to three hundred employees. CWM's books have never been better.

But what if . . .

What if I start living for me? Not give up my work ethic, but sneak in something that's not for others, something that's personal for me. *Juni.*

Nobody has to know unless we want them to. I put down the air freshener because maybe the smell is better than I want to admit. It might even be delicious.

Sitting on the couch, I pick up the phone and do the one thing we haven't done since the night we exchanged numbers. I text her again: *What are you up to?*

I fall back, realizing I just redefined the term lame.

But then three little dots roll across the screen, giving me hope I didn't blow it. And disappear.

Reappear as if to wave hello and boom—a message appears: *Nothing.*

Narrowing my eyes, I reread the message again. That can't be all there is. That took a long damn time to type one word. Call me pushy, but I reply: *Literally nothing or just nothing worth mentioning?*

Juni: *If you must know, I have an apricot mask on my face, and I'm in a hot bubble bath. Didn't think you wanted those kinds of details since you're my boss, so I deleted it, but now I've put it out there, so do what you may with the information.*

Despite pointing out that I'm her boss, she teases me with no fear of repercussion. Sitting by myself at eleven-oh-six on a Monday night, I'm here smiling like an idiot.

She does that to me, evoking other reactions as well. More specifically, by wearing that skirt, the shoes, the curve of her legs, and the sweet smile I catch playing on her lips right before she blushes. Juni is sexy without knowing it, and that makes her even more attractive by default. I feel more alive when I'm in her presence. I feel confused too, but that doesn't need to be worked out tonight.

Getting up, I pace around the couch, staring at my phone like it might catch fire. With her, it's all fun and games, but it makes me wonder if I'm crossing a line. I know the answer. The only debate is whether I do it anyway.

Another message shows up on the screen: *Was it the apricot mask? You're more of a matcha green tea kind of guy, right?*

The winky face she punctuated the text with doesn't do much to assuage my guilt, but no one has to know. I'm typing before I can change my mind: *I don't like tea.*

What the hell am I writing? Nonsense, that's what.

Juni: *What do you like, Andrew?*

Me: *I like ...*

I was so sure an answer would come easily, but as my fingers hover over the screen, I realize I don't have a response. I don't know what I like anymore because everything is different here. In LA, I had systems in place. Work, meetings, drumming up business, working out, meeting up with Dalen. Yet the only thing that's changed about my routine is Dalen.

I should miss her, shouldn't I?

We've known each other for years, but there was no . . . no heart involved. No plans set in concrete.

No commitment.

No feelings.

I should feel something from her absence—a hole or longing to see her—but I don't.

She isn't my person.

I stole that last line from my mom, but I know she won't mind.

I answer honestly: *I don't know anymore.*

There's no response and no dots to comfort me. I've never felt more alone than I do now. Not because of abandonment issues from my childhood because I don't have those. I can't blame Juni either for not rushing to reply with some filler to make me feel better.

My job placates instead of excites, and I don't feel like myself anymore.

I used to know who I was, and as much as I claim to have been steered into this career, I made the final decision to pursue it. I take responsibility for the decisions that got me here. It wouldn't be fair to take credit but leave out the disappointments. But this is different.

New York is becoming another Seattle—just another stop while keeping my real in California.

How is that a way to live? It's not. It's survival, something I'm really fucking good at.

The phone rings in my hand, and I stare at her name on the screen. Do I answer it? Texting was one thing. Sexting quite another. But is it crossing a line if we're just friends? "Hello?"

"You can't leave me hanging like that." It's good to hear her voice, calm washing through me from the frequency. She gets a little pitchy sometimes, but I like it.

I like her company, even if it's just listening to her. I grin, perching on the windowsill and looking out into the night. Wondering how far the distance between us extends, I ask, "Where do you live?"

"Oh no, you don't, Mr. Christiansen," she replies, a lightness caught in her tone as if she's dragged yesterday's sunshine into our night. The sound of water sloshing as if she's getting out of the tub is heard. "No changing the subject."

"And the subject was?"

"*Is.* The subject *is* that you don't know what you like. You can't name one thing?"

"I'm not trying to make you feel sorry for me. I just don't have time to worry about such things."

There's a pause, but undeterred, she asks, "What about ice cream?"

"What about it?"

"Do you like it?"

I move to the couch to settle in for a bit. "Who doesn't like ice cream?"

"Lactose intolerant people don't like it."

"I don't think that's true. I bet a lot of them do like it, but they can't have it."

She goes quiet. I listen to her breathing like a fucking stalker—it's airy with a musical quality to it. And then I hear it—music playing in the background. "Are you listening to classical?"

"Yes. Do you like it?" she asks as if she's on to something.

"Sometimes."

I can imagine she's rolling her eyes. "Me too."

The upbeat tempo is famous. "Is that Vivaldi?"

"Yes. I was listening to Puccini earlier, but he gets intense. I needed something happier." The sound of her shuffling through papers, keys, or coins and other odd noises cut through her words. "Back to the ice cream. What's your favorite flavor?"

This I know. It's remained the same since I was little. "Rocky road."

"Wow. I misjudged you, Mr. Christiansen." I like when she calls me that, but keep that *like* to myself. "I really had you pegged for a vanilla guy."

"What's with you pegging for anything—vanilla ice cream or matcha green tea?"

"You're right. You're unpredictable." Why does she not sound convincing? "What are you doing right now?"

"Talking to you. Ba dum dah. I'll be here all night, folks. Don't forget to tip your bartenders."

"You're a funny guy when you're not in business mode."

"What can I say? Numbers aren't that funny." My cheeks ache. I didn't realize I was smiling this whole time until the pain set in. This friends thing I have going with her isn't so bad. Not like I had a lot of other choices. I have Nick and Jackson. But even with them in the picture, I like my relationship with Juni.

"Very true. Now back to ice cream."

She has me craving a sweet treat. I look back at the kitchen, mentally tallying what will satisfy the craving. "You were saying?"

"Meet me outside the building in ten minutes."

"What? Why?" I spy the hands of my watch. "You know it's after eleven, right?"

"And it's a Monday night. We can come up with a million excuses, but all we need is one reason to have fun." A door squeaks, and I have a feeling she's getting a head start.

Popping off the couch, I rush to my room with the phone in my hand. "What's that reason?"

"Life, Andrew. We're going to live like we don't have work at eight in the morning."

"But we do." I drop my night pants and pull a pair of jeans on over my boxer briefs.

"No buts, just adventure. You have eight minutes left." The ding of an elevator overrides the last word.

Fuck. I snag a T-shirt and pull it over my head. "What happens if I'm not there?"

"I leave without you."

"Ah, fuck it. I'll be down there with time to spare." I hang up and finish grabbing my shoes before I rush to the bathroom and run my hand through my hair. I look like shit, but I don't care.

Hurrying back into the living room, I grab my keys and

tuck my wallet into my pocket as I head out the door. With only five minutes left, I debate if I should take the elevator. It's too damn slow, and currently, the number is stuck on the second floor. I can cover seventeen flights much faster.

I take off running and push through into the stairwell at the end of the hall. Running down the stairs, I use the railing to help swing my body around the corners even faster.

"Don't get up," I yell to Gil as I run through the lobby. Rushing out the door, I come to a stop when I see her. "I'm here. I'm here," I say through harsh breaths. Bending over, I rest my palms on my knees, trying to catch my breath. Sweaty with my hair hanging over my eyes, I look up. "Did I make it?"

She's grinning ear to ear. "You're right on time."

14

Andrew

"There's no shame in my ice cream game."

That was the last thing Juni said before she left me standing with a melting rocky road cone in one hand and her sweater in the other while she perused the counter for the next fifteen minutes.

After spending ample time debating each of the nineteen flavors, she looks back at me with her bottom lip tucked under her teeth, and then asks, "Maybe I'm in the mood for sorbet?"

"Ice cream," I reply, getting her back on track with this mission.

With her eyes locked on the prize, she proudly walks up to the counter, and orders, "Raspberry chocolate chip, please," like she won't ever get another opportunity to eat ice cream again.

I didn't realize this was going to be an event. Had I known, I would have mentally prepared better. But I have a feeling that I'll never be fully prepared for an adventure that involves Juni.

She insisted on paying. I argued but realized I wouldn't win that battle. I'm taking my last bite when she walks up. With her head tilted to the side, she drags her tongue along the deep pink cream. I lower my arm that has her sweater draped over it and clear my throat. "We should get out of here. It's getting crowded, especially for being almost midnight on a weekday."

"You're here," she says, as if that proves her point.

Blocked from opening the door properly, I stand on the opposite side and use my height to hold it open high above her head. She happily ducks under to exit, reminding me how small she is. She can't be more than five-two or three. "Late night, sweet treat."

I could call her the same. *I don't.* But I could.

We move out of the entrance and start strolling back toward my building. I say, "I haven't had ice cream in a long time."

"It's good, right?" Eager anticipation colors her expression, as does a chocolate chip above the right corner of her mouth. I subtly lick the corner of mine. Without acknowledging the act, her tongue dips out and sweeps the chocolate away.

"It was. I'm glad I came out."

Joy surges through her spine, causing a little wiggle, and she looks down at her feet. When I'm granted the beauty of her hazel eyes again, she whispers, "Me too."

I'm quick to pull her close when a boisterous group of teenagers hoards most of the sidewalk, leaving little room for others. She doesn't appear to mind my arm wrapped around her waist as though it belongs there.

I don't either.

Removing it is the right thing to do among friends. So, I do.

She asks, "How long has it been since you went out for ice cream?"

It's odd how that question hits sideways in my gut. Probably because it brings some truth to the surface. "I don't remember."

Although she had just taken a bite, which should bring pleasure, sympathy wriggles into her eyes. "I'm glad we're remedying that."

The moment passes, but I won't complain that the focus is off me. I prefer to be the one behind the scenes instead of in the spotlight. We continue walking. Her eyes are momentarily hidden behind closed lids as she savors the sweet flavor. When she reopens them, she catches me staring. Touching the side of her lips, she asks, "What is it?"

"Nothing."

"If it's nothing, then why are you looking at me like that?"

Chuckling, I reply, "I like how much you're enjoying that ice cream."

"See?" she says, confident the universe has her back. I have a strong suspicion it does. "We've gotten *two* likes out of you. Rocky road and me." She giggles. "Well, not me specifically, but . . ." She bumps into my side and taps her head to my arm in a nudge. "You're having fun, and that's what this is all about."

"I am. Thanks for insisting I join you."

"I didn't really have to twist your arm. You didn't waste a second getting downstairs."

Running is a good way to clear my mind, and lifting

weights helps maintain my muscle mass, but I rarely combine them. Yet getting down seventeen flights of stairs to beat her clock was worth the soreness I'll feel tomorrow. Shoving my hands in my pockets, I shrug. "It was no big deal."

We approach the coffee shop where we met last week. It's closed at this hour, but we still stop to take a peek. It's become a regular stop when I need something better than what's served at the office. She sits on the bridge ledge of the windowsill as she comes to the end of her cone.

"I shouldn't probably admit how boring my life is, but it's nice being out of the apartment." She sits, contentedly listening as I continue rambling. "I miss having an outdoor space, a patio to spread out on, or a short drive to the beach."

"Have you always only lived in Los Angeles?"

Nodding, I look down the street and then back at her again. "I spent a few months in Seattle before I moved to New York."

"The other CWM office," she says, filling in the blanks. "The other night, you said you were here for two years. What is that deadline?"

"Imaginary. It's just a mental note I keep."

"Because it's that bad living here?"

"No, because I left everything in LA, and some days, I get homesick. That doesn't sound very mature—" I turn to face the sidewalk to block her gaze that's determined to read me like a book.

"Being homesick isn't about maturity. It's about where your heart longs to be." Popping to her feet, she takes her sweater from me and puts it back on. "Thank you."

"No problem." Heading toward my place again, I look

around at all the apartment buildings in the area, curious where she lives. "What about you? Is your heart in the city?"

"I'm open to change, but there's no reason to right now."

My curiosity getting the better of me, I finally ask, "Where do you live?" She raises an eyebrow along with one side of her mouth but doesn't say anything. I add, "You don't have to tell me if you're not comfortable. I'm just guessing it must be close, considering how fast you got to my building."

"I'm close enough." I leave it at that, knowing I don't have a right to more than she's willing to give. "Does anybody call you Andy?"

Annnnd that comes out of left field. Entertained by how her mind works, I reply, "No."

"Did they ever?"

"Sure, when I was young and played baseball. Andy Christiansen sounded like a much cooler name to me at the time. My grandparents also called me that."

"When did it change?"

Each step I take has me slowing while searching for a thoughtful response until I stop. I glance at her. "You know, I don't remember. It wasn't something that I chose. It just sort of happened."

Nodding, she takes in my answer for a long moment, and then she says, "Andrew's a tricky name."

I laugh. It feels good to be kept on my toes. "I can't wait to hear this."

Without missing a beat, she walks quicker, matching the pace of her words. "Andrew is so grown up, but Andy is more like a kid's name. Where do you fall in the scheme of things? And what do you feel about that?"

"I guess I'm somewhere in between. And . . ." My name is currently the last of my concerns. Do I care? All I know is that I'm falling into bed alone. *Where on earth did that thought come from?* But right now, I'm not so lonely with her.

She says, "And?"

"And nothing." She chuckles as I continue wondering how my name changed without me noticing.

"If you could have any nickname, what would you choose?"

"I thought nicknames were something other people gave you?"

"I like Drew. I mean, oddly enough, I like the formal name, too. It's a win-win. Andrew is reliable, the guy you'd trust with not only your money but also your life. So, I think you're golden with either name you choose."

I'm drawn to the one she chose. "I like Drew."

"Next question," she announces with more pep to her step.

"Okay, shoot."

"Why'd you want to be CEO?" A few people—my brother, an ex-girlfriend, and a disgruntled employee, to be precise—think I only like to talk about myself. That's not accurate. I'm not a narcissist, but I am confident in who I am and what I have to offer. Although with Juni, the last thing I want to do is hear myself speak. I prefer to listen to her much more. "Why so many questions?"

"You ask a lot as well," she replies with a quick pop of the shoulders. "So I figured you were down with the get-to-know-you-stage of our friendship."

"I'm down with twenty questions, but all is fair—"

"This isn't love, and it's definitely not war."

I revert to my comfort zone and do what I'm accused of. I ask, "Then what is it?"

"I'm not sure, actually." She hooks her arm with mine, and we continue walking.

I could fill in the quiet air hanging around between us, but why? I like the sound of traffic and the bustling streets, when we talk and when neither feels the need. I like so much about her that she has me believing that eventually, I might like this city. Instead of doing anything else, I walk in the present with her on my arm.

We stop in front of my building, not close enough to have Gil jumping up, but where there's plenty of light drifting onto the street. I ask, "You're not going to let me walk you home?"

"No. How do I know if you're a stalker or not?"

Chuckling, I reply, "Easily, but if you can't tell, you're just going to have to take the risk to find out."

Stepping back, she crosses her arms and begins tapping her fingers. "Did you know there are only two plants in the entire office? And one's an aloe, so officially, it doesn't count since it's a genus of flowering succulents."

Her mind fascinates me. Her knowledge of plants is a very obscure party trick, or she's really into gardening. She probably has a garden covering her balcony or a fire escape jam-packed with plants. "Aloe doesn't count as a plant?"

"No, it definitely counts as a plant, but a succulent is—" She waves her hands, erasing the air. "Forget that. It doesn't matter to the actual point I'm making."

"Okay, what's your point?"

"That the other one is a faux philodendron that was shoved on top of the refrigerator in the break room like that's its natural habitat." Leaning in and lowering her voice, she whispers, "I have a theory."

"Do tell," I say, playing along.

"I think someone actually discarded it." I hear the offense in her voice when she covers her mouth, as if she can't bear the thought of it. An unrecognizable emotion flashes through her expression as she looks at the night sky. "Probably that asshat Justin." The conviction is gone, replaced by a quieter version of the woman I know.

Remembering what Nick told me about Justin crossing a line with Juni, though, has me calling him an asshole under my breath. I don't even know what happened, but I know I'm safe in the assumption. I could ask her, but is that a line I shouldn't cross? Should I talk to HR or keep out of it as I've always done?

With her continuing to stare up like she's waiting for a sign from above, I'm starting to wonder if she's purposely avoiding eye contact with me. I ask, "What happened with Justin?" *I cross that line like it never existed.*

That draws her attention immediately. "We should probably leave work at the office." I'm not granted a smile or a wink, no laughter, or even the sense of who Juni normally is with me.

It's then that I realize it's not the emotion that's unrecognizable. *It's her.* "Talk to me."

Moving farther away, she keeps her arms crossed when she turns her back to me, her stiffened body language keeping me at bay. "What do you want me to say?"

"I want you to talk to me as your friend."

It takes a minute, but when she looks at me over her shoulder, her body eventually follows. "As my friend, you'll keep this between us and not be CEO Andrew right now?"

"I'm always CEO Andrew, but what you tell me in private stays between us."

"He didn't say anything I can't handle." When her arms loosen and fall to her sides, her expression tempers. "Let's not ruin the night. I felt like I was just getting to know the Ice Cream *Drew*," she says with an emerging grin. "But there will always be a special place in my heart for bossy CEO Andrew."

I can get bossy if that's what she's into, but we're supposed to be platonic. I run my hand over my hair, not sure what to say. Everything that comes to mind is inappropriate. *Fuck.* Who knew ice cream could lead to thoughts that veer toward the gutter?

I probably did if I thought about it. "I'm not always the Boy Scout you think I am. Despite the tie I put on each morning, I'm a man with flaws. I've gotten in more than my fair share of trouble, but there came a time when I had to choose between instant gratification and long-term satisfaction."

Her expression is kind when she says, "I hate that you felt you had to be one or the other. You're so much more than a prestigious title." She starts backing away, but adds, "I can't wait to watch you unravel."

What would be considered an insult coming from any other person is a compliment from her. "Hey, where are you going?"

"We have work in the morning. I don't want to give my boss a bad impression."

Angling my head to watch her walk away, I rub my thumb over my lip, but then say, "You couldn't if you tried, babe."

A giggle escapes her, and she says, "I'll see you in the morning. *Babe.*"

There's so much more I want to tell her. That's a sign to walk away before things turn from platonic to erotic. "Want me to walk you home?"

With her back to me, she waves over her head. "Good night, Drew."

Drew. It's hard to repress my smile. *Why do I like hearing her say my name so much?*

I turn to Gil, who's holding the door open, and sigh. Two guys standing alone, one just witnessing the other getting shot down. "We're just friends."

He tips his head. "Keep telling yourself that, Mr. Christiansen."

I will.

15

Andrew

LYING TO OURSELVES IS SOMETIMES THE BEST MEDICINE.

I thought it would feel like any other regular workday when I walked into the office this morning. But disappointment set in the moment I saw the empty reception desk.

We're just friends . . .

Don't think about Ice Cream Drew or her tongue licking the pink ice cream. Fuck, that's going to be a hard memory to erase. It's just too good to forget.

So what if I enjoy seeing Juni Jacobs on a regular basis? That's normal. Men and women can be friends. Look at Dalen and me.

Just because I've had thoughts of having sex with Juni in my office doesn't mean a thing. I shake my head and hurry to said office to hide out before she shows up.

I'm so fucked.

I need to clear my head. I'm at work, for fuck's sake, and these kinds of thoughts could lead to me being fired. *Can I be fired?* Basically, Juni's turned me into an asshole.

Although she's not entirely to blame. I can squarely place a lot of responsibility on that damn black skirt of hers. I wish I'd never seen it. I wouldn't be losing my fucking mind if I hadn't.

I'm greeted by a few other early birds on my way down the hall. When I approach my door, I notice it's already open. That's odd. I distinctly remember locking it last night. Mary and the night janitor are the only two people with keys.

I slowly push it open and look inside to find Juni standing in front of my desk wearing another skirt that highlights her curves and high fucking heels again.

Nick is right. Juni is tempting me into an ethics code violation.

Although it's confusing to riddle through her different sides. I'm starting to get a fuller picture. She's become two sides of the same person. There's work Juni and then the one I hung out with last night.

Not sure I can say much since she pegged me as Ice Cream Drew and CEO Andrew. I knock and then walk in. "May I help you?"

She jumps, a gasp forced out as she holds her hand on her chest. "Oh my God, Andrew. Why are you sneaking around? You scared the crap out of me."

"I wasn't sneaking around," I say, peering outside my office just in case anyone heard her. Our office is full of lookie-loos and listening-lindas. What office doesn't love a little gossip?

Fortunately, it's still early enough that no one is in the area. "What are you doing in here?" I cover the distance to my desk in five steps and then settle into my chair. "And at work, you should call me Mr. Christiansen like everyone else."

"To your face."

Although I've been trying to avoid looking directly at her because I know my gaze will travel lower than her eyes, that comment has me locked on her. "What does that mean?"

"Nothing. Isn't that what you like to say?" Her sass is in full swing, and I'm wondering what's gotten into her.

"Is something wrong, Ms. Jacobs?"

"For future reference," she starts, her fingertips whitening against the wood of my desk. "Good morning is a nice way to greet someone you're seeing for the first time that day. Or good afternoon and evening depending on the hour."

I rock back in my chair, highly entertained by her, even if she forgot whose company this is. "Good morning, Ms. Jacobs."

"Good morning to you, *Mr.* Christiansen." My name leaves her lips like a dirty word she can't wait to spit. She presents two cups of coffee on the corner of my desk.

"Are we having coffee together?"

"Did you confuse me for Jen?"

Chuckling lightly, I like the fire she's burning inside this morning. You know what would be good to cool her down? *Deep. Pink. Cream.* "Is it hot in here?" I ask, tugging at my collar.

"No. It's seventy-one degrees. Just how you like it."

"How do you know that? I didn't even know that."

She smirks and sits at the edge of the chair in front of me. "Melissa gave me a manual."

"I could use a copy."

"Couldn't we all. Anyway, I brought you coffee to try. The brand served in the break room has a terrible aftertaste, and I also have noticed that a lot of employees are venturing to buy coffee in the lobby, or even more of a time waste—down the street—between two and four PM." She shakes her head. "Now, don't get me wrong. Getting out into the sunshine is a good thing. Sometimes we need a break. A little dose of serotonin goes a long way for a productive workday. But that takes them away from the office for about twenty-five minutes. Then they chat as they head back to their desks, which brings it in around forty minutes. According to the manual, a break outside of lunch should only take fifteen to twenty minutes max." She picks up the cups and sets them in front of me with a big smile as an accompaniment. "A or B?"

I'm still a little stuck on the serotonin benefits, and noticed break times my staff were taking. *Laurie was impressed with Juni for a valid reason.*

Just as I pick up A to try, she adds, "Be honest if you like it or not. This is just the beginning in the search for the perfect coffee, but I think I found a great contender in the Blue Ridge brand."

Seeing her proud of her efforts as she waits for me to pick my favorite has me wanting her approval. I don't know which one is the Blue Ridge brand. I taste the B cup. Now I'm thinking about her tits. *Fuck.*

I think she's bigger than a B, full C maybe. "B." I clear my throat and busy myself with business cards on my desk. I'm such an asshole.

Her hands fly together, clasping in front of her. "Really?"

"Really," I reply, keeping my eyes in front of me as I shuffle through six cards for window cleaners that Mary left on my desk yesterday. Why am I involved in that decision? Doesn't the building handle that?

Juni's still standing in front of me, silent as a mouse. When I dare to look up, she says, "I think the Blue Ridge is a nice upgrade, but not as smooth as I think we deserve. If we can keep employees in the office versus leaving, we can add more minutes of productivity into the day, thus potentially increasing the bottom line."

Studying the B cup in my hand, my gaze goes to her when she stands. "Wow, and here I just wanted a better-tasting coffee."

"That too." She taps my desk and then turns, walking to the door. "Also, Blue Ridge costs 12.48% less than our current brand. I love a good deal."

I thought the skirt would be a problem. I never saw her rattling off figures as the next weapon she'd use to distract me. *She plays unfairly.*

Thinking she was about to leave, I say, "Before you go—"

"Don't worry. I'm not going anywhere just yet." She turns and paces back, but then she detours to the couch, sitting down. "I've been thinking." Stealing a moment to herself, she glances out the window. Pretty sure I need to expect the unexpected with her after she works through her train of thought.

I click the main TV on but am quick to mute it. Stressing that someone might see us, I ask, "About?" hoping to move this along before more people arrive in the office.

"How this is going to work."

I turn on the other two screens that hang beside the TV, preparing to watch the market. "We already know how this is going to work."

"Which is?"

"You're going to fulfill your job duties, and I'm going to do mine. See? It was already settled the day we were hired. Unless you want to go above and beyond. That's always welcome at CWM."

"That sounds naughty. I'm going to need more details on that."

I can't say she's wrong, but we are at work, and I'm still wondering if we can push our private lives aside during business hours. "No. This is inappropriate on so many levels."

Leaning back on the couch, she crosses her legs as if she wants to spend some quality time together. "Also, for the record, when you're not grumpy, like just now, I feel like you've become smart-assy since we became friends."

"You might be right, or maybe we're just at a level to drop our pants." *What? Shit. I cringe inside. Did I really just say that?*

Her head jerks back on her neck. "Drop our pants? What does that mean?"

"Pretenses." *Do I really have to explain this? Play it off.*

"If it means pretenses, then why don't you just say drop all pretenses?"

Good question. "I don't know. It's a phrase that's out there, so I use it."

"Maybe it's used in a locker room where guys are dropping their pants, but not anywhere else."

We're getting bogged down in the nonsense. I also can't believe I slipped up like that. *Fuck.* She throws me off my game. "Let's move on from this conversation and pretend it never happened."

"I can agree to that."

"You should probably go to your desk."

She stands, maneuvering in this skirt better than the last time. Saluting me, she says, "Yes, sir, Mr. Christiansen."

Right before she reaches the door, Mary enters. Her eyes pivot between the two of us suspiciously. "Good morning, Juni. Andrew."

I'm hit with an evil eye from Juni just before she tamps it

down. She takes a breath and then grits, "Good morning," between tight lips.

Yeah, that didn't go over well. Pretending to look for a certain email, I keep my eyes on my monitor as my inbox lights up the screen. "Good morning, Mary."

Juni is almost through the doorway when I say, "I'll approve the plant expenditure, Ms. Jacobs."

She turns back with less anger in her eyes. "Anything I want?"

"You can get anything you want."

Pushing her shoulders back, she raises her chin. "Thank you, Mr. Christiansen."

Mary shifts to the side, including both of us. "Are we getting plants for the office? There's a pretty one in the break room."

"It's fake," Juni and I both respond.

Looking between us, she clears her throat. "Right then. I have your schedule."

Juni adds, "Have a great day, Mary." I receive a narrowed glare instead of warm wishes. I thought the approval for plants would make her happy, but I think she's thrown the first gauntlet. Or maybe I did when I told her to call me by my formal name but allowed Mary the opposite. Either way, a battle has begun, and I know one thing for certain—she's not going to let me live it down.

"You too, Juni."

The door is left open behind her when she leaves. Mary moves into action, setting the printed paper on my desk and sitting so we can confirm each meeting. My mind is elsewhere, though.

We work through the schedule, putting a game plan into place. I scrub over my face to wake up since I'm struggling to concentrate. It's only eight fifteen. I knew I should have gone to the gym. After being out late with Juni, I slept in and now look at me. It didn't do me any favors.

Mary stands with her pad in hand. "Any questions, or do you need anything?" Her eyes spy the two coffee cups, and she adds, "Looks like you're set for coffee today."

I'm quickly reminded of one thing that bugged me all night. "Did Justin get fired?"

Surprise filters across her face. Mary's not one to gossip, but she looks over her shoulder to check that we're alone. "I believe so, but I don't have any details."

"Thank you. That will be all."

I probably sit for thirty minutes before I send my chair rolling backward and stalk down the hall to Laurie's office. I hear Juni answering the phone when I pass the corner that leads to the elevators. I keep going, getting madder with every step I take closer to that asshole's cubicle . . . former cubicle.

After I knock twice, I hear, "Come in." Laurie stands when she sees me. "Yes, Andrew?"

Although she gestures for me to sit, I close the door and remain standing. "I heard Justin was fired."

"Ah." She sits back down and tucks her legs under the desk. "He was. He'd been warned twice prior. That was his third—"

"Why are we waiting for someone to commit three offenses against one of our other employees before it's handled?" I like Laurie, so I put my hands in my pockets, hoping it makes me appear less intimidating. Not that she ever has been, but by how she's exhaling so slowly, she appears to be trying to settle her nerves.

"That's standard practice, sir."

It was a simple answer and a great reminder. "We don't want to be standard. We want to be exceptional. I understand policy and procedure, but we also owe our employees a safe environment. Look into updating the policies and get with legal. Modern times call for change. Please have something on my desk by the end of the day."

"I'll get with Joseph right now."

"One more thing."

She asks, "Yes?"

"What exactly did Justin say to Ms. Jacobs?"

16

Juni

Two days later . . .

OH CRAP!

I drop to my knees, which is something I think I'm getting a little too good at lately. Shoving the chair out of the way, I scurry under the desk and attempt to tuck my limbs under, hiding from view. Sitting as still as I can, I try to eavesdrop.

The squeaky door Gil said he would oil last week is now my saving grace. I have a marker and steady my breath as I wait to hear the muffled footsteps of those familiar Italian leather shoes.

"Good evening, Mr. Christiansen."

"Good evening, Gil," Andrew says as soon as his shoes hit the marble floor of the lobby. "Do you ever take a day off?"

"Usually two days a week, but since Mike broke his leg last month, Pete and I are working overtime."

From the distance of his voice, I'm guessing he's a good ten feet from the desk, but I'm nervous that he's stopped to talk. And don't think I don't notice that Gil isn't moving him along in a hurry.

Andrew asks, "I've been meaning to ask you if you ever make it out to the games?"

Oh God, no! Andrew's found Gil's sweet spot. I'll be stuck under here all night if he gets Gil going.

Gil chuckles, and I know it's not because the conversation is so amusing. He finally says, "*Ju*—one of my residents gave me season tickets once. I felt bad for missing so many games because of work, but it was the best gift I ever received."

I'll just be here wishing I could hug him right now. Gil's the best. I've been fortunate to have him in my life all these years. I have a lifetime of memories in this building. As an only child, if I got bored upstairs with my grandparents, I would come down here and watch cartoons with Gil, or old sitcoms after school on the black and white screen TV. The Yankees playing were the soundtrack while I anxiously paced, waiting for my parents to pick me up after one of their research trips.

I didn't realize I'd closed my eyes until I hear Andrew speak. "I grew up going to a few Dodgers games. My dad worked a lot, so my mom would take my brother and me sometimes."

The sunlight slips back into my life, and I loosen the hold on my knees. He continues, "We were rambunctious boys, so she had us playing all kinds of sports to help burn through our energy."

Gil says, "I bet it didn't help."

"Not much, but it wasn't for lack of trying on her part. She had us take cooking lessons, we joined a painting club, learned to mow the grass. Anything and everything. She believed it was good for the soul."

"Sounds like she kept you busy and minds open to new things."

"She sure did." There's a pause, and then he chuckles lightly. "But we have a two-acre lot. Mowing was a full-time job when I was thirteen."

They share a good laugh, but their footsteps aren't moving away from me. Instead, they're coming closer. *Ugh!*

Gil has one job . . . fine, he has two—open the door for residents and don't let Andrew in on my secret. Coming around to the backside of the desk, Gil stands in front of me. I hear patting, and I know what it is instantly. He loves his tablet.

I gave it to him five years ago along with a stand and Wi-Fi, so he didn't have to suffer with this small box of a TV he had on his desk probably since before I moved here. "These days, I go to one or two of the afternoon games each season. But if the Yankees are playing, I'm watching."

"Do you have kids?"

"A daughter." When the sound of the metal frame nicks the counter, I know he's pulled out the photo he keeps next to the tablet. His daughter is like a cousin to me. I don't see her often, but when I do, it's like visiting family again. "Her name is Isabella." He pauses, and then adds, "I have another daughter. She's not mine by blood, but we're family."

Gil is my family in all sense of the word. Hearing him say it, though, which is something we rarely do, has me feeling loved. It's been a while since the emotion has filled my chest, and I realize now how much I miss it.

Andrew's words don't come fast. I can imagine him

taking in the information. He may get distracted easily when I'm around, but he's an observer.

He finally says, "My family means everything to me. I bet she appreciates having you in her life."

The toe of his shoe touches the side of mine. "Some days more than others."

Andrew laughs again. "You win some, you lose some."

"If that isn't the truth. Tell me, Mr. Christiansen—"

"You can call me Andrew." *Oh sure, he gets to.* I roll my eyes.

"You've been hanging around outside lately." Gil doesn't have to ask the question. We all know what he's doing, so I poke his leg. He's quick to shift around the desk away from me. "Are you—?"

"We're friends. Just friends." I'm not sure why that's a blow to my ego when he's only saying what I admittedly pushed for. *Andrew and I are friends.* And maybe if I say it a hundred more times, it will actually sink in. I just wish he didn't have to be so appealing or funny when he's off the clock. And how is he even better looking at the end of the day when most of us look like hell? No matter the hour, he's a walking *GQ* billboard.

Closing my eyes just for a moment, I can still feel his arm wrapped around my waist as he pulled me closer for safety. He doesn't say anything or make a production, but he always positions himself between me and the street. His acts of chivalry make my heart beat a little faster in a good way.

Gil's lucky I like him because if I didn't, I'd be furious that he's making me use my imagination, which is going wild with theories. The silence between the two men is killing me. I'm begging for a clue as to what's going on since neither is much of a talker.

"She's a nice girl," Gil says, causing me to halt on the spot.

"Oh, do you know her?"

Suddenly, Gil's very busy clicking a pen over again and picking up the receiver from the base and setting it back down. "I bet you have big plans for the weekend." He walks out from around the counter again.

"I'll probably work. Speaking of, I should probably get upstairs." Sounding a little disgruntled, Andrew adds, "I've been distracted all week and have a few hours of financials to go through before tomorrow morning."

"There will be storms tonight, but it should be beautiful by the end of business tomorrow, just in time for the weekend. There's nothing like springtime in Manhattan. Unless you're into fall, and it's pretty spectacular as well. My point is, it will be nice. I hope you get to enjoy it."

"Me too." Andrew's voice is distant, and that clues me in that he's finally at the elevators.

And then it dings. *Thank God.* My legs may not be as long as his, but they're cramped in this small space. A few quiet seconds later, Gil's head angles into my view. "Coast is clear."

I wrangle my way out from under the counter, my legs aching as I stretch them again. "Next time, can you send him on his way a little sooner?"

"Can't blame me that he decided today was the day to get to know each other." He sits on the chair and glides forward. "They eventually all come around for a visit. As for you, maybe the better decision would have been to face the truth, literally, and tell him you live in the building."

"Why would I do that?"

"Silly me," he says through deep laughter. The last of the light from the day disappears, but the fluorescents from the lobby shine in Gil's tired eyes. "I can tell you one thing, Junibug."

"What's that?"

"He's crazy about you."

I want to argue, to deny that such a man might think more of me than he's let on, but I can't. Andrew doesn't let his guard down often, but there have been two or three times when I've seen raw emotion written on his face. Maybe that's how I know there's more to him than he lets on as well. I don't just see it in his eyes. I hear it in his laughter. I watch how he moves with such ease around me. Seeing him at work gives me a comparison.

But the topic causes my hands to shake as a reminder of past pain takes over, and I shuffle backward toward the elevator. "You read the situation all wrong, Gil. You heard the man. We're just friends."

"My only advice is to be honest with him. A relationship built on lies doesn't stand a chance." He holds up my favorite pink box, bribing me closer. As soon as I take a donut and a bite, he looks right at me, all joking aside. "You're better than you believe yourself to be, and you deserve more than you allow yourself to receive. Remember that, kiddo."

I've sort of lost my appetite. Not because I'm upset, but because the truth can sometimes do that to you—sneak up when you least expect it. "Thank you," I say, conflicted about what to feel. Should I feel shame for accepting less in my life to keep me safe or sad that the walls I built to protect my heart are so high that no one is tall enough to see the real me?

"You've given me a lot to think about."

"The truth will come out. It always does. You have a

small window of opportunity to present it in the best light. It's up to you, though, if you take it."

"I know you're right. I'm just a little lost on what to do. I need some time to think this through."

"Life is happening whether you're ready or not. You're great at living each day as it comes, but what if . . ." He raises his hands in surrender. "Hear me out."

He's misreading my fear for impatience, so I take a quick breath and try not to let everything I'm thinking play out on my face. Softly, I reply, "I'm listening."

"You started making plans."

"There's a saying."

"No. I don't want to hear about life moving on while you're making plans or whatever it is. It's bull-cocky, Juni. Make the plans. Give yourself something to look forward to as well as living in the moment. Life is made up of many moments, but it's the memories that matter. I know you love Rascal, but you're not going to remember the time you took him to the grass patch on the roof. You might remember the time you took him to Brooklyn to get his portrait painted, though."

"I've never seen my boy look more handsome. Mr. Clark has that painting hanging near the front window. He only puts his most prized possessions by that window." I grab the watering can I had set down in the corner and head for the snake plants on the far side of the room.

"Don't push this conversation away, Juni. You're about to be twenty-six—"

I start watering, content in my focus being on the first plant. "Don't rush it, man. I have two months."

"Two months. Maybe that needs to be your deadline."

Turning back, I raise an eyebrow. "For?"

"I don't know. What I do know is that you have enough

money to hide from life for as long as you want. But what kind of life would that be?"

"I'm happy, Gil."

"And that makes me happy." Tilting back in the chair, his body language backs his beliefs. "Maybe I'm talking nonsense, but for all the joy you've created in your bubble, I just wonder what would happen if it were popped." Sitting forward again, he rests his arms on the lower desktop. Unable to settle, I relate. This conversation makes me just as uncomfortable. "I have a bucket list. Some things are big, like visiting Naples, where my family comes from, and others are small, like eating a hot dog down at Coney Island once a year."

"You can do that anytime, though."

"But sometimes, we need the reminder." Reminiscing cracks his normal steady and fatherly tone. "I don't get out there much, but when I do, I enjoy eating a dog in the salty air." How can I not smile? *He's right.* It's simple, but sometimes, we need to leave the safety of our little habitats. "Reminds me of my childhood and then later taking Bellabug." *Why does it always make me chuckle when I see this wonderful man misty-eyed when thinking about Isabella?*

Why does it also make me sad knowing my father never gave me a nickname? Or rarely called me at all. I'd always hear the same thing from my parents. *"There are no phones in the jungle."*

Listening to Gil, Coney Island must be the most magical place ever. I've seen photos and know what it is, but maybe experiencing it is different from watching videos. I've lived so close. I could have gone anytime as well. "I've never been."

"This isn't easy to say, but I'm going to anyway. You were abandoned by your parents. I understand that commitment scares you, but you had great examples from the people who stuck around. Your grandma, Marion, and your grandpa, Thad. You have me. The good outweighs the bad. But one day, I'll be gone, and I need to know that you're living the life you were meant to. Whether that is with someone or alone, I want it to be your choice. Not made from fear but from love."

He stands, and that has me looking outside. Mrs. Hendricks is approaching. He asks, "Do me a favor, okay, kid?"

He knows I won't say no, but to amuse him, I say, "Okay."

The door swings open, and he helps her with her bags. "Good evening, Mrs. Hendricks."

She stamps her cane down as if she just claimed the moon. "Hello, Gil. I needed a few things."

"Let me know next time, and I can help arrange a delivery service," he offers, charming her knee-high L'eggs pantyhose right off her. And yes, I know what brand she wears because my grandmother made me run an errand for Mrs. Hendricks when I was fourteen. *The memory stuck.*

She waves him off and keeps walking. "Stop pawing my bags. I needed some personal things and don't need some youngster knowing my business."

"Point made," he placates to settle her down because she's always been on the feisty side.

Noticing me in the corner, she says, "Why are you always hiding, Juni Jacobs?"

"I'm not hiding. I'm watering the plants."

"You're wasting time."

Moving to the third large pot, I reply, "The plants don't think so."

"Your life. You should be married and have a family by now."

Soooo tempting to roll my eyes. I don't. I don't even bother arguing with her either. It's not worth the sacrifice of my happiness just to feel justified. Gil puts her on the elevator, and I call, "Have a good night, Mrs. Hendricks." When she grumbles in return, she confirms I made the right decision not to waste my time.

As soon as we're alone again, Gil doesn't let up. "Make a list. Big things. Small things. Live, love, laugh things. Anything. I just want you to break your routine."

"I thought I had with the job at CWM." I'm not trying to be snarky, but that's more than a baby step. I mentally pat myself on the back for it.

"I'm going to let you in on a little secret," he says. I stop watering so I can hear his lowered voice better. "I've let you blame your parents for a lot of years gone wrong, and that didn't do you any good. It's time you look inward to figure out what's really holding you back."

Raising an arm out, I ask, "What am I missing?" It's a dumb, reactionary thing to say. I know what I'm missing in so many ways, but I try every day to be satisfied with the life I've created.

"That's for you to decide." When he sits down again, he settles in for the night shift. "Now stop wasting time with this old man. I'm sure you have something better to do than hang out with me."

As I head for the elevators, not needing an engraved request to give him peace, I turn back and ask, "Was all this a roundabout way of saying you approve of me dating Mr. Christiansen?"

A warm smile spreads wide. "Take it as you will." *My God, he is.* That is high praise indeed. I was joking when I asked that question, but I actually think that Gil thinks Andrew and I could work.

That has to be his own awesome marriage speaking. He and Nancy are a match made in heaven. *Rare.* Andrew's way out of my league.

Gil's gaze lowers to the desk, and he turns up the volume. Just when I step into the elevator, I hear the sports announcers talking about the bottom of the third. Yankees are up.

There's so much to digest from what he said. Albeit small, my world has always held such creature comforts—the apartment I was raised in, Mr. Clark and Rascal down the hall, and Gil downstairs. It's not like I don't leave this place. I leave it every day, but I have a feeling Gil means more than the walls that make up this building or the invisible ones that form my bubble. *As a matter of fact, I know he does.*

As soon as I enter my apartment, I think more about what Gil said.

"One day, I'll be gone, and I need to know that you're living the life you were meant to. Whether that is with someone or alone, I want it to be your choice. Not made from fear but from love."

Where would I be if he wasn't in my life? I'm sure I would have felt even more alone growing up. Is that what I'm doing? Making a choice from fear to be alone? Is it my choice, or am I hiding?

Is Gil disappointed in me for not being honest with Andrew? I can't have that. I send a text: *I was thinking I could come over.*

I sit down, gnawing on my lower lip, and wait for a response. Come on, don't leave me hanging.

A message pops up: *Apartment 17 B.*

I scramble to get ready—a casual dress, makeup, perfume—and burn some time since he's not expecting me to show up in two minutes. I wait around for ten and then sneak through the stairwell until I reach his floor. I've lived here long enough to know seventeen is one of the most expensive real estate in the building. There are only two apartments, and I'm standing in front of one of them.

Andrew opens the door and leans his head against the edge. "What brings you by?"

"We need to talk."

17

Andrew

THE TIMING COULDN'T BE BETTER.

I've not been home long, but my mind is already wrapped up, wondering what Juni is doing and if she'd want to go on another adventure tonight. After being locked away in meetings all day, I'm tired, but I'd make an exception for her.

I pour a drink, get more comfortable in sweatpants and a T-shirt, and sit by the window. *La bohéme* plays softly in the background as I sip and listen. The music builds, crescendos, and falls again, reflecting my life in more ways than I care to admit.

The whiskey doesn't soothe me, and the view is dull.

Even the soft material of my clothes doesn't have me feeling more at home in my skin than spending time with her does. But none of that makes sense. She doesn't fit into my plan, and I'm still not sure she didn't weasel her way into it from the beginning.

Does it matter now?

I take another long sip and then stare at my phone. With the message box open, I think about what I'm doing and why. Why? It's the one question I can't seem to answer. I finish my drink and then let my wants take the lead: *I was thinking we could hang out tonight?*

With my thumb poised over the send button, I pause, not sure why I'm holding back. She's different from the other women I've dated. Dalen is a Hollywood bombshell. She's intelligent, comes from money, and has become a sweetheart over the years. That's why we reconnected. It took a long time to get over her cheating on me.

The girls I dated in college were sweet but not driven in the same direction in life, one even telling me she couldn't wait to introduce me to her parents back in Kansas. We'd just fucked for the first time (*and last, I'll add*), and she was already making wedding plans.

I've dated women who had more ambition than I did—from sports agents to damage control PR reps for the latest scandals in LA to a restaurateur in the Bay Area. I saw potential for something more long-term with one of the Top 30 under 30 tech entrepreneurs in Seattle after our first couple of dates. The third time we went out, I learned she would never leave Washington State. That city is too rainy, too cold, too not LA. It was also only a pit stop in my journey.

Although I haven't been here long, it's long enough to know that I need to get out there. Maybe not like my mom would like or how Jackson dates—a man on a mission—but make a real effort to find more balance. That's something I've not been good with. Now's a great time to get it rectified. I delete the text and type a new one instead: *Would you like to go out with me on Saturday night?*

Before I press send, I rifle through my past, wondering

how someone with a heart of gold like Juni fits into my future. Do I really have time to dedicate to someone else, or will she get hurt? I'd hate myself for doing that to her, but I'm not sure I have the control to make that decision.

Christiansen Wealth Management is priority number one. I delete the text just as one comes through: *I was thinking I could come over.*

I stare at the screen, trying to calculate the chances of her thinking the same thing as I was.

Chance of being bitten by a shark: one in four million.

Chance of being struck by lightning: one in five-hundred thousand.

Based on recent history: *The chance of Juni and I thinking the same thing at the same time is incalculable.*

So maybe it's not by chance at all that she texted. Maybe the universe is playing her cards. As my dad would say about opportunity, "Open the door." I text: *Apartment 17 B.*

Who am I to tempt fate?

There's no need to stress. The apartment is still spotless from the cleaning crew that came yesterday. My clothes are comfortable. We're hanging out, not going to the ballet. I pour another drink and then make myself at home on the couch to wait.

The knock on the door isn't forceful but soft as if she's suddenly become shy. Not wanting a spoiler, I don't peek through the peephole. I just swing that door wide open.

But I wasn't prepared . . . I never am for her, it seems.

She doesn't have to try to be utterly breathtaking—she just is whether her hair is up or down, her clothes fitted or baggy, dressed up or casual. Those things are obvious. It's her smile and her hazel eyes that shine brighter than the stars on a clear night that have her stealing my breath and staring at her face. And everyone else she comes in contact with.

She just doesn't seem to notice or doesn't care that all eyes land on her. I couldn't help the chuckle the first day I saw the poor coffee shop schmuck who thought he had a chance with her. He probably didn't even have chest hair yet. *But it made complete sense. She's different from every other woman. She was made to stand out.*

The green of her eyes is brighter tonight. The other time I've seen that color take the lead was when she was laughing in the ice cream parlor and then inside the office when she brought me coffee.

The brown is showier, at least for me. Anger turns the golden centers to fire, and she struggles to hide the emotion, like when I called her a stalker or when Mary called me by my first name.

Juni may not be my girlfriend, but she has a jealous streak.

Dressed in jeans and an NYU sweatshirt, she says, "We need to talk."

I open the door all the way and step aside because Juni's a sight for sore eyes despite that ominous opening line. She has a flair for the dramatic—as if everything at that moment is the most important thing—so I'm not stressing yet.

There's no rushing in. She takes her time entering the apartment with wide eyes, studying everything she passes from the artwork to photographs, the furniture and the layout. Again, it makes me realize I have no idea where she lives.

What's her view like? Which floor does she live on? Does she prefer taking the stairs or the elevator? And when I really get going down this rabbit hole, I realize I don't know anything about her living situation, not even if she lives alone.

"Do you live with somebody else? Do you have roommates or live with family?" I shut the door but remain in the entry.

The question seems to take her by surprise, her gaze cutting through the distance to reach me. "What made you ask that?"

Signaling to her sweatshirt, I say, "You went to NYU, but I don't know much else about you."

"You know more than most." Her words aren't clipped, and she doesn't sound bothered. If I didn't know that she'd come here to talk about something else entirely, I'd guess this might be it.

I cautiously cover the next ten steps to get closer, but leave plenty of room for her to explore. "You're really good at hiding and a master at distracting, changing the subject, and easing out of any situation that makes you uncomfortable. Call me selfish, but I'd like to know more instead of less."

Worry creases her forehead, and she bites the inside of her cheek. "I came here to tell you. . ." Her breathing picks up, and her gaze falls to the floor. Her waterfall reaction has me curious to know how close I am to the cliff.

Is this it?

No more friendship?

"Would you like something to drink? I'm having whiskey." I find my glass on the windowsill and take a sip.

"Oh, um. Sure. What do you have that has more alcohol than water but isn't as strong as whiskey?"

"I'm pretty well stocked. Do you like wine? I have white or red."

"A glass of white, please. Maybe that's what I need." I'm

not sure I was supposed to hear the last part, but she's not rushing to hide she said it.

Attempting to read her is one of the hardest things I've ever tried to do. I usually have no idea what she'll say or what she needs. But I'm getting better. "Rough day?"

While I've been pretending we can actually be friends, the temperature has risen between us. I feel it, and I have a strong suspicion she does as well.

I'll still do just about anything for this woman even without knowing much about her. She's good. Her heart, her energy, and her intentions. In the short time I've known Juni, I've become an expert witness to it.

I'd kiss her if she asked, take her out if she wanted.

Whiskey has built my confidence.

But it's as though I can see her clearer than I did in the office or even in the park. She hides more than she thinks I realize. While I pour a glass of wine for her, I say, "You can tell me anything."

She comes into the kitchen, her fingertips tracing the charcoal veining on the top of the white stone counter. Stopping on the other side of the island from me, she rests her middle against it and says, "I live alone." She makes it sound like a sentence she's completing.

I slide the wineglass toward her, thinking this might be good timing. She probably needs something to take the edge off whatever's hanging over her head.

Taking a drink, she keeps her eyes on mine even when she sets the glass back down again. "I'll be twenty-six in two months, and I've never had a full-time job."

Not wasting the opportunity, I ask, "How do you survive? How do you live in the city?"

"My parents died when I was seventeen." Her tone isn't offish or cold; it's factual. *Damn, that's heartbreaking.*

And now I feel like shit for pressing her. "I'm sorry." I can't imagine what she's had to go through. It's easy to get caught up in the dynamics of my family—the good and bad, the ridiculous and stress that comes with being the kid of a highly respected couple. But I have Cookie and Corbin through it all. I don't want to think about a day when I won't.

"So am I." She takes another sip and then exhales a deep breath. "They had made a lot of money and had life insurance policies."

My mind goes to finances. It's my comfort, the place where I'm at my best. This is a damn nice neighborhood. My apartment went well above eight mil. If she lives nearby, that explains how she can afford it.

Why'd I ask that? Well, I know why—I let my curiosity overrule my mind. I deal with money for a living. Privacy is important in my business. But mostly, I had no right because she's not my client. "I shouldn't have pried. My apologies."

"It's okay. It's not a secret that I can hide. It's a fact in the public domain. I'm not trying to keep things from you, Andrew. I've just learned to protect my heart."

"I won't hurt you, Juni. I know that sounds like a line, but I want nothing from you other than to know you better."

"I can't promise you the same. I'm as skittish as an alley cat. But being friends means trusting each other. I haven't done that, though I've expected it from you. That's not fair."

It's a thing of beauty when her protective wall finally descends, exposing her heart. I reply, "Friends means honesty."

She nods. Picking up her glass, she taps it against mine. "Being friends means we're on equal footing."

While she drinks to that, I remind her, "I'm your boss."

"Not outside that office, you're not." An eyebrow raises in challenge, and there's that fire she carries inside her eyes.

"Touché." I tap her glass this time. "To equal footing. Outside the office," I shoot right back.

"I'll drink to that."

We both do. Her spirits have lifted, and although the wine could get credit, I'm hoping it's the conversation. Wandering through the living room, she ends up where I was before she arrived. It has the best view. You can see down the avenue in both directions and the sky above. "Andrew?"

"Yes?"

"If I tell you something, will you not make fun of me?"

"Why in the world would I make fun of you?"

She searches my eyes for a lie, but her expression eases. She appears satisfied not to find one. "Juniper."

"Juniper?" *Juni.* I'm grinning too wide to hide it. "That's your first name?"

"It is. You didn't look at my file?"

"Why would I do that?"

"Because you can." There's a remorseful pause, but then she giggles, and that pulls her pretty features away from shame. "Sorry. I would have snooped. Anyway, yep, I'm Juniper Jacobs. It's quite the testament to the love of alliteration" *That's what I thought.*

"It's a good name."

"If you love trees, which my parents did. Did you know that in some cultures, the juniper tree represents *enduring potential*?"

"That's a hefty expectation to live up to as a baby."

She rolls her head but is still smiling. "Tell me about it."

"I'd rather listen to you."

"Pfft. I'm not as interesting as you seem to think I am."

Her gaze extends through the window, but then she closes her eyes and sways her head to the soundtrack of our conversation that plays in the background. "I love *La bohéme*."

"Me too. Before we get sidetracked, what do you want to talk about?"

The dread she wore in her expression when she arrived is gone, and she asks, "What are you doing this weekend?"

18

Andrew

ANOTHER LATE NIGHT LEADS TO ANOTHER MISSED WORKOUT this morning. Though I can't blame Juni. *Juniper*, for it. She left just after eleven, insisting I stay put instead of walking her home.

The night was low-key, but there weren't any lulls in the conversation. It's been a while since I've hung out with anyone other than family. It was fun, relaxing. Unexpectedly so. That's not a bad thing. Quite the opposite. It felt . . . natural, like we've known each other so much longer than we have.

My mom once mentioned how souls find each other through the chaos of the universe. Drawn together. That we don't just have soul mates in this life, but souls we connect with on a different level.

Tonight was the first time I felt the truth in that. For a few hours, I was my old self. The surfer, the rowdy kid cruising Sunset on a Saturday night, the guy who used to know how to have a good time before the responsibility kicked in. *It was good to get a glimpse of me again.*

I also found out, after losing fifty bucks, that Juni's as serious about blackjack as she is about ice cream. She's a card shark, and I learned not to bet against her.

Pretty sure that's accurate in life as well. *Even though she's not had it easy.* She is still an enigma, yet I don't feel threatened by that.

Last night was good, but every night is good with her.

The problem is that I spent hours unable to fall asleep after she left. With a million tasks on my mind and falling behind with work, I lay in bed and strategize my plan of attack for today. I need this meeting to go well.

I only get one shot at landing the account, which is why I missed my workout. I spent the time researching everything I could online and adding to the file my team created.

Dressed in my favorite suit, the one I was wearing when my dad promoted me to CEO, I step off the elevator, ready to tackle the day. *Wait . . .* I got off too soon and move backward onto the elevator again. But a quick glance to double-check the number has me realizing I'm on the correct floor already. "Sorry," I tell the other passengers as I walk off again, embarrassed I don't recognize my reception area.

Looking around, I finally look toward the desk at the other end for clarification. Christiansen Wealth Management in brushed brass letters hangs on the wall. Just beneath sits Juni, whose eyes are locked on mine. She waves to me, and says, "Please hold, and I'll transfer you."

As soon as she transfers the call, she covers the microphone with her hand and smiles. She says, "You said anything I want." There's a hint of smugness in her words.

"I meant a few plants, not the Amazon jungle."

"You think it's too much?" she asks, gesturing to the rain-forest she's created in a corner of the reception area.

"It's a lot of . . ." When I see her smile fall, I add, "of goodness," turning it around. I am learning not to underestimate this spitfire in front of me. *This* can be handled on another day.

Her smile returns, brightening my day but not success-fully distracting me from that mess of leaves behind me. She says, "I'm so glad you like it. I was worried."

"No need," I say, freaking out on the inside. "It's like a casino in here pumping in the fresh oxygen."

"More oxygen increases productivity," she sings the last word.

I scan the room once more. "I'm sure it will." Trying not to lose my composure, I decide it's best if I leave while I'm ahead. "Have a good day."

"You too, *Mr.* Christiansen."

Stopping in the doorway, I see a plant on every desk in the office—little flowering plants, succulents, miniature versions of the ones in the lobby of my apartment building, and other familiar varieties. Taking a deep breath, I slowly exhale, and then reply, "Ms. Jacobs," without turning back and continuing on my way.

When I reach Mary's desk, I say, "What are we going to do?"

She starts laughing. "Well, you did give her free rein." I value that I don't have to explain to Mary what I'm upset about. She just comes along for the ride, taking my brain's detours in stride.

"I did, and I won't take it back, but we have to do some-thing about all those plants. I half expected an anaconda to slither out of there. That's not the first impression I want clients to have upon their arrival."

Her laughter wanes but then picks up again. "I'm sorry, Andrew. It's like a transformation gone wrong. I'm not sure what her vision was when she ordered all those plants, but her heart was in the right place. She gave me a peace lily. Isn't it lovely?"

Half-heartedly glancing at it, I reply, "Yeah, sure. You really think I should just let it go?"

"Yes," she replies, so certain it's not a big deal. "So what if they think we're all a bunch of plant lovers? We could be called worse things." When her laughter picks up again, I shake my head and go inside my office. Leave it to Juni to turn my most loyal employee against me.

Juniper Jacobs is good. *She's very good.*

Before I settle into my morning routine, I find myself standing next to my chair, staring at a sunny yellow pot with a plant sprouting out the top sitting on my console table.

Not just any plant—*a phallic-shaped cactus covered in sharp needles.*

Did she run out of the regular plants before she got to me?

Bending sideways, I take in the sight before me. I'm pretty sure, judging by this cactus, Juni thinks I'm an asshole, or a dick more specifically, by the shape of it. Getting the only plant in the office that can stab you is not a good sign for our relationship.

I drop my stuff on the desk and head for the door with the yellow pot in hand. But as soon as I open it, I find Juni standing there, ready to knock.

"I was just coming to see you," I say.

"Jinx, you owe me a coffee."

I can't even say my patience is worn thin because it's nonexistent this morning. "You got me last time, but this time, I have to say something. That's not how jinx works."

My tone is short, and when I see Mary watching our exchange, I whisper, "May I speak with you in private?"

With a simple nod, we move into the office, and I close the door. Despite my irritation, she looks like a movie star ready for her close-up, and I've known a few, even dated one. Her hair flows over her shoulders in soft waves. Soft pinks highlight her cheeks and lips while black lashes bring out her eyes. The short-sleeved black sweater has a rounded neckline, and the pleated black skirt flares out.

I triple-checked the dating policy yesterday. Dating her wouldn't break any rules, but as Nick pointed out, there is an "expectation" of upper management, and you can't get more upper than me. A friendship with Juni isn't prohibited, but these thoughts I've been having would not go over well with our board members if they found out.

They won't find out.

I'll make sure of it.

Breaking my train of thought that was fixated on her, she asks, "What is it, *Mr*. Christiansen." She's going to do that every time, isn't she?

I thought the formality of the name was a good way for us to remember the parts we play in each setting of our day. Apparently, I thought wrong. The way she's taking her anger out on me has twisted, and it's sounding dirty coming from her lips. *So fucking hot.*

Forming a T with my free hand and the plant, I call a time-out. "Okay, okay. Point taken. We can drop the mister part. Ow—shit!"

She moves quick, taking the plant from me and setting it down. Turning back, she says, "Let me see."

"I'll be okay."

Taking my hand anyway, she analyzes my open palm as two tiny blood spots appear. "Do you have a first-aid kit?"

"It's no big deal. I don't need tending to. I'll survive." Green. That's the dominant color of her eyes in this light as she looks up at me under the aforementioned dark lashes. Even the diamond stud earrings she's wearing can't compete with the sparkle in her eyes.

"I know you will, but I can clean the blood. That way, it won't get on your contracts." I hadn't thought of that.

"There's a small plastic kit in the bottom left drawer of the console."

Moving around me, her skirt balloons over her legs as she kneels. "Found it." She returns to where she left me standing with the kit already open. Setting it aside, she rips the foil packet of the alcohol swab. "I was having fun with the cactus." Although she was smiling when we started this conversation, it's now faded. "I'm sorry you got hurt."

"It's nothing."

She dabs not just the two spots where needles got the better of me but my entire palm, taking her time. "It's a joke gone bad."

"I'm going to live."

Dragging the swab slowly across my palm with care, she says, "You have a long lifeline."

"My mom's always been happy about that."

"And you're not?" she asks, a smile playing on her lips while holding my hand like it's precious cargo.

Standing this close to her as she cares for me, I find my breath deepening. While she gazes at my hand, I stare at her. She raises her chin to look up at me, and whispers, "Drew?"

She's too close—the floral scent of her perfume is delicate like her, those lips pale pink and so damn kissable, but it's her proximity, the feel of her pressing her body just shy of mine that has me pulling my hand away and returning to my desk. "I think . . ."

I don't know what to think, but the thoughts I do have are fucking with my brain. Juni confuses me. We say we're one thing, but I'm starting to feel very different about her, and that makes me question everything.

What the fuck am I doing?

I have a Fortune 500 company to run. My employees—*my family*—depend on me to be focused. *Deep breath.*

While she stares at me with what looks like shock, I try to get myself under control. She can't call me Drew in the office. I have to draw the line. Surely, she understands that.

I point at the phone as if that's an excuse, and say, "I need to prepare for my meeting."

A light knock is followed by Mary entering. "Sorry for interrupting." It's a welcome disruption to the crazed thoughts I've been having. "Are you ready to go over your schedule for today?"

Juni nods as if she's somehow inconsequential in this situation. If she only knew, to me, she's the opposite. I'm realizing now that I'm invested in a relationship, whether it ever grows beyond friends, more than I should, considering our positions.

"Thank you for the plant, Ms. Jacobs."

I see Mary's attention shift to the plant on the desk. Hiding her smile behind her hand, she's at least respectful enough not to laugh out loud.

Juni says, "You're welcome, but I realized I put the wrong plant in your office." She hurries out and then returns quickly. The clay pot is green, and the leafy vine overflows on the side. "It's a pothos ivy. They bring wealth and fortune."

When she sets it on the edge of my desk, Mary says, "That was so thoughtful, Juni."

Swiping the cactus by the pot, she adds, "It's nothing, really." But I feel the heat of her gaze. There's no fire or anger, not sadness or sympathy. There's nothing at all, making it impossible to read her genuine emotions. And I hate it. Hate when she hides herself away from me.

But, *thank God*, I catch the connection we still share hanging by a thread in an exchanged glance just before she reaches the door. "Thank you, Ms. Jacobs."

19

Andrew

After being out of the office for most of the morning, I return to my desk before noon to find my mom's list for me printed and lying on my desk. "Mary?"

She pokes her head in. "Yes?"

Holding it up, I ask, "Where did this come from?"

"Your brother. Nick stopped by about an hour ago. He said your mom made him do it."

Grumbling under my breath, I sit down and stare at the list I've read over a million times. It's stuck to my fridge, haunting me every night when I'm home. Glancing up, I say, "Thank you. That's all."

She went to the effort to put it front and center, so I'll give her the courtesy of another quick review. Only to humor her, though.

1. Lie in the grass in the nearest park at 9:17 AM on a sunny weekday.

   2. Eradicate negative vibes from the apartment on the sixth Thursday after arrival.

   3. Perform in front of an audience. *(Work doesn't count, Andrew)*

   4. Read Shakespeare on the steps of the New York Public Library just after midnight.

I DRAG my pen across the first one, glad I accomplished one.

Number two: I check the calendar. That's coming up in two weeks. I note that in my appointment software—*voodoo the spirits out of the apartment.*

Number three: Running a meeting doesn't count, but what will? Does she want me to run naked through Central Park or perform at Madison Square Garden? More thought needs to be put into that one.

Number four: This is easy. Juni likes off-the-wall activities. Maybe I should get her to tag along. I doubt she'd even think it was weird.

And, of course, the ridiculously hilarious number five makes me roll my eyes. I don't think I've ever read anything more outlandish than that.

This list is still a thorn in my side. With the original at home, I didn't need the reminder. I wad this one up and aim for the wastebasket. "He aims. He shoots. He—ah, fuck." Yep, that's about right. After bouncing off the side of the bin, it rolls a few inches in front of my desk.

I'll deal with it later.

Five minutes after Mary and most of the office have cleared out, there's a soft knock on the door. Juni swings it open, and says, "Heard the big meeting got postponed?"

It's hard to keep my eyes on hers when I want to run my

gaze down her body and take her in. I manage, but it's a struggle. That's not something I've ever had trouble with prior, especially when it came to the office. "The clients moved it to Monday. They had to fly out of town."

"Sorry to hear that."

"It gives me more time to prepare."

"Always looking on the bright side." *Why do I detect a note of sarcasm?* I'm not a negative person . . . a little irritable when I'm at the office, but I have a lot on my plate. I let the comment slide. She says, "Rumor has it you rarely eat lunch."

Lowering my gaze to the contract in front of me, I reply, "You heard correct, but how do people know that, much less talk about it?"

"Watercooler small talk and the manual."

"Ah, the manual." That's right. *This mysterious manual.*

"Also, I'm taking advantage of the sign posted outside your door."

Not following, I ask, "Which sign is that?"

"That you have an open-door policy. I don't exactly have anything specific to discuss, but I think it's good for you to spend time with the commoners like me." Holding up a bag, she wiggles it in the air. "Anyway, I brought you lunch. Two birds with one stone."

I set my pen down and look up. "I don't consider anyone who works for this company a *commoner,* as you call it. Every person here is talented in their field. And you didn't have to bring me lunch."

"I know, but I did it anyway. Do you like tuna?"

"It's fine in a sandwich."

"Fine?" she hums, leaving the door wide open. "What an odd answer to a fish question. Most people are less neutral on the topic."

And just like that, the old Juni is back. "Even though you didn't ask, I hate it." When she sits, she pulls two sand-wiches from a deli bag that look a lot like tuna. "Don't worry, it's chicken salad. I wouldn't stink up your office with fish."

"Juni, I appreciate you thinking of me, but I just don't have time today."

"I know you're busy." She stands. "I can go. Taylor invited me to eat with him in the break room." Speaking softer, she adds, "He just broke up with his girlfriend and could use a friend."

"He needs to get his own. You're mine." No one moves a muscle—*not her, not me.* I don't even think either of us is breathing. *Fuck.* Dragging my gaze up one millimeter at a time, I finally reach Juni's eyes. "I didn't mean—"

She whispers, "I know."

The awkwardness still surrounds us. "I'm sorry."

"Don't be."

Our words are stilted as discomfort takes hold of me. I grab the sandwich and say, "I love chicken salad."

Her lips lift into a genuine smile. "Me too."

Gesturing to the chair, I ask, "Will you have lunch with me?"

A gentle nod is followed by her sitting down again. Before she takes a bite, she notices the ball of paper on the floor just shy of the wastebasket. Reaching down, she picks it up. "You missed."

"I seem to do that a lot lately."

"I don't know about that. I think you're doing well." Tantalizing pink fills the apples of her cheeks, making me want to reschedule the rest of my meetings and dedicate my time to discovering what exactly causes her to blush.

I tap my pen to a pad several times. "At least one person doesn't think I'm failing."

Her eyes leave mine in a flash, and she takes a staggered breath before slowly exhaling.

It's not a big reaction, but it's seen in the slight adjustments, her happiness disappearing in the undertow of thoughts she keeps locked inside. I ask, "Is everything all right?"

She looks up, and a long pause keeps our eyes connected. For a moment, I think I might be able to read her thoughts, or maybe it's her heart that I'm tuned into. But then she says, "Yes," breaking the spell. She holds the paper in front of her. "May I?"

"It's nonsense. Just something frustrating I have to deal with."

Unwrapping the paper, she then flattens it on top of her thigh. "So says you." Her voice calming as she begins to read. I just took a bite when her gaze lifts to mine again, and she asks, "What is this?"

I swallow the food down, my stomach begging for more of the delicious sandwich. A little embarrassed, a lot feeling the need to justify, I set the sandwich down. "I'm just going to preface this by telling you that not only will this sound crazy but it's utterly ridiculous."

A grin tickles her lips. "I'm prepared. Now tell me everything."

"My mom made me pinky promise."

"You pinky promise with your mom?"

I'm not sure how to respond. Bashful takes the lead for how I'm feeling. At this rate, I'm probably turning pink. "I do."

As if the sun embodied her, her whole expression lights up. "That has to be the sweetest thing I've ever heard, Drew." It's foreign, the twist I sense in my chest every time she calls me that name. I just feel different, exposed in a good way, like she's taken a shovel and discovered a buried treasure. She says, "I love that you're so close to your mom. Says a lot about the bond you have with her."

"She's pretty great." Eyeing the crumpled paper, I add, "Unless she makes me do embarrassing things."

"Is that what this is? A list of ways to humiliate you?" I can hear the teasing in her tone.

Maybe it's not as bad as I'm making it out to be. "She doesn't want to humiliate me. She's created a list of ways for me to step out of my comfort zone. I was given the assignment before I moved to New York."

Curiosity keeps her eyes on mine as if this is the most fascinating thing she's ever heard. "Why would she do that?"

"Because she knows if I have my way, I'll work twenty-four seven."

"Your mother knows you well." She reads over the list again, pausing on the last one. Pointing at it, she asks, "Number five?"

"We're not discussing number five."

Her hands go up in surrender, and she giggles. "Fair enough. For now."

"No. Forever."

"Depends, I guess, on if you choose to break the pinky promise." She tears a piece of bread and eats.

Sighing, I say, "Not you too."

"Oh, there are others?" she asks, too entertained for my liking.

The sandwich is practically calling my name. I take it in hand, ready to stuff my face, but first say, "My brother, Nick, has joined in the fun. Any chance to tease each other and we take advantage."

"Speaking of Nick, we've never really talked about that relationship."

"There's not much to say. We get along better than most and have the good fortune of working together." I'm starved, so I take a bite so big that I have to cover my mouth.

"You're very lucky to have a sibling. I don't have any."

My chewing slows as we dip into heavier territory. When I finally swallow, I then ask, "Do you mind me asking what happened after your parents passed?"

Although I prefer the joy she seems to live in, I'm wondering if some of it is a façade. She mentioned protecting her heart, from me, from life, from everyone. The ex sounds like a distant memory, but he left her more damaged than she lets on.

Tugging the crust from the sourdough, her eyes stay focused. "I lived with my grandmother at that point already, so not much else changed."

Her parents passing away must have had a bigger impact than she's letting on. I have a feeling the time we have left of lunch isn't enough time to dig that deep. Although, I can't help but feel that we shouldn't be having this impromptu lunch at all. Not at work. Not when I'm CEO Andrew. *When I'm not Ice Cream Drew.* But how do I stop this? *Especially when I like her company.*

She's smart to leave the door open and disguise it under policy. I know the truth, but thankfully, it's not obvious to anyone else.

When she holds up the list again, I let her change the subject, knowing she needs to. She says, "I could help you with this list. Well, everything but the last one, of course. That one you have to figure out on your own."

Why does accomplishing these tasks sound more intriguing when she offers? "I'm not doing any of them. It's not a priority of mine."

"It is of your mom's, it sounds like."

"Well, yeah, but she's fixating on something that doesn't need fixing. I'm focusing on a billion-dollar company."

"You're right. They're both equally important."

"Wait, that's not what I meant."

"We should jump on number two tomorrow. Meet me at nine in the lobby."

"N-No. That's not what I have planned."

"What do you have planned on a Saturday at nine AM? Work?"

"Yes. I was planning on coming into the office to get a few things wrapped for this week and make headway on my research for the meeting on Monday."

"As thrilling as that sounds, this," she says, waving the piece of paper in front of me, "is important. You know what this list really is?"

"Punishment for the time I told Mrs. Whipple that my mom didn't like her prized fruit salad?"

"Prized?"

"She won the Women's League Cold Salad Division two years in a row with that fruit salad. She pinned her blue ribbons to her Louis Vuitton, so everybody knew she'd won." *Only in Beverly Hills . . .*

Setting the list down, she finally picks up the sandwich and says, "I'm going to need more details. Go on." She takes a big bite, keeping her eyes on me—wide and intrigued.

Why'd I open this can of worms? "After Mrs. Whipple found out about my mom's dislike of her salad—"

"Because of you."

"I was nine," I say, begrudgingly, "but yes, because of me. Seeking revenge—"

"The plot thickens."

Lowering my voice and telling the rest of the story like there's a campfire between us instead of a solid mahogany desk, I say, "Mrs. Whipple told the entire country club that my mom had paid for me to win the science fair that year."

Juni gasps. "She didn't?"

"She did. Well, Mrs. Whipple did. It was a low blow. I remember how mad my mom was, but how it felt like a reflection on me. I had done the work on my own, but with one cruel attempt at revenge, that was put into question."

Reaching over, her hand covers mine, making me wonder if the hurt feelings remain evident on my face. "I'm sorry, Drew."

"In my mom's defense, not only did she not pay for my project to win, but Mrs. Whipple refused to get her eyes checked and often confused the salt canister for the sugar one. We learned the hard way when she tried to teach my brother and me how to make sugar cookies."

"Yuck."

"You're telling me. To this day, I can't look at a sugar cookie without feeling dehydrated." I clear my throat. "Would you like a bottle of water?"

Lifting in her seat, she eyes behind me. "You hiding goodies back there?"

"I sure am." Waggling my eyebrows, I swivel around and open one of the console cabinet doors to reveal bottles of water and an entire tray of snacks and candies. "I never know if I'm going to need a sugar high or host a client who wants something stronger." Handing a bottle of water to her, I also take one for myself. Remembering the taste of those cookies like it was two minutes ago, I down half a bottle before taking a breath.

"Thanks for the bottle and the stories, but you're not going to distract me with cute childhood memories."

I furrow my brow. She might be the weirdest woman I've ever met. "What exactly is cute about salt cookies?"

She snaps twice. "We're not talking about cookies. We're talking about this list and what it is."

"What is it?"

Her expression anchors sideways. "Nice try, Christiansen. You know but let me remind you." She holds it up and waves it. "This is a list of life or, more importantly, getting one."

"I have a life, a very full life, I might add." I take hold of the sandwich again, ready to devour the rest.

"You, sir, have a life full of work."

I'm never going to finish this sandwich at this rate. I set it down and sit back, preparing to be here a while. "And the problem is?"

"You need a personal life."

"You're assuming I don't have one already. We've spent time together outside of this office. That's called a personal life."

She slow blinks, not amused by my sad attempt to convince her otherwise. "If spending time with me is the only fun, and yes, I know you had fun and will take full credit for said fun, but if that's it—"

"I went out with my brother and Jackson," I reply pointedly. "You saw me that night. I was out with the guys for hours."

Appearing to concede, she nods. "That is true. I'll grant you that time as well."

"And we made plans for this weekend. It's like my whole life is one big party. Anyway, what are you doing when you're not here or with me?"

"Okay, settle down. Let's not get carried away." Sitting back in her chair, she says, "My point—"

"Ah. I see your point. What's good for the goose—"

"Is not good for the gander." Placing her hands down on

my desk, she stands. "We can play cliché games all day, but wouldn't it be more fun, and productive, I might add, if we just do what your mom wants and complete the list?"

Now I'm rolling my eyes. "My mom would have me running around this city if she has her way, and then my dad would serve my ass on a silver platter to the next guy in line for this job."

"What kind of dad do you have that serves asses on platters, much less uses the good silver? Your family's weird. No offense."

We're the weird ones? I scoff, but a chuckle comes out after, sounding more like a mutated bark. Trying to play it off, I cough. "None taken."

Concern threads through her forehead. "Are you okay?"

I clear my throat again. "I'm fine. Just a little chicken stuck in—" I cough again for added effect.

"You're good. You're fine," she sing-songs. "Are you ever great? Like top of the morning, kick your heels in the air great?"

"Like a leprechaun? No. But I am great at my job. Yes."

Her eyes glide toward the windows, and she says, "At least one of us is," sounding distracted.

"Probably not something you should admit to your boss. Anyway, you've proven otherwise to everyone at CWM."

I see a smile settle in place before she waves me off, embarrassed. "I have a proposition for you." *The queen of sidetracks strikes again.*

"I'm not sure I'm ready for it."

"It's easy, no worries."

"Last time I was told not to worry, I was flying across the country to save a merger. So you'll have to excuse my concern when someone says not to worry."

"I'll let it slide. Look, you're new to New York. I've been

here my whole life. I can help you check each one of these oddball requests off your list in no time. You've already done number one. And quite honestly, I'm glad to find out this is what you were doing and that you're not just some nutball with a grass fetish."

That's what she assumed? "As much as I appreciate the offer, who says I'm even finishing this ridiculous list?"

"We met because of number one. I'm sitting here now because—"

"A temp agency placed you."

"You can say that all you want, but I'm not convinced that we weren't supposed to meet on purpose."

"Everything happens for a reason."

"*See?* You do believe."

"I believe in what's right in front of me. I believe the tangible and seeing things with my own two eyes." Not letting her get out of this without hearing what's on her mind, I loop back around, and ask, "What's the proposition?"

"A date."

20

Juni

TRUE COLORS DON'T STAY HIDDEN FOR LONG.

"I thought you were going to come see me at lunch?" Taylor leans against the high counter of my desk like it's his job to support it.

Did I miss something? Why does he sound annoyed with me, as if he wrongly presumed our lunch in the break room was a date? "Sorry, Taylor. I had other plans." It's not a lie. I ended up with plans in the end.

Tapping the counter to an annoying beat that doesn't have a predictable melody, he says, "A lot of us are going to The Watering Hole after work. Do you want to join us?"

Wonder who 'a lot' is? Drew? Laurie? Mary? Or Joseph? Suddenly, I'm caught in what sounds like a nativity scene. Or *The Wizard of Oz—oh my!*

Not wanting to pursue a religious avenue or Hollywood classics, I consider the invitation. I've not spent time with many others, but I wouldn't mind getting to know most of them better. I can practically see Gil high-fiving me for getting involved and developing more relationships. Completing my office supplies order, I finally give Taylor my undivided attention. "I'll pass. Thank you."

Baby steps.

He checks his watch and then starts to leave. "Too bad. I was looking forward to talking with you." I guess he's not familiar with what we're doing now. "It's five o'clock. Time to blow this joint."

I'm no empath, but that guy comes off like an asshole. What is it with accountants in this company? I answer the last call of the day and then place my order online for a delivery on Tuesday. Melissa had her way of doing things, but I've already formed a few habits of my own. I don't use the clip-on box and answer calls while assisting others. I've found that although I can multitask that aspect of my job, it's disruptive to others when I'm walking around answering calls. So if I need to leave my desk, I send the calls to the service.

I like to get to work early as well. Not only is it peaceful but I also have time to organize the coffee supplies before they get messed up by the zombies showing up needing a first cup.

At the end of the day, it's nice to say good night to everyone. Well, everyone who leaves before five thirty. That never includes Andrew and only occasionally includes Nick. The Christiansens are all workaholics from what I've witnessed.

Though sometimes they surprise me . . . while other employees pass by, saying good night as they head home, Nick Christiansen stops by my desk. We haven't spoken much in these past few weeks, but it's enough to be on a first-name basis. He says, "Hi Juni, some of us are going to The Watering Hole. It's a place around the corner."

"Yes, I've seen it."

"Oh, good. Laurie and Joseph went early to grab some tables. It's a last-minute plan, but will you be able to join us?"

He's very good-looking, strikingly so, tall like his brother, dark hair, similar soulful brown eyes. His wife is a stunner herself. When his assistant was out sick, I was asked to take notes. That's when I saw a photo of his wife on his desk.

But he's no Andrew . . . I think it's best if I don't dwell on something more potentially happening there. I'll only end up disappointed.

I drag my purse from the drawer. "I appreciate the offer, but—"

"I'm ready," Andrew says, filling the doorway. Not bothered by the witnesses waiting for the elevator or that his brother is standing there, he adds, "I hope you're coming to the happy hour, Juni."

"Absolutely."

Nick carries forward, chuckling, and we both follow. "It will be good to unwind and visit with everyone outside the office." There's a similarity in how the Christiansen brothers make you feel special, like no one else is around when they're talking to you.

The elevator opens, and as soon as the door closes, Nick adds, "I'd like you to meet my wife."

Oh great! No pressure. Just me and Natalie St. James, now Christiansen, former Manhattan socialite who never much cared for the spotlight. I've read *Page Six* a few times over the years.

I'm close to asking why he wants me to meet his wife, but with eight people standing like sardines in this tin can, I think silence is best.

The doors open, and a guy announces, "You can fit two more," before he and another guy push their way onto the elevator. The rest of us take a step back, making room we didn't have to spare.

I hadn't wanted to look around. Making eye contact in a confined space is one of my least favorite things. It becomes awkward quickly. Do I make small talk? Or pretend the other person doesn't exist? Acknowledge them and then move on like they're dead to me? Elevator etiquette is so confusing.

But in this frenzy of what to do, I hadn't noted that Drew was behind me, taking up the back corner. *Until now.* One step back has my back pressed to his chest, his body so close that I can feel him breathing, almost certain that his heart is pumping as hard as mine.

When the elevator jolts to a stop on the eighteenth floor, it causes us to shift with it. Sometimes, I regret wearing my nicest heels, four and a half inches of black leather Louboutins. *Not today.* When I'm thrown off balance, his hand catches the underside of my arm, and his other hand steadies my hip closest to the wall. No one knows. No one but him and me. My arm is released although his other hand lingers a few seconds longer.

My heart's been racing since the moment I touched him, and my body's temperature is rising. It's stuffy in here. *Just me?* I run my finger under the collar of my sweater and look around.

Everyone looks uncomfortable and ready to be out of this hot box. I'm not sure most of their faces would be any different if we were in the fresh air. Dipping my head forward, I swipe the hair from my neck, pulling it over my left shoulder. I close my eyes and swear I feel the ghost of his hand caressing my skin.

The pressure of his fingers dragging straight down my

spine. His lips a breath away. "Ahh." The sound escapes without permission, and my eyes snap open again.

Nine sets of eyes are staring at me. I'm feeling confident to include Drew, though there's no way I'm turning around to verify. I find my safe place in Nick when he grins sympathetically. The doors open to the lobby, and then he moans loudly. "Thank God we're here. I hold my breath, too."

While I stand in awe of what he just did to cover for me, a few chuckles are heard. But the rest rush forward. Only the three of us are left then, and Nick and Drew both wait for me to exit first.

I want to thank him, but Julie from the brokerage division says, "I was the new girl until you arrived. How are you settling in?"

"I think I'm mostly settled." As we walk, we talk, our large group scattered in the horde of other New Yorkers just getting off work. I only glance back once to see Drew, Nick, and Jackson St. James talking as they walk together.

It's then that I notice Drew isn't wearing a suit jacket. He's rolled up his sleeves, exposing his forearms and the Rolex I remember from the park. His tie is loose and hanging slightly askew on his chest. Basically, the man's trying to kill me, or at least weaken my knees.

And he's succeeding.

Inside the bar, Julie introduces me to many of the employees from the brokerage. Joseph is trying to handle his second beer and failing. Lightweight. And I've had this weird feeling that Drew is avoiding me, which causes me to hesitate before approaching him. But every time I find him in the crowd, his eyes are on me.

Half the bar's eyes are on him. Understandable. But after he staked claim to me when it came to Taylor earlier, I've been motivated a few times to stake claims of my own.

That would be wrong.

So wrong.

I'd lose this job, a job I wasn't even sure I wanted to keep a week ago. Here I am, trying to figure out which department I want to join when Melissa returns.

It was one mental reference to Taylor, nothing even spoken out loud. And there he is, coming toward me with a shit-eating grin and a beer in hand. "Thought you were passing?"

Not that I feel the need to justify my change of mind to him, but I say it anyway, hoping it satisfies his curiosity, "I got talked into it."

"That's cool. I'm heading over to talk with the boss man. Want to come?"

Now, this is the kind of offer I can get on board with. Leaving space between us gives others the opportunity to join in as well. Drew is in full-on CEO Andrew mode right now, so I flip that switch in my mind and try to keep my thoughts in line.

It's just so hard when I can still feel the warmth of his breath on the back of my neck, the heat of his hand imprinted on my hip, and those eyes that intimidate any guy who dares to look my way. Yeah, I've noticed. *How is it possible that he's even hotter when he's protective of me?* Damn him.

I don't think I cared how long it had been since I was with a man until I met him. Owning toys might get the job done, but there's no passion when it comes to anything requiring batteries and an instruction manual. I miss the emotion, someone telling me I'm beautiful, falling asleep in someone's arms, and sitting beside them on a lazy Sunday, even if they told me I had overstayed my welcome.

Dating in New York is tough. Most men want a girlfriend

but not a wife, a whore in bed but not a significant other come morning. I've had one-night stands and don't judge others for trying to fulfill their own emptiness. I miss the other stuff, the life that comes after when you connect on a deeper level—good morning kisses, coffee, and a scone in bed together, or losing a day lost in each other.

It's not just what I miss. It's what I want.

Gil was right. I'm ready. I've just been my own worst enemy.

Julie makes talking to the head honcho look so easy. Her light laughter and expressive arms as she talks with Andrew about the recent wild ride of the market. I attempt to join in as a group of stockbrokers talk shop with him but somehow get cut out of the conversation.

I take a sip of my water and look around. Making eye contact with Nick, I'm reminded I want to thank him. When he waves me over, I'm about to work my way around the table but stop and turn back when I hear my name being called in that deep tone that makes my tummy tighten.

Andrew says, "Do you want to join us?"

I know he wants me here, but the collective expressions of the others tell me to stay back. "Thank you, but I was just going to visit with someone over there." I point indirectly to an area that could really signify half the bar, but he's not dumb. He knows an excuse when he hears one.

The group returns to slobbering at his feet, and I head in Nick's direction. Nick has his arm around his wife but lowers it to her waist when I approach. "Juni, I want you to meet my wife, Natalie. Natalie, this is who I was telling you about. Juni Jacobs."

Natalie practically gasps, her lips parting in the same shared excitement Nick has. Reaching forward, she holds my forearm. "I've heard so much about you. Also, you have an incredibly great name." Leaning back against her husband. They make a beautiful couple, but it's the love that you can see shared between them when they're together that is most notable.

My heart squeezes, letting me know it's there.

"Thank you, but you're making me curious what was said."

They laugh, but I'm still not in on the joke. Making our circle smaller, she says, "Nick has told me you've been quite the asset to CWM, but before that, you helped Andrew out on one of Cookie's missions."

"What's a cookie mission?"

Nick gets pulled away, but Natalie stays to chat as if we're allies, ready to give me the insider's scoop. "Cookie Christiansen is Nick and Andrew's mother."

"I've heard about her, but I'm not sure I knew her name was Cookie. That's unique."

"It is, like her." She takes a sip through the straw of what looks like a vodka soda with lime, and then adds, "You'll love her. She's amazing."

"She sounds like it, but I'm not sure I'll ever meet her. I'm just covering the reception desk temporarily while Melissa's on maternity leave."

Her perfectly arched eyebrows pull together. "Oh, I thought you and Andrew were. . ." She looks across the tables at Andrew standing at the other end, the confusion deepening in her skin. When she turns back, she says, "My apologies. I think I misunderstood."

"It's okay. Drew and I have become good friends." I'd love to confide in someone and share how cute he was eating rocky road ice cream, or how he called me babe when he was drunk, and now it's a running joke. Or even that he slips and allows kismet into his life when he's not busy rejecting that it exists. There are so many things I'd love to talk to a friend and share, and I'm pretty sure Gil doesn't want to hear them.

Although she seems to understand the reality of my relationship with her brother-in-law, her expression soon changes, and a good-natured grin appears. She takes another pull from the straw like she just might not believe me. "That's sweet that you call him Drew. You're the only one."

I didn't realize I had slipped with his name. "Oh, um—"

"I shouldn't have said anything. I didn't mean to make you uncomfortable. Nick's said so many nice things about you and Andrew that I thought it was . . ." She glances at the group nearby, and then whispers to me, "Not so private. But I can imagine that's best when you work together."

Before I have time to process that she's practically welcomed me into the family by assuming Drew and I are having some torrid love affair, she asks, "Do you like shopping? I've built a business around it, but my best friend, Tatum, and I are meeting for brunch on Sunday and then going shopping. I'd love for you to join us. By the way, your outfit is to die for. From the Louboutins to the Chanel sweater—impeccable."

"The sweater was my grandmother's. She loved fashion but was conservative in the way she dressed. She has a closet full of Chanel and St. John."

"It's vintage? It's gorgeous. And there's nothing like the classic round toe pump."

I like her. She could be a model from her beauty alone, but her kindness makes her approachable. I haven't talked about clothes or even cared about them since my grandmother passed away. Lately, I've chosen what to wear the night before, and I'm pretty sure it's because of Drew. The name alone has me scanning the crowd for him. When our eyes meet, he smirks. There's something mischievous, something naughty about it, but I know it's just for me.

I smile right back and then take a drink. Talking clothes and shoes, shopping, and brunch with women around my age sounds amazing, so I say, "I'd love to come on Sunday."

"Great. It will be so much fun." We exchange numbers before she rejoins Nick's side and gets caught up in a conversation with her brother, Jackson.

Close to calling it a night, I head for the restroom. When I come out, I see Drew standing near the entrance to the main part of the bar. "Are you waiting for me?" I tease with a wink.

"Yes." There's no deviation in his tone. He's dead serious, or sexy serious, which fits him better.

His answer surprises me, and my mind starts spinning, wondering if I am reading this situation all wrong. "Am I in trouble?"

"By the looks of it." I don't quite catch on until it registers that he's referring to himself. *That's the hottest thing I've ever heard.*

My lips part, allowing me to take the breath I need to calm my racing heart. It doesn't work, so I lean into it, the thread of friendship narrowing with every minute we spent together. I almost wonder if we've been fooling ourselves all along and were always destined to end up like this. "I was just leaving."

"What a coincidence. I've already said my goodbyes."

21

Drew

I CAN'T BLAME THE ALCOHOL.

I'd only had one drink. That's my professional limit when I'm with colleagues. Clients are different. When they're trusting you with their money, they want to know you can hold your liquor. How one equals the other has never made sense, but I didn't make the rules. I just have to play by them.

Play . . .

Is that what Juni and I are doing? *Playing?* It's a game we'll lose if we're not careful. But caution was left at the bar along with my code of ethics.

Being a man is no excuse for wanting her the way I do, but I'm not alone in my thinking. I've seen the way she gets jealous. Michelle about had Juni blowing steam out her ears. That was good for my ego and a turn-on, but it's been silent in the back of the car, leaving me to second-guess myself.

I shouldn't be doing this. Sleeping with my receptionist

is not only a cliché but could also end badly. I need to drop her off and go home alone.

The neon signs from outside pass in a flash, leaving shadows in their wake. We stop at a light, and I look over at her. "Juni?"

"Drew?"

We speak at the same time. Laughing, we both reply, "Yes?" in unison.

"Jinx," I add, which makes her smile. "You go first."

As I work through her body language, she appears to be relaxed. There's no tension found in her shoulders or anywhere else, but then she asks, "Are we doing the right thing?"

"I was just wondering the same." I reach over and take her hand. "I don't want to mess up our friendship. I enjoy our late-night adventures and seeing you at work. If we do anything, that would all change."

"That's what I was thinking."

"I promise you it's not from lack of attraction or wanting to be with you sexually."

Her fingers wrap around mine, holding tight to my hand. "That's just it. I feel the same. Doesn't that mean it's already too late?"

"That's a fair point." I'm not sure what else to say.

But she does. Leaning forward, she tells my driver, "Mr. Christiansen's place, please."

My driver knows what this is but doesn't judge from the comfort of the driver's seat. He replies, "Yes, ma'am," but his eyes never leave the street ahead. It's a first for me having company come home as much as it is for him to witness it.

She sits back again. This time, a little closer. I'm not sure if it's on purpose, but I'm not going to complain. The car pulls to the curb, and Gil runs out. He opens the door and says, "Welcome home, Andrew."

I slide out and then bend back to help Juni. Gil's reaction is strange when he sees her, words escaping him. So her feelings aren't hurt, I say, "Gil, this is Juni," hoping he'll show her the same courtesy he always shows me.

"Uh . . ."

Juni smiles, and though it seems a little tighter than usual, she's still so beautiful. "Hi, Gil."

"Hello," he replies, curt in a way I've not heard him before. His departure is just as abrupt.

I glance at her, and quietly say, "He's usually friendlier."

"He was perfectly cordial. What do you expect? A life-long support system? Someone who will lie for you even if they promised their mom on her deathbed not to? How can you possibly expect a man to have your favorite donut on hand just in case you had a bad day or need a sugar pick-me-up?" She releases my hand as if that will win her a point and then raises her voice. "Geez, Andrew. Give the man a break. That's a lot of responsibility to put on the shoulders of the doorman."

I force myself to blink because I can't make any sense out of how this turned into an argument between us. "I don't expect anything of him," I reply like I have to explain I'm not a total asshole to Gil. "Just opening the door is great. But if I'm being honest, I don't need someone to open a door for me. I know having a doorman is a thing to brag about in Manhattan, but I'm perfectly capable."

I'm poked in the chest, and then she wags her finger at me. "Well, keep that to yourself, mister, or you might risk his job, and he has a family to support."

"What? I'm—I, uh. I'm not reporting him." I spy Gil out of the corners of my eyes, and now I'm thinking about his life outside this building, and his daughter, Izzy, his wife, and the girl he considers his daughter. He gives us privacy, keeping his gaze aimed straight down the avenue. More importantly, how did I manage to upset her? I'm beginning to think we're not going to make it upstairs.

Remembering a time when my dad sat Nick and me down for a heart-to-heart, I didn't understand what he meant back then. Now I do and say the one thing he told us to say if a woman is ever mad at us. "I'm sorry." It doesn't matter what we did or didn't do. Take the blame, pay the price, but always apologize.

Juni drags her hand down the side of her hair, taming flyaway strands, but the puzzled expression aimed at me is unmistakable—narrowed eyes and pushed-together brows form a little line in the middle. "Why are you sorry?"

"For upsetting you."

"I'm not upset." The scowl on her face tells me otherwise.

Scratching my head, I stand there watching her walk toward the door. I'm so lost that I don't think I can get this train back on track when it comes to her, but I'll make the effort and follow her.

Juni and Gil are whispering when I approach. Gil clears his throat and holds the door open wider for us to enter. They're both acting weird.

Once inside, we head for the elevators as Gil sits down behind the desk. He turns up the volume on what sounds like a Dodgers game. Names of some of the hometown players are called out and up to bat. I ask, "Who's winning?"

His gaze stretches across the lobby, and he eyes Juni. "Apparently, not me."

"Huh?" I've never seen him like this. He's usually so happy-go-lucky, but I guess we all have our off days. Fortunately, the button has been pushed to call the elevator because this is getting uncomfortable.

"It's not looking good for the Dodgers," he replies after a delay, glancing down at the screen propped on his desk.

Trying to lighten the mood, I laugh. I'm a terrible actor, but I stick with it. "No surprise. They're always the underdog. Makes it more exciting to root for them."

The elevator door opens, and just before Juni steps inside, she looks back at Gil, who's ripping a bite of a pink donut off like a bear ripping its prey apart. The door closes, and she says, "He seems nice."

He seemed out of character to me, but Gil is not who I want to be thinking about right now. Wanting to forget about whatever that was and focus on more interesting riddles to unravel, I slide my arm around her middle. Unlike in the elevator at work, I don't have to hide how she turns me on this time. Rubbing my thumb along the curve of her waist, I ask, "How are you feeling?"

"Good."

Still not sounding like herself, I press for more, "Is something wrong?" Dipping my head down, I nuzzle the top of her head. Closing my eyes, I take in the feel of her. This is the closest we've ever been, and right now, I don't want to think about anything other than kissing her as soon as we reach the apartment. Though her smelling of flowers on a spring day has me tempted to do it now. I lower my gaze until I meet hers. "Good is unlike the great Juni Jacobs I know."

Her gentle laughter rattles her shoulders, and she angles my way, bringing us closer. "I'm great because I'm with you." Her hand runs along my lower back, and she asks, "How are you?"

Nervous.

Excited.

Not knowing what comes next.

I'm always in control of every aspect of my life, so I'm not used to letting things play out organically. Before I have time to collect my thoughts, she adds, "You're from California. Aren't you supposed to be more laid-back, all love and going with the flow?"

"Have we met?" I volley.

Her laughter erupts and entices me to cut myself some slack. I don't have to be so serious all the time. My job is just that—my job. It's time to show her who I really am. And as the laughter dies down, I note that it's easier to breathe as I relax. My lungs feel like the vise has released them, and my shoulders are lighter.

I like Juni. I like her energy and enthusiasm, but I envy her freedom. I want a taste of that good life where I can be 100% me. And Juni's the one I want beside me.

Alcohol isn't controlling this night, so fuck timelines and old-fashioned dating conventions. I know her, and I want to be a part of her crazy schemes and late-night escapades. I want to get coffee on the way to work with her and sit together on the couch in the evenings talking about our day.

Is this premature? Maybe, but I'm willing to take the chance tonight to see where it leads me.

Taking her hand in mine, I spin her away and then bring her in again, keeping my arms wrapped around her this time. We've known each other a few weeks, so why have we been fighting our attraction? Holding her in my arms feels like this is how it should have always been. I'm not going as far as to say it's kismet or destiny, but I'll give fate a little nod of appreciation.

Although I know we're most likely headed to bed, I want more than sex with this woman. I want to be her date because she wants me there, not just as a bargaining chip. Next time she has a function to attend, I want her to ask me because I'm her person. Nothing more to it.

I can only be so fucking lucky.

She asks, "Are you going to open the door?"

"Huh?" I look at the door in front of me, too lost in my thoughts as we walked. "Oh, yeah. Sorry. Caught up in my head."

"You're not having doubts, are you?"

Pinching her chin between my fingers, I'm so close to kissing her but don't want to do it in this hallway. "I have no doubts." I push open the door and lead her inside. As for the privacy of my apartment, I'm quick to cup her face, kicking the door closed behind me. I press her back to the door, this time, leaning down with my lips almost touching hers and her breath becoming mine on each exhale.

That black skirt she wore the other day comes to mind, the shoes she's wearing now, the way her sweater reveals her curves, and those eyes looking hungrily into mine. *Fuck, she's doing me in.*

Her hands cover mine, and I'm given the gift of seeing her eyes again, hazel in this light. We're so close, but I just want to take her in. She whispers, "Are you going to kiss me?"

"I am. I just want to commit this to memory to add to my file."

"What is that?"

"How gorgeous you are the first time I kissed you." Just as she sighs sweetly, I close my eyes and press my lips to hers. Plush and accepting, her lips caress mine, and then they part for our tongues to meet.

We'd been good about keeping our distance in such a way that it was platonic, but it wasn't because I didn't want this. It's because I didn't allow myself the chance to give in, to follow a desire I've had since the moment we met.

The dance starts slow with our tongues and then works its way through our embrace. It's the way her hands roam my back and her lips start to claim ownership that has me pressing my hips against her, needing to stake claims of my own.

She pushes me back, stealing enough space to slip away. Hurrying through the entry, she reaches the living room and spins to face me again. Like a siren, beckoning me to her, I cover the distance in three enormous steps, sweep her into my arms, and head toward the bedroom.

"Living room. Kitchen, and I can't wait to show you the bedroom." The tour is fast, but neither of us seems to care.

"Alrighty then." Her laughter fills my ears as the dim light from the lamps welcoming me home shines like stardust in her eyes. She says, "Let the record show that you *actually* swept me off my feet the first time you called me babe."

"You liked that, *Babe*?" I kiss her lips.

"I do. I like being your babe."

"I like being your Drew."

She caresses my face, her smile growing. "I really like this friendship, especially if it comes with benefits." When she bites that bottom lip, I kick off my shoe before I even set her on the bed.

"Oh yeah?" My gaze follows her every move. "What else do you like, babe?"

She stretches with her eyes fixed on mine. "I like you looking at me like I'm a steak, and you're famished."

I yank the tie from my neck. "So fucking famished." I lean down and kiss her because fuck, if I don't touch her in some way, I'll blow my load just from looking at her. I lift and take a step back from the mattress, needing to slow things down and take care of her first.

But then she had to tease me with her foot. She rubs my hard dick, and then says, "You're not going to leave me alone on this bed, are you?"

Her hair of golden and brown strands flows in waves across the dark blue blanket, the night covering her in moonlight. I thought I'd seen beauty in the sun setting on the water's horizon, in the snowy peaks of the Swiss Alps, or feeling the rain cool me after a run through the city. That wasn't beauty. That was a gift from nature.

This woman is stunning, like nothing in nature can compare.

Juniper Jacobs steals my time during the day, causing my nights to be jealous. Not tonight. "Tonight, you're mine." I lean over her, and whisper, "Only mine," before kissing her again and pulling her into a deep embrace.

When our breaths are heavy, and our hands are frenzied to feel heated skin, she says, "That's what I want to be, Drew. *Yours*."

22

Drew

"*Ahhh.*"

That damn moan of hers after slipping off her shoes has me rock hard and undressing even quicker. Like in the elevator earlier, the sound stirs everything inside me. Then I was so close to kissing her neck, rubbing her hips, and pulling her back so she could feel how she affects me.

Now, I'm about to.

Lying on the bed with her arms spread wide, she says, "It feels glorious to take those off. I love those shoes, but twelve hours is torture."

"I'd have to agree, but for different reasons." I keep working on the buttons of my shirt, about to rip the fuckers off, when she props up on her elbows.

Not ashamed to stare at each button as it comes undone, she smirks before her gaze slides up my chest to meet my eyes. "What are your reasons?"

"It's torture when you wear them around me. I struggle

to think about anything besides how those shoes would feel on my back when your legs are wrapped around me." She falls back as if she needs more room to breathe than she was getting in the other position. "You know what else tortures me on the daily?"

"What?" she breathes out heavily, her lids hanging low as her body wriggles. In that position, it's easy to imagine her hand dipping between her legs to seek relief. *Fuck.*

I move to undo my pants and give my cock more room to expand. "Your tight skirts, the ones that tease me when you bend over, or are so tight, you can't stand without relying on me."

Folding her hands behind her head, she asks, "So you like the damsel in distress act?"

"No. I just like the damsel herself." I pull my shirt down over my shoulders and then tug my undershirt over my head, tossing them both to the side of the bed. Bending down, I kiss her lips and then lower to that delicate curve of her neck that was teasing me earlier. "Mmm." I give the craving a sound, wanting her to feel my vibration against her skin.

The tips of her fingers weave through my hair and then clasp together, holding me where she wants me. Tilting to the side, I kiss behind her ear. Intoxicated by the perfume scenting her skin, I'm urged to explore even more of her.

The frenzy of earlier has calmed, and though I don't want her any less, I like that this pace feels natural for us. Did I expect anything other than unique with Juni? No, that's why I find her so sexy. That and when she whispers, "Don't hold back. I want you, Drew."

"I want you so much." Anchoring her knee to my side, I push her skirt down that leg until it puddles at her hip and then wedges between her legs. Too many clothes still divide us, but she's so enticing that it's hard to go slow. Discovering what drives her wild is part of the fun. When I lift, I discover a small smile on her face. "What is it?"

Her fingers dance through the hair on my chest, and she says, "I'm happy."

The simple and direct words hold so much more weight than I'd expect. She's happy. She's happy to be here, to be with me, to be moving from friendship to more with the act of sex to bridge the leap.

But in her words, I find I feel that as well. "I'm happy." Sure, it slows things down that were heating up, but I can tell her how I feel without it changing what's happening now. That's Juni. She runs off her emotions and whims and deserves to know how she's made me feel. "You make me happy, Juni."

While her fingers spin my chest hairs, she reaches up with the other hand and runs it along the side of my neck, grasping in the back. "I think we've had a breakthrough, Mr. Christiansen."

"You do excellent work, Dr. Jacobs." Through a giggle, she adds, "I like that you have hair on your chest. You're definitely all man, Drew." Her hands round my shoulders, and she pulls me down to her again. We kiss and become more intimately acquainted when we start grinding together.

In everyday life, Juni is funny, a bit quirky, and definitely entertaining. She wears clothes that cover most of her body and makes no apologies for being who she is. In this bedroom, in *my* bedroom, the humor is stripped away, revealing someone not afraid to take what she desires. I'm just the lucky bastard she wants.

The vixen.

I stand to strip down my pants and toss my socks to I

don't know where. *Who the fuck cares?* I feel alive for the first time in years because of this woman. I don't want to waste a damn second where I'm not focused on thanking every inch of her body.

She unzips her skirt at the hip, and when it puddles to the floor, her sweater comes over her head. She climbs back on the bed, moving toward the upholstered headboard. Resting her head on a pillow, she lies in a bra and matching underwear.

The red against her pale skin is something naughty that feels opposite of the outfit she was wearing. "Did you dress for me?"

Her body squirms in reaction, arms raising above her head and thighs sliding together. "Would you be mad if I said I did?" Her tone is teasing like that little grin on her face.

"Only mad that it took all day to see you like this." In just my boxers, I climb on the bed and settle over her.

With a nudge of my knee, her legs butterfly open as an invitation to get closer. I hold myself over her, kissing her, but my hips thrust enough to get her body begging for more. When her moan escapes, I capture it on my tongue and kiss her again, consuming her breath, her moans, and her need.

She kisses and then whispers, "Every day, I dress for you."

"Like a present waiting to be unwrapped."

Her smile blooms again as I pull the lace cup of her bra down and take her nipple into my mouth. "Drew . . ." My name comes on the edge of a breath, and I suddenly miss her calling me Mr. Christiansen. I'll save that role-play for the office.

Her pussy rubbing against my dick makes me crave her

even more. Jagged breaths pant against my ear, and I start grinding against her again.

She makes it hard to focus when her scent and sounds captivate my senses. Lowering the other cup, I take but a second to admire her great tits before I kiss each hard bud and scoot down the bed.

I kiss her belly and then her hip. Looping the tips of my fingers around the lace sides of her underwear, I look up, and say, "I need you naked."

"Do you want to take turns—"

"Now."

The abrupt answer doesn't faze her, and she licks her lips. "Yes, sir."

"Fuck it." I rip the lace on one side and then the other to the sound of her fits of giggles.

The tips of her fingers scratch lightly against my scalp, and she says, "Those cost over a hundred and fifty dollars."

"I'll replace them," I reply with my face between her thighs. Her legs are clamped around me, and when I kiss her skin to move forward, she loosens them, allowing me entrance.

Tipping my tongue between her wet lips, I taste her and cover my nose in her scent. A swipe and then flick has her arching her back. But I want more. I want all of her body to react. I enter her slow and steady, pinning her hips to the mattress as her fingertips drag along my biceps.

I kiss her pussy, staying there until she can't sit still, pushing her buttons and drinking her up. When my tongue fills her entrance, she pushes her hands against my head. I look up, but she shoves me back down. "Don't stop."

Her legs clamp around my head as I thrust inside her to work her body until it's on the edge of a release. Using my shoulders, I wedge her legs apart and am granted the sound of her sexy little moans. "Please," falls off the tip of her tongue as I fuck her with my mouth.

When my hair is pulled, and she sucks in a harsh breath, I replace my tongue with a finger. First one and then another, her body aching, writhing as she begs for more. "I want you. I want you . . ."

Dragging my tongue on the inside crease of her leg, I kiss her, fucking her with my fingers until her back arches and her head's thrown back. Her body tenses as she sucks in another sharp gasp, and then she trembles around me and releases—pent-up tension, jagged breaths, and then falls to the bed. "Oh my God," she says, her breathing erratic and her heart pounding. Her eyes are still closed, but she adds, "That felt amazing."

I may have brought many women to orgasm over the years, but seeing the satisfaction on Juni's face makes me feel incredible. She's mine to please. And I will, as one orgasm is not enough for this beautiful girl.

I kiss her belly and then cover each breast again, working my way to her mouth. Our lips embrace, and our tongues taste as my heart races. Pulling myself away, I reach to the nightstand, open the drawer, and grab some condoms. I'm not sure I'll need four tonight, but I'm happy to put the effort in.

I'm quick to remove my boxer briefs, but she takes her time to remove her bra. I have a feeling she's still steeping in the bliss of the orgasm she just had. Those curves she's teased me with through clothes, the baggy ones that hid her altogether, do nothing compared to seeing her bare before me.

Watching me rip open a foil packet, she asks, "You don't want me to—"

"I do, but later. Right now, I just want to be inside you."

Her fingertips graze around my ears, and she drags her tongue over her bottom lip. "I want that, too, but I want to be on top."

I move to my back, and say, "Come on then."

She anchors herself on top of me. "Are you ready?" Secure in her own need, she hasn't asked how many partners I've had or worried about what happens in the morning. She's here in the present, taking what she wants and giving me what I need.

"So ready."

Planting her palms on my chest, she kisses me once on the lips, licks them, and then lifts back up. When I'm positioned, she slowly slides down, then stops to take a breath. Moving again, she exhales until she's seated at the base of my dick. *Holy. Shit. She feels so good.*

Her heat engulfs me.

The sight of her bare tits.

The shape of her hips.

Her hourglass waist inspires me to run my hands up and then back down again. With her eyes closed, she takes in a few deep breaths before she lifts and slides down again.

Seated at the base of my dick, she leans forward to kiss me again and then angles to my ear, and whispers, "Show me why you're CEO, Mr. Christiansen." *Oh, fuck! She knows how to get me going.*

Fast as lightning, she doesn't know what hits her when I flip her to her back and start fucking her. "God, yes. So dirty," she says, her pleasure punctuated with each word. Her eyes close, and her body opens. She becomes everything as I get lost in the feel of her around me, taste the sweat on her glistening skin, and make love so she'll never forget this night.

A push and pull, I thrust and give. She takes and gives back even better. "Harder," she pleads.

Taking her wrists, I hold them against the headboard as I fuck her with everything we've been through—the good times we've had, my bad moods, her ass in that skirt, and when she arches that eyebrow to challenge me. Our rhythm is found, but it's too much for me to hold back. "Fuck." I come to the sound of our bodies sliding together and the melody of her moans.

Just as I release, she comes until her body sinks into the mattress with me on top. Our breaths are heavy but align. When I fall to the side of her, she exhales, and then a giggle comes out. With her arm draped over her head, she turns to look at me. Her eyes are bright, the green shining, and she wears a smile that reaches deep into my heart, evoking my own. "I could get used to this."

"If I have my way," I say through uneven breaths, "you will. So much that you'll be bored stiff."

She rolls toward me, and her hand dips under the covers. "Speaking of stiff . . ."

Whoever said paybacks are hell hadn't met Juni.

We lose another hour before she's lying next to me. "It's late," she says, her eyes dipping closed.

I kiss her because I can. Her lips and eyelids, her neck and toes. I'd kiss her all night, every inch of her if she'd let me. Though I have to admit she's not arguing with it now.

Her hand comes around the back of my head, and she holds me close. Whispering, she says, "You never told me what your prize is for calling jinx earlier."

"I didn't need a prize. I have you in my life."

With her arms wrapping around me, she kisses me with the same devotion I've just shown her entire body. "You say the sweetest things."

"I say what I feel for you."

"It's mutual." One more kiss is placed on my cheek before she closes her eyes again.

This time, sleep sweeps her away, leaving me no choice but to whisper, "Sweet dreams."

Drew

THUMP.

Thump.

Thump.

Pounding in my head drags me from a peaceful sleep. I fight to remain in the fuzzy state, warm from Juni being next to me, my body still exhausted from having sex again just past two. But efforts fail as the sound of trumpets blaring from a mariachi band win this round. Slamming my arm on the side of the mattress, I growl, "That's it!"

I roll to my side to apologize. "Sorry. It's my annoying neighbor and their nighttime cooking concerts."

At least one of us can sleep through anything. *Or I just wore her out.* I'll take the credit.

Last night was nothing less than spectacular. And I'm not just talking about the sex, though that was as well. I can't pinpoint the moment I knew I wanted to be with Juni because if I think about it, I believe the attraction was bubbling under the surface all along. Were we fooling ourselves that we could remain friends? Wasting time having conversations about remaining platonic? It seems that way, and now we've boiled over.

There's no going back from here.

I don't harbor regrets when it comes to the past couple of weeks because in the scheme of things, we figured it out pretty damn fast. So I don't have a complaint regarding how we got here. It's figuring out where we go from this point on now that we know we're more than we once intended.

I lean forward to kiss her head, but my lips end up pressed to a pillow. When I reach out to touch her, though, the bed is empty. That's odd.

I turn toward the bathroom. The light's still out, but the faintest of lights is slipping down the hall. I flip the covers off and land on my feet. Grabbing my boxers from the floor, I slip them on and head for the door.

The music is louder, and the sound of a pan scraping against the metal grate reaches my ears. The scent of cumin and the onions cooking fills the air. I keep walking until I see the light of the kitchen shining bright against the backdrop of night.

The smell of the food.

The beat of the song.

The hour.

All is too familiar.

I rub my eyes, making sure I'm not imagining things or trapped in a nightmare. I see her first—a white T-shirt that looks like one of mine. Her hair is down and the strands a mess from rolling around in the bed. She's incredibly sexy. If she wanted to distract me, she's doing an excellent job.

It would be so easy to tempt me back to bed if suspicion —*confusion*—wasn't sitting like a rock at the bottom of my stomach. I'm tired and not thinking clearly. That has to be because this is just too familiar. *And extremely odd.*

While she's happily humming, not in time with the song at all, under the bright lights of the kitchen, I try to figure out how to approach without startling her. I'm not sure how to make my presence known otherwise. I move from the shadows and grip the back of a dining room chair. "Hi."

Whipping her gaze to the side, she finds me in the dim lights, and joy fills her eyes. "Hi there, sleepyhead. Thought you'd never wake up."

"Most people are sleeping at four thirty in the morning." I hate how serious I sound, cautious as if she's a snake ready to strike. Innocent before proven guilty, I remind myself. "What are you doing?"

"Making tacos." Her tone is lighthearted as if this is perfectly normal. "Since you didn't have tortillas, I'm using lettuce wraps and calling it taco fusion." Pondering that thought, she adds, "Maybe they should be taco wraps?"

"That works."

She browns the ground beef as I take in the scene before me.

The island is covered with containers and the knives and utensils she's been using to cook. A part of an onion is chopped on a cutting board, and diced tomatoes fill a bowl. Cheddar cheese is grated on a plate, and leaves of lettuce are drying on paper towels. "How long have you been awake?"

"Not long," she replies, trading the spatula for the knife on the cutting board. After a few chops, she lowers it as she comes closer. "I like to think I can cook better than I do. I'm a work in progress." It's the first I get of the full view of her. Legs that haven't seen the sun for a while dip out from under the hem of the shirt. They're toned, shapely, and I have visions of how they looked wrapped around me that make me hard again. She says, "No kiss for the chef?"

I kiss her, wishing I was kissing her like earlier in the night. But trust has diminished, and I don't deal well with lying despite my dick's wishes. She licks her lips and asks, "Hungry? I'm starved." Dicing the rest of the onion, she says, "I don't know if you realize, but we missed dinner."

"I didn't."

"Neither did I until my growling stomach woke me up."

"Do you cook much?"

She sets the knife down to tend to the skillet, not letting me stop her one bit. Clicking it off, she says, "It's done. Now we eat." So easily distracting . . . but is it on purpose?

Moving to the other side of the island, I say, "I don't."

"You don't what?" Handing me a plate, she adds, "Help yourself seems rude since it's your food. But yeah, help yourself or I can make you a plate?"

I fucking hate that my stomach growls, my traitorous body making it difficult to stay on track. I have to. This conversation is long overdue.

"One or two tacos?" she asks, holding up the lettuce.

"Two." *Yeah. Yeah.* I know. I'm such a guy who's easily pleased. *Sex. Food. Money.* I'm that asshole. Seeing her take such care in putting the toppings on each leaf of lettuce has me softening the accusations in my head. *Why am I mad?*

She's never told me where she lives. Technically, she hasn't therefore lied. *I think. Yet* . . . this doesn't sit right with me.

Why is she hiding something so basic as where she lives?

I stare at her, trying to figure out my angle, but then my gaze dips to the taco buffet. The best approach is direct, kind, and on a full belly. But this is so incredibly confusing.

My gut has never led me wrong, but I'm starting to think I'm just hungry.

Carrying her plate, she kisses my bicep when she passes. So much sweetness in the gesture that I hate to ruin the mood. I watch as she settles on the couch and starts to eat. I'm blowing this out of proportion. It has to be a coincidence —the music and food, cooking at odd hours.

I don't let people into my life this easily. Once I got to know Juni, her intentions were pure. Innocence coated her every move. She looked at me for a friend, and I was happy to oblige. Well, after we realized the inevitable. The universe gave us signs. Did we read them all wrong?

There's only one way to find out . . . right after I finish a taco. I wipe my mouth with a napkin, and say, "It's really good. Thank you for making them."

She leans forward with pride filling her eyes as she rubs my knee. "My pleasure."

I finish one taco and toy with the other casually . . . as nonchalant as I can be without this coming on like an attack. If given the opportunity, I believe she'll have a perfectly good reason for not telling me. I can't think of one off the top of my head, but it is five in the morning. I say, "I usually wake up at this time to fit in a workout."

Nodding, she swallows a bite, and then says, "I don't love working out. I'll do it when I have to. It's a necessary evil."

"I like it. Guess we're different that way."

The comment doesn't seem to bother her, but she is eyeing me. "Are you all right?"

"Fine. Yeah, *I'm fine.* So where'd you say you live again?" Subtle. As subtle as a bulldozer.

She levels me with a glare. "What?"

"Huh?" It's not that I'm afraid of her, but I don't want to lose what we've become. *Whatever that is.*

She gets up and heads back into the kitchen. "All that cooking has made me tired."

I reach for her, but she eludes me. Setting her half-empty plate on the counter, she asks, "Do you mind if I clean the kitchen tomorrow?"

"Juni?" I stand, not sure what the fuck I'm doing. I could destroy everything if I'm wrong. If I'm right, she already did. I just wasn't made aware until it was too late. "Where do you live?"

"Why are you asking this at five in the morning?" She starts for the bedroom. "Let's get some rest, and we'll talk in the morning." There's a noticeable tremble to her voice, and she moves quicker.

She's doing what she does best—distract from the topic at hand. I struggle not to let her win. Anything I do to disrupt the status quo means I lose, even asking her. "We said honesty and trust were pillars of our friendship." Stopping with her back to me, she crosses her arms over her chest. "Now we're more, or I thought that was the direction we were headed."

When she finally turns around, she says, "We are. Last night was so good."

"Then why won't you tell me." She makes no move to come forward. "Do you live downstairs?"

"Yes." I barely hear her. She crosses her arms and tugs her bottom lip under her teeth.

Offering nothing more, I ask, "Did you know this entire time we've been seeing each other?"

"I didn't know at the park. I didn't know at the coffee shop."

I don't know why I'm so angry, but it's hard to keep inside. But with a steady voice that I conjure from dealing with work catastrophes, I say, "Our relationship doesn't span years, not even months. We're a few weeks in, and you've already lied. And for what? There's always a gain in play, a reward for winning. What'd you win, Juni?"

"I've wanted to tell you—"

"Then you should have."

"It was a lie that snowballed."

"I'd call it an avalanche. The one thing I don't do well is allow people into my life. I allowed you."

"I don't understand why you're upset." A plea coats her tone as she covers the distance between us. "So I live in the same building." Touching my chest, she says, "That's good news, right? Now we can be close."

She makes it so hard not to comfort her, to make the welling tears that glisten in her eyes go away. I resist. "This wasn't a little lie." I move to the window, remembering all the times just outside. "You dragged it out. You walked down the sidewalk like you were going to another building. You know Gil and pretended you didn't." I rub my temple and take a deep breath. "Look, Juni, I have enough stress in my life. I got caught up in this chaos, but I think it's best we end this now."

"End it because you don't like me, or end it because you do, and that scares you?"

I cross my arms over my chest, digging in my heels. "It doesn't matter now."

Her lips part, but she struggles to speak, her eyes closing as if in disbelief. When she reopens them, a glare full of daggers is aimed at me. "You're upset because you have feelings for me. Well, guess what?" When I don't say anything, she adds, "I did, too." She pads down the hall in bare feet, leaving me to stew in the feelings I was so close to denying.

It doesn't take but a minute before she has her skirt pulled on and her shoes, purse, and sweater in her hands.

She looks smaller in her pain. Stopping in the doorway to the hall, she doesn't look back, but says, "This is why I didn't tell you."

"And that's why we're saying goodbye."

The door closes, and the automatic bolt locks in place—me on one side, her on the other, and deceit left between us.

24

Juni

THAT DIDN'T GO AS PLANNED.

Maybe the problem is that there was no plan how we would play out at all, so the only direction was down.

I walk off the elevator to find Gil napping on the job. I don't blame him. I step lighter, not wanting to wake him. I had hoped a shower could make me feel human again or lying down in bed would make me feel better. Neither worked, so I sit on the couch across the lobby from Gil, needing advice from my best ally. But after a while, I get hungry and wonder if he has a donut back there for me.

Tiptoeing over, I'm quiet as soon as I reach over the counter. My hand is lightly smacked.

Snapping it back, I say, "Hey."

"Hey, yourself." He slides his feet off the desk and onto the floor, sitting upright. "No stealing."

"I thought you said you got that for me?"

"I did," he replies. "To bribe you into spending time with me. Not take it and run." Despite my inner turmoil, he makes it hard not to smile. "You sticking around for a few minutes?"

"I need your advice."

He holds up the pink box. "Then take two." I laugh. It's light but feels like a good release of some of the turmoil swimming around in my stomach.

The one will do. "Thank you." I take a donut and plant my elbows down on the counter. "By the way, you don't have to bribe me to spend time with you."

I only got one taco wrap before this night went off a cliff, so the sugary sweet is a nice addition to fill my stomach.

Studying me, he says, "Wet hair. PJ's. Five thirty in the morning. What's going on, Juni?"

I'm sure I'm a shining example of an emotional catastrophe, but I appreciate that he's willing to tackle my issues head-on. "He found out."

"*He* found out? *Ah.* Mr. Christiansen," he says as if that's the complete answer. Actually, I thought he was for a short time, like tonight. "He found out you live here? He found out that Rascal's not your dog? He found out that—"

"Okay, let's not get carried away. You hit the bull's-eye the first time." I rip a piece of the donut off, trying my best to savor something that usually brings a little joy. It's good, but it can't fix my troubles this time.

"I've been wondering how that would go over."

"Why? We like each other, so me living in the same building should be a good thing. Why is he upset?"

"A lie's a lie, Junibug. You know how I feel about them. Even little lies can cause significant damage."

Maybe I'm tired. I rub my forehead, thinking the hour is messing with my head. That's the only thing that can explain why I'm so emotional right now and explain the tears forming in the corners of my eyes. "I feel terrible," I say, sniffling. "Worse than terrible, Gil."

He gets up, the chair squeaking along with his bones working out the kinks from sitting too long. "Come here, kiddo."

I let him wrap his hug around me and rest my head on his shoulder. "You warned me, and I didn't listen. Now I'm paying the price." I hadn't cried until now. It's a whimper, pretty pathetic if I were being judged. It's not like Drew and I were so far gone we can't turn around. "I liked him more than anyone else."

"Sometimes, if we're really fortunate, that happens." He grabs a tissue and wipes under my eyes. "You're strong. You always have been. I think you had to be, so I know what happened. You didn't let him inside."

"How could I? He didn't know where I lived."

"Your heart, Juni."

Pointing out the obvious is sometimes necessary. I've avoided deeper feelings when it came to Drew, but tonight is a prime example of why I did it.

Why would I let him inside so soon after meeting? We were friends and coworkers. It's fun to hang out with him, but did it become more without me realizing?

I ask, "How was I to know he'd mean more? Sure, he was cute with Rascal, and he lets me barge into his office at work anytime I feel like it. He gets protective when other guys look at me . . ." I finish the donut, shoving it in my mouth as if that will stop the twenty reasons that justify exactly why Drew and I can't be friends. He's grumpy but adorable. Grumpy-adorable? Whatever that means, I like it.

I like him.

Gil says, "Love—"

"Love? Let's not get carried away, Gil."

He chuckles, but it's light, befitting the conversation that weighs on the heavier side. "Listen," he says, gesturing his hand in front of him. I've learned that means he's serious. "I know why you're protective. You were done a disservice as a kid. I'm protective over you because of it, but if you like him, maybe like the new job, you show him. Love only blooms with an open heart. And if it's not love, you'll find out real soon."

His words unexpectedly reveal a new side of the situation—*Drew's.*

Drew welcomed me into his world, his private sanctuary. He didn't treat me as if I were only temporary. He treated me like I belonged there with him. "Always coming in with the good advice. How do you know all this love stuff?"

"I've been around the sun a few turns, and what can I say? I have less than two hours until I go home to my sweetheart after a long shift. She'll have a hot meal waiting, and then she'll lie beside me until I fall asleep."

They're the sweetest. "Nancy's always been a great cook."

"Hey," he says, pretending to pop his collar. "I'm not so bad myself."

I've been to his house a few times over the years. He grills out back, but the kitchen always seemed to be Nancy's domain down to the rooster décor. "Do you cook for her?"

"When I wake up to start getting ready for work, I have enough time to make her dinner. I usually leave a little note for when she gets home."

Finishing my donut, I ask, "What does it say?"

"I'll see you in the moonlight."

That's about the most romantic thing I've ever heard. "Does she leave you notes?"

"Yes," he says, his tone reminiscent of something special he's experienced. "I'll see you in my dreams."

I can only dream of finding someone as special to spend my life with.

While Gil takes a rag to the top of the desk, I look back at the elevator. Maybe it's that I'm more awake, or that I have food on my stomach, but my mind and heart are clear, giving me a new perspective. "Gil?"

He stops and looks up. "Yeah?"

"Thanks for the chat as always."

"Always here for you."

"Too much, in fact," I joke but also mean it. I start for the elevator, knowing I owe Drew an apology. Now I understand why he was so upset. A lie is a lie, no matter how big or small or the intention behind it. We told each other trust and honesty, and I broke that promise.

I can't be mad if he doesn't forgive me. It will hurt, but I have to give him that right to do what he feels is best for him.

Gil says, "Family is always there when you need them."

My parents used an unorthodox method of parenting, one that involved leaving me behind. So family isn't always there, but Gil has been. We don't tell each other I love you or get into the deep feels for each other, but we know we care without the words. "Good night."

"Take care."

The elevator door opens on the seventeenth floor, and I use the distance to his door to go over the things I want to say and try to predict a better outcome than the dread I'm feeling inside.

The night started with me still convincing myself we could be friends. That was a lie I was telling myself. As if I repeated it enough times, I would believe it. The teasing, the fun, and spending time together was already moving us past that stage. The physical attraction was always there, but somewhere along the way, my heartstrings started attaching to his.

I knock, light at first, and then wait. Dread digs its claws in deeper with every passing minute. Not able to stand there and wait, my fears have me knocking louder when he doesn't answer.

Lowering my hand, I know it's still early, and I look down the hall at the other door. I don't have a right to disturb his neighbors just because I screwed up. Leaning against the solid wood door, I say, "Drew? Andrew?" I'm not sure if I have a right to the nickname right now . . . or at all since it's become personal to him. "Mr. Christiansen?"

What am I doing?

We were making love three hours ago. Even if he is mad, surely, he'll be okay if I call him by his first name, for Pete's sake. Knocking lightly, I call, hoping he can hear me through the wood, "Andrew?"

Nothing.

No answer.

No reply.

No acknowledgment at all.

Anger tries to rear its ugly head as the insult of being ignored burns through me. I take a breath, drowning the emotions that make this about me instead of him. I should have told him the truth. He was owed that. I knew it all along. Is cutting me out with such finality my repayment? Now I start to worry about my job come Monday.

I like that job. A lot. But I'd give it up if it meant we could pick up where we left off earlier tonight in bed. "I'm sorry." Pressing my face into the corner of the door, I whisper, "I'm sorry I lied," hoping he can hear me.

Stepping back, I wait a few more minutes, silently begging him, willing him to open the door. When he doesn't, I decide I need to walk away. Not for me, but to give him the peace he's seeking.

I bypass the elevator and push through into the stairwell. It's only one flight down, but I'm dragging my feet. When I swing open the door to my floor, I stop. Down the hall on the right, long and muscular legs in fitness shorts stretch before him with sneakers on his feet. His T-shirt hanging loose around his torso might be the most casual I've ever seen him dressed. He wears it well like everything else.

Drew might be the most handsome man I've ever laid eyes on, but his mood permeates the hallway. His presence fills wherever he exists, and it's easy to get consumed by it. Right now, I'm willing to take the chance.

The door comes flying closed and whacks me in the ass, sending me stumbling forward. "Ow!" *Graceful.*

He turns, and the recognition filling his eyes has him scrambling to his feet as fast as he can. "Where have you been?" There's no harsh tone but one of worry.

I rub my ass and then toward him. "I've been waiting for you upstairs. I knocked. *A lot.* Probably disturbed your neighbors. After a while, I finally came back down."

"The same."

I cover the last few feet and ask, "For how long?" Call me a romantic, but it matters.

"Until you opened the door."

I'm not sure I'm doing a good job of hiding my smile when I twist my lips to the side, but at least, I'm trying. "Why would you do that?"

"Because I was an asshole, and I wanted to say I'm sorry."

"You weren't—"

"I am, actually. I'm an asshole in life, a miserable jerk

who cares more about a company than my own life. But you know what, Juni?"

I'm surprised to be having this conversation so quickly, so honestly, so easily. That has to be a good sign if we're trusting in those sorts of things. And I do. I lean on the wall across from him. "What?"

"I'm not such an asshole with you. And I don't mean *to* you, if you can momentarily forget my behavior upstairs, but to everyone because of you. You make me less annoyed with the world. You make me see the little things, the important things, everything I ignored before." He steps closer, but each is tentative. "Instead of getting upset, I should have given you the benefit of the doubt. I'm sure you have a good reason for not telling me you live here."

Glancing back, he scans the door and the wreath hanging on the outside. It's dusty, and I should have packed that away, but my grandmother loved it, so here it's stayed. I pull my key from my pocket and move forward, knowing I'm totally letting him into my small corner of the world if he'll stay. "Actually, I don't have a good reason, other than you called me a stalker on day one, so I did everything I could to make you believe otherwise." I roll my eyes just listening to myself admit that out loud. "You know, like a stalker would do."

Shoving the key in the knob, I unlock it and open the door.

But then he does more than I could ever ask of him. He says, "I was willing to wait all night for you. I think I'm the stalker, after all." He takes the heat off me. I might have hearts in my eyes. *Fine, I do.*

"Since you know where I live, psycho, come on in?"

"I'd like that, but first, I hope you accept my apology for how I treated you. So many excuses from being tired to realizing you're the one who has kept me up so many nights with your cooking concerts to the lie have run through my head. But I failed to acknowledge my part in all this."

Taking my hand in his, he brings it to his mouth to kiss, and then again. "I'm sorry, Juni, and I'm sorry for not making you feel safe to share the truth. I never thought you were a stalker." The smirk comes first in a direct hit to my knees. Why does he have to be so good at everything, including weakening me? Then the wink. "But," he says, playing it off in that non-bragging but totally bragging way, "you're not the first woman to follow me home."

My smirk pales in comparison, so I give him my best smug grin. "I bet I'm not. I can only imagine all the girls tripping over themselves when you were in high school." When I move closer, his arms envelop me without hesitation, bringing me against the soft T-shirt that covers his hard chest. I close my eyes, absorbing everything I can about this man. We are friends, but we're becoming much more, and I recognize that now.

"I did all right back in high school." He strokes the back of my hair. "But Juni, I would have been a one-woman man if I had known you back then."

Looking up, I rest my chin on him. "Magic happens when two forces join. This feels good because of us, not because I'm so special." He kisses my forehead, still appearing to bear all the wrong of the night on his shoulders. I add, "It feels good to joke with you, but I want you to know that I'm sorry I lied. I won't do it again." And I do need to explain to him why I held back, but I need more time to figure that out myself. Is it because I've never felt safe in a relationship before? *Safe enough to let someone into my heart?* I have a lot of thinking to do.

He caresses my cheek, looking into my eyes. "I believe you, but I'm going to need you to do something for me."

"What is it?"

Holding his hand up, he says, "I've never pinky-promised with anyone other than my mom. Not even Nick when we were little. But I will with you if you will with me."

When his pinky stretches out, I burst out laughing. "Hell yeah, I'll pinky promise with you." Our pinkies wrap around each other's, and he bends to give me a kiss. I kiss him because in the span of an hour, I went from thinking I blew it with this amazing man to being in his arms again.

He kisses me once more. I revel in the sweetness. And then he says, "Thank you for giving me another chance."

I could point out that I'm the one who lied and kept secrets, but I wrap my arms around his neck and say, "It's okay. We'll call it even." That wins me a chuckle that I'll happily take all day, every day, and in the middle of the night in the hallway. "Come in, and I'll give you a tour."

I shut the door behind him and let him wander on his own into the living room. A smile comes easy, and he says, "I like it."

Not wanting to let another moment pass, I go and kiss him because I can. Our lips meet, and his hands slide over the sides of my pajamas. But then he leans away from me, appearing to be confused. After he bends down, I ask, "What are you doing?"

Clapping his hands twice, he turns back to me, and asks, "Where's Rascal?"

Oops! "About that . . ."

25

Juni

I'VE NEVER HAD A MAN IN MY BEDROOM BEFORE, OR IN MY BED FOR that matter.

But there Drew sits at the end of my bed in quiet contemplation. I imagine this is something he does quite often. He tends to be a serious guy.

Since he doesn't know I'm awake, I take a moment to study him. The muscles in his back are defined but not big like Thor, more like Captain America in the earlier movies. Those are the muscles that tease me when he takes off his jacket. Shirts are tight but tailored for me to admire his body.

The black band of his boxer briefs isn't graffitied with a designer name. I like that for some reason. And when he looks toward the windows, I notice how dark the stubble covering his jaw is, tempting me to rub up against him like my own personal scratch post. I'm reminded how raw my thighs feel and now I know why. I'll take this feeling anytime if it means I'm with him.

Friends ... I was such a fool for thinking we could remain friends. We're friends, of course, but there was always something more between us. I smile, not from the sex, though that is worth a standing ovation, but from the fact Drew thought I was worth a second chance.

I can't bear to not see his eyes again. I nudge him in the buns with my big toe.

He turns around, smile growing, and grabs my foot. "Hey there," he says.

"Couldn't sleep?" I gently clear the grogginess from my throat.

Chuckling, he glances at the daylight fighting the blinds to sneak in. "It's almost noon."

A quick check of the clock verifies the truth. Snuggling the blanket to my chest, I roll to the side, having a hard time not grinning while looking at him. "I guess that sex, cooking, fighting, making up, and making love took it out of me."

"Yeah. Me too." He angles toward me and rests his weight on his hand. "I was thinking about how you asked me what I was doing today. Are we still on?"

With all that went on last night, I'd almost forgotten. He didn't, and that makes me swoon a little. "Definitely." I sit up and crawl to him, bare naked, and sit on his lap.

I like the way he takes his time tracing over my body, not coy about his gaze lingering longer in some places more than others. He doesn't make me feel shy or ashamed, but the opposite. I feel brave and sexy around him. I feel empowered.

His body's reaction also speaks volumes about his thoughts. I wiggle a little and then ask, "Are you in a hurry?"

Like a tiger protecting his pride, he rolls us over with such ease and care. His hand is under my head as he lays me down gently. Hovering over me, he pushes some wild strands of hair away from my face. "Do you know what I thought the first time I saw you?"

"Why is this crazy person yelling at me?"

"No." He chuckles, but then takes his sweet time peering down my body and then into my eyes again. "I thought you were stunning. Your cheeks were pink from running and your hair was in a loose ball on your head. But the first things I noticed were your eyes and the happiness within them. There was something so incredible about that moment, like I finally knew what I'd been missing."

His voice had grown softer through the confession, a sadness overcoming him.

I push the hair that's fallen over his forehead to the side, and ask, "What were you missing?"

"Something to look forward to." He kisses me quick and then pops off the bed. "I have no idea what you have planned, but let's get dressed and go."

When he disappears into the bathroom, I flop my arms out wide, and say, "And here I thought we were going to make love again. Silly me."

The shower is started, and then he fills the doorway, leaning against it. Waggling his eyebrows, he calls me to him with a bend of his finger. "Who said we weren't."

It doesn't take me more than a second to head into that bathroom. I fly into his arms and am pressed against the back of the door. He kisses me like we have all day to do it. We do, but it's nice to see the busiest man I know slow down. He asks, "Are you going to tell me where we're going?"

"Nope." I zip my lips and toss the key behind me.

He unzips my lips and then kisses them. "I like hearing you too much to ever zip those pretty lips. Always make sure you're heard, babe. The one thing this world needs more of is you."

Why does he have to be so sweet when I was hoping to get dirty in the shower? Now I just want to hug him. When I press myself to his body, I *feel* he's ready to get naughty as well. Dragging him by the hands toward the shower stall, I say, "Don't worry about me. I'll make sure the entire world hears me." I wink. "Or at least the building."

I spin under the water and spy him watching me. "This isn't a spectator sport," I say, soaping my body. "Get in here, *Mr.* Christiansen, and participate."

Calling him that name is a great motivator. I could spend a few minutes analyzing why the formal gets Drew moving faster than The Flash, but I think it's how he's wired, feeding into his bossy nature.

The tile's cold, but he's so damn hot I forget about it and pretty much everything else when he kneels before me and lifts my knee over his shoulder. Looking up at me, he says, "Brace yourself."

One hand goes to the tiled wall and the other to the small ledge. When his mouth takes charge between my legs, my head drops back, and my eyes close. I find a new appreciation for this CEO—chief erogenous officer. "Yes, Mr. Christiansen. God, yes." Every time I throw a prefix on there, his tongue works harder.

When his fingers find my entrance, I grip the ledge and the top of his head harder. "I'm so close." The words are lost in my arousal.

My release is fast and has me melting against the wall. When he sets my foot back on the ground, he holds me by the waist. "I was thinking we could go out for lunch."

Not ready to reenter the actual world, I slowly drag my

eyes open to find him smirking. I have no regrets coming back to him. "I thought you just ate?"

"I did, but I was thinking about you." Kissing my cheek, he takes my hand and wraps it around his erection. "I thought you might want something more filling. Something to wrap your lips around. Suck. On."

And there he is . . . Ice Cream Drew is joining the party.

Sexy. Funny. Intelligent. A great dresser. Tall. Dark. Hot as sin. How'd I get so lucky? "I'm starving."

Screwing my boss has never been more fun. Well, to clarify, I've not screwed any other bosses. Only him. But since I've crossed that line—*four times now*—I could do worse than the CEO. *And oh my my, how I like doing him.*

"This is the surprise?"

And apparently not a good one by how disappointed Drew looks. I can work with this. I have his expectations so low that the actual surprise will be even better now. Unless I'm misunderstanding the pursed lips and furrowed brow.

Maybe it's fear creeping into his eyes as he stares at the motto stuck on the window—new tools for age-old problems. "No, this is a pit stop."

"For?"

"You know what for. You've been in New York for five weeks. Let's just call the three prior to me purgatory—"

Shoving his hands in his jean pockets, he nods, looking satisfied. "It sort of was."

"Sort of?"

The toe of his shoe bumps the side of my Converse, forming a connection. It's the little things with this man that mean so much. "It was." Despite the grumpier moments he has, I love how agreeable he can be sometimes. "And the two since knowing you?"

"We'll call those the best time of your life."

He chuckles but then leans over and kisses the top of my head. "It wouldn't be a lie."

"That's good because we hate those."

"We sure do."

I drag him by the hand under the ragged purple awning and inside where a lady dressed in a long, purple silk robe is standing in the middle of the store. The red and white flowers on her chest are definitely attention-getters and the fabric on the sexy side. I'm now debating if we should have come here.

When she raises her hands in front of her, rings adorn every finger. She taps the tips of her long, red nails together and aims her eyes at Drew. "Welcome to New Age Innovations. What is your spirit seeking?"

His hand tightens around mine, and when I look up at him beside me, I'm thinking he's close to running out the door to escape. I'm not sure which verb fits this situation better because I'm a little freaked out as well. I say, "We're looking for a smudge stick."

Her hands fall to her sides, and her shoulders sag. Nodding to her left, she replies, "They're in the back corner." The creepy voice she was using has been replaced with a Bronx accent. That's disappointing. Not that she's from the Bronx, but that it was an act. *Anything to sell your goods, I guess.*

Standing in front of the curio cabinet, we read what each one does. Drew stops and looks over his shoulder before whispering to me, "Why are we here?"

"Number two."

"You need the bathroom?"

I balk in laughter. "No . . . oh great, now I do. Ugh. Thanks for bringing it up." He shrugs innocently enough so I can forgive him. I say, "Number two from your mom's list for you to get a life."

Annoyance stiffens his back, and he stands to his full, glorious height. "I have a life. *See?* I'm here with you in this weird shop on a Saturday. You know what I'd be doing on a normal Saturday?" He doesn't even bother keeping his voice down.

So I don't either. "Going for a run in the morning and then getting a coffee on the way into work?"

"Okay, you don't need to make me sound so predictable."

Crossing my arms over my chest, I raise an eyebrow.

He mimics my body language, but it only takes a few seconds in a standoff for him to lower his arms again, lean in, and whisper, "Fine, you win. That's what I'd be doing, but you know, I'm really fucking good at it."

"You say that all the time as if that's all you are, though. That's why this list is important. If it weren't for that list, you wouldn't be standing in this strange store in the middle of the Bronx at two on a Saturday afternoon."

"Hey," the lady calls from behind the counter where she's burning skull candles. "It's not strange."

I nod. It's freaking strange, but if she digs it, that's cool. I open the jar of the stick we need for our mission and take one out.

Drew says, "Yeah, me not standing in this strange place."

"Really?" silky robe lady says loudly. "I can still hear you."

Hitting me with a glare, he tells her, "Sorry." Lowering until his eyes are level with mine, my tall Redwood giant of a man whispers, "I wouldn't be here. That's my point." If emphatic can be managed in a whisper, he masters it. He really is skilled at so many things. His parents must be very proud.

"Oh wait," I reply, realizing I didn't think this through. "I think we're arguing the same point, or I'm lost at this point, voiding all other points altogether."

Taking the stick from me, he says, "That doesn't void my point," and then heads toward the register while tapping on his phone.

I follow him. Resting against his back as he pays, I say, "Point taken."

The small shake of his shoulders and soft chuckle make me smile.

When we walk outside, he asks, "Why did we get this again?"

"Number two on the list."

"Right." Holding hands, we walk toward the curb. "The negative vibes thing."

"On the sixth Thursday." His mom sounds like such a character. I'm sure we'll get along like a house on fire. I'm sure she'd approve of me bringing him here for the smudge stick—known for eradicating negative energy from places. Just getting creative.

What I find more fascinating is that she knew her eldest would have negative vibes to eradicate to list it as a task.

"Are you going to burn this with me?"

I stop and lift on my toes. Kissing him once, I drop back down, and reply, "Thought you'd never ask."

26

Juni

NOT ALL SUPERHEROES WEAR CAPES.

Sometimes they carry caffeine because you're dragging after a long night of fantastic sex. After walking a few doors down from New Age Innovations, we find a coffee shop.

"Was that Chris Evans?" Drew disappears from my side, and I look back to see him stopped like a tourist and staring at a man inside the shop where we just came from.

I try to follow his gaze, but I don't see anyone—*oh wait!* A man walks out with two coffees in his hands. "Oh my God, it's Chris Pine, right?" Squinting, I try to get a better look. "No, not the *Star Trek* Chris. He's the Chris with the famous ass. It *is* Captain America."

"I don't know about the ass part, but I met him once at a movie premiere."

Leaving the guy alone with a bunch of paparazzi following him, I walk back to Drew and point at the ground. "Are you going to pick up that name you dropped or leave it for someone else to try on for size?"

When he rolls his eyes, I feel like I've just been rewarded. Not only do I bring out his humor—*sexually speaking*—but now he's rolling his eyes like a champ. I ogle him with pride, and then say, "I knew one day you'd catch on."

"Are we talking about superheroes or eyerolls?"

"Both." I slip my hand in his and start dragging him toward the subway. "Also, that's so weird we saw him. I've had superheroes on my mind all day."

"Oh yeah?" He stops, pulling me to a halt with him.

Invading his personal space, I say, "And every time they came to mind, I was thinking of you. Come on, we have a train to catch."

"I'll take the compliment, but . . ." he says, keeping me from rushing away. "I have a better idea."

"Go on."

He comes around and holds me from behind, running his hands over my denim-clad hips. Taking my earlobe between his teeth, he sends a delicious shiver up my spine. "We have a car on demand to take us wherever we want." He signals to the curb. "I'd already called him."

"Dating you definitely has its perks." We hop into the car, and I see the same driver as last night. "Hi." The man knows Drew and I had sex, so I'm not sure if I should be embarrassed, but I can't seem to find any shame, even if the entire planet knew.

The driver looks in the rearview mirror with eyes that reflect his smile. "Ms. Jacobs. Mr. Christiansen."

I lean forward and slip him a piece of paper. Keeping this a surprise took some pre-planning. He nods and says, "Yes, ma'am," and we're off to Brooklyn.

Just over two hours later, we've walked the boardwalk and eaten a hot dog. I say, "There are a lot of people here."

"It's Saturday," he replies like that explains it all.

Maybe it does. I just feel like I let Gil down by not falling in love with Coney Island. He described it in such a romantic way, harkening back to his childhood and bringing Izzy. It's great that he has those memories, but I guess it just feels foreign to me.

Drew says, "New York is this busy all the time. Is there any place in the city where you can find peace?"

"Are you wanting to be alone with me?"

His arm comes around my shoulders. "It wouldn't be the worst way to spend the day."

"As charming as that is, have you thought about what this is? What we're doing?"

I liked his warmth wrapped around me, but I understand the need to close in a bit. It's a protective gesture I sometimes take as well. He shoves his hands in his pockets and looks around. I can't see his eyes behind his Ray-Bans, but I can feel the heat of his gaze when his eyes return to me. "I've thought about it, about us. We should keep things professional at the office. We've already established a working relationship. I don't want undue attention on us."

"No one will find out from me. The last thing I want to do is hurt your career."

"What about you? I've also been thinking about what you want."

There's always a bit of Andrew, even when he's dressed casually. I slip my hand under the front of his button-up and run my fingertips over his abs. He doesn't have to tense his muscles. They're hard as rocks. He gives his body the same attention he gives his work. Both pay off for him. *And for me. Don't hate the player. Hate the game.*

He leads me to a bench where we sit facing the ocean. We're close, but with our eyes directed ahead, it's easier to think clearly. "I was kind of playing it by ear. I'm happy to cover the front until Melissa returns. From there, I'm not sure."

Reaching over, he slides his hand against mine. "Juni?" When I turn to look at him, he asks, "Do you mind if I ask about your parents?"

"I'm not sure how talking about a job got redirected, but sure."

"I was thinking about something you said a while ago that hinted that you had little say in doing what *you* wanted when you were young. I'm guessing that had something to do with your parents. Will you tell me about them?" Our fingers fold together, and he brings my hand to his mouth for a kiss. "Anything you're comfortable sharing."

The waves are rougher today, not just choppy but angry. Sometimes, I can relate when it comes to my parents. But he has a right to ask, and he's giving me all the space to answer. "Honestly, it's a story I've told a million times to the press. I leave out a bunch of details because no one's usually interested in those. Not when they're trying to highlight my parents in a story."

"I want to hear your side, not the one you tell other people. The one that lives inside you."

I look at him, wondering how he always knows how to make me feel so special I lift his sunglasses so I can get a good look at his eyes. He chuckles, probably because people don't normally do this. I've not found a lie hiding in his eyes yet, and today is no exception. Lowering them back down, I turn my attention to the memories I want to share, the facts that are out there, and maybe some of the in-between that ties it all together.

Sliding my sunglasses to the top of my head, I'm frustrated when they fail to keep the wind from whipping my hair around. I take the elastic from my wrist and twist it around until I have a knot on top.

He asks, "You said you've been interviewed by the press. Were they famous?"

"They were, but not like the Hollywood celebrities you're used to. My parents were world-renowned botanists."

When he tugs his sunglasses off, he reveals that look of the dots being connected. I've witnessed it before many times. No one thinks they know anything about botanists until my parents' names are mentioned.

I know what he's going to say before he says it because I've heard it so much in my life. I can quote it. Turning to me, he says, "The plants in the lobby, the dick cactus you gave me, the reason that fake plant in the break room offends you . . . That's why. Your parents."

Well, I didn't see that coming.

"I have a gift for plants."

Nudging with his elbow against mine, he says, "And you're a plant gifter. See what I did there?"

"I sure did." I try not to laugh. There's literally nothing funny about what he said but seeing him enjoying that bad joke entices me to laugh with him. "And it's not a dick cactus."

"Does it matter what the official name really is?"

"No."

Moving closer, I enjoy touching him and being as close as I can. "Sex does things to you."

"Are we talking biology or botany?"

"No getting sidetracked. Let's talk about botany, baby." His arm comes around me again, and we sit like an old married couple on the boardwalk. "Teasing aside, my parents flew to every corner of every continent. They met in college, competing for the same scholarship. My mom didn't need it. Her parents were well enough off, but she just refused to lose to my dad. I should say they hadn't met until that point. Then they did, and the rest is history. Botany history, to be exact."

"Jacobs."

That's it. That's all he says.

A heavier emotion has taken hold of him, and standing, he paces. He stops, mumbles something to me, and then paces again.

"Are you all right, Drew?"

"I . . ." He circles the bench and then finally sits on the edge like he's ready to bolt at any second. "Juni?" His hand is large, his palm eclipsing my knee when he holds me there.

"Yes?" I rest my hand on his, feeling it adds to the drama.

Running his other hand over his head, he says, "You know how I mentioned the science fair and my mom?"

Nodding, I reply, "Mrs. Whipple accusing her of buying your win? Though wine might have rhymed better there."

He sits back. "Good memory and probably."

"Thanks." I prop my knee between us on the bench sideways to face him. "It's hard to forget Mrs. Whipple."

"True. I've tried many times, but that's another story." He's cute when he's a bit perplexed. More importantly, why does he seem puzzled?

"If that story is being left for another day, then what's this story?"

He says, "Jacobs." I sit up a little straighter, hearing my name. "Juni Jacobs."

"Okay, yeah?"

I'm used to seeing this kind of intensity in his eyes when he's at work, but out of the office, it makes me wonder if I need to be concerned. "Your parents were Daisy and Chris Jacobs?"

"Daisy and Chris Jacobs."

Though we say it at the same time, neither of us claims victory with a jinx. I nod again like I'm in on his revelation.

He says, "You're kidding, right?"

"Why would I kid about my parents?"

"Juni, my science fair submission that year was how sap and water move through the Tracheids at different speeds."

"That's my parents' theory, the one my mom started in college when she beat my dad in that competition. It was also the subject of their first published paper together, their first grant, and the reason they made their first trip to the Amazon. That was the basis of their relationship." He doesn't answer the question I'm sure I buried in there, so I'm more direct, and ask, "Using my parents' theorem, you won the science fair?"

"Water moves quicker, though the sap is to a plant like blood is to us. Jacobs' Tracheid Theorem."

They had other, and far greater, discoveries during their careers, but that one put them on the map. "They never had to beg for grant money again until a bioscience periodical did an article about them. It said they cared more about the fame than the planet they preached to want to save."

"I'm sorry to hear that."

"They'd drop everything, including me, to go on a research trip. Obsession comes in more forms than the obvious. To most, they're just plants. To my parents, they were an insight into another universe. They believed plants could be utilized to save civilization. Not in a nutty way, but if specific plants could be packaged in a certain way, there was potential for them to be replanted on another planet. We could have farms on Mars or fields of wheat on the moon. It was longshot stuff that included a lot of chemistry in reorganizing the plant cells to maintain the benefits of their genus while being able to adapt to the different environments in outer space."

"Those are lofty goals. They sound like geniuses."

I release a heavy breath from my chest, surprised I remember so much. It's taken up so much space in my life that, like the breath did, it feels good to release it. "The space station currently houses twenty varieties of plants packaged based on my parents' research. I wish they could see their goals brought to fruition."

He pulls me into a hug and rubs my back. "They were ahead of their time."

I nod against his shoulder, not sure why I'm tearing up. I'm usually much better at handling my emotions. When I look up, he cups my cheeks and gently runs the pads of his thumbs under my eyes. "My parents were supposed to be at my competition the day they died." When I struggle to hold his gaze, I drop my head to his shoulder. He places several kisses on my head. "They promised. They'd missed almost all the others, but this one was for state. The winner would get a $20,000 grant and a full-ride scholarship to any New York public university. The prize I wanted to win even more was the chance to study in the Amazon with the great Jacobs that summer."

Leaning back, his hands still hold my face, but confusion now fills his. "You entered to win a chance to spend time with your parents?"

"I did." I laugh humorlessly. "It was a two-month study program. If I didn't win, I wouldn't be there. I'd be in New York missing them like always. So I took their research and dived deeper to discover that the veins in certain genus can expand to allow the sap to flow better. They contract when water is sensed. How crazy is that?"

"It is amazing." It's not like he'd feel pride or anything,

but he sure is looking at me like he does when tenderness shapes his expression. "You're amazing." Confusion still enters his eyes right after, but I get it. This isn't usually a topic discussed at the dinner table. He asks, "What happened?"

"They came to me just before midnight the night before the event to tell me they'd gotten a call. They didn't have to say more after that. I knew how it would play out. It was the same every time. They were gone before I woke up in the morning. My grandmother came and picked me up from the Brooklyn house and drove me to the competition like she had done every other time when I wasn't living with her."

I sense his discomfort in the way he shifts and glances at the ocean. It's never easy for me to share, but he has me wanting to make him feel better. The truth. That's what I owe him, so he'll understand more of what he's dealing with when it comes to me. But then he lifts me and holds me on his lap, his arms secure around me, and asks, "Are you okay? You don't have to talk about anything you don't want to."

Why is the option to shut down so appealing? With Gil in my head, pushing me forward, and Drew wriggling his way into my heart, I say, "It was my turn. I stepped into the spotlight on the stage, ready to present my findings, but that's when I heard a sudden murmuring rush through the audience. A few gasps. I heard them and tried to figure out what was going on.

That's when my best friend, my boyfriend, who was competing there that day, came out and whispered in my ear." Digging into my hip he holds me closer. I say, "Your parents . . . the Amazon . . . the plane . . ."

Turning to find the comfort I desperately need from him, tears roll down my cheeks, and I push myself to continue, "They couldn't get to the crash site for five days. For five days, I waited to have confirmed what I already felt inside." For those five days I was numb. I cried and felt so lost. *Alone.* Betrayal didn't come until later. *That was all on Karl. Because as the murmurs had quieted and I'd been led from the hall, he presented my paper as if it was his own.* Claimed it as his own.

This time, I don't hide my eyes. This time, I find the peace I need in the soulful warmth of his admiring browns. "I'm sorry, Juni."

My tears dry as a little water glistens in his. And somehow, a little piece of my soul begins to heal. I'm not sure why or how, but solace is found in sharing my story with someone after all these years. Maybe because for the first time, there isn't the withdrawal of the microphone or phone, saying the information wanted was gained. Maybe because this time, there is someone to hold me while I grieve.

27

Drew

THE DAY'S BEEN BUSIER THAN I EXPECTED, BUT WITH JUNI, I always crave more time. Her honesty, the raw emotions, and her trust were placed in my hands when she opened up about her parents.

She's made me an insider. That's a role I don't take lightly.

After sex, well, duh, and a short nap, I'm woken up by my phone buzzing across the nightstand. Nick. I'm tempted to let it go to voicemail, but he usually just texts. So the fact he's calling has me curious as to what's going on.

Grabbing the phone, I slip out of bed and go into the bathroom so I don't wake Juni. "Hey, what's up?"

"Did you forget? You forgot. Fuck, Andrew, I promised Natalie."

I catch a glimpse of myself in the mirror. I look like shit with my hair in disarray and my unshaven face. Great, I silently grumble. I'm turning into a New Yorker. "Slow down. What did I forget?"

"Dinner at my house. I told you about it weeks ago."

"That's on the twenty—*oh fuck*."

"Yeah, the twenty-fourth, also known as today. You better get dressed and get over here, but I'm not letting you back out even if I have to come drag you over here myself."

Peering back at Juni sleeping, I keep my voice low, and ask, "What time is dinner?"

"You have an hour. I can stall for another thirty minutes, but after that, Natalie will lose it if her meal is served cold."

"You still have me down for a plus-one?"

"If it's Juni, yes. Anyone else, I don't want to do the dog and pony show. I just want to have a relaxed and fun night surrounded by people we know."

I know what he means without the details. Not only is he cursed with the tycoon last name of Christiansen but his wife and her family are Manhattan famous. Reminded of Juni and her parents and the fame that came with that has me glad she's been able to live in relative peace all these years. She carries a lot of burdens, but she's good at keeping her last name in relation to her parents on the down low.

I had no idea, so I assume most people don't. It's become her story to tell, and I'm one of the lucky ones to hear it. "I'll see if she's up for it."

"Okay, but I'm warning you, Andrew. You better show up."

"I will. You have my word." My word is as good as gold, too. He knows that.

When I return to the bedroom, Juni asks, "Where are we going?"

Fuck. Why does she have to look so good and be naked saying it?

I shift my dick, willing it to stay down when it overrides my ruling and stands at full salute just for her. With a mischievous grin settled on her face, she struts past me and starts getting dressed. "Nick's?"

"Yes," I say, grabbing my shirt from the floor and trying to hide my erection.

It doesn't work, but it's the effort that counts.

"When do we leave?"

"Forty-five minutes. Is that enough time?"

"I'll be ready." She slips on her shoes, leaving the laces untied. "Meet you down in the lobby?"

"That works." Every answer is more clipped than the previous one.

She laughs and then blows me a kiss. "See you soon, handsome."

I hurry to the hall just to get another look at her shaking that great ass. When the front door closes, I return to the bathroom and put the shower on cold. It's the only way I can hope it will keep me from ravaging her until we get home, and I have little faith it will work.

Feeling loose after the low-key day, I don't bother shaving or putting pomade in my hair. I like the feel of Juni's fingers grazing across my scalp, and she only does it when it's not perfectly in place.

I look in the mirror once more before I head out the door. I may not have done some of the things I've added into my routine since moving here, but I still want Juni to look at me the same as when I catch her ogling me with that hint of lust in her eyes.

The lobby is empty when I arrive five minutes early. I was taught never to keep a woman waiting, and the lesson has served me well. I was expecting to see Gil, but a guy I don't recognize enters dressed in the doorman's uniform. Jolly with red cheeks, he says, "You must be Mr. Christiansen. I've heard about you."

"Hope it was all good."

"It wasn't all bad."

Funny. I think I'm going to like this guy. We shake hands, and he says, "I'm Mike, the other doorman. I was out with a broken leg, slipped on the sidewalk after a late winter freeze."

"Are you doing all right?"

"Good as new." There's a mobster quality to his accent and the raspy, smokes a lot of cigarettes a day tone and a hacking cough threading through his words don't dispute the image. Leaning over like he's going to tell me where Jimmy Hoffa is buried, he adds, "I also needed to get out of the house. I couldn't take my girlfriend, Adrienne, doting all over me. I couldn't watch a program on the big screen without her wanting to cuddle. It's good to be out of the house again." The back of his hand hits against my arm as he passes. "Know what I mean, Mr. Christiansen?"

Not at all, but I nod anyway. Once he's seated and the chair stops squeaking, he asks, "What can I do for ya?"

"I'm actually waiting on . . ." The elevator doors open, drawing our attention. Black fitted pants stop just shy of her ankles, and the jewel-toned green top has thin straps that tie on her shoulders. The gold strappy heels bring her a lot closer to reaching my mouth, and she has a jacket draped over her arm. She looks spectacular, but it's her hair and makeup that have my mouth hanging open. "Wow."

Her hair is long and straight, all the colors from brown to blond are on display while a soft wave frames her face. The makeup is light, but those lips . . . those full red lips are going to have me fantasizing all night.

Before I can say anything to Juni, Mike is headed her way. "June, it's good to see you." I mentally note that he called her June. Barry the barista down at the coffee shop did that, and she never corrected him. I'm thinking the same has happened here.

She says, "Mike? I wasn't expecting to see you. You're back." Rushing to him, they hug, and when she steps back, she looks down. "How's the leg?"

"I survived."

"You sure did." Her eyes finally meet mine, and her smile lights up her expression. "Have you met Mr. Christiansen?"

My insides tighten like Pavlov's dog to her calling me that. Work should be fun come Monday . . .

Mike whacks me on the back. "Yeah, we're old friends now."

"We sure are," I reply, entertained by him but bitter that I missed the moment to appreciate her properly. "I bet Gil's happy to have a night off."

Moving toward the door, Mike says, "He wasn't upset," and then opens it. "Have a nice night."

We can take a hint. I hold my hand out to Juni, and whisper for only her ears, "You look incredible."

She reaches up and weaves her fingers through my hair just above my right ear. "I like your hair like this." After a quick rub over the scruff on my face, she adds, "And this. You're looking every bit California tonight, Drew, and I approve."

"That's why I did it."

She takes my hand, and we hop in the car to go to dinner.

Together.

On a date.

Like a couple would.

I kiss her when we're tucked in the back of the car. It's not something I felt I could do in the lobby and has me now wondering what we should or shouldn't be doing at all. My brother's house is a safe place. I'm not worried about us going tonight. I worry about work on Monday and how we'll separate the two parts of our lives.

"Drew?"

"Yeah?"

Still holding hands between us, she says, "Where'd you go off to?"

I push down the what's-to-come scenarios playing out in my head and refocus on what's happening right now. "I'm here with you."

Accepting my answer, she nods and then stares out the window.

Are we making a mistake?

Or is it too late?

There are so many ways this can go wrong.

But I don't want to dwell on those. I want this night with her, my family, and my friends.

We walk up the stairs of the brownstone with our hands still clasped together, and I knock. The large wooden carved door opens, and my mom throws her arms wide. "Andrew!"

"Mom? What are you doing here?"

"I flew in to surprise you, and Nick and Natalie. I've been missing you guys so much. It's too quiet at the house. Come here."

Releasing Juni, I embrace my mom. "Oh wow. Yeah, it's a surprise, all right."

She squirms, and I know what she's about to do. Juni never stood a chance to escape before my mom is hugging her, too. I say, "She's a hugger."

Juni's grin is as wide as her face when she hugs her in return. "It's so nice to meet you."

Standing back, my mom still clings to Juni's arms. "You

too. Natalie was telling me about you." Shooting a glare full of daggers in my direction, she adds, "Because my sons don't think it's important to talk about anything but work."

When my mom takes Juni's hand, Juni says, "That sounds just like Drew." She's led inside, leaving me on the stoop staring at these two women becoming fast friends.

"I love that you call him Drew. We tried to get that one to stick when he was a preteen, but he's only ever wanted to be called Andrew."

They move into the living room while I shut the door and hang Juni's jacket up. When I reach the kitchen where everyone—Natalie, Nick, Jackson, Tatum, my mom, and Juni—are hanging out, Nick greets me with a whiskey neat, and says, "I swear I didn't know."

"Mom meeting the woman I'm dating on the first date I take her on . . . yeah, make it a double."

When I see my mom showing Juni her crystal necklace, I'm on the move. "Excuse me, Mom, I need to speak with Juni in private for a minute."

My mom smiles like I'm trying to get away with kissing my girlfriend in the closet. Actually, that's not a bad idea. "Take your time." My mom winks at Juni. Oh God, this night is going to be long.

Juni and I step outside on the back patio, and I close the door behind us. The lights and the group's laughter stretch out here, but I know we'll have a few minutes to ourselves.

With a glass of wine in hand, she asks, "What is it?"

"Don't tell my mom about the science fair project being tied to your parents' theorem. She'll flip out, and we'll never hear the end of it."

"It's pretty unbelievable." Juni believes in fate and all that, maybe not to a New Age guru level, but more of the romantic notion side of things. I don't want to hurt her, but I'm just not a believer in that stuff.

If I had known my mom would be here, I would have prepped Juni in the car. The words race from my mouth on borrowed time. "It is, so she'll jump on that bandwagon and talk about recognizing the signs when you see them, and that will lead to talk of the list—"

"The ex-elementary science fair champion and the daughter of the winning topic's discoverers now seeing each other . . ." She shakes her head and takes a sip of wine. "Yep, no signs there."

She glances up to the stars and adds, "I know you don't believe in destiny. You've made that clear, but if there is magic in the universe, I'm glad it brought me here."

The two things I didn't want to do were hurt or disappoint her, and from her tone, it sounds like I've just done both.

Natalie pokes her head out the door, and says, "Dinner's ready."

I say, "We'll be right in."

Before the door closes, Juni says, "We're coming now."

"Okay," Natalie says, her eyes volleying back and forth between us. She leaves the door open when she returns to the kitchen.

Stepping closer, I catch her arm. "Juni?" When she looks back over her shoulder, I say, "Why are you upset?"

"I guess I thought there was more to us than what's on the surface. Is it so wrong to want a little magic?" She goes inside, but I stay a minute, needing to process what just happened between us.

Juni's not a fact or a figure, a report, or a stock I can analyze. I need to stop treating her like I can.

When I go inside, Nick hands me the freshened drink

and then gives my shoulder a squeeze. "It's going to be okay. Now drink up. You just need to relax."

"You're right." I walk to the empty chair across from Juni and next to my mom.

My mom is already regaling the small group with tales of me in a suit and tie at one year old. "He'd cry if I took his gavel away. He called it gav gav. It was so cute. Of course, he didn't pursue law. Nick did. I think the boys ended up in careers that played to their strengths."

Tatum asks, "Did it ever surprise you to see Andrew become CEO of the company?"

Cookie loves to talk about *her boys* and knowing she's proud of me as CEO has always given me confidence. But I know she's also had concerns about what it takes from me to run the company. She watched the toll it took on my dad. *So, perhaps her answer won't shock me.* "It doesn't surprise me he's in a position of power at the company. It surprises that he wanted the job in the first place. He doesn't show the other side of himself to people outside his inner circle, but there's so much more to him than CEO. What do you think, Juni?"

Shit. Juni's gaze is slow to meet mine, but she sets her silverware down and takes her time to think through her answer. Looking from my mom to me, she replies, "I haven't known him long, but I do see that other side of him, the man under the armor of the company."

Cookie's pleased. Not that it was a test question. My mom isn't devious like that. But that was a good answer, good like Juni.

That's when I realize I just really fucked up.

28

Drew

"IT'S SETTLED THEN," NATALIE ANNOUNCES. "COOKIE'S coming shopping with us tomorrow."

Normally, I wouldn't think anything of it until I realize the "us" includes my girlfriend. *Girlfriend?* That's the second time that's snuck into my vernacular. Is it wrong? I guess that's something I need to discuss with Juni. In addition to making it up to her from the earlier conversation.

I scrub my hand over my face not looking forward to spending the night trying to explain my side of things. Standing behind her chair, I lean down, thinking I'm going to need some time to make things right if we're going to have makeup sex after. "You ready to go?"

"Sure." She stands and starts to give hugs. Tatum loops her arm with hers as they start for the coat closet.

When I go to hug my mom, she stands and says, "I should ride with you. Do you mind?"

"No, of course not."

Nick's at the door already. We slap our hands together

and then bring it in. "I never got to thank you properly for doing Mom's dirty work and delivering that list at work."

"You don't have to thank me, brother. It was my pleasure."

"I just bet it was."

We have a good laugh about it because the whiskey's kicked in, and I care a lot less about that list right now. Juni's my priority. Kissing Natalie on the cheek, we say our thanks and make our exit.

Cookie and Juni are wrapped in their jackets. It's not cold but has gotten chilly. I could say the same about the temperature between Juni and me just as easily. No eye contact is the first clue. When she spends the car ride chatting with only my mom is the second. The third, Juni putting my mom between us.

I hate to interrupt their conversation about the garden club my mom used to belong to, but we're getting close to my apartment, and I don't want to backtrack. "Where are you staying, Mom?"

"With you."

"What? What do you mean?"

When she raises an eyebrow, she asks, "Did you not see my stuff in the spare bedroom? I went to the apartment when I landed this afternoon and got dressed before heading to Nick's."

"No. I never go in there." My eyes catch Juni's grin when a light from outside slides through the back of the vehicle.

Worry crosses my mom's face. "Hope it's not a problem. I just thought it would be one of the few ways I'd get to see you."

I tap her hand. "It's not a problem, but I would have picked you up from the airport or sent a car."

"I got here just fine. Thank you though."

"I'm glad you're staying there. It's better than a hotel. I get concerts late at night, and the night's special wafting through the vents."

She looks at Juni. "I must be tired because I'm not sure what he means."

Giving her forearm a gentle pat, Juni says, "Andrew has annoying neighbors." I catch the use of Andrew. She's definitely mad. "Lucky for him, they're in the loop and know better than to bother him."

By the bewilderment seen in the scrunch of her brow, I'm thinking my mom won't touch that one, but then she says, "That's too bad."

The car pulls to the curb, and I help the ladies out. Mike is already at the door with his hand ready to pull. "Nice evening?" he asks.

"Fine," I reply.

"Dandy," Juni adds.

My mom says, "That's such a handsome-looking uniform. Have you thought about adding a star right—"

"Mom?" I stop inside the lobby.

She looks up and then enters the building. "Sorry. I'm coming. Have a good night, Mike."

He tips his head for her. "You too, Mrs. Christiansen."

In the elevator, I push the button for my floor. As if it couldn't get more awkward, my mom asks, "Are you sleeping over, Juni?"

"Mom, please."

"Geez, Andrew. I'm just wondering if I should set the table for two or three for breakfast."

I want to hide. So embarrassing.

Juni reaches across the front of us and punches the sixteenth floor while giving me the evil eye. "No. I'm staying at mine. I'm the annoying neighbor."

By how my mom takes a step back, so we're not standing in a line, I'm thinking she'd like to disappear about now. When I look back, she's now very busy digging through her purse.

The floor dings, and Juni takes a step forward. "It was nice to meet you, Cookie."

"You too, dear. I'll see you tomorrow."

I get a half-assed backward glance. Just before the door closes, I say, "Good night."

"What did you do?" The accusation comes hard off her tongue, making me feel twelve again.

"*Me?* Why do you think . . . Fine, I fucked up."

The elevator opens on my floor, and we don't take two steps before she says, "Then why are you here and not there making this right?"

"Good question." I step back inside the elevator and punch the button. "I'll be back later."

"Don't rush home on my account and stop with the F-bombs. Love you."

"Love you." The door closes and reopens one flight down.

I knock, but there's no answer. I feel like we're repeating the same pattern. I could sit here for an hour or more, or I could go look for her. I take the stairs and check my floor. When I don't see her or hear any talking inside my apartment, I take the elevator to the lobby. "Hey Mike, have you seen Juni?"

"No. Have you checked the rooftop?"

Holding the elevator door open with my hand, it tries to close three times before it rings in alarm. "What's on the roof?"

"She planted a community garden up there, and sometimes that's where she takes Rascal."

"Thanks, Mike." Letting the elevator have its way, I punch the top floor button when the door closes.

I vaguely remember something about the roof when I was reading the amenities guide sitting on the bar when I first arrived. I've taken advantage of a few of them—the gym, the on-call barber, shoe shining, and the dry-cleaning service but I don't remember anything about a community garden.

The elevator arrives, and I walk down the hall to the glass door and push it open. I stop just outside to take it in —the lights strung like personal stars for our building, the garden to the right that's large enough to spend some time in, and the potted trees that give the feel of being in a park.

The woman beyond the garden holding a leash is the most beautiful feature of it all. "It's amazing," I say, not sure if she can hear from there.

She looks up, and I see a heavy breath wash through her body. "How'd you find me?"

"Mike."

"Never could trust him." I can't see her smile as I work my way across the rooftop, but I hear the teasing in her tone.

"What about me?"

She's dressed the same as earlier but is wearing black flip-flops instead of heels. "Remains to be seen, Mr. Christiansen."

"I much prefer Drew from you."

"Me too," she adds, sounding resigned to the notion.

Rascal doesn't notice me until I get closer, and then he yaps before tugging on his leash to reach me. I squat down, letting him jump up on my knee. "He's got good balance."

She sits on a bench, allowing the wind to sweep her hair from her shoulders. "He's little enough."

I pet him as he leans his front paws on my shoulder and

tries to get a few licks in around my neck. Setting him back on the grass again, I move to sit next to Juni. "I screwed up, and I'm starting to wonder if that's all I know how to do with you."

"Maybe, but instead of going down that path, have you wondered if I'm worth the effort?"

"You are."

"No, Drew. I don't need your confirmation to build my self-esteem. I'm good in that department. What I mean is am I, *are we*, worth fixing misunderstandings, worth fighting to get to a resolution, worth trying harder to understand each other instead of jumping to conclusions? I don't want an automatic answer. I want you to consider each one and come up with your own thoughts on the matter." Juni's a straight shooter. But right now, I don't know if that means she doesn't think it's worth the while to resolve whatever I did wrong.

"Have you?"

"Yeah," she replies, her smile coming easy. "Too much and I'm not mad at you. Well . . ." Reaching over, she slips her hand in mine. "Not anymore anyway." *Thank God.* Because I'm realizing that I want this. Her. *Us.* And I think I finally understand what went wrong tonight.

"I know I let you down. I'm not a romantic guy. I'm numbers and facts, and don't run my life off hunches, emotions, or notions." I hold her hand between both of mine. "If you can have patience with me, I'm learning."

"I don't want you changing for me."

"But I'm willing to."

"Why?"

"Because the last two weeks have been the best I've felt in years, and I owe that to you. It doesn't matter how this job or Seattle or even New York wears me down because you make me feel alive. You make me feel like *me* again." She wants romance and she deserves it, so I step out of my comfort zone and stand before her. "May I have this dance?"

She looks around. "There's no music."

Taking her hand, she stands before me, shorter than ever. I place her hand on my chest, and say, "There is. It's just in here."

We begin to sway to the music inside us when she says, "This is so spontaneous, Drew." A smile cracks her expression. "And I freaking love it."

"I've learned a thing or two from you."

She briefly looks down, but then on the end of an exhale, she says, "I feel like we've got the odds in our favor. We're two for two, after all."

"Which two are we speaking of?"

"Number one on your list since that's how we met and the science fair project that connects us."

I think she's right. The odds are in our favor. "I wouldn't be opposed to taking you to Vegas."

She stops abruptly. "To get married?" she asks, her voice pitching.

"No," I say, my hands flying in front of me. "No. No. No. To the tables. Gambling. We said the odds are in our favor—"

Laughing, she lowers her hand from her chest. "Yeah, I may need a little romance in my life, but I don't tempt the fates with that commitment nonsense. So Vegas, Atlantic City, and all the other quickie marriage locations are out of the question."

One minute I'm not sure how to move forward in the relationship, and now she's rejecting a marriage proposal that I never intended. I should be used to this craziness, yet I'm not.

Rascal is chasing his tail while Juni watches him. I sit down again, and ask, "What do you mean you don't tempt the fates with commitment nonsense?"

Her smile fades as she paces to the other side of the grass patch, taking Rascal with her. "Look, I know I have issues. Commitment is one of them. More long-term, to be specific."

"Then what are we doing?" The question seems to throw her as she shifts her head. "Two for two and all that. How do you believe in destiny and not believe in commitment?"

She moves the leash from one hand to the other, and Rascal lies at her feet.

"My parents showed me that being too passionate about anything always ends badly. They chose their work over me. If I allow every Tom, Dick, or Harry into my heart, where will that leave me? Alone, just like Karl did."

"What about a Drew? How does a Drew fit into your heart?" When she can't answer or chooses not to, I add, "We all have our issues. Mine are on full display, but I'm working on them."

"I took the job to work on mine. It may not seem like much to you, but ten weeks is a long time for me."

"Who's Karl?"

"He's the one who told me my parents were dead. He's the one who stepped into the spotlight and presented my research and discoveries as his own. And I let him. I stood there at the edge of the spotlight in too much shock to say a word."

"He won?"

She nods. That someone she cared about could so easily betray her makes me so angry. And perhaps that's the reason for some of her tears yesterday. But I understand betrayal—not quite to the extent of how that bastard treated

Juni though. But I understand how that can skew self-worth. How it stays with you for years after. "My high school girl-friend cheated on me. I was the most popular kid in school and she still cheated. This may sound cliché, but it wasn't about me. Karl stealing your moment wasn't about you, but you've willingly carried that burden for years. It's not yours to carry anymore."

"What happened with the high school girlfriend? Did you make amends?"

"Fuck no. I'm a guy. I started dating college girls my junior year in high school, fucking every one of them, and made sure she knew."

"That sounds healthy," she deadpans.

"Yeah, real healthy." I was only seventeen and had the brain of a gnat. Clearly. I walk over to the side of the patch where she retreated earlier and take the leash from her. "We're friends now."

"You are?"

"She was fighting her own demons back then. We ran into each other a few years ago and tried to date again, but we both realized we got it right the first time when we broke up." Dalen is complicated, but the one thing that's not is where she stands in my life. "We're friends now. You know why? Because I didn't feel about her the way I do about you."

She comes to my side and wraps her arms around my middle. "I like you, too, Drew."

Words don't always come the easiest when emotions are involved. Although I hadn't told her how much I like her directly, I'm glad she understands my language. I wrap my arm around her, holding her close, and say, "Karl sounds like a real asshole."

"He is," she replies, laughing. She bends down to pet

Rascal. He's looking sleepy lying in the grass. Glancing back up at me, she asks, "You know that proposition I made?"

"Trading your help on the list for a date? I think I'm still coming out ahead on that one."

All sadness is gone, and she says, "The date is an event in my parents' honor. Karl will be there."

"Good. I can't wait to show him how lucky I am. He's going to regret ever stealing your research, your grant, the scholarship . . ." I stop, too late, remembering the prize she really wanted to win. "I'm sorry."

"Don't be. I may not have won the money and other stuff, but I know it's my work that won it for him."

"Betrayal is a hard pill to swallow, but how you're looking at it is true."

She moves to the wall at the edge and looks over the side of the building. "You know what my parents would want me to do?"

"What?"

"Live life unapologetically."

"I believe they would."

Coming back over to me, she takes the leash and leads Rascal toward the door. "Come on. I have plans."

I jog to catch up. "Do they include me?"

"They absolutely include you."

Holding the door open for her, I ask, "Are you going to tell me?"

She lifts on her tiptoes and kisses me, and in Juni speak, I think that means I'm forgiven. Thank fuck. "I'd rather show you." *Fuck. Yes.*

29

Juni

"I DON'T UNDERSTAND."

I sound it out slower this time. "I don't have a condom."

"Why not?" Drew asks, staring at me like I'm an alien.

My defenses kick in, and I cross my arms. Even though it's over my bare breasts, he gets the message. "Well, for one, I haven't been sexually active in a long time. Secondly, you should have one as backup."

"Like carry one on me at all times? I'm starting to worry what you really think of me, babe. I'm not some sex-crazed animal roaming the streets. I might have slept with a few women over the years—"

"A few?"

His finger shoots up, noting my point for that round. "A lot, but that doesn't mean I can't control myself. Also, how did this get turned around on me?"

"Because we'd be upstairs right now if your mom wasn't visiting. And upstairs is where the protection is."

He sits up next to me on the bed and angles my direction. "Are you on the—"

"No. Reference number one again, the not sexually active with a human in many—"

"Months?"

I distract myself with the lights dotting the nightscape through the window and whisper, "Years."

"Years?"

"Okay, don't say it like that." My arms tighten because if I'm not getting any, he's not even getting the pregame show.

"Like what?"

"Like I'm a weirdo."

"I don't know how accusing someone of being a weirdo sounds, but it's not a bad thing that you haven't had sex with a human in years."

Grabbing the blanket, I pull it up to my chin. He's really close to getting my promise to *show him* revoked. "Wow, that did not sound convincing at all."

"I have an idea."

"I'm listening." *Fine*, I'm hot for him and weak to a good idea. *A little desperate as well.*

He gets out of bed and searches for his pants. They're in the living room, but I enjoy the show too much to stop him. "I'll go upstairs, get a condom, and bring it back down."

The lack of confidence in his suggestion is unrecognizable. "Why does this sound like an impossible mission?"

"My mom might be awake, and if she is, she'll want to talk."

I laugh. One of the biggest problems he's shared with me is that he has a parent who actually wants to spend time with him. I might be a little jealous of his family being so close, but I also love it. Everyone should feel that comfort of love.

This adventure is sounding fun. "Can I go?"

"No," he says, throwing his hands in front of him. "Don't leave this bed."

Getting out of bed, I head to my closet and yank a little sundress from the hanger. "I want to come."

"So do I. That's why I want you to stay just like this." His hands run over my shoulders and then down to my breasts. Men are so easily distracted. "I'll be quicker if I'm alone."

"Come on." I pull the sundress on over my underwear. "It'll be fun."

"Yeah, fun," he grumbles, pulling on his undershirt. "Do you know where my pants are?"

"Living room next to my shirt."

He disappears into the other room and then returns with the pants on. Without putting socks on, he slips on his shoes.

"I was surprised to hear your mom ask if I was staying over."

"I think it's hard for her to have her boys all grown up, but she tries to respect us as men as well." His gaze does a once-over on my body, and then he asks, "Ready?"

"Mission retrieve condom is on." On the way out the door, I slip my flip-flops back on. We take the stairs for convenience and probably because it feels sneakier.

He opens his apartment door slowly and scouts the surroundings on the other side before we enter. Using his hand like a map, he points at the top right quadrant of his palm and then gives me a thumbs-up before we start down the entry hall.

I have no clue what any of it meant, but it was cute, like we're on the same team and huddling. I really like huddling with Drew.

Pinning himself to the wall around the corner, he then

peeks backs and waves me forward. Unfortunately, the flip of my flop against the wood floor is loud, so I kick them off and make a run down the hall on my tiptoes. When I reach him, he bends and gives me a kiss because why the hell not? We're not actually in any kind of danger.

When we pass the guest room, no light shines from underneath the door, and I whisper, "I think she's asleep."

He's still not satisfied until we're locked inside his room. "I'll grab the condom."

"Grab two or three. Just grab the box. You never know."

"It's a bowl."

Pinned to the back of the door, I ask, "What is?"

"The condoms. I store them in a bowl."

"Wait, let me get this straight. You have a bowl of condoms?"

"It was here, so I used it."

I can't argue with that logic. "Grab the bowl, and let's get out of here." I head back down the hall, put my shoes on, and wait by the front door.

This has to be torture . . . waiting to get back to my apartment. I thought he'd give up after our tiff before dinner. That he'd retreat to being distant Mr. Christiansen. But the fact he pursued me, opened up a little more to me, has made my heart beat even stronger for him.

He's an underwear man, so I'd actually planned on teasing him a little when we got back to his apartment. Tonight's tease comes in the form of a black silk thong with two sweet pink decorative bows on the hips.

I wore them just for him.

I'm sexual to a point, but it's not been like this before. I crave his touch but need his cuddles afterward. The way he changes from angel to devil in the span of minutes keeps my body on high alert. I'm not above begging this man for an orgasm. He's that good.

God, now I'm turned on. I look up into Andrew's eyes, and I'm pretty certain he can see exactly what's going on inside my head.

I watch him as I run my hand between my breasts and then lower over my belly, making sure he can see very clearly how ready I am for him. "Drew . . ." I lean up and kiss him. Thoroughly. Soon we're both panting. "Why does the thrill of almost getting caught turn me on?"

"Are you trying to make me come right here in the entry-way?" There's a weakness in his voice that tells me I'm getting to him. "Fuck it." The bowl is set on the small table behind him. He takes a breast in his hands and kisses my nipple, teasing it with his tongue and then moving over to the other to repeat the technique.

His hands are enormous, like other parts of his body, and span my sides. So hot as he slides to his knees in front of me. "Is this what you, babe? You want to come on my mouth and have me lick you clean? Or maybe you want to fuck you right here against this wall? Tell me what you want?"

I run my fingers through his hair and then take a section and give a little squeeze. "Why can't I have both?"

As if he didn't already drive me crazy, the smirk comes first and then he takes hold of the silky string wrapped over my hip. He rips that one and then moves to the other side. This time. he pulls it away from my skin with his teeth.

He's about to shred it when a light comes on.

There's no time . . . we freeze, our gazes locked on each other. Then we hear his mom say, "Oh, I . . . um. Is that my jade bowl? Full of condoms? Not important. Not important. Pretend this never happened. *Right.* Good night."

Neither of us makes a move or says a word even after the lights off and we hear her door close loudly down the hall. I'm thinking she wanted us to know when it was safe again.

Just when I think our night of fun is over, I'm swept into his arms, and he sprints to the bedroom. *The Fast and the Furious* have nothing on him. My thong is ripped, and he's naked in seconds.

Remembering to leave a condom behind before he grabbed his expensive jade bowl of protection, he's covered and positioned in no time. "Do you need a warmup?"

"No." The word barely leaves my mouth before he's sinking into me.

We're not making love. This is sensual and desires sated, carnal to the core. His body moves of its own accord, mine taking and giving, opening for him. With him on top, thrusting his body as it glides against mine, I whisper, "You feel so good, Drew."

I thought Mr. Christiansen was his trigger, but Drew coaxes something else out of him—romance. He slows and kisses my cheek, wanting to make it last longer. I love it and could bathe in his charisma, revel in his care.

"Faster, Mr. Christiansen. Harder. I want you so badly." But then again, sometimes you just want to have it all as hard as you can. "Yes! Yes!" My head digs into the pillow, and I urge him on with my heels on his ass.

Whether it was the name or the speed or the pressure or all of it coming together at once, we do the same. Lying on the bed, we both stare up at the ceiling and try to catch our breaths.

I say, "I need a shower."

"Upstairs or downstairs?"

"My place." When I turn to the side to find him staring at me, he smirks. "I'll grab the bowl."

You would think sitting across from my boyfriend's mother . . . wait, boyfriend? *Is that what Drew is?* Do I have a boyfriend, or do I have a friend with benefits? And at what age do we stop calling them boys? I think Drew is my manfriend from here on out.

Back to the business at hand.

Although the rain outside put a damper on our shopping adventure, brunch is still on. I'm not embarrassed in the least sitting across from Cookie Christiansen at Sunday brunch. *Nope.* There's also no shame being here with his sister-in-law and her best friend, Tatum.

I think I'm too tired to care with the level of energy required.

I sip a mimosa and then finish my bacon and eggs before moving that plate to the side and making the small side of pancakes the star of the show. To be honest, I'm exhausted, but the last thing I should be doing is thinking about why. I was worried when our conversation turned to forever and marriage last night. But somehow, we got over that bump. And the sex afterward was sensational. He's glorious in bed. Attentive. Passionate. All that intensity turns into hot, provocative—I don't notice them staring until the conversation stops, and I look up with pancakes shoved in my mouth. I chew and then wash it down with more liquid. "Sorry, what were you saying?"

Tatum says, "I never thought of Andrew that way."

"What way is that?" I brace myself because I'm not sure if she's going to compliment him or go for the jugular.

Sitting back with an all-knowing grin, she says, "Don't get me wrong, he's gorgeous, like his brother." Her eyes momentarily connect with Natalie, who grins like a woman comfortable in her own skin. To me, Tatum says, "But the glow of your skin, your hair . . . You even cleaned your plate. Everything about you is . . . enviable." Leaning forward, she adds, "You looked beautiful last night, but today you look—"

"Like you've spent the day at the spa and had the best massage of your life," Natalie says.

I sort of did if three orgasms relax your soul.

"I need to meet someone." Finishing her mimosa, Tatum sets the glass on the table, and adds, "Sex with Andrew must be incredible."

Cookie raises her hand. "Check, please."

30

Juni

COOKIE INSISTED . . .

That I stay the night.

We have coffee together in the morning.

And to hear all about me, my childhood, and my family.

Drew called it. We found a list she created the night before for herself, so I had time to prepare—run, hide, or stick around and participate. He was kind enough not to hold it against me if I chose to leave.

I stayed.

She certainly loves to check things off lists and did with each item we accomplished. While Drew worked out at the gym at five in the morning, I got up shortly after to get in that bonding time.

I could handle the first two no problem. She even came down to the apartment after coffee to hang out and proceeded to pick out my outfit.

She has great taste—a spring pink, short-sleeved sweater,

and though it's still before Memorial Day, white pants because in LA they wear white year-round. In reality, I don't think Cookie makes excuses or justifies anything she does. If it makes her happy, she goes with it. She's easy-going like that.

Tucking my hair behind my ear, I walk into the living room where she's been looking around. I told her she was welcome to. Holding a gold frame, she shows me the photo. "This might be my favorite."

Out of all the framed photos my grandmother kept of her glamorous life, the photos of my mom, and eventually some of me, she chooses the one of me on my sixteenth birthday. The sun was setting at the country house in the Berkshires, and tall trees filled the background. It's a simple close-up photo, but you would have thought a professional photographer had captured the moment.

"I remember that day," I say, staring at a girl so different than how I feel today. Taking the frame from her, I admire the innocence in my eyes. "I had really hit my stride back then. I knew what I wanted and how I was going to achieve it." Setting it back on the bookcase, I add, "Funny how life can have a totally different plan."

"Plans are plans. Nothing more. They're not set in stone or carved into the universe. They're just ideas until they're set in motion. Women go through many moon phases as well. Some things are meant for us, and some things aren't despite the plans we made."

"There are plants that only bloom at night. I always thought it was because they craved the moonlight."

"The moon is a powerful force." She sets her empty mug in the sink, and asks, "It's not?"

"No, they open when their pollinators are most active. How romantic is that?"

"Very. It's as if they sense their soul mate and bloom for them."

She gets it. I knew she would. "You can leave the mug there. I'll deal with it later." Noticing the time, I ask, "Would you help pick out jewelry to go with my outfit? We can finish talking in the bedroom."

She's not flashy, though she has a rather large diamond ring, diamond tennis bracelet, and diamond earrings. She's wearing a fortune, but each piece is tasteful that nothing overwhelms, and she's the one who stands out.

I pull out my most prized treasures, gifts from grandparents to mark special occasions and others I inherited. Continuing our conversation as she looks at the tray of brooches and pins, I say, "My life was set in motion from the first word I'd ever spoken."

"And what was that?"

"Tree."

That makes her smile. "It's a great first word." Holding a brooch in the shape of a daisy, she says, "This is the one."

"My grandfather gave that to my grandmother the day she gave birth to my mom. He told her when he saw it in the store, he knew he was having a daughter. My mom's name was Daisy."

Rubbing my arm, she says, "Andrew told me about your parents. I'm very sorry."

"Thank you." Surprisingly, I feel relieved he told her. It's not something I want to go into every time someone finds out. I would have for Cookie, but I'm glad I don't have to.

"This brooch is so beautiful, like your mom's name." She pins it, not asking if the diamonds are real or crystals. I have a feeling she knows just from looking at it because she says, "I believe in wearing our fine jewelry without waiting for occasions. Every day should be celebrated."

I like Cookie. Just like Natalie said I would. She has a personality you're drawn to, something in her aura that tells you she's kind. I've missed having a mother figure around. I know that I've actually been very lucky having Gil and Nancy. They've given me a sense of family, even more so than my own parents did if I'm honest. I click more with Gil, though. Sports, people-watching, donuts. He and I just understand each other so easily. But I've missed a mother's presence in my life. Not that I think Cookie will be that for me, as there's no promise of forever with Drew. But if I were to wish for someone, it would be someone like Cookie. "Can I ask you something crazy?"

"The crazier, the better is right up my alley."

I couldn't ask just anyone, but based on the list she made Drew, I feel safe to assume I can ask her. "Do you believe our course is set before we're born?"

Her gaze moves past me to the windows as she remains still in thoughtful repose. When her eyes return to me, she says, "I think destiny plays a part, but you have to have an open heart and mind." With a laugh, she adds, "I'm sure you were warned about me. My sons and husband are more on the . . . how should we say, serious side of life. I think that's why they were drawn to their professions." Sifting through the open jewelry box, she finds dainty pearl earrings. "Classically beautiful."

As I put them on, she says, "The guys think they're humoring me, but it only takes one unexplainable event to occur, and they're coming to me wanting to know what it means." I slip on my heels as she sits in a blue velvet chair I have in the corner. "My husband trusts my instincts and now carries a crystal in his pocket. He'll be the first to say it was his hard work and my faith that it would all work out. Nick . . ." Her bond is revealed in a smile for herself.

We walk back out. "What happened with Nick? He and Natalie seem like the perfect match."

I grab a water bottle, and she stands at the island, and says, "They are. They have such a wonderful energy together. I knew if I could get him to open his eyes, he'd see what the universe was telling him. When he finally did, he met Natalie. It's quite a love story. I've encouraged her to write a book about it. The third time was a charm for them. No matter how many obstacles were thrown in their path, they just never got over each other."

"Sounds like a fairy tale come true," I say as I fill my bottle from the fridge spout.

She holds the straps of my bag before her. "You have yours already written in the stars. Going back to your original question, I believe in destiny, but sometimes, it needs a helping hand."

Taking the bag, I settle it on my shoulder. "You never told me about Drew. What was his first word?"

Pride bubbles up, and she says, "Leaf."

Leaf. He's speaking my language.

It's tempting to tell her about our other connection, the one with the science fair project and my parents. Not to mention how we first met, when I rambled on about removing grass stains, but since he asked me not to, I keep that to myself.

Not so subtly, she says, "I hear you're interested in botany?"

~

I HITCHED *a ride with the boss.*

It was my idea to be dropped off a block before we reached the building to be on the safe side. He refused at first but changed his mind when I promised to make it up to him by wearing his favorite shoes next time in bed or on the kitchen island. The location is yet to be determined.

I'm seated at my desk when he comes from his office, and says, "The lobby looks nice, Ms. Jacobs."

"Thank you."

I look around, almost forgetting that all those plants had homes on the two floors of CWM, but I hadn't had time to place them in their new homes in the office the morning they arrived. Also, the jungle vibe seemed to bother him, and I have a soft spot for that side of Andrew. So I might have accidentally on purpose forgotten to correct his assumption regarding the wildlife habitat in the lobby.

When I think about it, maybe I should be offended that he actually thought I'd leave a ficus mingling with a bamboo palm. My God, I'd have to be a lunatic to group a Dracaena with a Fiddle-leaf. They originated from completely different parts of Africa.

It's probably best if I let that go, though.

He lingers in the doorway while I take a call. After I transfer it, he asks, "Do you mind sitting in on my meeting this morning?"

"Is there something, in particular, you want me to do during the meeting?"

Acting unlike himself, he comes all the way into the reception area and leans on the counter like we're going to have a little chitchat. "I've been thinking about what you said about commitment."

I'm not sure where he's going with this, but I'll give him time to get there. He continues, "There aren't a lot of roles in the company, but we could start having you try them out. I heard you sat in with Nick recently when Barbara was out.

Mary has a dental appointment this morning, so I wanted to ask you first."

"I'll help however I can. If that's where you need me, I'll be there."

"I think," he says, cautiously, lowering his voice. "I want you to stay if that's something you want as well."

Kissing is out of the question, and so is hugging. Touching of any kind would be inappropriate in the office, but damn, does he make it hard to resist him. "I appreciate that, but you don't have to worry about me. I'm fine financially."

"I'm not worried about your finances. I'm worried about losing you."

The heat hits my cheeks like a spark to a match. "You're—"

The elevator doors slide open, and he's quick to move away from the desk, *from me*. Rousing hellos fill the area when three men step into the reception area. I watch as he greets who I assume are the Everest brothers, shifting right back into CEO Andrew. His posture tenses, his handshake firm from the veins in his forearms bulging.

All four men stand around sharing stories of a recent night out. I'd rather listen, but the phone keeps ringing, only allowing me to catch bits and parts.

Margie . . .

. . .Flirting with you.

You're a single man . . .

. . .You should get out more.

I guess they're more than clients, but also friends since they seem to know him so well. I'm a professional and can temper my jealousy, but it's tough with them still going on about it. Through the laughter, I catch Drew's eyes on me.

There's nothing he can say to make this situation better. We have roles to play, after all.

As they shift toward the door, he gestures to me and makes the introduction. "This is Ms. Jacobs. Ethan, Hutton, and Bennett Everest." With that simple deed, I feel seen again.

I stand to shake each of their hands and then offer to show them to the conference room.

So much money is verbally tossed about and not one of them bats an eye, not even Drew. This is his element, the arena where he performs his best. He's handling billions of dollars in their portfolios, and they're letting him. I find myself smiling, so impressed listening to him win their trust.

I don't know if I have a right to be, but pride swells inside just watching him. He's a masterful dealmaker, and his knowledge in his field is so sexy.

The meeting ends when lunch begins. More handshakes are exchanged, deals being sealed, and talk of contracts being sent over.

If I didn't adore Ice Cream Drew so much, CEO Andrew would give him a run for the money after that performance.

The men are escorted to the elevators. Drew stays until the doors close. Turning toward me, he says, "Will you stay?"

"I don't know," seems to be all I can say. "Answering phones isn't my dream job, but as much as I enjoy being by your side during a deal, I guess I never saw myself as an assistant either."

"Stockbroker? HR? Accounting? A financial advisor?"

"That you're thinking about me, I'm so touched, but I need to give this some thought."

Laurie comes through the door, staring down at a box in her hands. "Juni, you received a package from—*oh,* Andrew.

Sorry, I didn't see you there. May I help you with something?"

"No." Scratching the back of his neck, he says, "I'm good. Thank you."

Satisfied, she turns to me and sets a box on the counter. Agent Provocateur is printed across the box. When she glances at him again, he legs it out of there, "Excuse me." *I restrain my grin.*

She waits until he's out of earshot and even peeks to make sure the coast is clear before she taps the box with her nails. "I know you're not responsible for what is sent to the office, but receiving this type of gift—"

"What type is that?" I know the brand of expensive lingerie and own several sets, but I think it's good for her to be specific, if not entertaining.

"Sexy lingerie. It's not appropriate to have at the office. I didn't read the card, but I had to sign for it since you were in a meeting. Please ask your admirer to refrain from sending these types of gifts. Thank you."

She turns, not wanting a discussion but to deliver her policy. *Done.*

As for me, I smile as I read the card, but I'm not sure I understand what it means. I lift the lid and peel away the tissue to find two pairs of the same red lace underwear. *Ah.* Now the card makes more sense.

ONE FOR ME *and one for you.*

HE DOESN'T HAVE to sign it for me to know who the sender is, but I am surprised he's playing this daring game. I transfer the calls to the service and head for the restrooms.

Not sure what Drew's plans are for lunch, but I take a chance and check. Two can play this game.

"Come in," he says, his tone gruff.

When I open the door, he's quiet with his dark eyes steady on my every move. Closing the door behind me, I stay pressed to it with my hand on the knob. I'm not scared of him. I'm trying to remain a consummate professional. *Consummate?*

What an odd word. Even stranger that it's the same word for intercourse for sealing a marriage as used for skill and exemplary behavior. *Ugh.* This word is going to bother me now. Like platonically.

"Juni?"

"I received the gift. Laurie wasn't happy."

"Were you?"

"I can't wait for you to rip them to shreds." I click the lock.

As if a starter pistol has gone off, we both fly across the room, our mouths crashing into each other's as our hands fumble to get our clothes off. Within minutes, maybe even seconds, I'm bent over his desk, and he's rolling on a condom. "Now you have one handy?" I note in a bit of irony.

"I took a chance this morning and threw it in my wallet."

His breathing deepens as his hands slide up my back. Moving back down, he says, "You have the best ass." His mouth is on it, a lick and a gentle bite, and then he's nipping at my hip, teasing the red lace strap. "I knew these would look so fucking good on you."

The fabric gives under little pressure, and then he takes the other side and rips it as well. He pulls the remains slowly from the back, his hand replacing it in the front and teasing my clit. My smile is gone, and my mouth wide open. I close my eyes and let him work his magic.

The moment I reach the peak, he buries himself inside me. Kisses to my shoulders and whispers of how good he feels cover my back until . . . until . . . he can't fight it any longer. His orgasm hits hard, and his mouth closes around the skin on the back of my neck to keep the sound from traveling.

But it's too much—his heat, his breath, his desire for me —I come again right under him with his hand covering my mouth. As soon as I exhale, he stands behind me and lifts me in the aftermath. Moving to the couch, we lie together in each other's arms.

When I look up at him, I touch his cheek, knowing that sex may enhance emotions, but after spending the weekend with him, having time with his family, his mom especially, I feel as though I've seen so much more of Drew than he would normally allow.

He's sexy, without a doubt. He's handsome. He's intelligent and kind. Driven. But he floored me by sending lingerie to work, by taking a risk to make me feel sexy. *Naughty.* Part of what I feel is post-orgasmic glow here, but I'm fairly certain I'm falling in love with him. Whispering, I say, "I know you don't believe in destiny."

His finger presses to my lips. "I've been meaning to let you in on a little secret, babe." Not knowing where he's going with this, he has my full attention. "I'm beginning to believe because of you."

I kiss him, happiness bursting inside of me, and then curl a little closer to his side. We don't have long with most people out of the office, but we have this stolen moment that I'll never forget.

31

Drew

THE FIRE BETWEEN US WENT FROM AN EMBER TO A BONFIRE before we had a chance to catch our breath.

In three weeks, my life had completely changed—in a good way—because of Juni Jacobs. She's sexy but kind, fun, and keeps me on my toes in the office and at home. I can't say I fell in love with her the first time we met. There was shit involved, and a restraining order came to mind at another point.

No, she didn't come on strong. It was a creeping fire that she lit inside me. By the time I realized how deep I was in trouble, it was too late. I have feelings for her like I've never had for anyone.

Even now as she walks around my apartment with a smudge stick that has me worrying it will set off alarms, I'm dumbfounded she chose me to be her boyfriend.

Out of all the men in Manhattan, she could have her pick. Out of millions, we bumped into each other too many times to call it a coincidence, some may say. *Some . . . like my mother.*

I meant what I said to Juni, though. I'm thankful destiny chose Juni and me to mess with.

She says, "Now that I got it started, you have to do it, Drew." She hands the burning stick to me, and I stand there, not sure what I'm actually supposed to do with it other than walk around aimlessly. "I promised your mom."

My mom moved over to Nick's on Monday and then left for LA today. It was good to see her and have her meet Juni, whom she loved. She called me from the plane to tell me about first words and destiny, but I didn't catch the rest before she had to hang up. It was a strange conversation.

"Do I chant something?" That makes her giggle, but I'm not actually kidding. "What does it say to do again?"

"Number two. Eradicate negative vibes from the apartment on the sixth Thursday after arrival. It's the sixth Thursday since you came to New York, so we're all good. Just walk around with it."

I keep walking, stopping to look out the window as lights populate in the windows of the residential buildings across the avenue. "How much negativity could I have generated in six weeks?"

"That's not for me to decide, but I assume by your track record quite a bit. Six weeks is enough time for you to get so buried in work that you'd be dragging your stress home every night."

Moving behind her as she rests her elbows on the island has me remembering how fucking good it felt to be buried inside her then. I rub my hand over her ass. "C'mere."

She turns, her hair swinging in a high ponytail on her head. I hold the smudge stick away from her and wrap my other arm around her. She's only dressed in a T-shirt and jeans, but she still manages to steal my breath. She links her arms around my neck and rises on her toes. "Kiss me," she says.

I lean down and close my eyes. Our lips meet in a gentle caress. Sometimes it's soft, sometimes hard, other times fast and frenzied, or like now, slow and tender. Every kiss with her is steeped in meaning, and I'm memorizing each one.

"Ow!" she yells, jumping out of my arms and furiously patting the bottom of her jeans.

Looking down, I see the stick has left ashes on the floor, burning through the wood in several places. "Shit." Smoke fills the room by the time I drop the stick in the sink and douse it with water. The smoke detectors go off, and I say, "Call downstairs and tell them it's being handled."

I grab two bottles of water from the fridge and start dumping them on the floor. Before the first bottle is empty, the alarms in the hall sound. I look up to find Juni hanging up. "It's too late," she says. "The fire department has to come out to check for structural safety."

"Fuck."

Two hours later, a firefighter approaches, not looking happy with me.

Understandable. I'm embarrassed that I caused the street to close and that every resident in the building had to be evacuated. "Fortunately, the fire was contained to your apartment. The damage to the floor didn't spread after you put out the embers." He looks toward the flashing lights on the police car barricade, and then adds, "The building is safe and secured. We've already started to help some of the elderly back to their floors. You're going to receive a fine and bill from the city. I'd like to advise you not to play with fire, Mr. Christiansen. This could have been much more serious and deadly."

I'm not arguing with a man carrying an ax around, so I say, "I understand."

He leaves, and I start to look for Juni. The crowd is dense, and it's dark, but I spot her up ahead with Rascal under one arm and her other hooked around an older man.

"Andrew?" I turn to see Gil waving me over.

I run my fingers through my hair, mad at myself for causing this trouble. "Hey, I'm sorry, I—"

"It happens. We've had entire apartments burn through. I'm not letting you off the hook, but accidents happen, and fortunately, no one was hurt. Hey, do you mind helping Mrs. Hendricks back to her apartment?"

"Of course."

The woman must be in her eighties if I'm being generous. "Tall and handsome. Gil knows my type." She laughs, and I introduce myself. The wait for the elevator takes over an hour, so I sit with her in the lobby until it's our turn.

She asks, "Have I seen you spending time with Juni Jacobs?"

At the office, we're guarded, but in the building, we date openly. "Yes, ma'am."

"Her grandmother was such a lovely woman. I miss her. She passed away too soon."

I look around to see if Juni is near, but I think she was luckier and caught an earlier elevator. She's been coming and going through the stairwell all night helping, blowing me kisses here and there. She knows everyone and is a big part of this little community. Although I don't want to invade her privacy, I'm not telling her to stop.

There's a sadness that comes over Mrs. Hendricks' blue eyes, and for a moment, I wonder if she's going to cry. Unsure what to do, I lift my arm, not sure if I should give her support until she says, "It's been a long time since a strapping young man, such as yourself, has held me. Hint, hint."

Guess that settles it. I put my arm around her, and we sit there for a minute in silence. Then she says, "Her grandmother died a few years ago. Cancer. The incurable kind. My Artie smoked for sixty years, didn't even have a cough. Got hit by a bus crossing down at 42nd. I just know he would have outlived me if he'd made a different decision that day. So you just never know how you're going to go, but her grandmother deserved better. So did Juni. Such a sweet girl. I can still remember her with that Paddington Bear suitcase and this hat straight out of the jungle."

I catch Juni holding hands with a little girl who's carrying a teddy bear. She loads her onto the elevator with her mother and waves while the doors shut. She has so much love to give with her heart of gold. Invested in the story and more in the woman it's about, I ask, "When did you meet her?"

"Her grandmother, Marion, I met the day she moved in. I think twenty-five, thirty years ago now. Keeping time isn't something I'm keen to do anymore. Juni was seven when she came to live here. Her parents were botanists, famous even, but I guess they didn't have time for a little girl."

I've had a lot of thoughts about her parents since Juni told me her story. Some good. Some bad. At the end of the day, I think they were searching for a pot of gold that didn't exist. It came at the expense of their daughter, though. "That's too bad."

"It really is. Everyone in the building adores her, but we're also ready for her to leave."

"Why is that?"

"Oh, honey." She leans her head against my shoulder, smiling like a cat who caught the canary. "This is where we spend our twilight years, while for younger folk like you, it's just a stop on your journey. A great location in a prestigious building. But she needs to spread her wings and fly out of this place. She needs to live without the security of this nest and find her place in this world. She'd be missed, but we'll survive. Until we don't because we're old."

Mike calls, "Mrs. Hendricks. It's your turn."

I stand and then help her to her feet. She says, "She could do worse than you. Handsome and rich."

Laughing, I say, "I could only be so lucky to have the chance." I look at the empty elevator and then say, "Are you ready to go?"

"Since Artie passed away."

After the lobby is empty and everyone is safely back in their apartments, I drop on the bed next to Juni. "My body hurts. I must have run down twenty times." I never wanted to keep the elevator from picking more people up by calling it to take me down. Juni's idea.

"The good news is you don't have to work out tomorrow." She rolls to her side and props up on her elbow. "Don't be too hard on yourself."

I eye her out of the corner of my eye and then give her a wink. "I got distracted."

"It happens." She scoots closer and drapes an arm and leg over me. With her eyes closed, she says, "The good news. Number two is done."

"At least something good came from it."

We've had a lot of sex in the last week, but tonight, I just want to hold her. "What do you say we take a shower to get the smoke and sweat off, and we go to bed?"

"Sounds like heaven."

It is. She's heaven in my arms. I don't know yet what to do with Mrs. Hendricks's words.

But she needs to spread her wings and fly out of this place. She needs to live without the security of this nest and find her place in this world. She'd be missed, but we'll survive. Is that what Juni needs? To be set free? Free of commitment to a job. Free of commitment to a tiny dog. Free of commitment . . . *to me?* Mrs. Hendricks was definitely right and wrong about one thing, though.

She'd be missed, but I'm not sure if I'd survive.

Is there any way I can keep her here without it feeling as though I'm clipping her freedom-seeking wings?

~ One Month Later ~

"What is this?" I ask, walking into the reception area.

Juni looks at the booklet in my hand and replies, "The Unofficial Manual to Christiansen Wealth Management. That's a mouthful. It needs an acronym. UMCWM. That doesn't work."

I set it down on the counter of her desk. "We can figure that out later, but what *is* it?"

"You once asked me how I knew you liked the office at a freezing seventy-one degrees." She taps the top of the booklet. "That's how."

"Vaguely. I need more."

"You always do." I'm pretty sure that was a sex joke. The wink confirms it. She says, "Melissa started a manual about everyone's specifics, especially the bosses and Christiansens. I've added to it since I took this job. Figured it was my contribution to the next reception assistant."

Thumbing through the booklet, I find some relief that it's under a hundred pages. "Reception assistant?" I ask, glancing up at her.

"Receptionist feels dated. I thought a few minor changes wouldn't hurt."

I realize it's not like discovering a plant's veins contract and expand, but she's here, even if it's only temporarily, and improving the company.

I can't help but want her to stay, but at some point, Mrs. Hendricks's words need to come into play. Not just in relation to the apartment building but to this job that she's incredibly overqualified for, and simply isn't her destiny. Yeah, yeah. I said the d-word. *Don't tell her.*

"I like it, Juni. As for the booklet, why does it say not to bother me at 12:15?"

She clears her throat. "You know why."

"Ah." *Yes, I do.* That's when the office is the emptiest. Thank God there aren't cameras in here. We've been good about keeping our relationship on the down low. Is it what we prefer? No.

I could go public, but it's not a good look for someone in my position and could be easily misconstrued. Juni likes the secrecy, so we keep it contained when we're at work. Well, except for at 12:15.

Speaking of, I check the time, already looking forward to our lunchtime rendezvous. Not that it's every day, of course. Meetings offsite and staff meetings going overtime have prevented many meetups. Not only that, but we recognized that it would be more than risky if Juni was seen entering my office every day at 12:15 p.m.

"How many people have access to this book?"

"Me, and now you."

"That's good." I flip the page, still scanning for the things that pop out at me. "Why does it say not to bother Nick on Tuesdays and Fridays after 4:30?"

She transfers a call and then leans in. "That's when

Natalie stops by. You're not the only one having fun at the office. In fact . . ." She checks the door over her shoulder. "I think Laurie and Joseph are an item."

"Really?"

Nodding, she says, "I found this on the copier." She slaps a piece of paper down on her desk.

My eyes dart from the imprint of an ass with someone's cheek pressed to it to Juni. "How do you know that's them? How can you tell?" I angle my head sideways to get another look.

Taking a red pen, she circles a button. "Evidence number one, that's the button on the sweater Laurie keeps on her chair for when a certain someone tries to freeze the office. Number two . . ." She circles three dots on the smashed cheek. "Joseph has three freckles on his left cheek that always remind me of Orion's Belt."

"Have you considered detective work?"

She clicks the lid back on the pen and drops it in her pen cup. "Doesn't pay enough."

Just when I think she can't surprise me anymore. "And this job does?"

"No, but this job comes with perks. Reference 12:15 again." *She still does.*

I've found her quick wit one of my favorite things about her, and that's a long fucking list. "Don't forget it, babe."

"I never do, hot stuff." She winks with a cluck of her tongue. "See you in twenty."

32

Drew

"WHAT DO YOU THINK?"

I look around, thinking I don't recognize this place. Juni is industrious. I haven't completely left my CEO workaholic days behind me—I doubt anyone could simply eradicate the responsibilities on my shoulders—but I have certainly left the office earlier most nights than I used to. In fact, despite finishing at seven twice this week, I've rarely been there until ten or eleven in the past six weeks.

Baby steps.

I've come home to home-cooked meals, or we've eaten out and then crashed at mine. But Juni's often spent those nights making the apartment her grandmother left her, her own. The dusty wreath no longer hangs at the entrance, and the new door is more modern.

The knickknacks and picture frames have been pared down to a minimum and, from what I can see, put on two shelves of the bookcase instead of everywhere in the apartment. She even renovated the kitchen and bathrooms.

I'm not a jump in headfirst kind of guy, but it looks like she's planning on staying a while. "I like it. It fits you." I'm not sure if it fits *us,* though.

She beams and then sits on the couch, spreading her arms wide across the back. "I think so, too."

The thing is, thoughts about our future have become more frequent, the idea of settling down, whatever that means—*becoming more boring, more routine, staying home more often*—started sounding more appealing.

So when I look around her place and how she's decorated, the money she's spent, and the time she's dedicated to making it her own, I'm thinking she feels the opposite. Yet for someone who claims they don't like commitment, she sure is all in with this apartment.

I won't rain on her parade with the conversation that feels long overdue regarding us and her plans in life. I'm a planner by nature, so I won't be able to stay quiet for much longer.

"Drew?"

Shifting forward, I set my drink on the coffee table. "We should probably get going."

"Did you hear anything I said?"

"I'm sorry. I must have missed it."

She looks around as if she'll find someone else in here. "How'd you miss it when it's just the two of us?"

"I said I'm sorry." Pushing up, I grab my keys from the bar. "Are you ready?"

Her arms lower to her side, but she's not made any other effort to leave. "No."

"No?"

"I'm not going anywhere until you tell me what's on your mind."

I can't lie to her. I'd be pissed if she did to me. We're

heading out of the honeymoon phase of this relationship, and I had looked forward to us getting more serious. "I like what you've done. I love it. I think it will get over asking if you sell it."

Her eyes slide around the room as if the thought is unfathomable. "Why would I sell it? I just finished it."

"My apartment is bigger." I should have just said it instead of hinting around at what I've been thinking.

She scoffs, a humorless chuckle blending in at the end. "What does your apartment have to do with . . ." She stands —her jeans are skintight, and the hot pink top highlights her fantastic tits. Her chest rises and falls, and even though I know I shouldn't look, I can't stop myself. "Are you talking about me moving in with you? Upstairs? Living together? The two of us?"

"You can phrase it however it sounds best, but I've been thinking about it."

"You have?" She doesn't sound so mad right now. She comes to me and wraps her arms around me. With her head on my chest, she asks, "Why didn't you say anything?"

"I'm saying it now."

When she steps back, this time when she laughs, it reaches her eyes. "You're saying it now because I put your vague remarks together to form the big picture."

"Right, but it's out there . . . now." I tug at my collar. "Is it hot in here?"

"No. It's just how you like it. I always have the thermostat at the acceptable Andrew Christiansen temp just in case you come down to see me." Slipping on a coat, she heads for the door but doesn't open it. "Moving in together is a big step. I know we spend most nights together but living together is different. Even though you didn't ask, do you mind if I think about it?"

"Think about it like how you've been mulling over the job proposition for the last month?"

"Yes."

I shove my phone and keys in my jacket pocket and head out. When I pass her, I ask, "Why does this not surprise me?"

"I have no idea. That's really more for you to ponder than for me to answer."

"Stop." She does, five feet behind me. I don't know why that bugs me, but it does. I close three of the feet. "I'm not asking you to move in, Juni."

Fifty emotions flicker across her face, but the one that sticks is hurt. "That's what I get for assuming."

"I'm not asking you right now. I had planned to ask you soon, but you were so invested in making this apartment all yours that it made me think I was making a mistake."

"How soon?"

I close the rest of the distance and take her by the belt loops. "Last month."

"Oh that was really soon."

"And then I chickened out." I swallow my pride and give the woman credit where it's due. "The apartment is great, and since it's always at the perfect temperature according to many studies and national reviews of cohabitating in office spaces."

She straightens my jacket and then pulls me in for a kiss. "And cohabitating in your personal life?"

"Whatever makes you happy, babe."

"That's what I like to hear." I kiss her again. We argue very little, but we still have a few hurdles to jump. I push the button to call the elevator, and she says, "I think I'm turning in my resignation."

"What? Why?"

"Because you're right. I've been wondering what to do with my life for years. CWM gave me a soft place to land, but it's time I launch again."

We enter the elevator. I want to be happy for her, but I know what this means for me. I refuse to be selfish. One hint of fear or disappointment injected into the conversation and she'll focus more on pleasing others than doing what's right for herself. "Do you know what you want to do?"

"I'm going to return to research and working in labs as a botanist. I actually might even try my hand at working for one of the gardens around the city or in one of the other boroughs." She rests easily against the handrail, some of the burden she's been carrying now lifted. "Don't worry, though. I'll train the new reception assistant on everything." She nudges me. "Except on 12:15. That's our thing."

Chuckling, I say, "I'm going to miss our lunchtime dates."

"Well, you never know. I might be close enough to make lunchtime visits to a certain CEO."

"That *certain CEO* better be me, Ms. Jacobs."

"But of course, Mr. Christiansen. Only you."

I chuckle, but inside, I like that very much.

Our hands come together when we enter the lobby. Women love holding hands. I used to think it was their way of claiming them in a public way, but now I get it. It's not about stakes in the world. It's about the connection. Her skin is soft, her fingers entwined with mine, and there's an intimacy shared without saying a word.

And fine, it strokes my ego to be the one who gets to hold her hand.

We're taken to our table as soon as we enter Asado, the restaurant Nick's been raving about for months. We order drinks, and once we get them, we decide to look over the menu. I say, "I heard the empanadas are good."

"I love empanadas." She sips her drink but then chokes on it and starts coughing while looking over my shoulder. "Oh shit."

I'm rubbing off on her. I look behind me as Justin saunters over. Fuck. I turn around and whisper, "If he says one fucking word, I'm gonna knock him out."

Through a scratchy voice, she says, "I'll handle this." Coughing to clear her throat, she then gulps water. "What are you doing here?"

"No, hi, Justin, how've you been?"

My heart starts pounding. Not only from the sound of his voice but also from what he said to Juni that became the last nail in his coffin. He's all smiles, eyeing her like the fucking asshole he is, but he's failed to notice me. When he finally moves to the side of us, his shit-eating grin is wiped clean off his face. "Mr. Christiansen . . ." His gaze volleys back and forth between us. "Oh. Um." But then his eyes bounce to the drinks in front of us to the way we're dressed. "You guys are dating."

I want to remind him that it's not against policy, but he knows. It would be different if it were him dating Juni than me. He knows that too. I ask, "Are you working?"

"Very funny. I'm dining with friends. I don't have to be a CEO to afford dinner at a nice restaurant." His gaze returns to Juni. She shifts, and I know she's struggling with what she can and can't say just like I am. "From the silence, I take it I'm right. But let me ask you, did you have the ability to say no to your boss?"

Fuck.

My eyes stay fixed on her even when he leans down to taunt her. I keep my anxious fists under the table.

Her body angles toward him, and she says, "You have it all wrong. I wouldn't take no for an answer."

Standing back, he laughs. "A woman who likes to take charge. I can respect that, but the clients still won't look kindly on Andrew fucking beneath his station." *The fuck did he just say?* I stand as he walks away looking like the conceited ass he is, my chair rocking back on two legs precariously. I will not let that bastard walk away like that.

"Drew," Juni says, her tone firm. When I meet her eyes, she shakes her head. "We're not doing anything wrong."

"It's not about me. It's about you and your name being dragged through the mud. I don't want that for you."

She holds her hand out for me. I look back at Justin weaving through the restaurant to a table for four near the windows. When I turn back, she hasn't moved, her arm still raised, her hand in offering. I take hold of it and sit down.

Both her hands cover mine, and she says, "There's no proverbial mud to drag me through. I'm not Page Six-worthy material. Me sleeping with you won't affect my job aspirations. But for you, it matters."

"You said it yourself. We've done nothing wrong."

"In fact, you've done everything right." We don't order the empanadas because we've lost our appetite. "I think we should start talking, tentatively, about potentially moving in together."

I forget all else the moment she says that. The woman who has a fear of commitment just tentatively, potentially committed to me. I'll take it. *It's not a no.*

Juni

I'm not sure what happened.

One minute, I was making plans with my boyfriend to

move in with him, and the next, we're treading even more carefully around the office.

Justin talked all right, to anyone who would listen. But thankfully, most people in the office either didn't really care or didn't let on. Although I got a few dirty stares. I don't know why other than Mary became an ally, hinting the haters were jealous. She also said she'd known for a while and stopped staying during the lunch hour after overhearing something unmentionable. She actually coughed, but I got her drift.

Needless to say, we put a pause on the lunchtime rendezvous. No need to add to the potential fire.

Andrew's family didn't like the unwanted attention, however. They prefer to be the ones in charge of the narrative. They're okay. Cookie even sent me a text that read: *check please* and had a laughing emoji.

At least she has a sense of humor about it. As for me, I can still feel the same mortification I felt at brunch when Tatum said sex with Andrew must be incredible. *By the way, I told her it was.*

His family's support has helped both of us feel calmer and more . . . settled.

The past seven days have been weird, though. It's the most time we've spent apart since we met. I've slept in his apartment some nights, wanting that sense of being with him, but the past two nights, I've been back in mine. I'm missing him more than I thought possible.

It's Friday, and I'm still waiting for him to text me about how the meeting went with three of CWM's wealthiest clients, tech giants who live in Seattle. From what I can gather, it's been tough going.

33

Drew

I HAVE TWO DAYS TO GET BACK AND PACK MY SHIT FOR Seattle.

My suitcase is loaded in the back as I slip inside the car. I shut the door and angle my legs in the dark back seat. "Hi," Nick says.

"Fuck, dude." I grab my heart. "You trying to give me a fucking heart attack?"

The car pulls away from passenger pickup to start the journey home. *Home?* I think that's the first time I said that and meant it. I'm pretty sure that has more to do with a certain blonde than the apartment.

He says, "Actually, no, I wasn't." By his cackling, he's enjoying that he scared the shit out of me a little too much. "There was no other way to prepare you."

"How about a text that says I'm waiting like a creeper in the back of your car so don't freak out, okay?"

"I guess, but what's the fun in that?"

"None. That's the point." I still shake his hand, and we bump our shoulders together.

He chuckles. "Glad to see you, brother."

Now that my heart has stopped racing, I say, "Good to see you. To what do I owe the pleasure?"

"I heard you only have a few days in New York before you have to get back to Seattle."

Resting my back in the corner of the Town Car, I stare out the window. "I leave on Sunday because Monday is already booked with back-to-back meetings." I pause, and add, "I hated being there when I lived there. This week wasn't any better."

"I swear Seattle is becoming punishment for the dirty deeds we did in another life."

His tone catches me off guard. I'm used to my brother being happy-go-lucky these days, so the negativity is unusual. "It feels that way." His shoulders are at his ears from the stress that's riding him. His face unshaven and suit wrinkling from a longer workday in appearance than it's just gone five o'clock.

Something's going on. "I know you, Nick. You wouldn't have come all the way out to the airport just to ride with me back to the city. What's going on?"

"I thought you should hear it from family."

Mentally bracing myself, I say, "What is it?"

He sinks back in the chair and runs a hand through his hair—a Christiansen tic. "The advisory board wants one of us to consider moving there permanently until the buyout is finalized with Beacon and off the ground running smoothly." *What the fuck?*

"I spent months getting the operations division up and running. It runs steadier than the tides. The holdup isn't on our end. As for the buyout, it's a done deal. Two years in the making." I remember where I am and lower my voice. "No one knew the attorney general would deny the original application. We thought it was done then, but local governments want to keep their money local. You worked on the contracts. We added the addendum to never move it out of city limits. We've jumped through hoops and bent over backward for this deal. Why do we have to live there to secure it? I thought that's what we just did." My frustration is getting the better of me. I just stepped off a five-hour flight, working nonstop. I'm tired, and I want to get home to Juni, to lose hours making love to make up for the time I've been gone, and then sleep until morning because I'm so exhausted.

"It gets better."

I roll my head to the side to face him. "That's never a good start."

"No, it's not. They want us there for an extended stay to manage the next quarter or three of our biggest clients have threatened to pull their money and move it to the competition."

"That's bullshit. They were happy at the end of the meeting."

"Guess they changed their minds."

I scrub my hands over my face. "Fuck me."

"I'm just the messenger, but I'm going to put it out there —New York is my home now. It's Natalie's home. We're thinking about starting a family soon. We have no intention of moving."

"At the risk of your job?"

"Yes." His answer is firm with no wiggle room left.

If he's willing to walk away from the company for his family, there's only one other option. As the CEO, I already knew whose shoulders this would fall on. Anyway, I have no choice. We need their money to turn a profit. That's how we get paid, so I can't afford to lose them.

I just worry about what Juni will say.

"It's my responsibility."

"I'm sorry. I hate putting this back on you." His words are filled with remorse. I don't want him to carry that load as well.

"No, I'm used to it and would do the same thing in your shoes."

"What about Juni?"

We just started talking about living together before I left. Now what happens to that plan? "That's a good question."

Walking through the doors of the apartment building, Pete says, "Welcome home, Mr. Christiansen."

"Thank you."

I don't go to my floor but head straight to hers, so ready to kiss her again and have the feel of her soft skin under my hands. Dragging my suitcase down the hall, I stop in front of her door, unsure what I'm going to say about Seattle.

I need to say something, but what do I say? Nothing is decided. It's a board recommendation. They've asked us to consider it. I roll my eyes. I'm attempting to spin the truth and make it only a possibility. *I can't let my family down. Their legacy.* And if I *have* to *move*, it would only be for a little while, wouldn't it?

Knock.

Knock.

Knock.

Looking down, I wait. The door is a stark reminder of everything she was doing to protect herself, even from me, within the past few weeks. Then I gave in to her notions, in to her and my weaker needs, and started to think about the future together.

The door opens, and I'm kissed so hard that my shoulder blades hit the wall opposite her apartment. I give in, needing this, her, and the hope we can come out on the other side together.

Dropping to her feet with her arms still wrapped around me, she practically hangs from me like a swing from a tree. All smiles, she asks, "When did you get home?"

Home?

There it is again, but this time, it feels right. It's not the building; it's her. "Three minutes ago. That's all it took to get from the front of the building to your joy, beautiful." That earns a smile. I hold her around the lower back and try to see the differences since I last saw her. Carefree in a loose sundress that hides all the good stuff.

She still has makeup from going into work. Then I'm reminded how she still works at CWM to stand my ground and save my reputation. She stayed despite giving me her resignation. Any investigation would reveal she enjoys working here and never felt pressured by me or any other staff, excluding Justin, of course.

I say, "Let's get inside."

She's quick to roll the suitcase right into her life with no questions asked. She'd have questions if she knew I was leaving. Am I lying by omission?

She asks, "Are you hungry? I was thinking homemade meatballs and red sauce."

"That sounds incredible."

Since we've been dating, the cooking concerts have moved to a more sociable hour. I never complain anymore and score with the food created.

While she cooks, I shower, hoping some of the guilt will wash down the drain. I feel a lot better clean and on a full stomach. "I'm so tired. I never adjusted from East Coast time."

"We might be able to save you just yet," she says, reveling because I used to say my heart was West Coast all the way. It's been a long time since I've felt that way—since last April.

I'm tempted to hold her, but when we climb under the covers, one kiss leads to another and two orgasms. I can willingly admit that I felt no shame a few minutes ago as I lay in recovery. But then it sneaks back in without my permission. I'm not going to get a night's reprieve to enjoy our relationship before it falls apart.

I'm a realist.

I know her tendencies, and although I started to believe in the big d-word—destiny—I was a fool for letting my guard down. "Babe?" I whisper so slight, hoping she's asleep so we can tackle this tomorrow.

"Yes?" she replies, sounding roused from sleep.

"What do you think about Seattle?"

She traces figure eights across my chest. "I've never been."

"Would you want to go?"

"Sure." Maybe there's hope. She goes on, "We could visit Pike's Place, the original Starbucks. We could be regular tourists when we're there."

"We can."

"Could," she corrects so innocently. She was always whip-smart, and that includes when we're post-coital and even more so with her senses still on high alert. Kicking her arm up under her, she looks down over me. "What are you thinking, Drew? A visit? A quick trip? Or—"

"Longer than a quick trip?"

"Are you asking me? If you're asking me, I vote no."

My swallow becomes a gulp, and her eyes redirect to my

throat. When her hazels return to me, she asks, "Is there something you want to tell me?"

I nod once, still holding her around the back, her skin so soft just like I remembered. "On the way over here, I was told a trip I thought was going to be no more than two months has been extended."

"Two months?" Her mouth hangs open as shock shapes her features into disbelief.

"That was before."

"How long now?"

"Indefinitely."

"Indefinitely sounds like a move. You're moving to Seattle?" Her daggered stare penetrates mine where all the apologies lay. She closes her eyes, and then when her lids fly open, she climbs out of bed. "This isn't a discussion I want to have in bed." Slipping on a robe, she leaves a huff of anger behind as she walks into the living room.

I slip my underwear and a shirt back on before following her. "I know this isn't what you want to hear—"

"Me? You mean you don't care?"

"I care. I care a great deal. I'm the one being forced to leave."

"As if being left behind makes this easier? Spoiler alert —it doesn't. I've been the last one standing, and it's never fun. My parents left me. My grandparents. Fucking Karl took all he could and then packed his bags to go. So I understand the tough position you're being put in, but I'm the one being abandoned."

"This is business, Juni. I'm not leaving you. I'm leaving this city. That's all."

She positions herself on the other side of the couch. "It may be business to you, but it's the same as *it's just the science we need to discover,* which is what my parents said every time before they left me, too. You were becoming my everything."

"Not *were*. You *are* everything to me." I deserve this, to hear every word though I already knew what she'd say and what she'd do before she did it.

"Not if you're halfway to Seattle already."

"That's not fair—"

"You know what's not fair?" she yells. "Talking about a future that was never going to happen. Why would you even talk about living together when you knew you were leaving? Did you think I would drop everything, my life here, and run to live life in your shadow?" Her volume decreases with every word spoken. Not because she's less angry, but more, and she's trying to control it. She's trying to control her emotions and tuck them safely back into her world, leaving me out in the cold.

I move closer, coming around the couch. Her arms are crossed, and that fire in her belly is blazing in her eyes. She doesn't move, holding her ground. "This isn't about hurting you."

"But you're doing it anyway." Her voice is eerily low.

"I'm not abandoning you, Juni. I won't stay forever. Seattle's not my home."

"Neither is New York. So if you're looking for the location closest to your heart, you're heading in the right direction." Her arms finally uncross, and when a breath releases, her body's resigned. "You always talked about LA, and I sat here and listened. I sat here hoping that maybe I was different. Maybe I was the one who would make you want to stay."

"I want to stay with you, but I—"

"I know. You can't. You go do what you need to do, and I hope you find happiness." Her tone's not cruel. It's conflicting because it's genuine. "But I think you should sleep at your place."

Standing there, I want to argue, but I think I'm out of opportunities to convince her of my true intentions. Her mind is set tonight. "You're probably right. We need sleep. We'll talk tomorrow after we both get some rest."

She moves to the door and opens it wide. I take the handle of my suitcase and walk into the hall. I turn to tell her good night, but she says, "Good night," and closes the door before I have a chance.

I stare at the door a few seconds longer, trying to process what just happened. It feels a lot like we just broke up. That can't be right. We're running off exhaustion and heated emotions. After a good night's rest, we'll be able to think clearly again.

ANOTHER CHANCE TO have this conversation in new light didn't come. I spent most of my day hanging out in her hallway. It wasn't until night came on Saturday that I found her on the rooftop with Rascal. I started for them but stopped when I heard her crying.

I don't want to sneak up on her or Rascal, but I'm not sure how to approach them. I stop overthinking because I've lost twenty-four hours because of that and start walking. "Juni?"

She looks over at me and says, "Unless you've changed your mind, Drew, there's nothing to talk about."

"You say that like I have a choice."

Swiping at her cheeks, she raises her chin. "We all have choices, and it sounds like you've made up your mind."

"You don't understand the position I've been put in. I've worked my whole life for—"

"I know. You've told me. The thing is, I thought you'd changed."

"Change what? My career? How I make money to survive? What exactly was I supposed to change? I like my job. I know that sounds foreign to your ears, but just because someone loves what they do for a living doesn't mean they're lost to the dark side."

It was then, at that moment of anger, that I realized I'd crossed a line with her.

There wasn't fire in her eyes or a swift tongue to smart back. Her body language wasn't resolute, but the opposite. That was the exact moment I lost her, and I knew it.

Sorry wasn't going to solve this.

Begging wouldn't keep her here or get her to Seattle.

The choice had been laid before me without her having to say a word.

I was stuck between my job and family on one side, and Juni and New York on the other. *Yet I feel utterly and bitterly alone.*

JUST AFTER SIX thirty Sunday morning, I wheel my suitcase through the lobby. Gil smiles at first, and then I see his true allegiance. I can respect him for that. Juni's like a daughter to him, and I understand all about family loyalty. After all, isn't that why I'm about to walk out this door? Although, this is more than just family loyalty. Hundreds of jobs are at risk if I don't fix this insane issue.

I go to the counter where he remains sitting. I guess that's his way of taking a stand against me. Setting the envelope down on the counter, I say, "I was planning to give these to you at next weekend's barbecue for your birthday."

"You should keep your gifts, Mr. Christiansen."

Christiansen. That tide turned. "I still want you to have it."

He takes the envelope and peeks inside. "I can't take this. It's an invitation to watch the game from the owner's suite."

"It's yours for you and a guest to enjoy the first home game of the season."

Standing, he stares at the tickets in his hand and then looks at me in amazement. "How did you score this?"

"I know a few guys, pulled a few strings. Take Nancy or Izzy—"

"I'll take Juni." Hearing her name has my heart ping in my chest, and then it tightens.

I keep my composure, like I always do. "Or Juni. Prepare her. They only set out a flower arrangement on the buffet. There won't be any other plants in the area."

He chuckles lightly. "I'll let her know before we go." Pocketing the envelope, he asks, "You're really leaving?"

I take a breath that leans on the shakier side. It's odd because I'm usually much steadier regarding my decisions. "It was only supposed to be temporary."

"One week can turn into more so easily. When I started working here twenty-seven years ago, I was filling in for a guy named Chuck. I covered his shift, and we never heard from him again. Sometimes, I still wonder what happened to Chuck."

Now he has me wondering about Chuck as well. And Juni, and if she'll ever forgive me. "I'm not selling the apartment just yet." When I walk to the door, it's still closed. I look back at Gil who remains at the desk, and shrugs.

"Sorry, Mr. Christiansen."

"I can respect that." I push through the door, and add, "Take care, Gil."

I was hoping the car would be here, or what's the point in scheduling a time? A familiar yap has my heart beating faster. I turn toward the sound, hoping to find Juni there. I don't.

Rascal tugs at the leash until it's ripped from Mr. Clark's hand. I kneel to catch the wild papillon. "What are you doing, boy? You know better than to make a run for it, you little troublemaker."

"Hold on to that rascal for me."

"He's safe. No worries," I reply.

Mr. Clark finally arrives just under the awning. "I used to be faster, believe it or not."

Chuckling, I say, "I believe it." It's funny how I've never seen him walking the dog, only Juni until now.

"I recognize you. You're Juni's beau."

I've never thought of myself that way before but hearing him say it, it feels good to wear that title. "I am," I say, not sure if I have a right to the moniker anymore.

"Mrs. Hendricks said you were getting married soon."

News to me. I chuckle, but there's an ache in my chest that overcomes it. "No, we don't have plans."

"Why do young people wait so long to start their lives these days?"

I set Rascal down, holding on to the leash's handle. Mr. Clark doesn't seem to be in a hurry to take it from me. "I've been focused on my career."

"Pfft. I did that once. It got me shot down over open waters. Fortunately, a Navy ship picked me up. We lost the fighter plane, but they saved my life."

"Sounds like you were fortunate to survive."

He walks away. I'm not sure what he's doing, if he has

dementia, or if I should follow him. Sitting on a bench farther down the block, I look down the street to see if my car is coming and then wheel my suitcase and walk Rascal down to join him. As soon as I sit down, he says, "I was surviving only to return to my darling, Anne."

"Was that your wife?"

"No, she was the girl I'd left back home. Though she tried to get me to marry her before I was sent off. I was a dumb son-of-a-bitch for not jumping at the chance. I wanted to become a war hero, make her proud first, to honor my parents." He shakes his head with what I imagine is the same annoyance he felt then.

"What happened when you returned home?"

"I went to get the girl. I marched straight into that church and was given the sign I needed."

"What was it?"

"The minister asked if anyone had any objections. I marched down that aisle and said, I do. I objected to living the rest of my life without the prettiest girl in that church."

Holy shit. Mr. Clark was a wild man. Watching Rascal chase a bug on the ground, I note the apple doesn't fall far from the tree. "She was getting married?"

He laughs, seeming to relive the memory in his head. "No, but her cousin was. I didn't care. She didn't either. We got married right then and there. Her family disowned me for ruining the wedding." He waves it off. "They eventually came around in time to meet our first son." He looks me right in the eyes, and adds, "The point is, stop wasting your damn life on things that aren't worth retelling, or waiting for the perfect moment, and stop beating around the bush. If you love her, tell her. If you want to marry her, ask her. I promise the only regret you'll have is the time you wasted without her."

There are so many wise words tucked inside that advice.

The car pulls to the curb, and I stand. Handing the leash over to him, I bend down and pet Rascal one more time. I take the suitcase, and say, "That's a good story."

"It's not about collecting stories. It's about making memories worth sharing one day."

"Wise words." I start for the car but stop to say, "Thanks for sharing."

"Take care, Drew."

I stop to look back. Juni's the only one who calls me that, making me realize she's been talking to him about us. Maybe that story was told to me specifically, or maybe he's just good at reading people.

Either way, it makes me glad she's not completely alone. She not only has her makeshift family, but they're one hundred percent supportive of her. For a while, I felt like I was part of that family. A part of the group who wants to see Juni happy. Thriving. Finding her dreams.

I want to be the one who gets to come home to her.

As the plane takes off for Seattle, I lean my seat back and ponder Mr. Clark's words. "The point is, stop wasting your damn life on things that aren't worth retelling, or waiting for the perfect moment, and stop beating around the bush." Isn't that what Juni said to me about moving in together? Not to beat around the bush? *"I promise the only regret you'll have is the time you wasted without her."* But Juni has dreams and plans, as do I.

Seattle isn't forever. Fixing this problem with Beacon isn't forever. It's another hurdle, another work-related but salvageable problem. But that's not what Juni is. Perhaps she's my story. No, I want her *to be* my story. How do I make that happen, though?

How do I make sure *I* have stories worth telling?

34

Juni

His office has been empty for the past week.

I successfully avoided it until this morning when I had to put a letter on his desk. The sad little ivy on the corner of his console caught my eye, and even though I was ready to hightail it out of there, I returned to check on it. When I rubbed a leaf between my fingers, my heart ached. Not for the plant, though that did as well until I touched the dirt and found it still had some moisture. No, it was this office, the belongings, the smell. The man. I closed my eyes, and his scent, like his aura, filled the room.

Although there was a brief debate about leaving the plant alone since it had a corner office full of natural sunlight, I knew I needed to take care of it. I retrieved my watering can and let it drink up. Like me, it doesn't take much to make it happy.

Though lately, I haven't felt like myself. I stood in the middle of Drew—*Andrew's* office and let the memories wash over me. I didn't know then, but I think I fell for him the night I saw him drunk. He was just so cute and at ease in his own skin. Charming and a little goofy. It took a few whiskeys to get him to loosen up. That changed when he was with me. It took catching him off guard. Shrugging even though no one can see me, I try to justify it to myself.

There wasn't a smirk, but a smile that came from seeing me. He'd probably fib and tell people he doesn't remember that night. But I do. It's when I decided I'd judged him all wrong. I mean, sure, I totally nailed his personality, but I didn't expect to see the change in him. My affection only bloomed after that.

Where did that leave me?

In his office with him gone, now nursing the plant he left behind. Another thing I seem to have in common with the ivy.

I decide this is the best place for it to live and grow. Maybe visiting and watering it in here, being present in this space without Drew, will do the same for me.

When I walk out, Mary glances up from her desk. She says nothing and doesn't ask anything of me. She just lets me return to my desk in peace.

She's a good person, and he's lucky to have her. Even though her duties have lightened due to him having an assistant in Seattle, she keeps busy but not so stuck to her desk. I've seen more of her lately—in the break room or passing through reception at lunch—and sometimes, when I work late to organize the different stations around the office, she checks on me before she leaves.

She pops into reception around two, and asks, "Want to grab a coffee downstairs?"

Pointing at the headset on my head, I reply, "I'm not sure I can leave."

Laurie comes in behind her and punches the elevator

button. "Ready to go?" She's looking at me. This is different and exciting to leave the office. "Send it to the service," she adds. "We'll only be gone fifteen minutes."

Remembering my calculations from before, fifteen is usually forty-five, but who's counting. I've been invited to join the cool kids for coffee. I grab my purse and send the calls to the answering service. "Ready."

We score an elevator ride by ourselves. Only a few seconds tick by before I'm rethinking my decision to come along. Mary asks, "How are you doing, Juni?"

"I'm good. *I'm fine.*"

She laughs with a kind smile. "Andrew always says that."

I hate that my own smile falls from the mere mention of him, but my heart currently feels a little battered. "It's cliché."

Laurie nods, not like she's judging my word choice, but more sympathetic to my plight. What that plight is exactly, I'm not sure. In the softest voice, she says, "It's not against company policy."

And this *was clearly an opportunity taken advantage of.* Why did I choose to stand in the middle of them?

I eye the open doors button wondering how far I'd be willing to plummet to avoid this conversation. The elevator is on ten. That's death level. I'm probably wanting more broken leg or mild concussion outcomes from the second or third floors. "You don't have to whisper," I say, not whispering at all. "It was a terribly kept secret. Everyone knew—"

"I didn't," replies Laurie. "I actually don't think many people did know until that weasel Justin tried to get fifteen minutes of fame by leaking it to the press."

Deciding it's best if I don't try to escape, I'm resolved to the fact that I'm currently the hot story for office gossip. I've been down this road before with my parents. It will pass in time when something else more exciting or tragic happens.

The doors open, and we stand in a line that weaves a fair distance through the lobby. That means more time to talk about me and Drew. Yay! *Not . . .*

Rocking back on my heels, I point out the art I'd never seen in the lobby before. I'm usually rushing to get to the car. I miss the car rides with him. We gave up dropping me off, and now I just ran like the wind and ducked in the back. Pent-up sexual tension soon fogged the windows, and steamy make-out sessions behind the privacy glass became a regular thing.

I can afford a private car to drive me places, but it wasn't the car that was fun. It was the man.

The man.

The man.

. . . The man.

I'm not sure what's coming over me. I haven't cried once this week. There's pride found in controlling your emotions. But my heart starts racing, and my eyes are burning. "I have to get him out of my system."

Mary gives my hand a squeeze. "It's only been a week."

"A week of hell." My hand trembles, and I squeeze my eyes closed.

Breathe in. Breathe out.

Breathe in. Breathe out.

Oh no, not here. "I need to go." I rush back to the bank of elevators and hop on one that was just about to close.

As soon as I'm deposited back in CWM, I rush to the office, the one I won't name. I open the door and am hit with his scent again. Pain sinks as I go to get the ivy. I'm not leaving it here any longer.

I only make it to the doorway before I see Mary staring

at me. I take control of my emotions again, cuddle the plant to my stomach, and raise my chin. "I'm taking it with me."

She nods.

And just when I'm about to pass her desk, she says, "If you ever need anyone to talk to, it will stay between us."

My lip wobbles, but I nod, taking my broken heart and the plant to my desk.

I finally found the perfect spot for the ivy on the table in the waiting area. At least until I take it home later. "Hi, Juni, how's it going?" Nick asks.

Gesturing to the microphone on the headset I'm wearing, I mouth, "Sorry. Got a call."

Leaning over the counter, he points at the phone on the desk. "No lights."

"Dammit."

He rests his arms on the counter like he's going to stay a while. "Nice try. Are you avoiding me?"

Am I avoiding him and every other human with the last name of Christiansen? It's probably a safe bet, but he's still one of the company owners, which makes it hard to figure out how to play this hand. Mental gymnastics are rough when your heart is yelling louder. "Honestly?"

"Honestly."

"Yes."

He smiles, earning the Christiansen name. I blame Cookie for her sons' good looks. Of course, I haven't met Corbin yet. *Yet?* Probably never. *Definitely never.* "I want to make sure you're okay."

"I'm good. I'm fine."

He's staring at me, and when I realize why, I snap, "Drew doesn't own that phrase. Anyone can use it."

Maybe it's my bite on the last comment, but he takes a step back. "Absolutely, use away." He taps the counter, and I think it's the first time I've seen him nervous. "He didn't go willingly."

"He still went." I stand, disconnecting my headset, ready to finish my coffee in the break room.

"One of us had to. Natalie's job is here—"

"I appreciate the effort, Nick, but there was no compromise or talk of a long-distance relationship." I swallow hard, the pain of him leaving me still stuck in my throat. "He told me what he was doing, and then he left."

"I heard a different version. I'm not here to defend my brother, but—"

"But you're here to defend him?"

"Pretty much. He likes you, Juni, and I know he can be a real grumpy asshole. But you know he's all heart on the inside. He'd do anything for his family and friends. I know he'd do anything he can if you asked him."

"Except stay."

Straightening upright, he looks down with a laugh, but it lacks its usual joyous sound. "I know you're hurt and mad, but I'm asking you to hold off judgment until you two can talk things through."

I'm getting it from all sides today, it seems. "We're not communicating at all. That's how breakups work."

"That's too bad."

"It is, but that's reality."

Shifting toward the door, he says, "Interesting. Andrew was always the realist. I pegged you for more the dreamer."

"As fun as this banter is, you've delivered your message, and I need to get back to work."

He chuckles. "You sound like my brother."

"Apparently, we have more in common than we realized."

"You do, *did*." He stumbles through the right word to

choose. "I'm just gonna go before I screw this up even more." He leaves.

And I don't know why I do it, but I hop up and run to the door. "Nick?"

Turning back, he looks at me. I say, "Thank you," and receive just a nod, but it's enough.

The last few hours of work are uneventful. Thank goodness. And when it's time to go, I take the ivy with me and ride the subway.

If I were wearing my Louboutins, like I did for Drew, I wouldn't dare take the subway, but my flats are fine on a train. I haven't worn my heels all week. Originally, Mr. Fancypants inspired me to step up my work attire. When I saw how he reacted, I thought it would be fun to tease him. Looking down, I stare at the ivy in my hands, stroking the leaves and keeping it protected from others. "It's okay. I'll take care of you now."

When I reach my block, the door is opened before I reach the awning. It's Mike's night. He's fine, but he's no Gil.

I could really use a strawberry donut right now . . . *and some of Gil's great advice.* If I texted or called him, he'd be here, but it's his day off, and I need to give him a break. I'll just have to wait to see him tomorrow.

Comfy clothes are my sole mission as I hurry upstairs. I shouldn't, but just to torture myself a little more, I pull on a pair of his sweatpants, tightening the strings at the waist so they don't hang low on my hips, and tug my NYU sweatshirt over my head.

Twisting my hair into a knot on my head, I pad back into the kitchen to see what I can find to eat. It's not from lack of food, though. I started the week fully stocked. But for the fifth night in a row, I look in my pantry and fridge, and nothing inspires me. I don't know what happened, but I've lost my motivation. *Did Drew take my joy of cooking with him too?*

I check my phone, a bad habit I've picked up, but there's nothing new. *No messages. No calls.* So I set it back down on the counter. It's been hard not to text Drew when we used to have so much contact, to tell him about my day, to spend the night in bed together.

I'm still so confused. There were no other offers. Every decision he made was based on the business. What about me? I thought we were closer since we had just talked about moving in together. What a mistake that would have been. *Bullet dodged.*

Why wouldn't he even offer to split his time between the two cities? Am I supposed to pack my bags and leave indefinitely? *I would have. If he'd asked again.*

Although, for me to leave, I'd need to find a replacement, and that's not that easy. I could have contacted the temp agency to help find the proper fit.

I have a good reputation with them, and companies request me on a regular basis. CWM has put me out of commission for a minimum of eight weeks, and it sounds like Melissa was taking the extra two Drew gave her.

If there had been an offer from him to travel along, would I now be seen as a flake? It doesn't matter. If he would have asked me to go with him, I would have found a replacement. If he'd wanted me by his side, maybe there could have been a temp job in the Seattle office. Doesn't matter if I was working or not. I would have gone. I hate that I wasn't a thought—personally or professionally. I hate that I didn't get the choice at all.

But did Drew? *As CEO?*

My grandmother told me never to drink to comfort your emotions. I pour a glass of wine anyway. I'm angry, sad, frustrated . . . *lonely.* I drink half of it fairly fast and then pull up Drew's text chat.

A few sips more and the tears begin to fall. Seeing the photos we took and the memes we shared, the inside jokes we had, and the flirtations exchanged. Every emotion I restrained for the past week surfaces all at once.

It doesn't matter what I feel. It all comes back to him and the choice he made.

Am I looking at this all wrong? Did he leave because he didn't have a choice? Logically, that makes sense. He runs the company, and that branch needed his attention. But that doesn't help my heart. I trusted Drew and let him in to my tightly controlled world, proving Gil was wrong. It wasn't good to open my heart. It fucking hurts.

Why didn't Drew just leave me alone?

With wine clouding my rational thoughts, I get angry, remembering it was me pushing to be friends. Friends. *Fucking friends.* Nothing more has ever worked out for me, and I just proved it again. But the anger doesn't fill the hole in my chest.

Only he can.

Looking at the screen again, I type: *I miss you.*

But I don't send it. I'm confused. Why'd I type that? The lights are dim in here. Maybe I'm seeing it wrong. I click on the lamp, and yep, I typed that. Thank God I didn't send because Drew hurt me, and even worse, he continues to. I reach to delete, not willing to give Andrew Christiansen the satisfaction that I contacted him first.

I'm about to delete, but when I'm startled by a knock on the door, I accidentally hit send. "Oh my God. Oh my God. Oh my God."

What have I done?

35

Drew

DID SHE JUST BEAT ME TO THE PUNCH?

Don't get me wrong. Juni did what I couldn't. I give her full credit for that. I had a lame 'can we talk' sitting in our text box for three days and didn't have the balls to send.

After staring at her message for hours, I still don't know how to reply. Am I missing something? Well, other than her. I've tried to read between the lines, but it might just be that she misses me.

It's a big leap from not talking to me to missing me, but she was brave enough to take it. I text: *I miss you, too.*

And then send before I can second-guess my decision. It's gone. Sent. It's the truth, and that's what we need to share right now. I've been more miserable than the weather. Whiskey's become my friend in this pocket of the Pacific Northwest. It does what she used to do—keep me warm and my mind off how unhappy I am.

Juni was softer, sexy as all fuck without even trying. She made me laugh and threw me mental curveballs. Whiskey fails to do that pretty much on all levels. I'm thinking drinking my troubles away doesn't suit my type A personality.

It's not my friend. It's happy to remind me of all my failings. *How pathetic, Christiansen.* I get up and empty the glass I just filled.

Liquor won't help me get over the woman I lost . . . not lost. I didn't lose Juni. She was right there in my arms and in my bed, at my work, and filling my head with destiny. No, I didn't lose her. I put her second to my work.

Work—something a person has to do. *Has to do.*

Juni—*what I want to do.* Okay, besides having great sex, I want to spend time with her. It wasn't about entertaining me or stepping out of the box anymore. It was about her.

My day.

My night.

My life.

My world had begun to revolve around her sun.

Even now, I feel lighter just thinking about her, so why the fuck am I texting her when I should be calling. I grab my phone and do just that.

The worst thing I did was to put space, time, and distance between the woman who made me realize I deserve to be happy and me. Cliché as that might sound, it's true.

The company will not fold, the clients' business may or may not be salvaged, but CWM will stay strong. *And so will I.*

I run my hand over the top of styled hair, a quick check to make sure every strand is in place. It's a bad habit. She can't even see me, so I hold the phone to my ear.

Ring.

Ring. *Why am I getting nervous?*

Ring. *Come on.*

Ring. *Please answer. Please answer.*

Ring. *My chest begins to deflate.*

Ring. "You have reached my voicemail. Leave a message and have a great day!"

If a voice matched her beauty, that was it—sunshine and a pretty melody. My Juni.

Mine.

I pull up my chat box again and read the message two times over. My stomach is full from my heart sinking to the bottom of it, and for the first time in years, I have no fucking clue what to do.

Yes, I do. *I know.* I pick up my phone again and call the one other person who can help me through this. The call is answered on the second ring. "Andrew?"

"Hi, Mom."

"Hey there. I'm surprised, pleasantly, to hear from you."

"I just wanted to hear your voice, talk to you about this miserable weather, or whatever else."

"You don't sound like your usual self. What's going on?"

"I've been thinking about you, Dad, and Nick and Natalie." I don't care about my hair. I shuffle my fingers over it until bangs hang down. "I never saw myself getting married."

"Not everyone does. Not everyone feels that need. Some people prefer to live alone, and some have partners. The beauty of life is that you get to decide how to live it. Do you remember what I used to say to you boys when you hit your teens and were driving?"

For as laid-back as Cookie is now, she worried a lot back then. "Don't do anything illegal, be kind to others and yourself, and—"

"Live the best life you can. Are you living your best life, Andrew?"

My fear of failing grips me, and I hold my tongue. Truth and honesty are the pillars of my friendship with Juni and the words that give me strength right now. My mom only wants the best for me, even at the expense of the company. "No."

Her sadness comes through in a sigh. "How can you change that?"

"I don't want to let you guys down."

"You never have. Your happiness isn't a disappointment to us. Being miserable because you think you have to sacrifice that happiness is. We never wanted one or the other. As parents, we all fumble the ball now and again, but we still want to help you reach the end zone, whether that's carrying the ball or the team. It's all a win if you're happy." It's funny when my mom throws the random sports analogy into our conversations. She never grew to love the games, but as long as we were having fun, she loved watching us play.

She adds, "You've carried the team for a long time now, even before your dad retired. How about you let someone else run the plays for a while?"

"How so?"

"Leave Seattle, Andrew. Get out of there and go where your heart is happy. You always said it was LA, but I think that might have changed."

"I never thought I'd like New York . . ." I leave that there to lie between us.

"You sure it's the city you're liking?" I knew she'd pick it up and run with it. And maybe I wanted her to. "I don't know what it is with that city, and the women making the Christiansen men give it all up for them, but your heart knows its way home."

That's a big statement coming from her. My mom always wanted us near, even setting us up to always have a place to come back to—Nick got the beach bungalow when he got married, and the Beverly Hills home, the place where I grew up and where they live now, is in the will for me.

But she's right about cities, and women, and the place we call home. She knows if I get on a flight tonight, I'm going to the East Coast.

"Mom, I have another confession."

"Do I need to sit down?"

"I think you'll be okay. You know your list? I didn't complete it."

Gentle laughter reaches my ears. "Oh honey, that list isn't mine. It's yours. Whether you complete it or not is up to you. What I wanted the most was for you to open your eyes to more possibilities around you. Maybe you only needed to mark off the items that were most important for your life to change trajectory."

Two for two. Juni was a part of both of them. *Juni's entry into my life* has *done exactly that.* I just made a wrong turn. It doesn't mean I can't turn that back around, though.

It wasn't just Rascal who knocked the breath out of me when he landed on my stomach; Juni stole it altogether.

Lying next to me after making sure everyone was back in their apartments safely after the fire. Sitting with Mrs. Hendricks telling me that Juni needs to spread her wings. They didn't know, but she'd been doing that all along with me. From our friendship to a budding romance, she didn't crack the door. She flung it wide open and invited me into her world.

I won't discount that she took the job and made it look easy. She committed herself in so many ways that she doesn't even see it. Is she living on the edge? No, but for someone who's experienced so much pain, she still took the first steps and raised her wings.

"Mom?"

"Yes?" she replies, leading me to give more.

Pushing off the bed, I say, "I need to go."

"Oh, okay."

I grab my suitcase and open it on the bed. "No, I mean, I need to get to the airport."

"Ah. Yes. I think you do. Have a safe trip, and I hope you find what you're looking for."

"I already have if it's not too late."

"It's never too late to make amends. Love you."

"Love you, too, Mom." I toss the phone on the bed and open the wardrobe to grab my suits to pack. But then stop and look at them. They're suits. I'm not going on a business trip. I'm going to get a life back. *Everything I need is already in New York City.*

When I was a kid working in this company's mailroom, I remember a quote that hung above the door. Setbacks don't determine your fate. If you overcome them does.

I always thought it would make more sense if it said *how* you overcome them does.

But now I get it. Some people will hit an obstacle, and that's where their story ends. Others won't let anything stand in their way.

"I'm sorry, sir. There are no available seats on any flights to JFK or LaGuardia tonight. Not in coach, business, or first class. And the standby list is ten people long. We can usually only accommodate three or four. I'm happy to book you on the first available flight in the morning." Her eyes lower to the screen, and her fingers furiously tap on the keyboard. "I have first class on a six fifteen flight to JFK?"

Setting my card down, I say, "I'll take it." *Fuck. I need to get to New York. I need to get to her. I need . . .* Maybe I need this time.

I stop and think. Why couldn't I get the flight *I* wanted?

Maybe it's time I need right now.

I spend that time putting a new plan in place and attaching an ultimatum of my own. At three forty-seven in the morning, I push send to the advisory board, my parents, and Nick.

At three forty-nine, my phone rings. I know who it is before I see the name on the screen. Makes sense because he's three hours ahead. "Hello?"

"Brav-fucking-o, brother. That's the kind of message I like to wake up to."

I pack my laptop in my travel bag. "So you approve?"

"Not of you quitting. Of your list of demands, that was a CEO talking there. Either way this pans out, you win. I'm proud of you for taking a stand."

Even I, with the confidence of an elementary school science fair champion, still like to get my family's approval. "Thanks. How do you think Dad will react?"

"I think he'll be proud you finally figured your shit out." Nick gets up early to work out like I do, so it doesn't surprise me that he sounds wide-awake. "Upside, the plan from what I'm seeing right now is solid. If the account managers can't do their job and keep their clients happy, then you can take the larger portfolios. But you can do that from anywhere and just fly in a couple of times a year."

"That's why it's there. There's no need for me to sit in an office to placate a few clients." I'm proud of the proposal I put together. This had been on my mind all week, but traveling here had its benefits. Seeing where I'm best utilized cemented the direction I need to steer the company. I won't kowtow to a few clients on their whims. I have a record of success to back why I decide how to run this company, and it's time I take that power back.

I continue, "The bottom line is, this is not personal. It's business. If they want the best, I'll work with them directly. If they want to leave, that's their choice. But I have a say in my fate moving forward."

"I agree. I'll work on updating the client contracts for them and put you as the lead. It will be ready to sign on tomorrow."

"Thanks, Nick." Sinking down on the couch, I ask, "Have I told you recently that I think you're doing a good job?"

"You never tell me that."

"Probably best," I say. "It's good to see you motivated to please the boss." Laughter bellows from his gut he's laughing so hard. "Hey, you're doing a good job."

"Thanks. You're not so bad yourself."

"On a personal note, what do you think about Juni?"

"What I think doesn't matter, but if you're asking if I approve, she's a great girl and way out of your league."

I chuckle. "I know, but maybe she'll take pity on me."

"For you, I hope she does. I hear you're flying in. Want me to pick you up at the airport again?" His laughter builds. "I'm giving you warning that I'll be in the car."

"I think I'm good."

"I know, *you're fine.*"

"Actually, I'm great."

In fact, it's as if the stars aligned tonight. *And I finally saw them with clarity.*

36

Drew

"Morning, Mr. Christiansen. It's good to see you again."

"You too, Pete. It's good to be home." I'm not surprised to see Pete since it's the day shift, but I was hoping to run into Gil for some advice. After all, he knows Juni best.

I drag my suitcase into the elevator. Tired and running on autopilot, I reach for the button for the seventeenth floor but stop myself. I'm on a mission, so I punch sixteen instead.

My knuckles hurt from knocking on her door for so long. I don't know if she's purposely not answering or if she's not home, but I'm too anxious to sit here and wait for who knows how long. Looking down the hall, I haven't heard the little yappy dog, but I do get an idea. I drag my suitcase and knock on Mr. Clark's door.

When he doesn't answer either, I head upstairs to drop off my luggage and then catch the elevator back to the lobby. "Pete, why's it so quiet on a Sunday. I've ridden the elevator three times, and it never made another stop. Maybe it's my lucky day?" I'd like to think so, but I can't confirm until I speak with Juni.

"A lot of the residents and Gil are at the funeral."

I rush to the desk. "What funeral? Whose?"

"Mr. Clark. He passed away last week. He was walking Rascal down at the park and had a heart attack on his way back, just outside the building. Gil saw it all and tried to help, but . . ." His gaze lowers as he shakes his head. "Man," he starts again, his eyes watering. "I know he was old, but I don't know. You get used to having people around. Know what I mean?"

Juni. "I know what you mean. That's too bad about Mr. Clark. I didn't know him well, only met him once, but I know he had a lot of close friends in the building." Shit. Juni was close to him. She loved that old man. And given his comments about Juni, he'd adored her, too. Another person in her life who left her. His words have bounced around my brain the whole time I've been away.

"Stop wasting your damn life on things that aren't worth retelling, or waiting for the perfect moment . . . If you love her, tell her. I promise the only regret you'll have is the time you wasted without her."

Did destiny plant him in my life at just the right moment, too? And I'd still missed the point? *But not the pun about destiny and the plant. Seriously, Christiansen, your humor is so whack sometimes.*

I need to be with Juni. I need her to know that I'm not leaving her—abandoning her.

It's time to start writing a story worth telling. Our story.

"What time is the funeral?"

Checking his watch, he replies, "Starts in fifteen minutes."

I look at the door as if that can help me. "Where is it?"

"If you'd like to attend, here's a flyer Juni put together—" I snatch it from his hands.

"Thanks, Pete."

"Give my condolences."

I push through the door and run to the curb to flag down a taxi. As soon as one pulls over, I hop in the back, and say, "To this address. Hurry."

I'm a fucking asshole for not checking in on Juni this past week. I thought I read the sign for time correctly, but maybe following destiny is harder than I thought. Or maybe she's in a bad mood because we hit every red light in the city and an accident involving a honey truck that tipped over.

The cabbie looks at me in the rearview mirror, and asks, "You from around here?"

"No."

He hands the flyer back and rests his elbow over the chair when he looks back. "This funeral home is two blocks north of here and three blocks straight down. You'll get there faster if you walk it than sitting here letting the meter run. This honey truck isn't going anywhere soon. And the bees are coming."

I can walk. *Fuck, I'll run it.* If that means getting to Juni, being there for her, I'll do it. He turns on the windshield wipers when I take the flyer back and toss a bill to cover the fare. "Keep it."

Swatting a few bees out of the way, I start running, now wondering if bees are a sign of something. All this New Age destiny stuff is fucking with my head.

I'm a runner, dammit. I'm not usually running in jeans, fitted jeans at that. Not only is the denim rubbing me wrong in my crotch but it's also fucking hot today. I reach the funeral home, stopping on the steps out front to catch my breath. Wiping the sweat with the hem of my shirt, I try to

clean up out of respect. There was no time to change
clothes, so a white T-shirt and sneakers it is.

I march up the steps and open the doors. Gil turns to
offer a program, but when he sees me, he says, "Andrew,
you're back in town?"

Keeping my voice low like his, I reply, "Just got in and
heard the news from Pete. I'm sorry for your loss."

"He's been a resident in the building since before I
started working there. Nice man."

"How's Juni doing?"

He lifts up to see if he can spot her. Maybe that's all the
answer I need—to see her again. "She's sitting alone in the
first row if you'd like to see her."

"Thanks." As much as I would like to get advice on a few
things, now is not the time. I can't think about me, or us,
when I know she's devastated.

I don't get far before he catches me. "You know, Andrew,
she hasn't opened up about what's going on or what
happened, which is unlike her. But you know what that
tells me?"

"What?"

"She cares about you. A lot."

"I care about her more than a lot."

He grins, and maybe that's allowed at the funeral for a
man who lived a long and good life. I'm sure Mr. Clark is
already in heaven causing a scene and kissing his wife.

Gil whispers as the service begins. "Commitment has
always been a thing since her parents died. They were too
good at what they did, loved it, but obsessed. Even they
couldn't control their fate. But Juni somehow got it twisted
in her head that if she took herself out of the running, she'd
never be hurt again. I'm not telling you what to do, but when
pushed, she runs the other way. So, if you're thinking about

trying to get back into her life, you get one shot. Make it count."

I shake his hand. "Thanks, Gil."

He tugs me in and whispers, "Hurt her again, and you'd better stay in California."

Leaning back slowly, I see the warning in his eyes to back his words. I nod, surprised to see this side of him. I'm equally happy Juni has him. "I won't."

I don't join Juni on the front row, deciding at the last minute it was best to let her have this time to grieve. I also don't want to disrespect Mr. Clark's family and friends. *The one time I'm not Mr. Suit . . .*

After a long line of speakers wanting to share poignant stories of how Mr. Clark affected them or changed their life for the better, Gil grips the side of the podium and leads us in a moment of silence. Then he says, "There's someone else who would like to say a few words. Mr. Christiansen?" He steps aside, signaling me to come up.

"What?" I'm shaking my head. I barely knew Mr. Clark. If not for that last conversation before I left for Seattle, I wouldn't know him at all.

Out of the sea of people, Juni's head rises above all. Her eyes penetrate mine as her eyebrows knit together. "What are you doing?" She doesn't even mouth it but says it for everyone to hear.

While I panic sweat in this pew, Gil grabs the microphone again and says, "Now is your chance to say how you feel, Andrew."

Why's he doing this? He's the one who told me to—*shit*—make it count. I thought he meant for me to decide when that would be, not to be forced into it.

With everyone staring at me, I stand and walk slowly up the aisle. When Rascal sees me, he yaps and springs from his blanket in front of the casket to run to me. Tail wagging, tongue hanging out the side, and freshly washed by how his fluffy fur makes him look round.

I bend down and catch the little fellow. This time, I don't mind his slobber all over my chin. At least someone missed me.

Juni is seated again, and when I pass, I hand Rascal over as a peace offering. She takes him and holds him to her chest. He barks once more, but she's able to quieten him down as I step behind the podium. Looking at this packed house, I look down to try to gather my thoughts. Remembering what Mr. Clark told me, I step forward.

Here goes everything.

"Hi, I'm An—I'm Drew," I say, raising my hand. "I, uh, apologize for my lack of suit. Just came from the airport. Thought I'd say a few words off the cuff, if you don't mind." I hear a "go on" and "the floor is yours" from audience members. "I didn't know Mr. Clark well. We lived in the same building, one floor apart. But I knew Rascal, and I had the honor of hearing a story of his a few weeks back. One about his wife." People start shifting in their seats, looking bored. I clear my throat and grip the sides of the podium for support. "I'll never forget that conversation because although it was brief, it was memorable. He said that life is not just about collecting stories but about making memories worth sharing one day. Since that conversation, I've realized that with my current life trajectory, I won't have a story worth telling to my grandkids other than I went to work and came home. That's not living. That's not worth telling anyone."

I look right at Juni and make it count. "Juni, you woke me up from the sleep I'd been in. We haven't known each other long in the scheme of a lifetime, but I like creating stories, memories with you better than working seventy, eighty hours a week. I like when you wear your hair on top of your head, and it's a mess. I like the hard time you give me when I give too much of myself to the company. The green of your eyes first thing in the morning and the pink of your cheeks after we make love match the leaves of the rose Calathea."

She'd been steady in her expression, keeping it neutral until now. That pink I mentioned colors the apples of her cheeks, and the lines from sadness soften. Her gaze had stretched into the distance, but now her eyes are set on me.

I continue, "Mr. Clark was a wild man from what it sounds like, but it worked for him. I'm not sure I could get away with the same, but I think he's leaving a good motto to follow. He also said to stop wasting your damn life on things that aren't worth retelling. Don't wait for the perfect moment and stop beating around the bush. Solid advice for everyday life. Ah, a rhyme," I add, feeling the heat of embarrassment sink its claws in me.

This time when I look at Juni, she holds three fingers in front of her chest. With a proud nod, a full smile appears. I don't know why she's proud or why she's smiling, but it gives me hope that I'm doing something right, so I keep rambling. "I'm not sure how Mr. Clark knew the right thing to say the day we met, but this stuck with me the most. He said, if you love her, tell her. I promise the only regret you'll have is the time you wasted without her. Fuck, that's good stuff." Giggles ripple across the crowd. "Oh, sorry. Anyway," I start again, one of Juni's favorite words rolling off my tongue as if it's one of mine as well. Looking at her with tears in her eyes, the light that shined in them that first day I met her has returned. "I love you so much, Juni. I don't want to create stories with anyone else but you."

Feeling invincible, I push off the podium and walk to her pew. "May I?" She nods, so I sit beside her, perhaps taking my first real breath in a week. I don't say anything. There's not much left other than a few important details to work through privately. But when she reaches over and slides her hand in mine, I know I'll get that chance.

You'd think I was a superhero with all the back pats and congrats I was getting outside on the sidewalk. The mourners have gone, and Gil's been helping Juni wrap up after the minister spoke. He comes trotting down the steps and says, "Mr. Clark would have approved."

"What about you?" Gil's a father figure to Juni. His opinion matters to me.

He replies, "Way to make it count. I'll see you two tomorrow. I have a date at home."

"You didn't have to wait."

I turn to see Juni, dressed in a black dress, standing on the top step. Rascal sits at her side on his leash.

Shoving my hands in my pockets, I say, "I don't mind waiting for you." I don't think the double meaning is lost on either of us. A gentle smile works its way onto her face as she comes down the steps.

She stops on the last one, closer to eye level with me but not quite. "He left Rascal to me."

I look down at the dog who's staring at me like he's enamored. He's the strangest and cutest dog I've ever seen. "He knew you'd take good care of him. You already were."

Kneeling, she strokes the top of his head. "Who's a good boy? You are." When she stands again, she asks, "Did you mean everything you said?"

"Every word."

"You still left, Andrew."

I let the name slide because I understand she has

reasons to be mad. *Reasons to feel abandoned.* "I left because I didn't see there was an alternative. And I wouldn't have learned that had I not gone. I wouldn't have learned that I'm not indispensable and that although my role requires I look after the business and its employees, there are more important things in my life to me. You. *Us.*" Taking hold of her hands, I say, "Travel is required with the company, but if you give me this second chance, you'll know that I'll look at each scenario and consider more clearly if it's my pride that decides if I go or if I'm a necessity. Because you are essential to me."

She sighs, her chest laden with heaviness. "I don't want you to feel like you have to check with me to do your job. I just want to know that at the end of it, you're returning to me. That's what commitment means to me."

"Commitment means trusting that I will, not believing I won't."

When she nods and her shoulders lighten, she leans closer. "The wires were crossed in a chain of painful events. I confused commitment leading to abandonment. That's not everyone's fate. That was my parents. I had no right to project that onto you."

Her arms come around my neck, and there's only enough room for a small papillon between us. Juni says, "My parents lived a full life, lived for every day, and made the most of it. I thought they were selfish and didn't want me. But they were showing me how to live all along. No tomorrow is guaranteed. And like Mr. Clark said, the only regret I'll have is wasting time without you in it."

I wasn't sure if I'd ever get another chance to have my lips against hers again. And she kisses me.

When our lips part and she opens her eyes, she says, "I'm proud of you for accomplishing number three."

Left-field tangent. It's good some things never change. "I didn't understand what you meant when you held three fingers for me."

She comes down the final step and hooks her arm in mine. "You performed in front of an audience. It was a spectacular performance as well. Guy gets girl and then chooses his boring work over her."

"Destiny steps in, and he has a revelation."

"And what might that be?"

I stop and cup her cheeks. "I love you, babe." I kiss her again, and when I look into her eyes, they're watery.

"I love you, Drew." Those are the sweetest four words I've ever heard. And I don't know what's happening, but something must be in the air because my eyes are watery as well.

We don't dwell on the mushy stuff as we walk down the street to take Rascal to the park, but I hold her hand, not just because girls dig it, but because I want to be the one on Juni Jacobs' arm.

I am Juni's beau, after all. And maybe more one day.

Definitely more.

37

Juni

Five months later . . .

"I DON'T UNDERSTAND." I STOP IN THE MIDDLE OF THE
sidewalk and look at Gil to help me make sense of this.

Holding up the urn, he replies, "I have no idea. He left
me Mrs. Clark. I don't even know her first name."

"Anne."

We look at Drew standing with his hands in his pockets.
The weather turned with the new month. Gil eyes the urn
and appears satisfied by the grin. "Anne Clark."

I ask, "How did you know that?"

"He told me the story about their wedding."

"Oh really? Was it romantic?"

His arm goes across my shoulders, and he brings me
closer to his side. "The most romantic."

Drew guides me by my lower back toward the elevator.

"If you want to nap before tonight's adventures, we need to get upstairs."

As soon as the doors close, I say, "I'm getting in bed, but I have no intention of napping. Would you like to join me?"

His smirk never ceases to weaken my knees. His arms come around me, and he runs the tip of his nose behind my ear. "Thought you'd never ask."

We kiss, our lips caressing like the familiar lovers we've become. Drew's been quiet most of the day. Not sure what's going on with him, but I know he's had some stress at work and, since I left, a few frustrations with the new reception assistant.

Sitting in a lawyer's office for hours isn't exactly entertainment either, but it took five months for Mr. Clark's wishes, jotted down on a scrap of napkin left on his coffee table, to work its way through the courts and be deemed legal. Today is a good day, though. Not only is Rascal officially mine but in a surprise plot twist, Mr. Clark also left his apartment to me. His son hadn't been happy about that, but in the end, he realized that he hadn't been present in his father's life since his mom died, something he now regretted. More so because he realized that he'd missed out on those years of knowing his dad. He'd neglected to keep collecting memories worth sharing. Funny how death can teach us things.

We've yet to decide what to do with Mr. Clark's apartment, but we're considering keeping it for CWM staff who have to travel to New York for business. So that, when possible, they can bring their family with them rather than leave them behind. Andrew's certainly working harder at ensuring a better work-life balance for CWM staff and himself. *No wonder I love the man so much.*

Living with him the past five months has given me a new

perspective. My apartment, which I put on the market this week, might have reminded me of my grandparents, especially my grandma Marion, but I have the memories and our traditions and can take them anywhere.

Spoiler alert: We're taking them to a three-story brownstone right next door to Nick and Natalie. When the property came on the market, we didn't hesitate. It's a complete gut job, but despite my part-time research job at the Jacobs' Garden, I've started planning the landscaping out back. It's going to be magical.

The "boys" have also started surfing together on Saturday mornings. Well, when it's warm enough. Sure, The Rockaways, Lido, and Montauk have nothing on Southern Californian beaches, but it's more about time spent and memories made than the peaks and surf.

Just after midnight, a shower where we got down and dirty before we got clean, and a full Italian feast that I made to tide us over, we leave for our next adventure.

I push forward to see out the tinted window. "Something's going on at the library." Even under my coat, goose bumps cover my arms. I turn back to look at my guy. Again, so quiet today. "Drew, look how beautiful it is."

Sliding his hand under my hair, he caresses my neck. "You look more beautiful than I've ever seen you."

I can't help but remind myself of what I'm wearing. It's not something I wear a lot, but the little red dress has come out a few times. "I could have sworn you'd seen me in this dress before."

"It's not the dress, babe. It's you." Forget the flickering candles covering the steps, the orchestra playing La bohème. All of that pales in comparison to the love I have for this man.

"Thank you." I move into his arms, savoring the last few

seconds of having him all to myself before the car comes to a stop.

He asks, "Are you ready?"

"Never more." He might be nervous, but I'm excited.

Holding hands, we walk along the sidewalk and then stop to see what's going on. I ask, "Do you think they'll let us borrow a step or two?"

"Pretty sure they will." He used to be grumpy. *Now he's always so cocky.*

Why does that do such naughty things to my body?

He just walks up the center of the steps where an aisle was created with candles on either side. "Drew?" I whisper-yell, worried we might be crashing someone's wedding.

Reaching the first deck, he turns back to find me. "It's okay, Juni." His hand is out, and no one around seems to care, so I walk up the steps, meeting him there.

After clearing his throat, he announces, "I'll be reciting from Shakespeare's *Romeo and Juliet* this evening." His eyes find support in mine, and every word is spoken directly from his mouth to my heart.

"My bounty is as boundless as the sea, My love as deep; the more I give to thee, The more I have, for both are infinite."

My heart swells in my love for this man. He's reciting Shakespeare for me. *Gah!* So romantic.

He once told me he's fact and figures, but he would learn the other stuff for me. He's an excellent student.

He brought up the topic of checking off the fourth to-do on his life list a few weeks ago. *He brought it up.* Drew is changing, not for me, but for him. I knew it would be quite the sight to watch him unravel. I've not been disappointed one bit. "Mission accomplished," I say, giving him a hug. Still holding hands, I turn to leave and do a little dance on the way down. My excitement for him can't be contained.

"Wait," he pleads. Bringing me back to the platform, he says, "I have one more for you." His grip a little tighter, his eyes full of love. "Did my heart love till now? Forswear it, sight! For I ne'er saw true beauty till this night."

"Trying to kill with the heart swoons?" I tease. "Me thinks Sir Christiansen likes being the center of attention."

"If that's where you are, it's where I want to be." Digging something from his pocket, he dips to one knee. "Mr. Clark also told me if I want to marry you that I need to ask you."

"What?" The teasing is all gone. I look around suddenly, and some things don't make sense. Like Gil, Nancy, and Izzy, Cookie and Corbin, Tatum, Jackson, Mrs. Hendricks, and Rascal being there. The only ones missing are—

Natalie runs up the steps with her husband, and we're showered in rose petals. I'm more of a daisy girl myself, but petals work. Their velvet softness is due to their cellular structure rather than the other photosynthesizing parts of the plant that— Well, let's just say I get the appeal.

"Juni?"

"Yes?" I say to the man on his knee in front of me. I click my heels and enjoy this moment. It's one I never dared to dream until I met him.

"The first time we met was pretty shitty." Ah, we're peppering in some funnies. Look at my grumpy man. "But after that, I don't know what hit me."

"Nice rhyme."

"Thanks." His smile turns gentler, and as he holds both my hands in his with a ring box balanced on his knee, he says, "I knew there was something different about you—"

"Geez, thanks. Should have left it to Shakespeare." This time, I flash my winking skills at him.

"Special. You turned my world upside down before the moment we met. And then once we did, I couldn't stop thinking about you. I'll be honest, they weren't all good thoughts."

"Touché." I roll my eyes, though I relate to the honesty. Not all thoughts were good in the beginning. He was super annoying, in fact. But I'll leave that to tease him another day.

"But they made me feel. You made me feel for what felt like the first time ever. I don't know what kind of magic destiny wields, but it was used that day and every day since. I wake up excited not just about the next adventure we'll take, but because every minute I'm awake is another minute I get you. Today was about accomplishing goals, ticking things off a list of life experiences. Today was the day that I checked off two."

I run through the list that I've read a million times and committed to memory. See? I'm committing all over the place these days.

1. Lie in the grass in the nearest park at 9:17 AM on a sunny weekday.

CHECK.

1. Eradicate negative vibes from the apartment on the sixth Thursday after arrival.

Check. Check.

1. Perform in front of an audience.

Check. Check. Check.

  1. Read Shakespeare on the steps of the New York
     Public Library just after midnight.

Check. Check. Check. Check.

I GASP, my hands covering my mouth. Tears ping my eyes when I realize I'm number five. "I'm number five, Drew."

  1. *Fall in love like you won't get a second chance.*

DAMN THAT CHRISTIANSEN SMILE. "You are. May I?"

I nod like a crazy person with makeup running down her face because her manfriend never gave her the warning to wear waterproof mascara. Some friend he is.

Slipping my hand back in his, he says, "I didn't set out to fall in love, but sometimes the universe has a different plan. I may not have realized it then, but the day I met you, I fell in love like I wouldn't get a second chance. You're the one I want to spend the rest of my life—"

"And eternity."

He chuckles. "And eternity with. Through chaos and sunshine, we can survive anything together. Will you marry me?"

There it is, one of my biggest fears—commitment—wrapped with a bow and his heart on his sleeve. But now, because of my CEO Andrew and Ice Cream Drew, I don't have that fear. Everything I feel for him can be summed up in one word. "Yes."

And then two because *I do*, which will make it official. But we don't need to worry about that right now. That's way down the road.

Baby steps.

Or so she thought . . .

EPILOGUE

Drew

FOR SOMEONE WHO CLAIMED SHE WAS SCARED OF commitment, she sure did plan with this. The Jacobs' Garden officially opened to the public. My stunning fiancée planned every plant, designed the garden, and wrote the book to sell in the shop in her spare time. During the days, she furthered her research on her initial findings, which exposed the dirty tactics of her ex-boyfriend when he failed to produce the same results.

Sadly, I didn't get to punch his thieving face. *Maybe one day.* Either way, it was a great day.

Today is another.

The garden is dedicated in honor of her parents, Daisy and Chris Jacobs. It's taken healing and therapy, but Juni's come to realize that their passion reached beyond them. It's touched the world in so many technologies. She's grateful most days, like today, standing in the garden.

Others, she still wished she could have just had normal parents. Rubbing her tiny belly, she promises our baby that she'll always be there. Even when they're teenagers wanting to lock themselves in their rooms to play video games, she'll be there.

Can't wait to see how that plays out.

Right now, I'm living in the moment. The future doesn't matter. I say, "I do."

Gil walked her down the aisle, but when a breeze blew in on this hot September day, nine seventeen to be exact, to match the time the universe and Cookie brought us together, she held my hand and told me she could sense her parents smiling down on her.

Rascal runs in circles, making it really hard to get that ring from him. It was Juni's idea to make him the ringbearer. When Jackson catches him in a grass patch, the ring is saved but not Jackson's shoes, unfortunately.

"Andrew, Mr. Christiansen, my Drew. You *were* uptight. Controlled. Meticulous. Regimented. Scheduled. Grumpy. Handsome. Kind. Generous. And loving. You've been my biggest cheerleader and my greatest ally. Not a day goes by that I don't feel like the luckiest woman alive. I'm so in love with all of you. I love you so much it kicks."

"Kicks?"

"Oh my God, the baby just kicked." She shoves my hand on her stomach. "Can you feel it?"

My breath catches just like hers when we feel our little baby kick for the first time. Just one small thing . . . we hadn't told anyone. Her baggy sweaters had come in handy until we were ready, which was determined to be after the wedding. So when we look at our friends and family gathered around, we say, "Surprise."

"Jinx," we say in unison again.

Laughing, she says, "Double jinx."

"I didn't know there was a double jinx."

She says, "The official rules state it can only be used in the case of a tie." She shrugs. "I don't make the rules. I just play by them."

She's sounding a lot like me these days.

Instead of cake, we celebrate our nuptials with pink strawberry donuts and a taco buffet feast because that's what she was craving this morning. The caterer wasn't happy, but he didn't mind the big tip.

Just as Juni finishes a donut, she dusts her hands on a napkin and asks, "Do you want to tell your mom about the science fair connection now?"

"Another time. I'm rather liking this connection better right now."

"Oh, I forgot to tell you how cute it is that your first word was leaf. Leaf, Drew. That's another connection. I said tree. You said leaf."

"That's cute that you said tree since you're a Juniper and all. But my first word wasn't leaf."

Holding me by the rolls of my shirt sleeves, she kisses under my chin. "Yes, it was, babe."

I angle my head down to catch her pretty eyes. "No. My first word was tie."

"Tie?" she spits in disgust. "Like what you wear with a suit?"

"Yes. It's a good first word."

"Not as good as leaf."

Okay, now I'm a little offended. "I'm not sure why you thought my first word was leaf, but it wasn't," I say, standing my ground. "Why did you think it was leaf?"

With a glass of wine in hand, my mom comes to hug us. She says, "I could tell you two were meant to be the moment I met Juni."

Both of us look at Cookie at the same time, but Juni says,

"His first word was tie. I married him under false pretenses."
She struggles to keep a straight face.

I ask, "Why'd you tell Juni my first word was leaf?"

She takes a sip of wine and winks. "Sometimes destiny
needs a helping hand."

Wrapping my arms around my wife, I give her a kiss on
those delectable lips and say, "It all worked out in the end."

"It sure did."

The End

∾

IF YOU ENJOYED **The One I Want,** make sure to read/listen
to **Never Got Over You** where you meet Nick and Natalie.
This is a sweep you off your feet, feel-so-good epic
romance. Click here for more information: Never Got
Over You

Or, you can turn the page for a sneak peek.

NEVER GOT OVER YOU

CHAPTER 1

Natalie St. James

I'M THE FIRST TO ADMIT I HAVE NO BUSINESS TAKING ANOTHER shot.

Especially after the past two.

But what's a girl to do when a room full of strangers is chanting my name and a particularly wild best friend places the shot hat on my head along with a small glass of liquor in my hand?

I drink.

In a little hole-in-the-wall hidden from the main street in Avalon on Catalina Island, I down the liquid like a champ, then promptly proceed to fall from grace, also known as the barstool.

My eyes close, bracing for impact, except . . . someone catches me just before landing. With my breath caught in my throat, I hang in the balance of arms made of steel and open my eyes.

Laughter fades away with any drunken shame that threatened as I stare into the soulful eyes of a stranger.

"Hi," whispers the future hero of my dirty dreams . . . *oh, wait.*

Maybe I'm unconscious? Maybe I was knocked out cold, and I'm dreaming. I blink. Why are my eyes open? Letting my lids fall, I keep them closed long enough to pray, "Please let him be real. If he's not, I'm begging you to leave me in this dream a little longer." My lids drift back open to find him still staring at me.

"Are you okay?"

"Perfect," I reply. *I think.* I'm not sure if I actually voice the response or not. I feel pretty damn perfect in his arms, though, the response still fitting in any circumstance that involves me, him, and those arms wrapped around my body.

Naked would be nice, but I'll save that for our second date.

His brow furrows, but a smile curls the corners of his lips.

The fog of alcohol clouds my mind, creating a heavy blanket on my brain. Regardless, I try to calculate the odds of a ridiculously sexy stranger—the exact man I'd craft if Create-a-Hottie was an actual thing—being in the right place at the right time to catch me if I fell.

It's impossible, so the only logical answer to this conundrum is that either he is the best college graduation gift ever or I'm dreaming. "How are you so hot?" I ask, worried he'll disappear in a puff of smoke and mirrors. Clamping my eyes closed again, I whisper, "Dear Lord, please don't let him be a mirage."

"I'm real." *Yes!*

Does that mean my friend set up this encounter for me? She's always been a great gift giver. It is our job, after all. I squint one eye open, biting my bottom lip. "*Mm*, so real," I purr. *Too perfect to be real, though. I must be dreaming.*

His grin creates dimples that could compete with the Grand Canyon. *How did I know I liked dimples enough to add them into this delirium?* I don't know, but score one for me.

"I think you're going to be okay," my dream man says, his voice as delectable as his face.

Wait, what? No. "As for me being okay, not so fast, buddy. No need to rush toward the waking hours. Anyway . . ." I drape my hand across my forehead. "Dream or real, I'm going to need mouth-to-mouth resuscitation."

His dimples dig deeper. "Is that so?"

"*So* right," I pant.

"Do you think I should call a paramedic?"

"That's a little kinky for me, but if you're into it . . ." I press my lips into a pretty little pout to seriously consider this twist. "Nah. Changed my mind. I only want you. Just the two of us resuscitating each other."

"You want me?" he asks, surprise tingeing his tone as he cocks an eyebrow. He readjusts me in his strong, manly arms. "Circling back to the real part, you do realize you're not dreaming, right?"

I reach up and wrap my arms around his neck, wanting to melt in his arms again. Totally obsessed with how I fit so perfectly, I pull him closer and hold tight. "You do realize you're stupidly attractive, right?"

He chuckles, his grin lifting higher on one side.

That smirk would totally get me into bed, given what it's doing to me while dreaming. I close my eyes again. "I'm ready."

"For what?" His deep, dulcet tones vibrate through my body.

"Resuscitation. I'm ready. Resuscitate away."

When nothing happens, I peek one eye open. He's still

staring at me with the smirk I'm ready to kiss off his sexy face, and whispers, "I don't think you need me—"

"Trust me." Opening both eyes, I also run my fingers through his shiny, chestnut-hued hair, taking in the feel of the soft strands. "I really, *really* need you."

When he leans down, I prepare my lips with a quick lick before meeting his . . . or at least, that's the direction I hope this dream is going.

"I was thinking—"

"Yes?" My gaze floats from his mouth to his eyes again.

"We've been at this a while. Maybe we should get you off the floor?" His head tilts to the side, and the industrial lights above him shine bright in my eyes, almost like a place of business, a restaurant, or a bar would hang. My senses begin to return, starting with the stench of old beer scenting the air.

"Yuck." Next comes a wave of cedar-y cologne and salty air. That's a scent I approve of, but that's when something else hits me. *What if I'm not dreaming?*

"Up you go," he says, shadowing me again as he tries to lift me to my feet.

I don't budge. "Dream or not, I quite enjoy being horizontal with you."

"Are you always this, *should we say*, flirtatious?" he asks, laughter punctuating his question.

"Not when I'm awake, no."

As if he couldn't be more gorgeous, little lines whisker from the outer corners of his eyes, enticing me to drag my fingertip along each one. I don't, but I want to. "Are your eyes hazel or brown? It's hard to tell in this light."

"Brown."

"Brown does them a disservice. A kaleidoscope of colors

is trapped inside them. I'm going to need a closer look in the sunshine."

"The sun will be setting soon."

"Then we should hurry."

A restrained chuckle wriggles his lips. "You can stare into my eyes, but I have to warn you, once you do, you'll fall madly in love with me. And I'm leaving tomorrow, so if we're falling in love, you better get to the loving part since you've already fallen."

"Good point."

"Get up, Natalie," my best friend says, rudely barging into my fantasy and peering at me from beside his shoulder. "The floor is filthy! Now you're going to have to wash your hair."

My eyes shift her way. "Please go away and let me have this one little dream, Tatum."

Snapping her fingers twice in front of my face has me jerking my head back. "You're wide awake and making a fool of yourself."

Noise from the crowded bar filters into my consciousness. Instead of looking around to confirm, I stare into Dreamy's eyes a moment longer and then exhale as embarrassment becomes reality, returning me to the present. "You're real, aren't you?"

A slow nod accompanies a smug expression.

The heat of my cheeks has me pressing my hands to them in hopes of cooling my skin down. "Do you mind helping me up?"

"I need to know something first."

"What?" I ask, knowing I should leave before I'm sober enough to realize how absurd I've been behaving.

Still holding me in his arms as if I'm light as a feather, he leans closer with his eyes on my mouth. When his gaze rises to meet mine, he asks, "Did you fall in love?"

My heart rate spikes, and the sound of it beating whooshes in my ears. Maybe I did hit my head because I swear at that moment, the one with my dream man so close I can kiss him or even lick him if I want, I can answer honestly.

Despite all the physical signs of me feeling otherwise, I reply, "You know. I think it's time for me to go." *Before the last few minutes really sink in.*

My feet are set on solid flooring while his hands remain on the underside of my forearms to steady me. Like the perfect gentleman. "I wish—"

"Nat," Tatum says under her breath. She moves in and grabs my hand.

"What?"

Her hair catches the light when she flips it over her shoulder, an exhausted sigh following right after. Every blonde needs a brunette bestie, and Tatum Devreux was destined to be mine since our mothers exchanged silver spoons from Tiffany's as baby shower gifts. I'm not exactly the calm to her wild ways, but she can out party me any day.

"A party on a yacht down in the harbor. We have to go now, though."

Panic rises in my chest. I know I should want to hightail it out of here to save myself from further mortification, but I don't want to go. I'm perfectly content right here.

I'm not shy about it. I look straight at him, but I'm smacked with a dose of candor I wasn't ready for, my ego crushed under his expression that mirrors pity. Now I regret not making a quick getaway when I had the chance.

My stomach plummets to the floor I was just hovering

above. "Yeah, it's time to go," I tell Tatum, my hand pressing to my belly in an attempt to keep myself together. My hand is grabbed, and I'm tugged after her as she calls, "Ciao, darlings."

I turn back to catch Mr . . . *Dreamy, Smug, Sexy, Pity-er of Drunk Girls* watching me. I'm left with two options to make an escape without further incident. I *could* blame the craziness on a head injury, or I *could* just leave. "So . . . thanks," I say awkwardly as I back toward the door. *Yes. Choosing the latter.*

"Are you sure you're okay?" His voice carries over the lively crowd.

I dust the dirt off my ass. "I'm fine. Guess I'm not a tequila girl."

"You drank rum," he replies with a lopsided smile that could sweep me off my feet again if I'm not careful.

"Rum. Tequila. Same difference." I wave off the idea because it doesn't really matter. "I'm not good with liquor." That should settle it, but I make the mistake of daring to look into his eyes again. The five feet between us virtually disappears, and mentally, I'm back in his arms again, reading the prose that makes up his features. It would take me days to interpret, capturing not only his thoughts but a history that's worn in the light lines. He makes it hard to look away.

Stepping forward, he raises his hand and then lowers it to his side again as conflict invades his expression. "You sure you're okay? You might have a concussion."

I can't say I'm not touched by his concern. Grinning, I ask, "Does a concussion involve my heart?"

"What's happening with your heart?"

"It's beating like crazy."

Smiles are exchanged. "I think you're experiencing something else, but if you'd like me to call an ambulance—"

"Nope," Tatum cuts in, yanking me toward the door again, and laughs. "He's cute, but we don't want to miss the yacht." She whips the straw hat off me and tosses it to him.

I twist to look back. "Thanks for the lift. *Literally.*"

"Anytime," he says with his eyes set on mine. When he shoves his hands in his pockets, he looks like he's posing for a Ralph Lauren ad. Tan. Rugged good looks. Tall. Those dreamy eyes and a grin that call me back to him. But life isn't a dream. It's time to return to reality.

Goodbye, dream man. It was nice hanging with . . . onto you.

Click here to continue reading: **Never Got Over You**

To keep up to date with her writing and more, visit S.L. Scott's website: **www.slscottauthor.com**

To receive the newsletter about all of her publishing adventures, free books, giveaways, steals and more:

https://geni.us/intheknow

Follow me on TikTok: https://geni.us/SLTikTok
Follow on IG: https://geni.us/IGSLS
Follow on Bookbub: https://geni.us/SLScottBB

THANK YOU

Thank you so much for reading my book. Writing is a dream and wouldn't have come true without you.

Your support means the world to me. Please leave a review where you purchased your book.

My family has been incredible during this chaotic year. They are my biggest cheerleaders and I'm the most fortunate wife and mom in the world to have them.

What an awesome team I have. They are literally the best. Thank you Andrea, Jenny, Kristen, and Marion. You made this book so special and on a crazy deadline. I'm sorry about that. I love you!

To my audiobook production team at One Night Stand Studios and the incredible narrators - Sebastian York and Summer Morton: Thank you for bringing my books to life. I adore listening to you and working with you so much!

And finally, but not least, thank you to the Wildfire Marketing team and my Rockin' Readers. My heart is full because of you!

Printed in Great Britain
by Amazon

78906037R00215